The Shadows of London

Andrew Taylor is the author of a number of crime novels, including the ground-breaking Roth Trilogy, which was adapted into the acclaimed TV drama *Fallen Angel*, the Marwood and Lovett historical crime series and *The American Boy*, a No.1 *Sunday Times* best-seller and a Richard & Judy Book Club choice. He has won many awards, including an Edgar Scroll from the Mystery Writers of America, the HWA Gold Crown, and the CWA's prestigious Diamond Dagger, awarded for sustained excellence in crime writing. He also writes for the *Spectator* and *The Times*. He lives with his wife Caroline in the Forest of Dean.

X @AndrewJRTaylor
www.andrew-taylor.co.uk

By the same author

The Shadows of London

ANDREW TAYLOR

HEMLOCK
PRESS

Hemlock Press
An imprint of HarperCollins*Publishers* Ltd
1 London Bridge Street,
London SE1 9GF

www.harpercollins.co.uk

HarperCollins*Publishers*
Macken House, 39/40 Mayor Street Upper,
Dublin 1, D01 C9W8, Ireland

This paperback edition 2024
1
Published by HarperCollins*Publishers* Ltd 2023

A catalogue copy of this book is available from the British Library.

ISBN: 978-0-00-849417-9 (PB)

This novel is entirely a work of fiction. The names, characters and incidents
portrayed in it are the work of the author's imagination. Any resemblance to
actual persons, living or dead, events or localities is entirely coincidental.

Typeset in Fournier MT by Palimpsest Book Production Ltd, Falkirk, Stirlingshire

Printed and Bound in the UK using 100% Renewable Electricity
at CPI Group (UK) Ltd

This book contains FSC™ certified paper and other controlled sources
to ensure responsible forest management.

For more information visit: www.harpercollins.co.uk/green

For Caroline

THE MAIN CHARACTERS

At the sign of the Rose, Henrietta Street
Catherine Hakesby, formerly Lovett
Brennan, her draughtsman and business partner
Jane Ash, her maid
Pheebs, the porter
Josh, his boy

Infirmary Close, The Savoy
James Marwood, clerk to Lord Arlington, and at the Board of Red Cloth
Margaret and Sam Witherdine, his servants

Whitehall
King Charles II
Lord Arlington, Secretary of State
Lady Arlington, his wife
Joseph Williamson, Under Secretary of State
Monsieur Colbert de Croissy, the French Ambassador
Dudley Gorvin, clerk to my Lord Arlington

Madame des Bordes, the Queen's Dresser
Mademoiselle Louise de Keroualle, a Maid of Honour to the
  Queen
George Villiers, the 2nd Duke of Buckingham
Roger Durrell, his servant

Others
Robert Hadgraft, lawyer and speculator
Grace Hadgraft, his daughter
Mistress Susannah, her cousin, her waiting woman
Monsieur Pharamond, her French tutor
Willoughby Rush, Justice of the Peace and man of affairs
Thomas Ledward, his servant
John Iredale, clerk
Patience Noone, a servant in the house where Iredale lodges
Mr John Banks, a young clergyman of Cambridge
John Evelyn, Esquire, of Sayes Court

CHAPTER ONE

THE RAIN HAD stopped at last.

On Snow Hill, the miniature streams ran like watery veins among the setts and stones of the roadway. The open drain overflowed, its stinking contents rushing down to the Fleet River below Holborn Bridge. As the growing light bleached the shadows, the creatures of the night left their shelters and ventured abroad.

A black cat with torn ears and a sagging belly rounded the corner from Snow Hill to Chard Lane. She trickled, fluid as water itself, along the base of a wall on the left-hand side. The wall was seven feet high. She veered into the middle of the lane and turned to face it. She drew back on her hind legs.

With a clatter of claws, she streaked up the wall. She perched on the top, scanning the wilderness on the other side. There was no sign of the watchman's dog. She jumped down and threaded her way among the weeds.

The cat was too young to remember the old almshouse that had stood here five years earlier before the Fire. Most

I

of the buildings had been demolished to their foundations. Behind them was an irregular rectangle of waste ground where the inhabitants had kept a pig or two and grown vegetables.

In the angle between the waste ground and the almshouse site stood a dilapidated house and its yard surrounded by a wall of brick. The Fire had been capricious or perhaps the wind had changed at the last moment. Whatever the reason, the flames had left the house untouched.

The cat padded warily towards it. There were often scraps of food to be found in the yard – the watchman fed the dog there once a day. It was a clumsy brute whose method of eating scattered fragments of its dinner far and wide.

One of the spoil heaps was close to the house. During the night, the heavy rain had soaked into it, making the debris shift and settle. The cat picked her way across, pausing to defecate near the top.

Afterwards she raised her head and sniffed. Her tail flicked from side to side. She smelled blood. It was very near. And it was fresh blood.

Cat heard the men shouting. Another quarrel? They were worse than children.

Early though it was, she was already in the site office, preparing for the morning's work. Below her window, the watchman, Ledward, was sweeping the yard after last night's rain; unusual evidence of industry from him at this hour or indeed any hour.

She laid down her pen and pushed back the stool. The labourers had begun work on the other side of the wall under the nominal control of their foreman. There should have been ten men, but three hadn't turned up. Since the Fire, there was such a shortage of labourers in London, not just craftsmen, that you could never be sure they wouldn't be lured away with promises of more money for less work. They should have been shovelling the spoil into barrows and moving it into the waste ground. Instead they were squabbling again.

Unless it was an accident, not a quarrel – the men were clumsy at this hour, still half asleep. If she were unlucky, it would be a fight, though these usually happened after midday, when the ale the men took with their dinner could heat their passions.

Ledward paused in his sweeping as Cat came outside. He ducked his head and knuckled his forehead. 'Mistress Hakesby.'

'What's going on?'

'God knows. I mind my own business.'

She glanced at him to see if he intended impudence. Ledward looked gravely back with no sign of insolence in his expression. He was broad-shouldered, a long-armed man with black hair streaked with grey. It was hard to tell his age – anything between thirty-five and fifty. His forearms were bare, and there was a long scar running up to his right elbow; it looked like a sword cut that hadn't healed properly.

He opened the gate in the wall for her. Cat went outside. The men were gathered about the nearest of the spoil heaps. Three were standing on the far side, halfway up its slope, which made them invisible from the waist down. Brennan was below, shouting at them. Her business partner had a light voice, soft and reedy. His words were having no discernible effect.

Cat lifted her skirts and negotiated her way through the

mud. One by one, the men fell silent and doffed their hats. Brennan turned to her. He was very pale, and the freckles stood out on his skin like Smyrna raisins in a pudding.

'They've found a body.'

'Another one?'

'This one's different,' he said. 'You'll see.'

The main range of the old almshouse ran parallel to Chard Lane, separated from the roadway by a paved area and a wall. The spoil heaps lay some yards to the rear. The nearest had been piled into the rectangular enclosures made by the former chapel and the cemetery beside it. In the early days of its history, the almshouse buried its own dead.

'You.' Cat flicked her finger at the three men still on the heap. 'Come here.'

She watched them slithering over the rubble. The men had dug up partial skeletons of at least a score of people. They had been buried in their shrouds and nothing else. There had been one exception: a stone coffin containing a complete skeleton, perhaps belonging to the founder or his kin. A crucifix and a rosary had been among the bones, which meant he had been a Papist. The almshouse had been founded long before the Reformation.

'Pray give me your hand.'

With Brennan's support, she scrambled over the broken ground without too much loss of dignity.

'Probably the rain last night,' Brennan said. 'Something shifted, something gave way. The ground collapsed.' His grip tightened on her arm. 'Have a care. It may not be safe. You never know what's underneath these places.'

She obeyed; Brennan knew what he was about, and she had come to trust his judgement in such matters. Craning

4

her head, she saw a shallow cavity choked with rubble, broken bricks and charred planks. At one end, a yellowing bone lay among fragments of rotting wood.

'Not that.' Brennan pointed. '*There.*'

Cat followed the direction of his finger. She blinked and swallowed. She was looking at a hand, a man's by the size of it, still with its covering of flesh and skin. The index finger was at an unnatural angle, pointing at Brennan. She made out the calf of a leg nearby with thick black hairs sprouting from waxen skin. Then the curve of a shoulder between them.

'Can we move those planks?'

Brennan nodded, following her train of thought. He called down to the foreman for a couple of short scaffolding poles and a rake. In two minutes the man had dragged the poles up the heap while the rest of the labourers watched. They were muttering now, their voices growing steadily louder. Left to themselves, Cat thought, they would either sidle off to the alehouse or scrabble in the spoil heap in the hope the dead man had left behind his clothes.

She ordered the youngest labourer, who was little more than a boy, to look sharp and fetch the constable. She set the rest to moving the largest spoil heap to the waste ground. Shovelling rubble into barrows was backbreaking work. It would leave them little time to gossip.

'This won't please Mr Hadgraft,' Brennan muttered when the men were gone.

'First things first. We'll talk to him later.'

'And on top of everything else.'

Cat nodded. She looked at Ledward. The watchman was

leaning on his brush in the gateway that led to the site office. She wondered if he had heard.

'Bar the gates,' she said. 'Let no one in until the constable comes.'

'A body, mistress? Whose?'

'No one knows.' She turned back to the white-faced foreman. 'Lever up those planks. Mr Brennan will do the other side.'

It didn't take them long to expose what lay beneath. More rubble. More bone fragments. And more glimpses of the body. Brennan raked away more of the debris, exposing the whole length of the corpse.

The man was as naked as the day he had been born. He was lying on his back, his head turned to one side. The dome of his skull was covered by a ragged crop of short dark hair. Head lice had left reddish bumps and scabs behind the one visible ear. There were at least half a dozen stab wounds in the chest, which were rimmed with dried blood. He should have been staring up at them but—

The foreman let out his breath in a long, shuddering sigh and turned away to vomit.

The dead man had no face.

CHAPTER TWO

WHEN THE CONSTABLE arrived, he was not alone. He and the foreman's boy were a few yards behind a small upright man in a disreputable wig, a stained travel coat and a pair of mud-streaked riding boots. He walked briskly towards her, his sword swinging violently to and fro.

'It's the justice,' Brennan murmured. 'His name's Rush.'

'Mr Rush,' Cat said, curtsying. 'I wish you good morning, sir.'

He stopped in front of her and made the briefest of bows. 'Your servant, madam. Who's in charge?'

'I am. Mistress Hakesby.'

He frowned, his eyes flicking towards Brennan.

'My partner,' Cat said. 'Mr Brennan.'

'You may be aware I'm a magistrate. I was with the constable when your message came. What's this about a body? The boy had some garbled story, but I couldn't make head nor tail of it.'

'The rain last night dislodged some rubble.' Cat gestured toward the spoil heap. 'It exposed a body.'

'Found a few bones, eh? Scarcely unusual in a place like this.'

'These aren't bones, sir. This is a man. He's been stabbed. Recently, and many times. And his face . . .' Her voice trailed into silence.

'What about it?'

'You'd better see for yourself.'

Brennan stepped forward. 'This way, sir. Mind how you go. The ground's treacherous.'

'I can see that.' Rush threw a glance at the constable. 'Keep an eye on those men over there.'

He followed in Brennan's wake, cursing when he stumbled or slipped. He was surprisingly agile for a middle-aged man. He stared down at the body for at least a minute.

He glanced at Cat: 'Pray send for the watchman here. You have one?'

Ledward came forward from the gateway of the yard, still with the brush in his hand. He pulled off his hat and bobbed his head. 'That's me, your honour.'

'This body can't have been there long,' Rush said. 'No sign of rat bites. Have you seen or heard anything suspicious in the last night or two? Or yesterday?'

'No, master.'

'Where do you go at night?'

'I've a mattress in the house over there. Where the office is. But I go round the whole place on the hour, every hour.'

Rush grunted. 'What about your dog? You must have a dog.'

'Yes, sir. Though I ain't seen him today.'

'Ah. But you did last night?'

'He was here at nine o'clock. I turned him loose, like I always do. If there's strangers about, he soon lets me know.'

'But he usually comes to you when you do your rounds?'

'Not always, sir. He knows my step.'

Rush dismissed Ledward with a wave of his hand. He turned back to Cat. 'I know murder when I see it.'

'You're not alone in that, sir,' Cat said.

His complexion darkened still further. 'You'll stop the work until the matter is dealt with.'

'What? You can't mean—'

'I mean what I say. No more, no less.'

'What if we cordon off this area and carry on with the rest of the site? We're short of time. And every—'

'Tell your men to pack their tools and leave. I want the whole site cleared and the gates barred.' He scowled at her. 'I'll put in my own watchmen until the matter is resolved according to proper form.'

She hesitated, groping in her mind for an argument he might accept.

Rush tapped his stick on the ground. 'Are you questioning my authority?'

'Of course not, sir, but as a magistrate you must be aware that the coroner will—'

'The coroner?'

'Yes, sir. The City of London—'

'No. You are ill-informed.'

'We're within the City Bars, sir.' Cat felt her temper slipping away. 'Therefore, the—'

'You mistake me, madam. True, Chard Lane is by Snow Hill, and Snow Hill is in the City as every fool knows. But the Chard almshouse is a liberty. It does not come within the City. The whole site belongs to the Bishop of Ely. He has his own courts, and he will no doubt appoint his own coroner.

In the meantime, it's my duty as the King's Justice to ensure that the rights and privileges of his lordship are observed in a fitting manner, and according to the laws of the land.'

Cat stared at him. Rush had a small mouth, and at this moment the lips were pressed tightly together. But not for long.

'Clear the site, madam. The whole site. And do it now.'

Rush allowed them an hour.

The men were sent away. Cat wondered if she would ever see them again. Rush supervised the removal of the body, which was taken away in a cart by the constable's men. The outer gates to the site were barred and sealed.

Cat extracted one small concession from the magistrate. A variety of building materials was stored in the house they used as a site office and in the walled yard beside it. Some, such as salvaged lead, were of considerable value. There were also tools, drawing slopes and plans. Removing all this would take time. It would also require a waggon to be brought through the main almshouse site.

Moreover, she pointed out, was Mr Rush certain that the site office stood on land within the bishop's liberty? She understood that her client had acquired it through a separate transaction which had nothing to do with the almshouse trustees. The house might well be under the jurisdiction of the City of London, and therefore the Bishop of Ely and his coroner could have no possible interest in it.

Rush, having got his way in everything that mattered, made a great show of magnanimity and permitted Cat and Brennan to retain the use of the house, on condition that he barred and sealed the gateway from its yard to the main site. They would have to come and go by the narrow alley on the far side of the house, which was a public thoroughfare.

'And now for Hadgraft?' Brennan said, as they watched Rush leave with the constable hurrying after him.

Cat grimaced. 'We can't put him off any longer.'

'I'm surprised he ain't here already.'

Mr Robert Hadgraft lived in a neat, modern house not far from St Andrew's church in Holborn. The manservant who opened the street door was pink-faced and bright-eyed. He frowned at them as if they were an unwelcome distraction.

'Mistress Hakesby and Mr Brennan for Mr Hadgraft,' Cat said. 'Is your master within?'

Of course he was within. They could hear him shouting upstairs. Hadgraft had a high-pitched voice, and when he raised it in anger it sounded like the buzzing of a small, angry insect.

'What do you have to say for yourself? Eh? You ungrateful fool!'

Underneath the shouting was another sound: a woman weeping.

The servant put them into a small parlour off the hall and closed the door. Shortly afterwards, Hadgraft's brisk footsteps pattered down the stairs. He burst into the room and scowled at them. He was a small, narrow-faced man with restless eyes and a prominent Adam's apple.

'Well, Mistress Hakesby?'

'I fear we bring unwelcome news.'

'What now?'

Cat explained about their discovery this morning, and about Willoughby Rush's intervention.

'Rush?' Hadgraft spat into the empty fireplace. 'That rogue. Who's this dead man? How did he get in? And what was Ledward doing while all this was going on?'

'We don't know.' Cat hesitated. 'Ledward says he heard nothing last night, or the night before. Nothing during the day, either. But as far as we're concerned, the greatest problem is that Mr Rush has now stopped us working on the entire site.'

'He can't do that.'

'He thinks he can, and we can't carry on against a magistrate's orders. Is he right about the land being within the liberty of the Bishop of Ely?'

Hadgraft took a deep breath and reined in his anger. 'I'm afraid so. It's a detached fragment of the liberty around Ely House. It was originally an orchard, I think. The bishop granted the land to the founder of the Chard almshouse. But it's still within the Ely liberty.' His voice sharpened. 'I can't afford more delay. We'll have winter upon us before we know where we are.'

'And unless we pay our labourers for doing nothing,' Cat said, 'they'll leave. May I remind you that we have orders in place. We also have masons and other skilled men booked for three weeks' time. They won't wait for us. And once the frosts come . . .'

Hadgraft leant on the table, resting his fists on it as if he needed its support. 'Rush will know that as well as I do. He's doing this out of spite.'

Cat stared at the Adam's apple, which bounced up and down as he swallowed. 'Perhaps the bishop's coroner will move quickly. If we're lucky, we may lose only a day or two.'

'You don't know the whole of it,' Hadgraft said. 'At the

start, before I brought you in, Rush was to be my partner in the affair. He was to bear half the cost of it all. He would invest in the rebuilding of the almshouse and together we would reap the benefit when we developed the waste ground at the back. But he changed his mind at the last moment, when it was too late for me to turn back, too late to find another backer, and now he does everything he can to hinder me.' The movements of the Adam's apple became frantic. 'I carry the entire load myself.'

Including, Cat thought, the bills that she and Brennan would soon present. Which included the payments they had already made on Hadgraft's behalf, as well as the materials they had already ordered for him.

Brennan cleared his throat. 'Could Mr Rush be persuaded to change his mind, sir? Perhaps if you were to suggest an alteration to the terms of your previous arrangement with him?'

'The last time I saw him,' Hadgraft snapped, 'he told me that he hoped he'd see me rotting in hell. What do you think?'

'Strange,' Cat said as she and Brennan were walking away from Hadgraft's house. 'He wasn't really curious about the murder itself. It was all about Rush.'

Brennan was pursuing another line of thought. 'Do you think Hadgraft has already had to borrow heavily? To make up for the loss of Rush's investment?'

'I don't know. He's rich, but we don't know how rich.'

'But – I know it's unlikely – but if he were declared a bankrupt . . .'

'Then we'd be liable for what we've ordered on his behalf.

13

As well as losing what he owes us for the work we've done so far. I'm sure Hadgraft knows that as well as we do.'

They walked in silence for a few minutes. Cat had known Brennan for nearly six years. He was an excellent and conscientious draughtsman, though their relationship had not always been easy. But he had made it possible for her to continue the business after her husband's death – at the start, some clients refused to deal with a woman; though as her reputation spread, that problem was diminishing. He was an effective site manager too, as long as Cat took the major decisions.

Last autumn Brennan had married the daughter of a pastry cook in St Martin's Lane. He still looked like a mangy fox but now he was a fatter and more cheerful one. It was as if his wife had transferred some of her own surplus plumpness to her husband, as well as her surprisingly substantial dowry. The dowry was the reason that Brennan was now Cat's partner rather than merely her employee. He had bought into the business, which resolved their previous problems with debt at a stroke. But if Hadgraft went under, he would be even harder hit than she would.

'There was a woman crying upstairs,' he said suddenly. 'Did you hear? Hadgraft's daughter?'

'He usually dotes on her.'

'I wonder why she was crying then.'

'How should I know?'

Perhaps, Cat was thinking, Rush had been acting outside his authority. She knew nothing about him apart from the fact he was a magistrate and had money at his command for a substantial investment. There might be a way of putting pressure on him.

Brennan glanced at Cat as they walked. 'Have you seen

the daughter? I have. She's a beauty.' He might be married, but he still had an eye for a pretty face. 'Very accomplished, too,' he went on. 'They say she's even got a French tutor. That can't come cheap, can it? If Hadgraft's really so rich, his daughter will have money enough to marry anyone she wants, even if she weren't a beauty. And she is. So what's she got to cry about?'

'If we try hard enough,' Cat said, 'we can all find something to cry about. But I don't understand why Rush is making everything so difficult for Hadgraft.'

'But he is. That's all that matters.'

Cat shook her head. 'There must be a reason. And perhaps that's also why he withdrew his investment.'

They reached the site office. Brennan unlocked the door. 'We need someone who can make interest for us, don't we? Someone with a bit of influence. It's the only way to make Rush see sense. Otherwise we're at his mercy.'

She said nothing. He was right. She knew what he was going to say next, and she didn't want to hear it. But he said it anyway.

Brennan opened the door and stood aside for her to precede him. 'What about asking if Mr Marwood can do something for us?'

Cat and Brennan spent the rest of the day in supervising the closure of the almshouse site and ordering affairs at the house. After the labourers had gone, they locked up the site office and walked to the hackney stand by Holborn Bridge. With some misgivings, Cat left Ledward in the house as watchman. He had given her no reason to mistrust him, and there was too much of value to leave the place unguarded.

The coach dropped Brennan in St Martin's Lane – he was living in the house of his parents-in-law at present – and went on to Henrietta Street. The Drawing Office was on the top floor at the sign of the Rose, with Cat's private lodgings on the floor beneath.

The porter, Pheebs, let her in. She barely acknowledged his greeting. Suddenly weary, she climbed the stairs slowly, pausing at each landing.

Unless Rush changed his mind, their only other options were to go to law and try to force him to relent, which would take time and money, or to find someone with influence who could put immediate pressure on him to relax his restrictions.

Brennan had a point. Marwood was the obvious person to approach. He was employed as a confidential clerk at Whitehall and he knew many people at court. No doubt some of them owed him favours. Best of all, he worked directly for Lord Arlington, the principal Secretary of State and the most powerful man in the country after the King. If he would only speak on their behalf to my lord, then the matter might be resolved in their favour in a few hours.

The trouble was, Cat didn't want to speak to James Marwood. Not if it was to ask for his help. There was too much between them already, too many favours asked and granted on both sides, too many words unsaid, too much that was still unsettled.

Cat's maid, Jane Ash, was waiting to take her mistress's cloak and hat and remove her pattens, which were caked with mud after the rain. There was a fire burning in the parlour, and a pan of water warming on the hob. Since her mother's death, the girl slept in the closet off the bedchamber. She was so thin and insubstantial that she made little impression on the space she occupied. To tell the truth, Cat was glad of her company.

'There's a letter, mistress. Shall I bring it?'

Another cursed bill. 'Not now.'

Cat went into the bedchamber to change into slippers. When she came to open the letter later in the evening, she realized at once that it wasn't a bill simply from the quality of the paper. She broke the seal and unfolded the letter, releasing a faint perfume, richly floral with an underlying hint of musk.

Ma chère Madame . . .

The letter was from Madame des Bordes, whom Cat had met the previous year in France when she was working on a commission for the Duchess of Orleans, the sister of King Charles. Madame des Bordes had been the princess's *femme de chambre* and one of her most trusted confidantes. She was a kind woman, vastly knowledgeable about fashion, and she and Cat had become friendly. After the death of his sister, the King had offered her ladies a home in England. Madame des Bordes had taken up the offer and was now Queen Catherine's dresser.

. . . and it seems an age since I have seen you. Would it amuse you to come here one evening? It would give me so much pleasure to see you. Her Majesty is in Suffolk, but there is always an assembly here, though in her absence it will be smaller than usual. I think you would find much to interest you in the new fashions, particularly the shoes. We have had two deliveries from Paris in the past week alone. If the weather is clement, we might walk on the terrace. Friday would suit me best . . .

Cat threw down the letter. She could hear Jane brushing the mud from her cloak on the landing. 'Bring me pen and ink,' she called. 'And my slope.'

But when she had her writing materials in front of her, she sat motionless, pen in hand, for over a minute. At last she dipped the pen in the ink and began to write:

Dear Mr Marwood . . .

She stopped. She frowned at the three words. She drew a thick black line through them. But they were still legible. After a moment's consideration she drew a second line through them, and then a third and a fourth, until there was nothing to be seen on the paper but a glistening puddle of black ink.

CHAPTER THREE

THERE WAS DANCING. There were cards. There was flirting, discreet but unmistakable. But the Queen was away with the King on their Progress through Suffolk and Norfolk. As a consequence, there was a lacklustre quality to the evening's entertainments. Almost everyone who mattered was with the court, and the court was with the King.

Since Louise was a maid of honour, her place would usually have been with the Queen. But she was still weak from a fever contracted over the summer, and the Queen had commanded her to stay at Whitehall to mend her health. Perhaps the Queen had another reason for wanting Louise to stay in London: to keep her away from the King.

That evening she felt better, and her maid had told her that the Duke of Buckingham was paying a short visit to London before returning to Newmarket. She went downstairs and played at ombre, losing more than she could afford at the turn of a single card. She also took more wine than was altogether wise. But the Duke failed to appear.

At last, when Louise was folding her fan before rising to

leave, he arrived in the doorway, causing a brief hush in the drawing room. He paused as if to admire the effect he had had. He was a tall man, magnificently dressed, with a golden periwig and a bloated face dominated by a nose like an axe blade. She felt a stab of anxiety, mixed with a stubbornly irrational hope. She stood up and made her way towards him.

'Mademoiselle,' he said in French, 'you look enchanting. If the angels catch sight of you, they will whisk you up to heaven to join them.'

'Your Grace is too kind,' Louise said, curtsying to him. She didn't trust him, but the Duke of Buckingham was too influential to antagonize, and too rich. Also, he had agreed to do her a favour.

'I see you were leaving the card table,' he said. 'Did fortune smile?'

She stared up at his face and widened her eyes. She knew he would like that. Men were such fools. 'Not as much as I would have liked.' She paused. 'Have you news?'

'I've ensured the first steps are taken, mademoiselle. You need have no fear. This little irritation will be removed.'

'The *irritations*, sir. There are two.'

'You mustn't trouble yourself.' He smiled down at her. He had a wide red mouth with strong yellow teeth. Fleshy jowls hung below his jaw. When he smiled, he looked like a yawning mastiff past its prime. 'Everything's in train.'

'Pray, sir – don't let there be any unpleasantness.'

He smiled and wished her good night. At the doorway, Louise glanced over her shoulder. The Duke was now talking to Monsieur Colbert de Croissy, the French ambassador. Both men saw her looking at them. They bowed in her direction and resumed their conversation.

Madame des Bordes, the Queen's dresser, followed her from the room and caught up with her in the passage. The two women knew each other well, for they had both served Madame, the late Duchess of Orleans, before they came to England at the invitation of her brother the King. He had generously offered to take his sister's ladies into his wife's household. What the Queen thought of this arrangement was anyone's guess.

'I saw you talking with the Duke, my dear. I thought you disliked him after the inconvenience he caused you at Dieppe.'

'One must be polite,' Louise said. 'Goodnight.'

'Have a care – his word is not to be trusted. As you know.'

They went their separate ways at the end of the passage. Louise climbed the stairs leading to the apartments of the maids of honour. Her head hurt. She was uneasily aware that Madame des Bordes might be right. The Duke of Buckingham was not to be trusted. But she had to trust him. Because she had no one else now.

Cat slept badly, her mind pursuing a troubled course among the jumbled memories of the day. The dead man's face haunted her dreams by its absence rather than its presence, which somehow made it worse. She feared that when she opened her eyes she would see again the bloody mass of flesh and bone, the featureless lump of bungled butchery that had once been a man. The face that was not a face.

She spent the first part of Tuesday morning in the Drawing Office, making a schedule of overdue bills and writing polite but firm letters to their debtors. In her darker moments, she thought that her work was now more about trying to control the ebb and flow of money than about designing buildings and overseeing their construction. Her letter to Marwood was still on the table, tucked between the leaves of Fréart's *Parallèle de l'architecture antique et de la moderne*.

She heard women's voices below, and then footsteps mounting the stairs to the Drawing Office. There was a tap on the door, so unassertive as to be the next best thing to a scratch. The wraithlike figure of Jane Ash slipped into the room.

'Your pardon, mistress. If you please, Margaret's below.'

Talk of the devil. Margaret Witherdine was Marwood's servant. She acted unofficially as Jane's instructor in matters of housekeeping, general conduct and indeed life itself. She called at Henrietta Street at least once a week. Cat and Marwood were perfectly aware of the arrangement, though neither was supposed to know about it.

Cat reined back her impatience. 'Yes?'

'She brought up a parcel for you from Mr Brennan. Pheebs was taking it in when she arrived. She said I should give it to you.'

Cat beckoned, and Jane approached with a small package wrapped in the coarse paper they used for crayon sketches. It was tied with string and addressed to her. Cat knew what it was as soon as she felt the outlines of the contents.

She sent Jane away and tore off the paper. Inside was a man's shoe for the left foot, tapering and square-toed. It was shabby and stained, but she knew at once that it had cost someone a good deal of money: this had been made for a gentleman.

There was a note in Brennan's small, neat handwriting tucked inside. *The foreman found this by the spoil heap where the body was and left it in my office yesterday.*

The workmanship was excellent, probably French. Madame des Bordes would know. The leather must have been extraordinarily supple when it was new, though now it was wrinkled and stiff, spattered with mud and dust. The interior had been lined with silk, but there wasn't much left. The heel was low. Originally the flaps had been secured with two ribbons. Only one was left, grubby and frayed. It was missing a tassel from one end.

Cat turned the shoe over. The stitching was coming undone near the toe. There was a hole in the sole, and the heel had worn completely away on one side.

It was only then that the practicalities of the murder took shape for her. Killing the man must have been the easy part. The pattern of the stab wounds suggested that it had been done in a frenzy. Afterwards, though, the murderer had destroyed the face and stripped the body of its clothes and possessions, presumably to hinder identification. Not easy to do in the dark or at twilight. Next, he had dragged the body to the spoil heap and concealed it in a place where it might have remained undiscovered for weeks.

Had this murder been planned? How many people had been involved in its execution?

In the parlour below, Margaret laughed, the sound travelling up through the floorboards.

Cat glanced at the letter to Marwood. Margaret's arrival was a sign, a nudge from Providence.

Carrying both the letter and the shoe, Cat went downstairs, making very little sound in her slippers. Sharp smells wafted up the stairs and made her wrinkle her nose. Both servants were on their knees just inside the parlour door.

'Two parts vinegar to one part lemon juice,' Margaret was saying. 'If the quantities are amiss, the stain will go deeper. And you must remember to add a—'

Cat caught them unawares. The two servants scrambled

to their feet. Margaret was a sturdy woman with black hair and a square red face. Beside her, Jane looked like a child.

'It's this floorboard, mistress. Jane here happened to ask me how to—'

Cat cut her off. 'Is your master at home?'

'He will be this evening. He wants to talk to me and Sam about something.'

'I want to talk to him myself,' Cat said, and the words sounded awkward and misshapen as she spoke them, liable to misinterpretation, as words so often were.

'Nothing easier. Shall I ask him to call, or will—'

'No. That's to say, I've changed my mind.' Flustered, Cat went into the parlour. She screwed up the letter and tossed it into the fire. In the flurry of the moment, she contrived to drop the shoe.

Margaret stooped for it. A ball of paper was left behind on the floor. Jane picked it up.

Cat held out her hand. The paper must have been stuffed into the toe of the shoe. She unfolded it and found a scrap torn diagonally from the corner of a larger sheet. Written on it in a sprawling hand were four and a half words.

. . . *arage Swan by Holborn Bridge.*

A cock on his own dunghill, the innkeeper poked his chin in the air and surveyed them with lordly condescension.

'Ah – you mean old Ma Farage?' He was a small man who bounced on his toes to make himself look taller. 'Why didn't you say?'

Brennan flushed. 'Because—'

'Yes, sir,' Cat said. 'I fear I didn't hear the name clearly.'

24

'It's the house over there. She holds it by yearly lease from me.' The innkeeper pointed his stick towards the north side of the yard. 'See? Beyond the coaches. Looking for lodgings, are you?'

'Yes. For a friend from the country.'

'Well, she might find room if your friend can pay. You can't miss her. Face like a frog. Croak!'

He laughed at his own wit and strutted away to welcome a party come by the Oxford road.

Cat touched Brennan's arm. She had taken a hackney up to Chard Lane as soon as Margaret left. In the site office, she had surprised her partner eating an enormous venison pie, the work of his doting wife. One of the advantages of living at a pastry cook's establishment was that you had your own oven on the premises.

She explained her reason for coming while Brennan finished his dinner. He made it clear from his manner that he thought her plan was a waste of time.

'If we just sit here waiting for something to happen,' Cat had said finally, 'we'll lose much more time than this. If we go to the Swan, there's a chance we might find something.'

'There's more than a chance that we'll lose an afternoon's work.'

But Brennan had come, all the same. They negotiated the crowd in the yard and reached Mistress Farage's door. Their knock was answered by a servant, a big-boned woman with a smear of soot on her cheek.

'Mistress is out,' she said. 'Won't be back till this evening. If you're looking for lodgings—'

'We're not,' Cat said. 'We are looking for a man who may live here.'

'Why? Owes you money?'

'No, the reverse. To repay a debt, a tavern bill for this gentleman.' She gestured towards Brennan, who was now looking confused. 'The trouble is, he didn't catch his name, only the address.'

The maid considered her. Cat took out her purse.

'Four men here at present.'

Cat took out a ha'penny.

'Mr Fisher, Mr Iredale, Mr Bickerstaff and Mr Jones.'

'The man we want is perhaps thirty years of age.' Cat summoned up the unpleasant memory of the white body with the stab wounds in the chest. 'Or five or ten years older at most.'

'Mr Fisher's got white hair. Mr Bickerstaff's away in the country.'

The servant held out her palm for the ha'penny.

'Is Mr Jones or Mr Iredale within?'

The maid said nothing until she had the ha'penny in her hand. Then: 'No. But it must be one of them. You can leave the money here. If you like.'

'I think not,' Cat said.

The woman retreated into the house and shut the door in their faces.

There was a husky chuckle at Cat's elbow. She turned to see an old man sitting on a mounting block outside the neighbouring house and smoking a short pipe.

'That's Patience Noone for you, mistress,' he said. 'Won't give you the time of day unless you pay for it. You didn't pay enough.'

'Do you live here?' Cat nodded at the house next door.

'No. I'm just about the yard. Here and there, most days.

Make myself useful where I can. A man must find his meat and drink somehow. It won't find itself in this cruel world, mistress, and that's a fact.'

And it was also an unmistakable hint. Cat let the purse chink on the palm of her hand. 'Tell me, do you know the people who live in this house?'

This struck the old man as amusing. He coughed smoke. 'I knows everyone here. Anyone will tell you that for free.'

Cat gave him a penny. 'A man about thirty years—'

'I heard you, mistress. Patience told you the truth. Must be either Iredale or Jones. Jones is Welsh – if it was him, you must have heard it in his voice, it goes up and down all over the place. Did he sound like that?'

She sidestepped the question. She remembered the dome of the dead man's skull, with the scabbed skin and its shading of short, patchy hair. 'Does Mr Jones wear a wig?'

The old man shook his head. 'He has a fine head of his own hair. I wish I could say the same. Of course when I was younger . . .'

'Our man wore a wig.'

'Then there you have it, mistress. Your man must be Iredale.' He grinned at her, revealing toothless gums. 'I could tell you something else about him if you make it worth my while.'

Cat shook the purse. 'The more we learn, the more we pay.'

'For a start, Iredale ain't been home for three nights. I heard Mistress Farage asking Patience about him.'

'And there's more?'

'You're not the only ones looking for him.' The old man looked slyly at her. 'Did you know that? Maybe he lent someone else some money as well as you. And they want to pay it back to him as well.'

She let the mockery pass. 'When was this other one here?'

'Saturday evening it was. Two of them.'

'What were they like?'

He shrugged. 'I didn't get a good look. I was over there, by the arch to the stables.'

She gave him another ha'penny. Afterwards, she and Brennan walked back to the site office. He stopped on Holborn Bridge, forcing her to do likewise. They looked at each other in silence.

'Will you talk to Mr Marwood now?' he said.

CHAPTER FOUR

I HAD ORDERED MY servant Sam to light a fire in the parlour.

The house in Infirmary Close was always cold, even on the hottest days of the year, and tonight it seemed colder and damper than ever. The wind was blowing in the wrong direction, filling the rooms and passageways with the smell of the river at low tide and the stink of the hospital graveyard.

I lodged in the old palace of the Savoy, which was convenient for Whitehall and the river, and no more expensive than most. At one time I had counted myself lucky to be here, despite the graveyard at the side of the house. Now I disliked the place. It held too many ghosts and not enough warmth.

Since my return from Whitehall this evening, I had been writing a summary of recent correspondence with my Lord Arlington's steward at Euston Hall, his principal house in the country. The steward was prolix; my lord was impatient and he had set me to summarize the details. It was tedious work, though I knew men envied me my position: to be confidential clerk to Lord Arlington was to be someone at Whitehall.

When it was done, I rang the bell. Sam Witherdine appeared eventually, announcing himself with the thump of his crutch on the bare boards. He always made more noise with it when he was out of temper, which seemed to be most of the time these days. Like master, like man.

I tossed him the key to the cupboard. 'Bring me the wine – the sack this time, and a glass.'

He gave me a sour look and hobbled over to fetch the wine. He had done me good service in the past but at present he was trying my patience sorely. No doubt I tried his patience too, but at least I paid his wages, gave him a bed to sleep on and clothes for his back. With one leg missing beneath the knee, he would find it hard to secure another place, let alone one as comfortable as this; and we both knew it. His wife, Margaret, was another matter. She ran my household with exemplary efficiency. I couldn't have one without the other.

There was a knock at the street door. I nodded to Sam, who went to open it. I threw back a glass of wine. As I was setting down the empty glass on the table, he returned.

'Mistress Hakesby, master,' he announced.

I stood up in a hurry, suddenly aware of my slovenly appearance. The cuff of my gown caught the glass, which tumbled on to the stone floor and broke into a thousand fragments.

She appeared not to notice. She scowled at me. 'I'm obliged to ask you a favour,' she said.

Cat Hakesby didn't like asking me for favours. Or indeed anyone else.

She and I met every few weeks. When we first encountered each other six years ago as St Paul's burned in the Fire, she had been Catherine Lovett. A year or so later, she became Mistress Hakesby, a young woman with an old husband. But soon the elderly architect died in circumstances that still haunted my dreams, leaving her a widow.

Our shared past tied us together. It also weighed us down like an ill-digested dinner. Last year I had spent a night in her bed. Afterwards, I offered her my hand and my heart, but she refused them both. Yet we remained something more than friends. She and I would go to hear music or to the play. In finer weather we might venture on the river. And I was there when she needed a man to escort her. When I wasn't with her, she found her way into my thoughts more often than was either convenient or comfortable.

But now here she was, bringing me this matter of a face-less corpse and an obstinate magistrate, and suddenly everything was made easier. She explained why she had come in a cold, unemotional voice, like a physician describing a patient's symptoms to a colleague.

I summoned Margaret to sweep up the glass. Afterwards we sat in silence in my damp, evil-smelling parlour, haunted by the ghosts of the undeserving dead. Sam had built up the fire when Cat came in without waiting for my command. The flames flickered on the side of her face, and I thought how beautiful she had become with the passing of the years. She had accepted a glass of wine, but it stood untasted at her elbow.

'Well, sir?' she said sharply, banishing my foolish thoughts. 'Would you oblige me by putting in a word with my lord?'

'He's at Euston at present, and he's likely to be there for a few weeks. The King and Queen are due to stay there after they leave Norwich.'

'Write to him, then.' Cat sounded impatient. 'If Lord

Arlington would take our part, I'm persuaded our difficulties would vanish in an instant.'

'I assume Rush is right?' I refilled my own glass. 'About the Chard almshouse being part of the liberty of Ely House?'

'Yes. But the nub of the matter isn't a question of law. According to Mr Hadgraft, my client, Rush is acting out of spite towards him.'

'Why?'

'I don't know. Rush originally invested in the project, but Hadgraft says he withdrew at the last moment. I don't know the reason for that, either. It doesn't make sense. Nor does shutting us down.'

'Rush might argue that you could accidentally destroy evidence before the inquest.'

Cat shook her head. 'In that case he could have ordered us to cordon off the spoil heap. But why prevent us from working on the rest of the site?'

'It's his decision,' I pointed out. 'However arbitrary it may seem. As a justice, he's acting within his powers.'

'But in this case he's abusing his authority.'

I changed the subject. 'A naked man. Murdered, mutilated and thrown into a spoil heap in the middle of a fenced building site with a nightwatchman. It's hard to make sense of it.'

'There's also the watchman's dog,' Cat said. 'Which has vanished.'

'Have you any idea at all who the dead man might be? Or why he was killed? And why would someone take pains to destroy his face? So no one could recognize him?'

'I don't know.' She looked away and toyed with the stem of her glass. 'In any case, it has no bearing on this business with Rush.'

I wondered if she were right. 'These stab wounds. What are they like?'

'Quite big.'

'A sword?'

'Perhaps.' She looked directly at me, and the candlelight made her skin golden. 'There were at least half a dozen wounds.'

'And?'

'Surely one would have been enough?' she said. 'Or two to make sure. It's as if . . .'

'The killer hated his victim? Or the attack was the work of a madman?'

She took a sip of wine. 'Or both.'

'I can't understand why he left the body where he did,' I went on. 'He must have realized it wouldn't stay hidden for long.'

'Perhaps he was disturbed. Or they panicked. In any case, the murderer could hardly drag the body through the streets without someone noticing, even at that hour.'

'Is there anything else you can tell me?' I said. 'Anything at all? If I'm to help you, I must know everything.'

Cat had brought a bag with her. She pulled it nearer and took out a small bundle of linen. She unwrapped it and placed a man's shoe on the table.

'It was found by the spoil heap where the body was.' She nudged it towards me. 'I wasn't sure whether to mention it to you – my problem's Rush, not the murder. He and the constable must have missed it.'

'The victim's?'

'Probably. It can't have been there long. It's French, I think, and it's been worn so much it's falling apart. But it must have been costly when it was new.'

'Have any Frenchmen been seen in the neighbourhood?'

'I don't know. Brennan says that Hadgraft's daughter has a French tutor, but I've never seen him. He might not even be a foreigner. Besides, the shoe could be second-hand. Anyway, these days you can buy a French shoe almost as easily in London as you can in Paris.' She held up a crumpled piece of paper. 'This had been pushed inside. To keep out water, perhaps.'

She slid the paper towards me: . . . *arage Swan Holborn Bridge*. The scrawled letters might have been written by a child.

'A Mistress Farage keeps lodgings in Swan Yard,' she went on. 'Do you know the Swan? The big inn by the bridge. Where one of the Oxford coaches starts.'

'You've been there?'

'Brennan and I went this afternoon. One lodger hasn't been seen since Saturday night. He's the right sort of age, and he wears a periwig, as the murdered man did. His name's Iredale.'

'Who is he? What does he do?'

Cat hesitated. 'I don't know anything else about him. Apart from the fact that two men came to Swan Yard looking for him on Saturday evening.'

'His killers? Do you think—?'

'I don't know what to think,' Cat said, her voice rising. 'Indeed, I don't want to think about it at all. I just want to build an almshouse.'

CHAPTER FIVE

THE FOLLOWING MORNING, Sam and I found a hackney in the Strand. The traffic was barely moving and the coachman took us up through Covent Garden. On the way we passed along Henrietta Street. I drew back the curtain and looked across the road at the sign of the Rose, the house where Cat lived and worked. There was nothing to see, no faces at the window, no Cat. Only the porter, Pheebs, sunning himself at the street door. He did not see me.

Sam and I rattled through the streets. Progress was slow because of the traffic, and for much of the way the grating racket of other vehicles made conversation impossible. In a quieter patch, I explained to Sam that we were looking for information about a man named Iredale.

'Keep your eyes and ears open, will you?'

He nodded, looking more cheerful at the prospect of doing something out of the ordinary.

The coach dropped us by Swan Yard. A maid answered the door of the Farage house. She was a big woman with sweat stains under her arms. I said I was on the King's business and asked to see her mistress. She ushered us into a stuffy dining parlour on the ground floor, where Mistress Farage was sitting with her left foot up on a footstool.

'I'm looking for Mr Iredale. I'm told he lodges here.'

I showed her my commission, which vouched for me as Lord Arlington's clerk employed under royal authority. Sometimes the mere sight of the seal was enough, but she read every word, breathing heavily with the effort, her tongue poking from the corner of her mouth. As she handed it back, she glanced at my face and her expression changed. She had seen the scars.

'Yes, sir, Mr Iredale does lodge here. But he ain't in the house.'

'When did you last see him?'

'Friday? Or maybe Saturday morning?'

It was now Wednesday. I said: 'Do you know where he's gone?'

'No.' Her tone brightened. 'But have you tried his office? They'll know. It's in Queen Street, by Lincoln's Inn Fields.'

'What does he do?'

'He's at the Council for Foreign Plantations,' she said proudly. 'They can't manage their business without our Mr Iredale.'

That was bad news. An enquiry was always more complicated when a government servant was involved. The council was one of those subcommittees that the Privy Council spawned whenever it was unable to make up its woolly mind about something. But if Iredale were rich or important, he wouldn't live in a place like Swan Yard. The wig suggested that he was a clerk of some sort rather than a menial. Which meant that a patron had probably put him forward for his place. Which meant—

'What's he done, sir?' Mistress Farage asked.

Sam cleared his throat and spat discreetly into the fireplace. 'Nothing. As far as I know.'

'I keep an honest house. Truly. You can ask anyone.'

She told me that Iredale had lived there since last winter. He kept himself to himself. He paid his bills more or less on time, and no one had come after him for debt.

When I asked Mistress Farage what he looked like, she gave me a vague description that could belong to a thousand men in London. 'And he wears a wig,' she added. 'Bought it second-hand at Easter.' For a second, malice flickered on her face, as a tongue flickers in a snake's mouth. 'Very proud of it, he is.'

'Does he have many visitors?'

'No, sir. Apart from the foreign gentleman.'

Neither she nor the maid seemed capable of describing the visitor, apart from the fact that he had worn a vizard covering his face. Even his nationality was a mystery. He had called once or twice in the last few weeks.

'What about the two men who came on Saturday evening?' I asked. 'They talked to your maid.'

'What men, Patience?' said Mistress Farage sharply.

'Why didn't you mention them just now?' I demanded.

The servant looked so blank that I wondered if she were half-witted. 'They weren't *visitors*, master. They didn't come into the house, did they? They were just asking where he was.'

Perhaps by accident, the chop-logic reply came dangerously close to insolence, but I let it go. 'What were they like?'

She considered. Then: 'One of them was a rat of a man. The other was a big, fat fellow.'

I sensed that I had extracted all the information I was going to get. I asked to see where Iredale lodged.

'The girl will show you, sir.' Mistress Farage pulled a face, which increased her resemblance to a frog. 'The gout's terrible today.' She winced as if to supply outward evidence of this. 'As God's my witness, I can't manage the stairs this morning without a miracle.'

Patience led us up a narrow, gloomy staircase. Sam followed behind – despite lacking half a leg, he was remarkably nimble. Iredale's apartments were on the second floor, immediately below the attics. He had a big, low-ceilinged parlour overlooking Swan Yard. It was meanly furnished but the sloping floorboards had recently been polished, and everything was orderly and clean. An inner door led to a panelled closet.

Patience folded her arms and waited. She had a habitual stoop, as though from a lifetime of trying to make herself look smaller. Her face was too large for its features. The eyes, nose and mouth were marooned in the surrounding flesh, skin and bone.

I felt her eyes on me while I opened cupboards and peered at the few plates and cups arranged on the shelf. In the closet, a box bed was set into a curtained alcove, also panelled. A neatly pressed nightshirt lay folded on the pillows. The maid looked like a slattern, but she knew what she was about when it came to her duties.

Sam followed us into the closet. He wandered restlessly about, his eyes darting about the room, occasionally touching something with a fingertip. Meanwhile I went through Iredale's clothes, which were kept in a chest opposite the bed.

There was a worn suit, which had been recently brushed. His linen was mean stuff, but it had been freshly washed, ironed and neatly folded. Sam cleared his throat.

I glanced at him. 'What?'

The panelling ran into the alcove. He stroked one of the panels at the head of the bed. 'Seems out of true, sir. Maybe warped? I'd say it needs a bit of work.'

It was always a delight when Sam fancied he was being subtle. I gave him a nod and he set to work on the panel, probing and twisting and pulling and knocking. Like many sailors, he was good with his hands. If providence had arranged matters for him otherwise, he could have made a respectable living as a joiner.

I took the opportunity to observe Patience out of the corner of my eye. She was breathing heavily and rapidly, but her expression was unchanged. She showed no traces of alarm or even curiosity.

The panel was about a foot square. Gradually Sam slid it aside until most of it was behind its neighbour directly to the left. He stood back, looking smug, and waited for me to investigate what lay within. The brick-lined recess was about twelve inches high, nine wide and six deep. I put my hand inside. The hole extended behind the right-hand panel by two or three more inches. There was something soft and smooth in the bottom corner, resting against the back of the panel.

For the duration of a heartbeat, I thought it was the body of a young rat. But when I drew it gingerly into the daylight, I found a small purse of dark-green velvet, fastened with drawstrings and embroidered with a pattern of yellow chevrons edged with seed pearls. There was nothing inside.

'Have you seen this before? Did you know there was a hiding place here?'

Patience shook her head.

The purse must have been expensive. It looked unused. Why would a man like Iredale hide it? Why would he possess such a thing in the first place?

I asked Sam for the satchel. I opened it and took out the shoe from the spoil heap at the Chard Lane almshouse. I showed it to Patience.

'What about this? Have you seen it before?'

She sucked in her breath and then let it out in a shuddering sigh. Her face briefly lost its blank expression. 'No, master,' she said. 'Never in my life. It's not Mr Iredale's if that's what you want to know.'

I assumed Patience was stupid because she was a large, lumbering servant with few outward charms. But it was I who was stupid.

At Whitehall, the clock over the guardhouse struck midday.

Louise was still abed, with the familiar monthly pains upon her. In this strange country they called them 'those' for reasons she found unfathomable. Why could they not call it bleeding? Was it because Englishmen were particularly disgusted by the shameful leakage that afflicted womankind? Or were they simply afraid of it?

The bed curtains were still closed. The darkness smelled stuffy. Last night she had taken laudanum again to deaden the pain, and its fumes still drifted through her mind as aimlessly as clouds.

For the whole of yesterday, there had been no news from the Duke of Buckingham. She might see him again this evening, but there was no certainty even of that. Where the Duke was concerned, she was learning, there was no certainty of anything.

In the eyes of the world, though, it was undoubtedly certain that a young woman of good birth but no fortune had only two respectable choices: to find a wealthy husband, preferably of her own rank, or to retire from the world, which in Louise's case meant to enter the living death of a nunnery. Her eyes filled with tears as she contemplated her plight, and soon her cheeks were wet.

There was a knock on the door, a lifting of the latch. She stopped crying.

The hoarse whisper penetrated the curtained dark. 'Mamzelle?'

'Open the curtains,' she said, wiping her face with the sleeve of her nightgown. 'Bring me the pot.'

There was a rattle of rings on the rail, and light burst upon her. Louise covered her eyes with her hand.

'A letter, mamzelle,' her maid said. 'From the King.'

Louise sat up abruptly, ignoring the protesting pains in her belly. 'Give it to me.'

CHAPTER SIX

T HE HACKNEY SET me down at the corner of Queen
Street by Lincoln's Inn Fields. I was alone. I had sent
Sam back to the Savoy.

The Council for Foreign Plantations had leased part
of a house on the south side of the street from Lord
Bristol. It was a substantial establishment around a courtyard. It was now divided among several tenants. The
porter at the street gate directed me to a doorway in the
range at the back, close to an archway leading into the
gardens. The door stood open with its keeper visible
within. As I reached it, he turned away, distracted by
raised voices in the lobby beyond.

'. . . they were there on Friday afternoon,' a man was
saying in a clear, precise voice. 'I saw them with my own
eyes. They cannot have walked away of their own volition.'

A man's voice rumbled in reply.

I rapped my stick on the step.

The doorkeeper turned, his eyes swiftly assessing my
appearance. 'Does your honour have an appointment?'

42

'No. But my business is urgent. My name's Marwood. Is the Secretary within?'

'The council isn't sitting this morning, sir, and—'

The porter broke off. Behind him, a middle-aged man was descending the short flight of steps from the lobby. He was plainly dressed but had the bearing of a gentleman. At the foot of the steps, he paused, looking at me.

'Your servant, sir. Your face is familiar.' He snapped his fingers. 'Mr Marwood, is it not? My Lord Arlington's clerk.'

I recognized him too. It was Mr John Evelyn, whom I had seen more than once in company with Lord Arlington. I bowed. 'You, sir, I know, are a member of this council.'

'Indeed. As is my lord now, of course, though we rarely have the honour of seeing him here. Do you come from him?'

'Not exactly.' I chose my words carefully. 'But I'm enquiring into a matter that may require his attention. I scarcely like to trouble you with such a trifle, but is a man named Iredale employed here?'

'I've no idea. In what capacity?'

'I don't know.'

Evelyn looked sharply at me and then at the doorkeeper. 'Well?'

'Mr Iredale's one of our copyists, sir. He's not here today – in truth, I've not seen him for a day or two.'

'I'm anxious to find him,' I said. I lowered my voice. 'I fear some harm may have come to him.'

Evelyn was too discreet to question me further. 'Mr Davis is upstairs – he's one of our clerks. I'm sure he'll know about the man. Come with me.'

I followed him up the steps to the lobby. Another flight of steps led to the first floor.

'Do you have the whole of this side of the house, sir?' I asked.

'Only the first floor – though that's commodious enough, as you'll see. We have seven or eight rooms as well as a share of the gardens and the stables.'

In the first room, a servant was setting turkey-work chairs against the wall.

'Have you found them yet?' Evelyn asked him.

'No, master.'

'It really won't do. Someone must have taken them. It's your task to find out who.'

We left the servant muttering behind us and passed into the next room.

'It's a tiresome, trifling matter,' Evelyn said, flushing with annoyance. 'We have a cupboard where the councillors keep our commons in case we need refreshment during our meetings. I had a bottle of Madeira and a Cheshire cheese in there. They have vanished. It's possible that one of my colleagues took them but not likely. It's not the things themselves, you understand, sir, but the principle of the matter.'

I murmured sympathetically. Evelyn struck me even on short acquaintance as a man for whom both order and principle were important.

He escorted me through a long gallery hung with tapestries and lit by a bay window overlooking the garden. The council chamber was beyond, a stately room furnished with globes and map cabinets. Charts hung on the wall, and a large atlas lay open on the long table. A slight man in a brown coat was tidying the paper, pens and inkpots in a large standish on a smaller table at the far end of the room. He looked up as we entered.

'Mr Marwood,' Evelyn said in a stately way, 'may I present Mr Davis, our chief clerk? We couldn't manage our business without him. Mr Marwood is from Lord Arlington's private office.'

Davis came forward. 'Your servant, sir.'

He was a brisk fellow with quick, decided movements. Evelyn explained why we were here.

'Iredale? I'm afraid he's not in the office.'

'He's not at his lodging, either,' I said. 'When did you last see him?'

'Saturday. He did his work as usual, and then he left with the rest of us. None of us was working last Sunday. He didn't turn up on Monday morning.'

'Did you enquire at his house?'

Davis shook his head. 'We've been much occupied. I intended to send a messenger this afternoon. I thought he might have been called away to see his parents if there had been another crisis in their affairs. They live in Paddington, he told me once. They are poor folk, and not in the best of health.'

'What exactly does he do here?' I asked.

'We have a considerable volume of correspondence, and he's one of the three copyists who deal with it. He's also on the rota for recording the meetings.' He gestured at the small table with the standish. 'We sit there, noting in shorthand what's said by the council, and we make fair copies for them to sign afterwards.'

'Are you happy with his work?'

Davis glanced at Evelyn, who nodded and turned tactfully away to look down on the garden. 'Well, sir, since you ask . . . Iredale is undeniably quick, and he has a lively intelligence. And a fair grasp of the French tongue, which comes in useful. But he is not always as industrious as I should like and between ourselves he's a coarse fellow. And his copying is sometimes slapdash.'

'But you keep him on . . . ?'

'Yes, sir. In the circumstances, it would be awkward not to.'

I was coming to like Davis. He shared a way of speaking that was common at Whitehall, where spoken words were often less important than the meaning that flowed like an invisible stream of intelligence beneath them.

'Ah. Perhaps he was put forward for his place here by a member of the council?'

Davis grinned. The change of expression was so sudden and unexpected that I found myself grinning back. We might have been a pair of schoolboys sharing a piece of mischief.

'You have it in one, sir. He was commended to us by one of the Duke of Buckingham's people. I understand he'd rendered the Duke some small service in France.'

I stopped grinning. Davis looked curiously at me but said nothing. Despite the immense difference in our stations, the Duke of Buckingham knew me, and I knew him: he despised me, and he wished me nothing but ill.

'An empty purse?' Cat said. 'Why hide that?'

Marwood dropped it on the table. 'It's worth something. Just in itself.'

She picked it up and felt the quality of the material and examined the stitching. 'At least a pound or two. Very well – so it's worth keeping safe. Perhaps the servants are light-fingered.'

'But it's not something you'd expect a copyist to have in the first place, is it? Iredale can't earn more than sixty or seventy pounds a year at best. His lodgings are neat enough but there's nothing of value in them.'

'Except this.'

Marwood veered on to another line of thought. 'Perhaps he'd hidden other things behind the panel. Perhaps he was in a hurry when he took them out, and he overlooked the purse. It was tucked away at the side. You couldn't see it in there.'

Neither of them spoke for more than a minute. It wasn't an uncomfortable silence. They knew each other too well for that.

They were sitting in the parlour of Cat's private apartments at the sign of the Rose. She had sent Jane Ash out to buy wine. The table was near the window. The evening sunshine glanced against the left side of Marwood's face. Unless you looked for it, she thought idly, you hardly noticed the scarring now, for all he was so absurdly conscious of it. But the fire that burned his face and neck had left other scars, and she doubted that those would ever heal completely. Even now, years later, he preferred not to stand too close to a fire.

'The purse is like that shoe,' Marwood said suddenly. 'It doesn't *belong*.'

'Why don't I show them to Madame des Bordes?'

'Who?'

'She's the Queen's dresser. A nice woman with a taste for gossip. I met her in France last year, when she was *femme de chambre* to the King's sister. If the shoe's French, she'll probably know who made it. She asked me to Whitehall on Friday to see the new fashions. I wasn't going to go, but perhaps I should. I'll write to her.'

'It's worth a venture.'

Cat's mind had darted off in another direction. 'What worries me . . .'

'What?'

She shook her head. 'It doesn't matter.'

Marwood had an unwelcome habit of not letting her retreat into the safety of silence. 'The brutality? The way the face was smashed to pieces, obliterated?'

'That wasn't what I was going to say,' Cat snapped. Nevertheless, she winced at the memory.

He smiled, which threw her off her stride. 'What then? Oh, I know. The work.'

She nodded, though it was only part of the truth. 'We haven't found anything that could strengthen our hand against Rush. We've only made matters worse. I don't even care who killed that poor man. All I want to do is get the ban lifted. Every day we don't work is a day nearer winter. Every day that goes by, we either have to pay men for work they don't do or watch them drift away to other jobs. We've already laid out a small fortune on Hadgraft's behalf. But he won't pay us a shilling until we do something.'

Marwood leant closer across the table. 'But we have learned something. We know Iredale is missing, and there's a very good chance that he's the victim. We also know that Iredale has a connection to the Duke. There's also the masked foreigner who called at Swan Yard. Arlington will be interested in that for its own sake. I'm sure of it. Which means that I shan't just be asking him a favour on your behalf. I'll be reporting something he will want to know about. Besides,

I have to tell him about this to cover myself – Mr Evelyn may tell him that I called at the council today.'

'*John* Evelyn?' Cat said. 'You met him today?'

'Yes. He's on the council. Why?'

'Nothing. I know him by reputation.'

'Obviously, when I talk to my lord, I'll mention your difficulty too,' Marwood went on. 'Perhaps I can persuade him to let me write to Rush on your behalf.' He paused. 'And there's one other thing. I'm probably making something out of nothing, and perhaps . . .'

'What is it, sir?'

'It's those men asking for Iredale at Swan Yard. The maid said one was a little rat of man, and the other was a big fat fellow. And Iredale got his job as a copyist through Buckingham's interest.'

She stared at him. She couldn't find words to say. She felt suddenly defenceless.

'There must be hundreds of fat men in London,' Marwood said softly. 'Thousands. Why should this one be Roger Durrell? Anyway, he's probably dead. He lost a hand, remember?'

'And what about Buckingham?'

'Cat, the Duke's everywhere. Hardly a day goes by without his name coming up. It probably means nothing.'

Marwood went on talking, and she allowed herself to be soothed. A little later, there were steps on the landing, and Jane came in with two bottles in her basket. She was looking slightly furtive, as she generally did even when she had done nothing wrong.

He stayed for a glass of wine but he did not linger, to Cat's unspoken regret. It was typical of him that he had put his

49

finger on what really worried her. It was typical that she had been unwilling to talk about it because that might make it real, and also typical that he wouldn't allow her to push the subject aside. And typical yet again that he wasn't here when she wanted him to be here.

The delay on the Chard almshouse project was a problem that she needed to solve if she and Brennan were not to risk financial difficulties, even ruin. Even if it came to that, however, she had faced worse things and survived. She was not without friends, including Marwood himself.

But the other matter was not a problem that could be solved, or whose possible consequences could be predicted or faced. It belonged to a different category.

Was Iredale's fat man the same as Roger Durrell, the man who had been in the employ of the Duke of Buckingham three years before? Durrell was the creature from Cat's nightmares. You couldn't use reason against the monsters within your own head. Even my Lord Arlington would be powerless to help her. Even James Marwood.

Durrell had been in this very room, her own parlour. Durrell had manhandled her down the stairs. With foolish, unexpected bravery, her elderly husband had come running after them in the hope of rescuing her. And Durrell had killed poor Mr Hakesby as casually as a man squashes an ant under his thumb.

I wrote to Lord Arlington later that afternoon.

I had served my lord in his private office for a little over a year. During that time, my duties had grown into a role that combined those of a confidential secretary and of an intelligencer. I usually worked at Goring House, the

Arlingtons' London residence at the Westminster end of St James's Park, rather than in his office as Secretary of State, which was in the Privy Gallery at Whitehall. Many men envied me but I was not altogether happy in his employ, despite the money and the influence it brought. I had previously worked in the office of Mr Williamson, my lord's Under Secretary, and I had found his manner of doing business more to my taste.

In a few dry sentences, I described how Mistress Hakesby had asked my advice about the corpse of a faceless man discovered at a building site off Chard Lane. I mentioned that a shoe of French manufacture had been found near the body and that an address concealed inside it had led me to the lodging of a government copyist named Iredale, who was now missing. Before his disappearance, a masked foreigner had paid several calls on him. I explained how the local magistrate, Mr Willoughby Rush, was using a legal quibble to halt work on the whole site for as long as he could, purely to spite the developer. Mistress Hakesby would be for ever in his lordship's debt if he were to write to Mr Rush and request him to lift his ban.

Arlington knew of my connection with Cat, though not, as far as I was aware, of the full extent of it. She had built his infant daughter a splendid poultry house in the garden at Goring House. Last year he had commissioned her to design an even grander one for the King's late sister, and there had been talk of a further commission at his country mansion in Euston Hall.

He was reasonably well-disposed towards Cat, but I knew what his response to her request would be as if he had dictated it to me in person. Before he could help her, he would say, he would want to know who the dead man was, and why he had no face. He would also want more information about the foreigner and the copyist.

Only then, perhaps, would he condescend to help her. But at least I had tried.

CHAPTER SEVEN

C AT SAT AT a window in the house off Chard Lane. She had chosen this room on the first floor partly because it was well lit, and partly because it gave the best view of the site as a whole. From here, she could see the spoil heap where the body had been concealed. To the right stretched the waste ground. To the left were the few remains of the original almshouse.

The plans for the new one had been completed months ago. The trustees had also granted Mr Hadgraft a long building lease on the wasteland behind it, together with a right of access from Chard Lane. Once the almshouse was built, Hadgraft wanted Cat to lay out a street of brick houses, eight on each side, built to conform to the new regulations since the Fire. Such a large a parcel of land lying close to the City was immensely valuable. The houses, conveniently placed between Newgate and Holborn, would undoubtedly prove a very good investment once they were built. Two men had already put down substantial deposits for leases.

So near, Cat thought, so far. The work was waiting.

Everything was ready. But that cursed magistrate had made them stop.

She returned to the papers in front of her. She was going through the figures in the hope of finding ways to economize or at least delay the payments that had already fallen due.

There was a knock on the street door, followed by Ledward, the watchman, clumping down the passage. A little later she heard footsteps on the stairs. Cat put down her pen as the door opened without the courtesy of a knock.

'Mistress Hakesby!' Grace Hadgraft stood on the threshold. Her waiting woman hovered on the landing behind her. 'I find you hard at work!' She made this sound slightly indecent. 'Pray forgive me for interrupting you.'

Cat rose and curtsied. Grace, her client's daughter, was barely eighteen. But she was already a beautiful woman, the sort that turns heads in the street and makes men into beasts. Her clothes were beautiful too. Her father used her appearance to advertise his wealth.

'There's nothing to forgive, Mistress Hadgraft,' Cat said. 'And how may I serve you?'

Grace coloured prettily. She did most things prettily. 'My father doesn't know I'm here.' She made a moue, pretending to be shocked by her own naughtiness. 'Pray don't mention it to him. I happened to be passing, you see – I'm going to my glover's – Susannah says I have nothing fit to wear for winter, don't you? – and I – I had a sudden notion to see how things progress here.'

'Not very well.' Cat gestured through the window at a landscape empty of figures. 'As you can see.'

Taking this as an invitation, Grace glided across the bare boards and stared over the building site. Her long fingers played with the ermine collar of her cloak. 'Such a pity that Mr Rush is being obstinate! My poor father is distressed beyond measure. It makes him so cross with everyone.'

The waiting woman remained by the door. Susannah was older than Grace, a small, sallow-skinned woman with restless brown eyes. Cat had encountered her at Mr Hadgraft's house more than once, though she had never had occasion to speak to her.

Grace's hand flew to her mouth. 'Oh, Mistress Hakesby! Is that where the body was found?' She shuddered and gestured in the direction of the spoil heap. 'Down there, on that pile of rubbish?'

Cat joined her at the open window. 'Yes – the rain made the rubble shift. That's when we found it.'

'And – and the face was quite gone?'

'Someone had beaten the features to pulp,' Cat said.

Grace cried out. Tears brimmed in her eyes. 'How – how terrible.'

Cat knew she should feel guilty for upsetting the poor, spoiled woman. But she didn't. 'It may well have been done after death,' she said soothingly. 'So he would have felt nothing.'

Grace turned and bolted from the room. Her footsteps clattered down the stairs, followed by the sound of the yard door opening. The waiting woman's eyes met Cat's for an instant.

'My mistress has been a trifle unwell lately,' she said. 'Since the master sent Mr Pharamond away.'

'The French tutor?'

'Yes, mistress. That's right. One of these mounseers. I believe he was unsatisfactory.'

Then she too left the room and sedately followed her mistress.

Cat went to the window. Grace was in the yard below, leaning with one hand against a stack of timber. Her head was bowed, and her cloak had fallen from her shoulders to the ground. Susannah was a few yards away, making no attempt to go to her mistress's assistance. Instead she was watching her with every appearance of indifference.

Grace Hadgraft retched, her whole body racked with the effort. She retched again, and again. At last she vomited, partly on the ground, partly over her skirt and partly on the cloak with the ermine collar.

Mistress Farage smacked her wide, wet lips together as if catching a fly. 'I can't go,' she croaked. 'You could not be so cruel, Mr Marwood, so unmanly as to force me?'

Iredale's landlady stared reproachfully at me. We were in her parlour. The air smelled fetid and weary. Her bandaged foot was up on a stool.

'I've a coach at the door.' I needed someone to tell me whether the body was Iredale's, or even if it might be. But I wished now that I had gone first to Queen Street and found someone who worked with him instead. 'You'll be back before you know it.'

'It's quite impossible.'

She groaned loudly, squinting up at me to see the effect her performance was having.

'If you please, sir.' Patience Noone, the maid, stepped forward. 'I could go in her place.'

'Of course!' Mistress Farage cried. 'Why didn't I think of it?'

'I'd know him, sir, I'd know him anywhere. It was me that waited on him.'

A glance passed between the two women.

'So you did, girl,' Mistress Farage said. 'So you did.'

We went first to Mr Rush's house. The magistrate lived not far from Chard Lane in one of the new houses in Hatton Garden, which was on the other side of Holborn Bridge. I needed his authority to inspect the body.

While Patience waited in the coach, Rush received me in his dining room, where he was making a late breakfast. He was a compact, middle-aged man, with a high colour and a face much scarred with smallpox. His features were irregular, as if they had been carelessly reassembled after some childhood catastrophe had smashed them into fragments. He took his time inspecting my commission, but afterwards he was civil enough.

'Of course you may see the corpse, sir.' He had a hard, staccato way of speaking that lent emphasis to his words. 'But you realize that it cannot be removed without the permission of the bishop's coroner? Or whomever he delegates his authority to.'

'Of course not. I merely wish—'

'And for the same reason' – he tapped the handle of his knife on the table – 'I cannot allow work to continue anywhere on the Chard almshouse site until after the inquest. In case the coroner finds that the location of the murder is germane to his enquiry.'

'I understand you perfectly. Where is the body?'

'You won't have far to go. I keep it in an outbuilding. I can keep an eye on it there.'

57

'We know a particular man is missing. I've brought a servant who may be able to identify the body, if it is him. She's waiting in the coach.'

'I rather doubt that anyone could identify this fellow.' Rush scratched the black-and-silver stubble on his chin. 'By the way, you're not the first to be curious about this corpse of mine.'

'Mr Hadgraft, perhaps?'

'He'll get nothing from me, and he's not foolish enough to try. No, this was someone else, a mean-looking fellow who waylaid one of my people in an alehouse. Fell into conversation, bought him a drink, and then started asking questions. Wanted to know where the body was, and when the bishop's coroner was due. That sort of thing.' Rush smiled smugly. 'He wasted his money. I choose my people well.'

'May I talk to your servant, sir? Perhaps he—'

'No.' As if to make up for the blunt refusal, he went on, 'But if you come across this man, you won't mistake him. He's a big ugly rogue.' The magistrate gestured with his arms, indicating that the size had to do with width as much as height. 'Wears a sword on his right side. That's because he's only got a left hand. He's mislaid the other one. Wears a spike instead.'

Willoughby Rush was looking at me, expecting a reaction. Surprise, perhaps, or even amusement. But I gave him nothing at all.

Rush's house had a narrow garden surrounded by high brick walls topped with spikes. With Patience Noone trailing behind us, we walked towards a door at the end. Rush explained that the garden backed on to a court that opened off Holborn.

He had taken a lease on a cottage and a former workshop and inserted this doorway into the wall.

'I don't care to be overlooked, Mr Marwood. I've spent time at sea, and that's given me a taste for minding my own business and expecting others to do the same.' He glanced sharply at me, as if to make sure I was attending. 'And I need storage for my own affairs. I've a contract with the navy to supply them with belts.'

A navy contract was bound to be lucrative. It also suggested that Rush had useful friends.

We came to the door. He knocked on it with the head of his stick. It was opened in a moment or two by a tall man with a shock of red hair. He gave a salute of a vaguely military character.

'We want to see the body,' Rush announced. 'Fetch a lantern and a couple of candles.'

When these were ready, he led us down a flight of steps to a stout, close-fitting door, which he unlocked with a key from his pocket. For a moment he and I stood in the doorway. Patience Noone was behind us, craning her head to see into the small, low-ceilinged cellar. I covered my mouth and nose with my sleeve. Patience whimpered softly.

The body lay on a makeshift bier, a door resting on trestles. The air was cooler down here than in the garden, but not by much. The first thing I noticed was the smell. It would soon grow worse, for the weather was still mild. The ventilation, such as it was, came from a small grille set in the ceiling near the far wall.

Rush handed me a candle. 'Already on the turn, I'm afraid. Anyway, there's your man.'

Shielding the flame of the candle with my hand, I walked

slowly around the bier, forcing myself to concentrate on small, harmless details in an attempt to distract myself from the horror of the whole. The body looked well nourished. The limbs were lean and well-muscled. The hands were clean enough, and the skin lacked calluses. The man had been of medium height. I estimated him to have been in his thirties, for the body was not that of a youth. He had been stabbed seven times – four times in the vicinity of the heart, and thrice in the belly.

I forced myself to look at the face, or rather where the face had been. It was now a wilderness of broken bone, dried blood and shreds of flesh. The eyes were gone. Why go to such lengths? To conceal the man's identity? In a frenzy of hatred? Or both?

'Patience.' I held out the candle to her. 'Do you know this man?'

She stared at the wreckage of a man before us. 'How can I know? How can anyone?' Then she crumpled to the floor, making no more noise than a pile of dirty sheets pushed off a table.

The morning went from bad to worse. First Grace, then her father.

Grace blamed her sickness on a dish of oysters she had eaten last night. When she recovered, she left the site office with her waiting woman. Cat returned to her work. Ten minutes later, Hadgraft appeared, announcing his arrival with a fusillade of knocks. Ledward let him into the house.

'Why didn't you notice anything that night?' Cat heard Hadgraft shouting. 'Were you drunk again, you worthless creature?'

She went downstairs to greet her employer. She found him waving his stick at Ledward, who was backing away towards the door to the yard.

'Answer me, you knave!'

'God's my witness, master, I don't know. Maybe they cast a spell on me. Or put something in my beer to make me sleep. And where's my dog? What have they done to him?'

'Get out of my sight!' Hadgraft turned to face Cat. He was red in the face, and the Adam's apple bounced in the scrawny throat. 'Well?'

'Have you news, sir?' Cat said. 'Do we have a date for the inquest?'

'No we do not. And you?' Hadgraft advanced a step closer. His head was on a level with hers. 'What about your friends at Whitehall? Can't you ask them for help?'

'I'm doing what I can.' Cat felt her temper rising. 'I want the matter dealt with as much as you do.'

'I doubt that, madam! I doubt that very much.' His anger radiated from him like heat from a fire. 'Have you any idea—' He broke off suddenly, for there had been another knock at the street door. 'Where's that damned rogue to answer the door?'

Cat pushed past him and opened the door herself. Marwood was outside. He looked paler than usual.

'Who's that?' Hadgraft demanded, glancing at the new arrival and finding nothing to like.

'May I present Mr Marwood, sir, of my Lord Arlington's private office? And this is Mr Hadgraft, my client.'

'Oh!' The anger vanished like a punctured bubble. Hadgraft bowed hastily. 'Then may I venture to hope that my lord himself has taken an interest in our difficulty?'

'That remains to be seen, sir.' Since he had gone to work for my lord, Marwood had learned the trick of running his eyes over people in a manner that suggested that he did not find them very interesting. 'His Lordship is in the country at present. I wish to make further enquiries before I trouble him in this matter.'

'Mr Marwood is my lord's confidential clerk,' Cat murmured. 'You may be assured of his discretion.'

'Of course. Naturally. Pray allow me to assist you in any way I can. Perhaps I may offer you some refreshment? My house is but a step away if you would honour me with a visit.'

While Hadgraft was speaking, Cat manoeuvred herself behind him and on to the first step of the stairs. She nodded vigorously over his shoulder, hoping Marwood would take her meaning. She had had more than enough of her client for one day.

'I'd be happy to, sir,' Marwood said.

It was only after the two men had left that she wondered why Marwood had come to see her.

CHAPTER EIGHT

'MARWOOD?' MR HADGRAFT said as we walked across Holborn Bridge, raising his voice to be heard over the noise of the traffic. 'The name's familiar. Was there not an Alderman Marwood in the late king's time?'

'There was,' I said reluctantly. 'My father's uncle.'

He looked at me with sudden interest. 'Indeed.' We crossed the top of Shoe Lane, and he led me into the quieter streets next to St Andrew's church and Thavies Inn. 'A most worthy man,' he went on. 'I didn't have the honour of his acquaintance myself. But I knew him well by reputation.'

So did I. Great-Uncle Marwood had been apprenticed to a wealthy grocer. He must have been a plausible fellow for he married his master's daughter, his only child. The old man died, leaving the bulk of his estate in trust for any children his daughter might have. My great-uncle lived high on the hog for a few years and was briefly an alderman, a tribute to his father-in-law's wealth and his wife's ambition rather than to any merit of his own. Then he too had died, long before I was born. The marriage had been childless. His widow soon married again and produced a brood of healthy children. My father, who before his wits went wandering was no fool, always said that Uncle Marwood was a sly, godless fellow who would lick the arse of the Devil himself if it earned him a shilling.

Hadgraft lived in a comfortable, brick-built house. It stood just outside the area touched by the Fire. He led me into a study overlooking a pretty little garden. There was a summer-house set against a south-facing wall. Two women were sitting there with their backs turned to us.

'You'll take a glass with me, I hope?' Without waiting for a reply, Hadgraft unlocked a cupboard set in the panelling. He poured the wine and we toasted the King.

'Mistress Hakesby told me she would see what she could do,' he said as he set down his glass on the desk. 'But I confess I had not dared to hope that she would bring a gentleman of your standing into the business.'

'You have shown much discernment in your choice of architect,' I said blandly, returning flattery for flattery. 'She's a lady whose work attracts increasing interest at court. Lord Arlington is among her clients. I hear the King himself admires her designs.'

'Most gratifying, sir, and particularly for one such as I. Unlike your honoured self, I was not born into a prosperous family. My origins are humble. But by God's grace I have prospered. In the last few years, I've adventured some of my fortune on the seas, and my voyages have made happy land-falls. In return for God's bounty, it seems only fitting that I should lay out a portion of my wealth on those less blessed.' He shot a glance at me. 'I tell you this not to boast, you understand, but in case my lord enquires more deeply into my situation.'

I inclined my head in what I hoped was an encouraging manner.

'I prayed for guidance,' he went on, 'and God led me by degrees to the understanding that the best way to do this was to rebuild the Chard Lane almshouse to His greater glory. And to relieve the suffering of the destitute, of course.'

I guessed that Hadgraft had made this speech, or something very like it, on previous occasions. It had a suspicious fluency, a well-rehearsed and almost rhythmical quality. Not that his words were necessarily insincere. But my life in recent years had bred in me a cynical tendency. I wondered what he hoped to gain from the project.

'The Fire destroyed the old, almost ruinous place,' he was saying. 'Perhaps that was a blessing. With the agreement of the trustees, I shall erect a commodious set of buildings with a particularly fine chapel and a neat house for the warden. It will shelter the poor for generations to come while promoting the values of the Established Church.'

'The Bishop of Ely must surely approve of that.'

'No doubt. But his lordship may not even know of the project. My agreement is with the Chard Lane almshouse trustees. The fact that this parcel of land remains within the bishop's liberty is an unfortunate accident. But alas – it means that the bishop's courts may have the right to adjudicate in certain legal disputes that occur there. I was bred to the law, sir, and I fear there is no disputing that point.'

It was a common difficulty in London, both the City and its environs. Such pockets of ecclesiastical privilege dated from before the Reformation. The monasteries were long gone, and so were many of the town palaces of the bishops; but their privileges often remained, though they varied widely in nature and extent. Often the grounds on which they had stood were legal sanctuaries, and in some cases they had become the refuge of thieves and fugitives, debtors and whores. I knew something of the liberty they called Alsatia, not far from my house in the Savoy. It was the place to go if you wanted to have somebody maimed or even killed, or if you had stolen goods to sell or a need for a drunken clergyman to conduct your bigamous marriage. On the other hand, you risked having your purse stolen and your throat cut while you were there. The liberty of the bishops of Ely in Holborn was not as lawless as that, but I was unsurprised to learn that it was a legal quagmire.

I stirred in my chair. 'Even a case of murder? Isn't that something for the Crown to deal with, not the bishop?'

Before he answered, Hadgraft refilled my glass with canary. When he spoke, he picked his words with care. 'You would think so. But it's possible that in the first instance the bishop has the right to appoint his own coroner in the case of an unexplained death. I've applied to examine both the original grant of the liberty and any later modifications. But all that will take time. And time is in short supply for us because winter will soon be here. Which is where we come to the heart of the matter. Has Mistress Hakesby told you about the unreasoning obstinacy of a man named Rush?'

'Yes. The local justice.'

'While he waits for a reply from Ely, he's placed an interim interdiction over the entire site – not merely the place where the body was found. He claims this is in case the coroner should find the environs to be material to the murder. There is no rational ground to suppose that. Meanwhile my workmen are drifting away and I lose money with every day that passes.'

'Why would Mr Rush do that?' I asked.

'He's actuated purely by malice. By an unreasoning and spiteful hatred of myself. We've had some business dealings in the past and I suppose he must feel himself ill-used in some way. All nonsense, of course.'

I changed my line of questioning: 'Have you noticed any foreigners in the neighbourhood?'

'What?' Hadgraft swallowed, taken by surprise, and his Adam's apple wobbled. 'Why?'

'My Lord Arlington is always interested in the movements of foreigners.' I waved my hand. 'They are so often rogues or malcontents. They cause trouble wherever they go.'

'I suppose there must be some in the neighbourhood. But I know nothing of them.'

My eyes strayed to the window, to the two women in the summerhouse. 'Doesn't your daughter have a tutor for the French tongue, sir? Is he a Frenchman?'

Hadgraft snorted. 'Oh him! Yes, he is. And a damned coxcomb too!' He hesitated, and I sensed that he was deciding what he need tell me. 'I thought you meant strangers, you see – he's been here for months. But I had to dismiss him the other day. The fellow's stuffed with his own inflated consequence yet he barely has two pennies to rub together. I . . . I caught him trying to steal a silver spoon from me. I was merciful – I merely had him thrown out of the house.'

'When was this?'

With sudden violence, Hadgraft raked a nail across his forehead, leaving a red trail below the line of his wig. 'Saturday evening.'

'And his name?'

'He calls himself Pharamond. You – you don't think he might be . . . ?'

'The dead man? Or even the murderer? I don't know. Where does he lodge?'

'You'll find him at the Three Crowns near St Sepulchre's.'

'Off Snow Hill?' I said. 'Above Newgate?'

'Yes.' Hadgraft had risen to his feet. He went to the window. 'Ah – I see my daughter below, walking with her waiting woman. Allow me to introduce you.' He rapped on the glass and beckoned frantically. 'She will be with us directly.'

I could hardly refuse the introduction without seeming rude. 'One more question, sir. Have you encountered a fat man with only one hand? He wears a sword. But he's a rough fellow of no breeding.'

Hadgraft stared at me. 'Why do you ask?'

'Have you?'

'No, as it happens, but pray satisfy my curiosity. Who—'

He was interrupted by a knock. Two women entered the room. The first was Grace Hadgraft. She curtsied and gave me a slow, calm smile.

I bowed. Her father was saying something to me, but it passed over my head. A pearl, I thought, what a perfect pearl of a woman.

I left Hadgraft's house soon after I had been introduced to his daughter and her waiting woman. I tried not to betray the fact that the arrival of Mistress Grace stripped me of my hard-won assurance. Her perfections made me conscious of the scars on my face and my neck. I wished I had worn a better coat.

Not that Mistress Grace had appeared to notice anything

amiss. She was true to her name, gracious indeed. She was more than beautiful and kind. I fancied I saw sadness in her eyes, and her sadness tugged at something deep within me. I was a practical man, I reminded myself, a man of business. I could not afford to be otherwise. Grace's father was a rich man. That too was a great point in her favour.

But I had work to do. With some difficulty I put the thought aside and retraced my steps over Holborn Bridge. On the other side, I cut through the smaller streets, passing the old house where Cat's site office was. I needed to warn her about Roger Durrell, but not now.

I turned into Chard Lane, and in a minute or two I came to the bustle of Snow Hill. The old Three Crowns, hard by St Sepulchre's, had been consumed in the Fire, but the inn was now rebuilt on the old foundations. It followed the usual pattern for such places. The ground floor was occupied by shops. There was a tavern on the first floor and a yard at the back. The second floor, I learned from the tavern's landlord, was let out for lodgings. I enquired after Mr Pharamond.

'Ah – it's the mounseer you want, is it, sir? Does he owe you money too?'

'How do I find him?'

'Ask Mother Gribbin – she's upstairs. You can't mistake her. Looks like she's got a mouthful of pickles. But I warn you, the mounseer owes everyone money. You won't get a penny out of him. He's all fine words and an empty purse.'

Mother Gribbin was mending bedlinen with the assistance of a maid who looked about ten years old. She was a small, elderly hunchback who had lost most of her teeth. Her lips were almost invisible.

'Mr Pharamond? He ain't here.'

'Do you know where I may find him?'

'No.'

I persevered. 'When did you last see him?'

'Who's asking?'

'My name's Marwood.' I showed her my warrant. 'Here's my authority from the King.'

Mother Gribbin bit off a thread and spat it on the floor. 'That ain't no good to me, is it? I never been much of a reader, and I'm too old to start now. All I know is that he ain't here. And he owes me nigh on seven shillings.'

'But he does have lodgings here?'

'Lodgings? Is that what he calls it? It's a garret. Even I can't stand up in it.'

'I want to see it.'

'Well you can't. How do I know you're not a thief? If the mounseer don't pay my seven shillings, whatever's up there is mine. I'm not letting anyone else get their hands on it first.'

'Mistress, my warrant—'

'The girl will see you out.'

I stared at the old woman for a moment. She was one of those you couldn't bend and you couldn't break. Perhaps she had been born contrary and life had made her more so. I would have to return with authority to force my way in. I followed the maid to the door.

On the landing, she stood on tiptoe and whispered in my ear: 'Master? Has the mounseer been murdered? Is it him up at Chard Lane?'

I glanced down at her avid face. I didn't reply.

'I could tell you something. If it's worth something in return.'

'I'll be the judge of that.'

'Someone else came here, wanting to talk to him, wanting to go up to his garret. Said the Frenchy owed him money.'

'Who?'

She shrugged. 'I didn't see. It was after dark on Sunday. Ma Gribbin sent him off with a flea in his ear.'

I tossed her a penny and clattered down the stairs.

CHAPTER NINE

I N THE AFTERNOON, Cat decided that she had had
enough of waiting. If she left the business to Marwood and
Hadgraft, it would never be done. She told Ledward she was
going out. The watchman unbarred the street door for her.

'I won't be long. If Mr Marwood calls, ask him to wait.'
She wanted to tell him that she had written to Madame des
Bordes, accepting her invitation to Whitehall tomorrow
evening. There had been no opportunity when he had rescued
her from Hadgraft this morning.

She splashed through the streets to Holborn Bridge, walked
up to Hatton Garden beyond what was left of the bishop's
rambling establishment, and knocked at Rush's door. The
house was well enough, but the windows were dirty and the
doorstep needed cleaning. When the door was opened, she
gave her name to the servant and begged a word with his
master about the Chard Lane almshouse.

Rush received her in his dining room. The floor was dull
from want of polishing, and glasses had left grey rings on
the table.

'Mistress Hakesby.' He was courteous enough to stand and bow. 'How may I serve you?'

'I think you may be able to guess, sir.'

He waved her to a chair. 'You want me to change my mind about the almshouse, don't you?' His lips set into a tight line. 'If so, you've had a wasted journey.'

'I wouldn't presume to question your decision,' Cat said as meekly as she could.

Rush was still standing. 'Then why are you here? Don't think to wheedle me, madam.'

'Of course not. I merely wish to ask if you would consent to modify one small restriction that can have no bearing on this terrible murder. I beg you to allow us to work on one small part of the site – the waste ground at the back, which is nowhere near where the body was found, and nowhere near the ruins. If we could at least mark out our foundations and begin to—'

'No.'

'Sir, it would mean—'

'I said no.'

Cat hardened her voice. 'May I ask why?'

'You may ask, but that's no reason for me to answer. It's enough for you to know that I do my duty to the King, madam, and I act according to the law and my conscience. There's no more to be said.'

Cat rose to her feet. In the last few years, she had learned the painful lesson that it was sometimes wiser to curb her tongue and bide her time.

Rush crossed the room to the door. 'By the way, were you responsible for my visitor this morning? My Lord Arlington's clerk?'

'I'm not privy to Lord Arlington's arrangements, sir,' she said coldly.

He hesitated, his hand on the door. Unexpectedly, he smiled. 'I can't blame you for trying to change my mind. Let me at least give you a word of warning for your pains: don't trust Mr Hadgraft any further than you can see him. Everything he does is solely for his own advantage, including your project for him in Chard Lane. Take care he don't cheat you. He has no more honour than my dog.'

After I had dined at an ordinary in Cockspur Street, I called again at the almshouse site office. I found Cat taking off her muddy pattens. She told me that she had just returned from a fruitless visit to Rush. We went up to her room.

'He hates Hadgraft and he warned me not to trust him,' she said when we were closeted together. 'I wonder why he's so bitter. Apart from that, which we already knew, I got nothing from him. I couldn't alter his mind even by an iota.'

I told her that Rush had allowed me to view the body and to show it to the maid from Iredale's lodging. But the face had been too mutilated for her to hazard an identification.

'How did you get on with Hadgraft?' she asked.

'He gave me a glass of wine and talked about the almshouse. He blames Rush's obduracy on a business deal between them that went sour.'

'Then we've gained nothing,' Cat said.

'Not quite. Did you know Hadgraft dismissed his daughter's French tutor on Saturday? For stealing a spoon.'

'Are you thinking of the shoe we found in the spoil heap?'

I nodded, pushing the thought of Grace to the back of my mind. 'His name's Pharamond. He lodges at the Three

Crowns by St Sepulchre's. His landlady hasn't seen him since Saturday. He owes her seven shillings and she wouldn't let me search his room.'

'Two missing men,' Cat said. 'Not one. Iredale and Pharamond.'

'Rush says a stranger tried to pry information about the body from a servant of his.' I hesitated. 'A big, bulky fellow wearing a sword. With a spike where his right hand used to be.'

'Oh God save us all,' she said, briefly terrified into piety. 'Roger Durrell.'

The clock over the guardhouse had struck six o'clock before I reached Lord Arlington's office in the Privy Gallery. His chief clerk, Mr Gorvin, greeted me with a smile. He was the nearest thing I had to a friend at Whitehall.

'What can I do for you?'

'I wondered if there's a letter for me here. From my lord.'

It was just possible that Arlington would have had time to reply to the letter I had sent him yesterday afternoon. When he was away from London, he was too wily to cut himself off from Whitehall. He knew that if he let slip the reins of power even for a few hours, someone else would snatch them up. His couriers called daily at both Goring House and the Privy Gallery office to collect and deliver letters of importance. The couriers rode post on my lord's own horses. They could reach Euston in six or seven hours.

Gorvin shook his head. 'Nothing, I'm afraid. But in any case, your letters usually go to Goring House.'

'Nothing there, either.'

'Anything I can help with?'

'I wish you could.' I took his arm and drew him out of earshot of the junior clerks in the outer office. 'It's about the Chard Lane murder. Have you heard about it?'

'Who hasn't?' Gorvin wrinkled his nose. 'Nasty business. I didn't know you were involved.'

'Between ourselves, two men are missing who might possibly have a connection to the matter. One's a copyist at the Council for Foreign Plantations. The other's a Frenchman.'

'In that case I can see why my lord might take an interest.'

I hadn't mentioned Cat's part in this business, which had brought me into the affair in the first place. Though I trusted Gorvin as much as anyone here, Whitehall was a place that bred caution.

I hurried on, 'The Duke of Buckingham got the copyist his place at the council. And one of the Duke's ruffians is almost certainly engaged in the matter. Both before and after the murder. There's another odd thing: the local magistrate is making things difficult. The body was found on a big building site for a new almshouse. There's a delay about the inquest, and the magistrate's using a legal quibble to put a stop on all work on the site. It's quite unnecessary, and he knows it. People are lobbying to make him lift it.'

Gorvin shrugged. 'If I were you, I'd talk to Mr Williamson. He'll know if the Duke's making mischief if anyone does, and as Under Secretary he has the authority to make decisions when my lord's away. I saw him walking in the Matted Gallery not ten minutes ago.'

'I suppose I must.'

Gorvin gave me a sympathetic smile. 'No love lost, eh? Even now?'

'He's not a man who changes his mind easily.'

'I wager he'll tell you to tread carefully with the magistrate. The City won't thank us for using the King's authority without good cause. It would be seen as interference, and we're unpopular enough in that quarter as it is. What's the man's name by the way? Anyone I know?'

'Willoughby Rush. He lives in one of those new houses in Hatton Garden.'

'Ah. Your Mr Rush is not without friends at court. He sailed with Prince Rupert during the Protectorate, and the Prince speaks highly of him. He distinguished himself in the Dutch wars too. My Lord Sandwich got him a patent afterwards, I believe.'

'A contract for the supply of belts to the navy,' I said sourly.

'No doubt. And Rush was in the House of Commons for a year or two. You'll be interested to hear that he generally voted with the Duke of Buckingham's people.'

Afterwards I went in search of Mr Williamson.

The Matted Gallery lay at right angles to the Privy Gallery. It ran above the Stone Gallery along the east side of the Privy Garden, with the King's apartments at one end and the Duke of York's at the other. It was a popular place to see and be seen, an indoor promenade for gossip and for the exchange of whispered secrets.

As usual at this time of day, it was crowded with people strolling about. I looked for Williamson, but he must have left already. As I turned to go, I stood back against the wall to allow a couple to pass by me. I recognized Monsieur Colbert de Croissy, the French ambassador. The ambassador was intimate with Lord Arlington and a frequent visitor at Goring House.

He had a young lady clinging to his arm and was murmuring something to her as they went. The lady's eyes were lowered. I did not see her face, which was shaded by the brim of her hat. But as I passed them, she glanced up. I saw a pretty face, sweet and childlike, with dimples at the corners of the lips.

As for her, I didn't know what she saw. She looked straight through me as though I were invisible.

'I rejoice that your health has improved, mademoiselle,' Monsieur Colbert said, leaning so close to Louise de Keroualle that his wig brushed her cheek. 'The King was most concerned.'

'He did me the honour to enquire how I did,' Louise said. 'Yesterday he sent me a note in his own hand.'

'So I hear.' The ambassador smiled, and she wondered whether he had bribed her maid to report on everything Louise said and did. 'Were you aware that he has also paid that trifle you lost at cards the other night? Where you're concerned, his generosity knows no bounds.'

Colbert paused to greet a couple of acquaintances passing in the opposite direction. They walked on. 'Shall we go?' he murmured. 'We shall never have a moment in peace. My wife won't mind if we're before our time this evening.' He led her back down the gallery, bowing to right and left. 'Dear me, I believe your acquaintance is grown even larger than mine. The other day, I heard Lady Castlemaine say that there is now no lady at court whose society is more sought after than Mademoiselle de Keroualle's.'

Louise did not reply. With Colbert, she had learned, the words he spoke often meant one thing on the outside and something quite different within. Lady Castlemaine had been the King's principal mistress for many years and she had taken care to make the most of it. Even now, she retained her titles, her houses and her pensions; and her children, the King's bastards, had been ennobled. It was a reminder of what had been gained, what could be achieved and what was at stake.

The ambassador steered her towards the stairs. 'Whitehall is already at your feet. And you're so young! So untouched by the world! His Majesty finds that particularly enchanting.'

So untouched by the world: Louise knew all too well what those words meant to a man like the King.

'But you mustn't keep him waiting too long,' Colbert said quietly as they walked downstairs. 'He won't wait for ever.'

They parted to prepare for the evening's entertainment at the ambassador's house. In half an hour, Colbert called for her at the lodging of the Queen's maids of honour. He escorted her down to the Pebbled Court. His coach was waiting for them in the street beyond the gate.

The courtyard was busy, for at this hour there was much coming and going before the main business of the evening began. The Duke of Buckingham was talking to a cluster of gentlemen by the gate. The men's voices were strident and their faces were flushed. The Duke's voice crowed with laughter above the others, a cock preening on his dungheap.

'Ah,' Colbert said in a colourless voice. 'His Grace is making merry already.'

After a glance in Buckingham's direction, Louise avoided looking at him. It was almost three days since they had talked. He had promised to deal with the delicate matter that threatened both her peace of mind and her future prosperity. But she had heard nothing from him since then. She wondered how she could have been so foolish as to trust someone who had already failed her. But she knew why. A drowning man will clutch at anything that might save him.

Ahead of them, a plainly dressed man emerged from the Privy Gallery and walked briskly towards the gate to the street. Buckingham's head turned towards him, and then away. He spoke a few words to one of his intimates. As the stranger neared the gateway, the group drew closer together – not quite blocking the man's way but nevertheless impeding his passage and forcing him to slow down.

'Why, gentlemen,' the Duke brayed. 'it's the Marworm. Alas, he looks even more marred than usual. Pray have the goodness not to tread on him.'

The man took no notice, except to change his course to avoid walking through the group. There was a flurry of movement. One of the gentlemen seemed to stagger and fall against the stranger, pushing him against a wall, at the foot of which was a puddle. Muddy water splashed his shoes and the hem of his cloak.

'Your pardon, sir,' the gentleman said cheerfully. 'On my honour I didn't see you there.'

Buckingham caught sight of Colbert and Louise. He broke away from his friends and came to them.

'Mademoiselle de Keroualle,' he said, 'dare I hope you are recovered?'

'Thank you, Your Grace, yes.'

'Ah!' He laid a hand on his chest and raised his voice like an actor declaiming on a stage. 'Such a weight from my heart. From so many hearts.'

Louise was filled with a powerful desire to puncture the armour of the man's vast self-conceit. But all she said, driven by an instinct to disturb him, was, 'Who was that, sir? The man who passed you just now?'

'Nobody, mademoiselle.' Buckingham smiled wolfishly at her. 'A mere nobody.'

CHAPTER TEN

O N FRIDAY MORNING, Sam and I rode out of London
on a pair of hacks from the livery stables at the Mitre.

I should have spoken to Mr Williamson first, as Gorvin
had suggested, in case he knew anything about Durrell's
presence in London. But I persuaded myself that it would be
wiser to ride out to Paddington, where Iredale's parents lived,
while the day was fresh. It was possible that he was hiding
at their house.

In truth, I was reluctant to wait on Mr Williamson unless
I had no alternative. He was Lord Arlington's Under
Secretary, a man of great influence at Whitehall. I had been
one of his clerks until last year, when my lord desired me to
work for him instead at Goring House.

During my years in his office, Williamson had come to
trust me with much work of a secret nature, as well as with
the day-to-day management of the *London Gazette*, the
government newspaper. He had not taken my departure well,
choosing to believe that I had sacrificed loyalty to ambition.

Sam and I passed the gibbet at Tyburn and took Watling

Street north towards the village of Paddington. The road was busy – it always was – but the way was dry, and we made good time. Like many sailors, Sam managed a horse in an unorthodox way; his stump meant he rode askew on his mount; but he kept the beast under tight control.

A passing labourer directed me to the cottage of Iredale's parents. It was a cramped building in poor repair, standing by itself in a lane leading north from the churchyard. It had its gable end to the road and a tangled garden on one side.

When I knocked on the door, a shutter slid back.

'Who is it?' a woman said.

'Mr Marwood from London. I work with Mr Iredale for the government. I understand his parents live here.'

'They don't want to see anyone.'

'Is he here?' I said.

'No.'

'I need to speak to his parents. I have a warrant here—'

The shutter closed. Silence fell.

'We could force the door if you like, master,' Sam suggested. 'But it might be faster if I smash a window.'

'Don't be a fool.'

He grinned at me. We rode back to the village. I routed out the parson, a plainly dressed man in early middle age with a long, humorous face. I showed him my warrant and explained our difficulty.

'You mustn't blame them, sir. The old people have learned to be fearful. Their cottage stands on its own, and two ruffians tried to break in on Tuesday evening.'

'Thieves?'

'Who else could they be? Old Iredale discharged a fowling piece out of the window and it frightened them off. They were not to know that the poor man is blind, and there was no one else in the house except his wife and their maid.'

'What did the men look like?'

He shrugged. 'It was dark. But there was one odd circumstance. They were mounted. The Iredales heard them riding away.'

I agreed that was curious. Most thieves were beggars or deserters or tinkers or the like. In other words, they were opportunists likely to be on foot.

'But why are you looking for young John?'

'He's not been seen in his office at the Council for Foreign Plantations,' I said. 'They're concerned about him. All the more so because some of his work is confidential.'

My explanation seemed to satisfy him. We walked back to the cottage with Sam trailing behind us. On the way, I asked the parson if he himself knew the Iredales' son.

'Yes – a good enough fellow. I gather he prospers in London. He was in service in France last year, so we hardly saw him for a while. He came back to England last autumn with the Duke of Buckingham's people, much to his parents' relief. I understand that His Grace found him his present employment. Clearly he thinks highly of him.'

I nodded and smiled.

'Now he's back in London,' the parson went on, 'he often walks from town to see them. He's been a good son to them.'

We knocked, and the parson persuaded the maidservant to open the door. She was a slatternly girl with a sullen face. She led us into the kitchen, where Iredale's parents were huddled over the fire. The father turned his face to us as we entered. His eyes were covered with a dirty white film, and a rusty fowling piece was propped against the arm of his chair. He said nothing when the parson introduced me.

'Have you seen my son?' the old woman asked. She was wrapped in shawls, though the room was stiflingly hot. 'Have you a message?'

'No, mistress,' I said. 'I thought I might find him here. When did you last see him?'

'Two weeks ago . . . He said he'd come on Sunday. He often comes on Sunday. Mr Lane knows that.'

'Indeed John does,' the parson said. 'He shows a very proper filial regard. He makes sure all is well. He often brings little presents for his parents, too.'

'He's a good boy,' the mother said loudly, as if we had dared to suggest otherwise. 'A *good* boy.'

'He'd have sent them packing,' the old man said. His voice creaked like a hinge in need of greasing. 'Cursed rogues.'

'*You* sent them packing, Father,' said his wife. 'You fired your gun out the window.'

'Aye, but John would have chased the devils and killed them.'

He subsided in his chair, dislodging the fowling piece, which fell to the floor with a clatter. By the grace of God it did not discharge itself. He turned his head in the direction of the parson. 'Who d'you say this man is, sir?'

'His name's Marwood. He works for the King and Lord Arlington. I've inspected his warrant. It's all in order.'

Iredale grunted and appeared to lose interest in me. He scratched his leg with a long, horny fingernail.

'Do you keep a particular chamber for your son when he's here?' I asked Mistress Iredale.

'Oh yes, sir,' she said. 'All neatly furnished and aired. Everything ready for when he comes.'

I glanced at the parson, who struck me as no fool. 'Would

you allow Mr Lane to show it to me? I have been to your son's lodging in London, but perhaps you make him more comfortable here.'

'Best room in the house. No more than John deserves.'

The old man muttered under his breath. I thought he might object but he held his tongue.

'Then perhaps I might show it to Mr Marwood,' the parson said. 'If you would permit.'

'The King himself would sleep like a baby in that bed . . .'

Her voice trailed away. The parson gestured upwards. 'Shall I lead, sir? I know the house.'

I said a word to Sam and left him to keep an eye on the maid and the old people. The parson took me upstairs and into a low-ceilinged chamber. There was a layer of dust on the furniture and the air smelled of unemptied chamber pots.

'The old people can't manage the stairs,' the parson murmured. 'The maid does no more than she has to. She bestirs herself when John sends word that he's on his way. I wonder sometimes about her honesty.'

'You understand that I have to search this place,' I said quietly.

'I thought you might.' He gave me a wry smile. 'I've seen your commission. I've no power to object.'

I looked inside the chest and behind a faded, moth-eaten tapestry that masked damp plaster on the wall behind. I examined the bed, including the curtained frame. I paced over the floor, looking down at the boards for signs of a hiding place beneath.

'You've done this sort of work before, sir,' the parson said in a studiously neutral tone.

I nodded, without looking at him.

'Pray be careful what you say to the old folk. If your duty allows, of course. They dote upon the boy. I don't know what young Iredale has done, but he pays the rent on this house and the maid's wages.'

'They have nothing of their own?' I said.

'The father used to keep an alehouse in the village, but he grew too infirm and lost the business. If it weren't for John, the parents would have to go on the parish.'

I looked up at the ceiling. There was a modest canopy over the bed, from which the curtains were suspended. At the bottom end, a dense network of cobwebs stretched from the top of the canopy to the ceiling. But there were no cobwebs at the head of the bed.

A chair stood against the wall. I used it as a stool. The canopy was supported by a wooden framework. Most of its upper surface was grey with dust and littered with decaying flies. Sitting on top was a box bound with iron. I drew it slowly towards me. At either end was a handle, which was useful because the box was as heavy as sin.

With Lane's help I lifted it down, carried it to the kitchen and placed it on the table. I didn't trust the maid. I told Sam to take her outside to help him search the outbuildings and the garden. I kept the parson with me. He might be useful if I needed a witness or simply to reinforce my authority if the parents objected.

The box formed a flattened cube, with a base roughly twelve inches square. The lid was secured with a single lock.

'This was concealed above your son's bed,' I said. 'I'm obliged to open it, and I'm authorized to do so by the terms of my warrant from the King. Mr Lane has inspected my credentials and finds them in order.'

'Can he do this, sir?' Iredale said.

'I believe so,' said the parson. 'Best let Mr Marwood do as he wants.'

The old man made a sound like a smothered growl. 'And if I don't?'

'He'll do it anyway. Now or later. It's better that he does it now, with me here.'

'If he must then.'

'Thank you,' I said, speaking more gently than before. 'Believe me, I wish your son no harm. I will have to force the lock, I'm afraid. I'll call my man in to do it.'

'No.'

Iredale fumbled at his throat, his swollen fingers burrowing beneath his coat, his waistcoat and then the neck of his shirt. He brought out a key attached to a string. He lifted it over his head and held it out to me.

'John gave this to me for safekeeping. Pray God I'm right in letting you have it.'

I thanked him and inserted the key in the lock of the box. 'Do you know what's inside?'

He shook his head. 'We didn't even know it was up there, sir. Or that there was a box. And that's God's truth.'

The key turned easily. The parson came a step closer. I angled the box towards him.

'Pray open this for me, sir,' I said.

Lane lifted the lid with both hands. Both of us drew in our breath sharply. It seemed to me that the kitchen had suddenly become a richer, brighter place. The interior of the box shimmered with gold.

CHAPTER ELEVEN

POINTED TOES, CAT thought, green silk lining and three-inch heels. Not much more than a year ago she had loved these shoes almost as much as life itself. But they were no longer à la mode. They were dreary. Old-fashioned. Badly made. And, for what it was worth, they had never been comfortable either.

Over the summer, Cat had occasionally worn them for want of anything better. But they were clearly impossible for the Queen's drawing room at Whitehall, even if the Queen herself wasn't there. Fortunately, Cat now had her new shoes. Monsieur Georges had made them for her. He kept a shop in the New Exchange in the Strand, where he charged prices that only fools and ladies of the court would pay.

The new shoes were made of the palest cream leather, soft and supple, with a delicate design of cherries, leaves and blossom. They had tapering, two-inch heels. A ruffle of white lace, ribbed with green ribbon, ran around the opening, circling the wearer's ankles in a soft embrace. The strap was ornamented with a single pearl.

Cat perched on the bed and put on the shoes. They had arrived yesterday, along with a bill that she had hidden from herself in the back of her copy of Vitruvius. The problem was, she hadn't had time to try the shoes, even about the house. It wouldn't matter if they turned out to be uncomfortable – what was a little pain, after all, in the pursuit of beauty? – but what if they made it completely impossible for her to walk or, even worse, what if a heel fell off in the middle of the drawing room?

The rest of her appearance was less critical, partly because she had no real choice. She angled the mirror on her dressing table and inspected her reflection. Her best gown – pale blue silk – was older than she would have liked, but she could set it off with the Brussels lace that Marwood had given her. The present had embarrassed them both. Marwood had muttered something about its having come into his possession by chance in settlement of a card debt, an implausible story because he rarely gambled. But it was an extremely fine piece of lace and it would make all the difference to the gown.

She heard someone knocking on the parlour door, followed by Jane's footsteps and the sound of Marwood's voice. Talk of the devil. She felt flustered, like a child caught in a misdeed. Jane tapped on the door and poked her head inelegantly into the room.

'It's Mr Marwood!' she said in a voice that was part whisper, part squeak. Her eyes widened as she took in Cat's appearance. 'Oh mistress! You look . . . you . . .'

'Tell him I'll be with him directly,' Cat said repressively, aware that her voice would be audible next door. There was no time to remove the lace. If Marwood had to call at such an inconvenient moment, at least she was looking her best.

When she went into the parlour, he was standing by the fireplace. 'Madam,' he said, 'I'm honoured that you should make such an effort for your humble servant.'

His face was grave, but she caught the hint of amusement in his voice. 'Have you come here merely to insult me?'

'Is that the piece of lace that I . . . ?'

'Jane?' Cat said. 'Go downstairs and wait for the coach. Let me know at once when it comes.'

'Where are you going?' he asked.

'Whitehall. The Queen's drawing room. Not that the Queen will be there.'

The parlour door closed, leaving them alone.

'To see your friend? The Queen's dresser?'

'Yes – Madame des Bordes.' She lowered her voice. 'But there's nothing she doesn't know about clothes and shoes, men's as well as women's.'

'Take the purse as well as the shoe,' he suggested. 'The one from Iredale's lodging.'

'I already have it.' A silence grew. 'My coach will be here at any moment. How did you fare with Mr Hadgraft yesterday?'

Marwood cleared his throat. 'He told me the history of his life. Then he said that Rush was being malicious in banning work on the site because of a business quarrel between them. It appears that he discharged his daughter's French tutor, a man named Pharamond, on Saturday for trying to steal a spoon. The only other thing I know about the tutor is that he owes seven shillings to the keeper of his lodging-house.'

Cat said, keeping her voice elaborately casual, 'And did you chance to meet Mistress Grace while you were at her father's?'

'Briefly.'

'A beauty, don't you agree?'

'Yes – she's well enough, I suppose.'

It was a suspiciously dismissive reply. Cat probed him with another question, as one probes a sore tooth with a tongue. 'Did you know that she's her father's only child? She will get everything when he dies. He has no other family apart from that waiting woman, who's some sort of cousin. I can't see her getting anything.'

'No doubt,' Marwood said and changed the subject. 'I know you're pressed for time, so I won't keep you long. I went to see Iredale's parents in Paddington today. They were expecting a visit from him on Sunday, but he didn't turn up. And then, on Tuesday, after nightfall, two men on horseback arrived and tried to enter their cottage.'

'Could it . . . ?'

'Could it have been Durrell? It was too dark to see. But there was something else: Iredale had hidden a box there. It contained at least sixty pounds, mainly in gold.'

'Where did he find that sort of money?'

'God knows. Perhaps when he was in France. More than half the pieces were louis d'ors. I also found these in the box.'

While he was speaking, Marwood had taken out his pocket-book. He extracted two folded papers and smoothed them out on the table. Cat picked up the first. It was a list of a dozen names in a neat, regular hand. About halfway down were two she recognized, one below the other: *Mr Hadgraft. Mr Rush. Mr Rush* had been scored out with a single line of the pen.

'Is that Iredale's writing?'

'I don't know yet,' Marwood said. 'Look at the other paper.'

The paper had been torn from a book. It was a blank page to which had been gummed a bookplate bearing a familiar coat of arms: the lilies of France, with a label, a mark of cadency, to differentiate the arms from those of Louis XIV. She had seen similar plates in the books she had consulted last year when she was working for King Charles's late sister in France. They had come from the palace library of St Germain.

'The arms of the Duke of Orleans,' she said.

'Turn it over.'

Cat glanced at the other side of the sheet. A column of pencilled figures ran down the left-hand margin, with a total of fifty-three at the bottom. Beside it had been scrawled a few words in ink: *Dieppe, le 15° Septembre 1670*.

'Dieppe?' she said.

'The parson at Paddington told me that Iredale came back to England with the Duke's people. It's likely enough that he sailed from Dieppe. As for the rest, a bill perhaps? Or a list of debts or assets? But compare it with this.'

He retrieved the torn scrap from the pocketbook and handed it to her: . . . *arage Swan Holborn Bridge*: Iredale's address, from the toe of the French shoe found at the almshouse site.

'It could be the same writing.'

'It almost certainly is.' Marwood had been apprenticed to his father, a printer, and he had an eye for such details. 'Look at the "e". And the capital "S".'

She bit her lip. 'Now we have the King's dead sister and a missing Frenchman, as well as a link between Hadgraft, Rush and Iredale. And a box of gold.'

'Together with Buckingham,' Marwood said. 'And Roger Durrell. Perhaps.'

Footsteps were running up the stairs. Jane Ash burst into the parlour, her face red with exertion and excitement. 'If you please, mistress, the coach is here.'

'Fetch my cloak and the overshoes,' Cat said. Now the time for departure had arrived, she was struck with panic. 'Hurry.'

Marwood was already on his feet. 'May I escort you downstairs?'

'No. Thank you, but no.' She didn't want him to distract her at a time like this, or to see her in such a state. 'Pray go.'

He bowed, suddenly stately in manner as if to match her appearance and her destination. 'Goodbye, madam. I hope your evening is agreeable as well as useful.'

Her mouth was dry. 'Thank you.'

He paused at the door and looked back. He said in his normal voice: 'You look most elegant, madam. Faith, I . . . Believe me, you look very well indeed. I swear you will outshine them all.'

The drawing room looked out over the Thames. The weather had been fine all day, and there was not enough wind to stir the long taffeta curtains. Even now, at past six o'clock, the air was warm enough for people to stroll on the terrace outside the windows.

The sun was sinking. There were golden glints on the grey water. The tide was high, which meant that the river covered the foreshore and reduced the smell of sewage.

'Pouf,' said Madame des Bordes as they paced up and down.

'Whitehall is not the Palais Royal or St Germain, but on an evening like this, I admit it's quite agreeable.'

She had been waiting near the door when Cat arrived and she had taken her under her wing. A few gentlemen were playing at cards in a corner of the room, but most people were circulating, listening to a word here or dropping another in an ear there. In these surroundings, her blue silk seemed quaintly modest, even dowdy.

According to Madame des Bordes, the drawing room was a place where much business was discreetly transacted with a nod, a wink or the press of a hand. 'But this is nothing,' she said dismissively. 'There's hardly anyone of importance this evening.'

To Cat's alarm, the tall, golden-wigged figure of the Duke of Buckingham was standing by the fireplace, looking as if he owned it, and indeed the entire palace. He had not yet seen her.

'When the Queen is here,' her hostess was saying, 'there are four or five times as many people. Even the King comes. Here he comes and goes almost as a private gentleman. In his wife's drawing room, he moves about and talks to whomsoever he wishes, with no formality.' She lowered her voice still further. 'The Queen may not have given him an heir, but she's no fool. She's made a place for herself at court, and he's grateful for that. Indeed, I think he cares for her in his own way, despite the mistresses.'

Cat turned her back on Buckingham and faced the river, as if admiring the view framed by the window.

'That's a pretty piece of lace,' Madame des Bordes said. She stretched out her hand and fingered it. 'Where did you find it?'

'It was a present,' Cat said, her spirits lifting.

'Ah. From a gentleman?'

'In a manner of speaking.' She wouldn't call Marwood a gentleman for all his newly acquired airs and graces. Nor, for that matter, would he.

'Don't be coy, my dear. Oh! Show me those shoes. New?'

Cat nodded. She raised her skirts a fraction. Madame des Bordes circled her. 'Charming. Monsieur Georges?'

'How did you know?'

'No Englishmen could have made those. Besides, Monsieur Georges loves cherries. He used to have a workshop in Paris, but he's Protestant, poor soul, and he feels more comfortable in London. Shall we go outside?'

They walked out on to the terrace and stood looking at the broad, grey river.

'Talking of shoes,' Cat said, 'I've brought one to show you.'

'Another purchase?'

'No – it's a man's shoe. I think it's French.'

'Then why . . . ?'

Cat explained some of the circumstances surrounding the shoe's discovery. 'It's possible that the dead man was French.'

'*Mon dieu!*' Madame des Bordes cried. Her hand flew to her bosom. 'How they hate us here! If they had their way, they would murder us all in our beds.'

'Not in Whitehall, surely,' Cat said.

'This dead man's shoe . . .' Madame des Bordes wrinkled her nose. 'Where is it?'

'In the anteroom with my cloak.'

'Show me later, then. When you leave.'

'I also have this.' Cat felt in her pocket for the purse that Marwood had found at Iredale's lodging.

Madame des Bordes stared at it. 'Was that found with the shoe?'

'No. Somewhere quite different. What do you think of it?'

'A lady's purse, of course.' She took it from Cat and turned it over and then inside out. 'Charming. Beautiful stitching. Where did you get it?'

'A man had hidden it in his closet.'

'This Frenchman?'

'No – an Englishman. No one of importance.' Cat lowered her voice. 'But he may have had something to do with the murder.'

'My poor late mistress the Duchess of Orleans gave purses like these to her maids of honour a year or two ago. I can't swear this is identical, but it's certainly very like. The materials. The stitching. That little design at the corners.'

'Then one of her maids might have brought it to England when the King offered her ladies a home in the Queen's household?'

'Perhaps. Most of them are with the Queen at present.' Madame des Bordes glanced through the window into the withdrawing room beyond. 'But there's one still in London. Over there, talking to our ambassador. Mademoiselle de Keroualle.'

Monsieur Colbert leant closer. 'Now you are restored to health, mademoiselle, there is no time to waste.' The ambassador had a soft, viscous voice, which seemed to insinuate itself into Louise's ears like drops of olive oil. 'In the general way of things, there would be no reason for you to go to

97

Suffolk if not to attend the Queen. But I have discussed the matter with Lord Arlington, and I believe we have hit upon a scheme that will answer very nicely. We—'

'That lady looks familiar,' she interrupted. She was desperate to find a diversion, to postpone this conversation. 'On the terrace. Talking to Madame des Bordes.'

The ambassador frowned at her. 'In the blue dress? I don't know her.'

'Quite a pretty face,' Louise said dispassionately, with the unassailable objectivity of an acknowledged beauty. 'But there's nothing to her. Oh – I know – I saw her at St Germain last year, and once at Dover Castle too. I can't remember her name, but she was advising my mistress on some building work.' Louise laughed, finding relief in the absurd. 'She's a sort of architect, monsieur! Can you believe it?'

'By profession?' Seeing Louise's nod, Colbert went on, 'How strange. But to return to your own situation: the difficulty is that, now you're well, you must resume your duties with the Queen, but she will soon leave Euston. However, we must not allow you to put too much strain on yourself before you are fully recovered. A week or two in the country will give you the refreshment you need before you attend Her Majesty again. Lady Arlington has already written to beg her permission for you to come down to Euston with my wife and myself. Nothing could be more pleasant. Don't you agree?'

'How delightful,' Louise said.

Colbert nodded. His smile dropped away, and he said in a lower, harder voice, 'This is your chance, mademoiselle, and it may be your only one. Take it.'

CHAPTER TWELVE

'WOULD YOU INTRODUCE me to Mademoiselle de Keroualle?' Cat asked. 'I'd like to ask her about the purse.'

Madame des Bordes glanced over her shoulder. 'Not just now, I think. She's deep in conversation with the ambassador.'

As she was speaking, however, Colbert turned aside to greet a middle-aged gentleman with a thin, unsmiling mouth. He introduced Louise to him.

'You see,' murmured Madame des Bordes. 'Colbert is the soul of tact – he barely knows Monsieur Evelyn, and yet now he seizes upon him.'

'John Evelyn?' Cat looked at him with interest.

'He will be at Euston too – Lord Arlington values his taste greatly. I cannot say I agree.'

Her voice had become sharper than usual. Cat glanced at her. 'The gentleman's not a favourite with you?'

'We have had our disagreements. He does not appreciate the importance of a well-made shoe or a well-cut coat. Instead, he prefers to play at gardening. He also pretends to know all there is to know about trifling artistic matters. But he's a useful man to know unfortunately. That's why the ambassador is trying to bring him together with Mademoiselle de Keroualle.'

Cat now had a clear view of the maid of honour. She was small, plump and very pretty. She was staring up at Evelyn as he talked, her lips slightly parted. Two other men joined the group around them.

'She looks so . . . so timid, doesn't she?'

'Don't be fooled by the baby face, my dear. Leave that to the gentlemen. She has to marry well. That's why she's in England. There's nothing wrong with her birth, or she wouldn't be one of the Queen's ladies. But her family hasn't two penny pieces to rub together. If she can't find a rich husband, she'll end her days in a convent. Particularly if . . . Well, it's growing chilly. Shall we go in?'

'You can't leave it there,' Cat said. '*Particularly* . . . What does that mean?'

Madame des Bordes sighed. 'The silly girl spends as if she were rich. And she has a weakness for cards.' She brought her head closer to Cat's and lowered her voice to a whisper. 'There were rumours of unsuitable attachments in France. But that girl only has one thing to sell, and if she doesn't find the right buyer, she's ruined.' She brought her mouth closer to Cat's ear. 'The King pays her the most improper attentions. He means to make her his mistress.'

When they went back into the room, Buckingham noticed Cat for the first time; he gave her a sardonic glance and turned his back on her.

'Do you know His Grace?' Madame des Bordes asked.

'We've met,' Cat said. 'I don't care for him. Nor he for me.'

'There's something strange going on between him and *her*.' She glanced towards Mademoiselle de Keroualle. 'She was to come to England in the Duke's yacht last year. But he left her stranded in Dieppe for nearly two weeks. She ran out of money. She thought she was quite abandoned in the world. In the end they sent one of the King's yachts instead. She felt the Duke humiliated her on purpose. Yet now they whisper together in corners.'

'It's Mistress Hakesby, isn't it?' A middle-aged man who had been talking to Evelyn broke away from the group and came smiling towards her. 'What a pleasant surprise to see you here. Do you remember me?'

'Why, yes. Mr Gorvin.' Cat turned to Madame des Bordes. 'Of Lord Arlington's office. We had dealings over the plans for his poultry houses.'

She was well-disposed towards Gorvin. He had handled her business with Arlington promptly and efficiently. Also, she knew he was a friend of Marwood's.

When the introductions were over, Gorvin said, 'I gather you're to go to Euston next month.'

'Am I?'

'It will be after Their Majesties have left. I understand that Lady Arlington will write to you. They want to consult about the stables.'

'And if I can't spare the time?' Cat said, irritated by the bland assumption that her time was at the Arlingtons' disposal.

Gorvin's eyes crinkled at the corners but otherwise he kept a straight face. 'I expect you will be able to. Mr Evelyn will be there to advise about the gardens. Do you know him?'

'Only by reputation.'

'Then allow me to present him to you.'

Madame des Bordes cleared her throat loudly. Her face had lost its usual good humour.

Gorvin brought Evelyn over and made the introductions. 'Mistress Hakesby is an architect.'

Evelyn bowed. 'It's fitting for a lady to indulge in a pastime that encourages the study of beauty.'

'For me, sir,' Cat said, 'it is not a pastime. It is more in the nature of a profession.'

'Mistress Hakesby took over the business of her late husband when he died,' Gorvin said. 'She designed the poultry house for my lord. Dr Wren speaks highly of her work.'

'Indeed.' Evelyn bowed again, his face unreadable.

'And you may see each other at Euston.'

'I shall look forward to it,' Evelyn said with chilly politeness. 'But would you excuse me? Monsieur Colbert is leaving, and I must say goodbye.'

'And so must I,' Gorvin said, adding tactfully, 'with regret.'

Madame des Bordes gazed at Evelyn's retreating back. 'Well!' she whispered. 'Did I not tell you? Is he not disagreeable?'

But Cat was not listening. The company was thinning out, but Buckingham was still there, and now he was openly staring at her. It made her uncomfortable. She touched Madame des Bordes' arm. 'May I show you the man's shoe now?'

They went into the anteroom, off which was a closet where three servants presided over the cloaks of the ladies and managed the screens and the chamber pots. Cat retrieved her bag and they settled in a window embrasure where they could not be overlooked. Cat gave her the shoe.

Madame des Bordes shuddered. 'It's strange to think a man was wearing this at the very moment he was murdered.'

'We don't know that, madame. It may have nothing to do with the murder.'

The Frenchwoman turned the shoe in her hands and then set it on the broad windowsill. 'Shoes like this were everywhere in Paris a year or two ago.' She poked the leather with a finger. 'One used to see them at court.'

'Then it is French?' Cat said.

'Probably. Or at least made by a Frenchman like your Monsieur Georges. Shall we go back in?'

'Forgive me, I'd rather not run the risk of meeting the Duke of Buckingham.'

Madame des Bordes raised her eyebrows but she didn't ask questions. 'Very well, my dear.'

'On another occasion,' Cat said slowly, 'would you introduce me to Mademoiselle de Keroualle?'

'Why? Or is that another secret? You're full of secrets.'

'I wish I were not,' Cat whispered.

Madame des Bordes patted her hand. 'Everything passes. Even secrets.'

They kissed each other and parted. Ten minutes later, as Cat was going down the stairs, she heard a man say her name. She glanced over her shoulder. Buckingham was bearing down on her.

'Ah, God be thanked I caught you before you left,' he said in a soft, caressing voice. 'Faith, Mistress Hakesby, you're like the wood nymph, flitting shyly through the thickets of Whitehall. I glimpse you so infrequently that I think you must be a divine creature who only rarely condescends to take human form.'

'I'm pressed for time, Your Grace,' she said.

She tried to hurry away but he laid a hand on her arm. They were on the bend of the stairs, and there chanced to be no one in sight. His fingers wrapped around her wrist. They stared at each other, all pretence gone.

'Let me go.'

'You irritated me before, madam,' he said, his grip tightening. 'And you irritate me now.'

'I can't help that.'

'Have a care, won't you? A solitary lady is so weak, isn't she, so defenceless? And the world is so cruel, so full of malicious accidents.'

Cat struggled to rein in both her fear and her anger. 'Is that what you tell Mademoiselle de Keroualle?'

He dragged her closer to him and brought his head close to hers. 'Why do you ask that?' Drops of spittle landed on her cheek. She smelled the stale wine on his breath. With sudden violence, he shook her. 'What do you know of her, you whey-faced little bitch?'

There were footsteps above them. Cat snatched her arm away. Mr Evelyn appeared round the turn of the stairs.

'There you are again, sir,' Buckingham said, his face a mask of courteous benevolence. 'I've been telling Mistress Hakesby to have a care on these stairs. It's so gloomy, and it would be easy for a lady to stumble. Why do they not bring lights?'

'Sir,' Cat said, taking a step towards Evelyn, 'this is well-met. I had hoped to tell you upstairs how much I treasure your translation of Fréart's *Parallèle de l'architecture antique et de la moderne*. I have my late husband's copy, and he used to tell me that he found more of value there than he did in Vitruvius himself.'

The three of them walked downstairs, with Evelyn murmuring modestly about the shortcomings of his translation. The Duke left them in the Pitched Court.

'A beautiful evening.' Evelyn hesitated, then: 'Forgive me, madam, you seemed a trifle uneasy.'

'A little, perhaps. I – I'm not familiar with this part of Whitehall.'

His face was thin and unsmiling. He held out his arm. 'Then permit me to escort you to your coach.'

'Thank you, sir,' Cat said. She took Evelyn's arm, and he led her towards the street.

It was nearly midnight before the sedan set me down in the Strand. I made my way slowly down the cobbled slope towards the gate of the Savoy, where a lantern burned feebly over the archway. It was almost completely dark, and the cobbles were slimy underfoot. The familiar smell of the river washed up to greet me. I wished I had paid the bearers extra to carry me down to the gate.

I had gone to the Duke's Theatre with my friend Gorvin that evening, to see a tiresome tragedy translated from the French. He was late – he had been detained at Whitehall, where he had seen Cat in the Queen's apartments. But he was determined to go to the play, this play, because his mistress was playing one of the principal roles. He applauded like a madman when she died bloodily in the final act while making several long speeches both before and after she was stabbed.

Later we supped with her and a friend, another actress. It would not have been difficult to prolong my acquaintance with the friend in a more intimate setting, but tonight I had no appetite for the dangerous delights of Venus; and so I came home.

After all, I thought smugly, the services of a woman who was little better than a whore had few charms for a man who might soon be in the grip of the tender passion. I tripped over a cobble and recovered myself with some difficulty. 'Grace,' I murmured like a magical incantation, 'gracious indeed.'

I tried without much success to picture her face and to remember her precise words to me, few as they had been. Instead, I had an inconvenient but very clear memory of Cat's expression a few hours earlier when she asked me if I had chanced to meet Mistress Grace. *A beauty*, Cat had said in a carefully neutral voice. *Don't you agree? Did you know that she's her father's only child? She will get everything when he dies.*

In fact, Cat herself had looked very fine this evening in the blue gown and the piece of lace I had given her. She had been brought up a gentlewoman and she knew how to carry herself. The lace had been absurdly expensive but I had known she would like it, and she had swallowed my story that it had come to me by chance in settlement of a debt. But there was no point in thinking about Cat. I had asked her to marry me last year, and she had rejected my advances in no uncertain terms.

What did that matter now? Perhaps it had been for the best. 'Grace,' I whispered again into the night, 'gracious indeed.' Not only was the girl as beautiful as the day, she would make a fine match for any man. Moreover, I told myself, God did not intend me to be celibate, and a wife would keep me from falling into temptation.

A man cleared his throat a few yards away. I glanced towards the sound but I could see nobody. Half a dozen lights hung over the doorways, but you could have hidden a troop of horse in the deep pools of shadow between them.

I quickened my pace towards the gateway and the lights of the porter's lodge. As I walked, I rapped my iron-shod stick against the stones to give me courage.

There was a sudden rush of footsteps behind me. I began to turn towards the sound but I was too late. Someone seized me by the neck and flung me to the ground. I grazed my knuckles as I fell and lost my stick. My hat and wig fell off. I rolled on to my side, curling up to make myself as small a target as I could.

But the footsteps were running up the slope, towards the bustle of the Strand. Why hadn't the attacker gone for my purse?

'Marwood?'

The voice was coming from the other side of the lane.

I scrambled to my feet. 'Who's that?'

'You know me.'

Of course I did. The deep, hoarse voice was unmistakable.

'Durrell.' I tried to speak calmly, but my breath was ragged. 'So you are alive.'

'And so are you. For now.'

'What do you want?'

Roger Durrell took a step forward, a step closer to me. 'It's what the Duke wants.' He took another step. 'If it was me, I'd cut your throat now and let you bleed to death. But the Duke says no, not now, not yet.'

I swallowed. 'That's kind of him.'

'He says you'd be more trouble dead than you are alive.

For now. But that might change if you keep asking questions.' Durrell hoicked up a mouthful of phlegm, which he spat on the ground in front of me. 'Live down here still, do you? Infirmary Close, the house by the Savoy graveyard. I remember. I wanted to make sure you was still there. In case we need to find you.'

Not five yards way, he emerged from a doorway and walked slowly towards the Strand. The light from a lantern, brighter than the rest, threw his shapeless shadow before him.

CHAPTER THIRTEEN

THE SAME ARGUMENTS, the same debate, the same underlying rancour.

'We do have other commissions,' Brennan pointed out. 'I tell you, Chard Lane will lead to ruin if we're not careful.'

'But if we withdraw now,' Cat said, 'we lose everything we've already laid out. If we give it a little longer, it may still come right.'

It was Saturday morning, a bright start to the day but a bleak prospect before them. She and Brennan were in the Drawing Office at the sign of the Rose in Henrietta Street. They sat side by side on the stools in front of their slopes. Paper, pens and inkpots were ready on the table, along with crayons, drawing instruments and rulers, and the folders and the books were on the shelves nearby. The tools of their trade, Cat thought, the instruments of their dreams. Or in this case nightmares.

'I saw Mr Gorvin yesterday,' she said. 'He said Lady Arlington means to send for me.'

'You know what I think about your grand clients. More

trouble than they're worth. They don't pay their bills half the time.'

'Lord Arlington paid for our poultry house.'

Brennan shrugged. 'Miracles happen.'

'They've asked me to Suffolk. Only for a day or two, probably, and I would not like to disoblige them.' Cat had to tell him sooner or later, and why not now when there was already bad feeling between them? 'They want me to advise on the stable block at Euston Hall. They've mentioned it before. It could be a major commission.'

'More likely it could be throwing away your time and labour for no return.'

'It's worth my going,' Cat said. She wished, not for the first time, that she hadn't taken Brennan into partnership; but he had a stake in the business now, and he quite reasonably felt that it bought him a share in its management as well as its profits. It didn't make it any easier that sometimes his arguments were proved right. But she persevered, knowing that she wouldn't change his mind: 'Euston's one of the greatest mansions in the country. It's near Newmarket, so everyone goes there in the autumn. Including the King and the Queen.'

'They don't pay their bills either,' Brennan said. 'Someone's coming.'

They had both heard the footsteps on the stairs. There was a knock at the door, and Marwood came in. He bowed to Cat and nodded to Brennan, who muttered something under his breath.

'I wondered how you did yesterday evening, madam.'

Cat hesitated.

'Oh, don't mind me,' Brennan said in the voice of one who

did mind. 'I'm going out. Someone's got to deal with the guttering at Dragon Yard. I told you we hadn't ordered enough for the end house.'

He seized his pocketbook, stick and cloak. They listened to him thundering down the stairs.

'What ails him?' Marwood asked.

'He thinks we should cut our losses at Chard Lane. He could be right, but I don't want to do it yet. Your coming in didn't help, either. You know he's never much cared for you.'

Marwood shrugged Brennan away. 'I had a note from Mr Hadgraft this morning: Rush had an express from Ely. The bishop's appointed a coroner.'

'Thank God,' Cat said with uncharacteristic piety. 'When's he coming?'

'I don't know yet. How did you do yesterday evening?'

She told him what little she had gleaned at Whitehall. 'The man's shoe is probably French, and of a pattern worn at court a few years ago. But that's as far as it goes. On the other hand, the purse is very similar to those that the Duchess of Orleans gave to her maids of honour last year. The King offered a home to his sister's ladies after she died. Some of them are now at Whitehall, attached to the Queen's household. It seems that the King is particularly interested in one of the maids of honour. Mademoiselle de Keroualle.'

'Interested?'

'What do you think?' she snapped. 'He means to make her his mistress. She's one of these soft, pretty women who make men think they cannot survive in this hard world without their protection. I imagine that the King finds her amorous glances irresistible.'

'And what does she think about him?'

Cat's mouth twisted. 'He's twice her age, at a hazard, and probably pox-ridden as well. On the other hand, he's the King, and he can give her almost anything she wants, if he pleases. Except marriage. All she has to offer in return is her virginity. That and her languishing looks. Do you think it's a fair exchange, sir? Which of them has the bargain?'

Marwood said nothing for a moment. Then, 'There's nothing fair about it. It's the way of the world.'

She said more quietly, 'Then the world mistakes the way it should be.'

'Perhaps.' He was not foolish enough to dispute the matter with her. 'But is there more? Has this woman something to do with Chard Lane?'

Cat sank back on her stool. Her anger vanished as swiftly and mysteriously as it had come, leaving her drained and sad. 'I don't know, Marwood. I don't know.'

'What about the Orleans bookplate I found with Iredale's gold? That might connect her with the murder.'

'Mademoiselle de Keroualle was stranded at Dieppe on her journey to England. The figures on the back of the bookplate were dated from Dieppe. She was to cross the Channel on Buckingham's yacht. But the yacht never arrived. She was angry with him at first, but lately they seem to have made friends.'

'Buckingham,' he said slowly. 'We know that it was thanks to him that Iredale got his place at the Council for Foreign Plantations.'

'I saw the Duke at the drawing room. As I was leaving, he made vague threats against me.'

'Why?'

'He didn't say.'

'Unlike Roger Durrell when he waylaid me last night outside the Savoy. He and another man attacked me.'

'Oh God.' Without thinking, she put a hand on his arm. 'Are you hurt?'

'No. Only a bruise or two. He didn't mean to hurt me. He wanted to remind me that he knew where I lived.'

Cat took her hand away. 'Why?'

'It was a warning.' Marwood perched on Brennan's stool. 'The meaning was clear enough: keep away from him and his master's business.'

'Why now?'

A pool of silence spread between them. The ripples expanded.

Marwood sighed. 'Because we've touched Buckingham at a sore point. Almost certainly it has something to do with this murder. And the odds are that it also has something to do with your French maid of honour.'

'The devil's up to his old tricks,' Cat said.

'And we're in his way. Again.'

An hour later, I was at Scotland Yard, the sprawling collection of offices, residences, storehouses, stables and much else that lay on the river immediately to the north of Whitehall itself.

Mr Williamson, Lord Arlington's Under Secretary of State, was installed in a set of offices in one of the quieter court-yards. Here, he and a handful of clerks dealt with the *Gazette* and with the correspondence designed to disseminate the government's policies and achievements throughout the kingdom. They also gathered information from a variety of sources, many of them secret, and collated the material for the King, Lord Arlington and a handful of other members of the Privy Council.

It was still early, but there was a good chance that I would find him at his desk. He did not take his duties lightly, and he expected those who worked for him to do the same. The porter nodded affably to me, and I went upstairs to the outer office, where the clerks were at work at the endless copying that their jobs required. I knew that Mr Williamson was here by the industrious hush among his people. One or two of them smiled or waved at me, but no one spoke. I took a deep breath and knocked on the door of the inner room.

I heard the familiar growl within and entered, closing the door behind me. Williamson was writing, his heavy wig hanging over the paper before him as if shrouding it from invisible snoopers. He did not look up but continued writing until his quill ran out of ink.

'Marwood,' he said, raising his eyes at last. 'I thought it was you.'

'May I beg the favour of a private word, sir?'

'I suppose so,' he said ungraciously, his hard Cumberland-bred voice roughening the vowels. 'What is it?'

'Roger Durrell is in London. The Duke of Buckingham's man.'

'I know he's in London.' Williamson stabbed the quill into the ink pot. 'If you came to tell me that, I'm afraid you've had a wasted journey.'

'Is he alone?'

'You mean is he with his old master? The broken-down parson?'

'Yes, sir.'

In the past, Durrell had always been in the company of a man named Veal, an obstinate Yorkshire clergyman who had been ejected from his living for his failure to conform to the Thirty-Nine Articles of the Established Church.

'Veal's dead,' Williamson said. 'Fell off his horse in Skipton last year.'

I felt an unexpected stab of regret. It has ever been a maxim of mine that the better I know a man, the less inclined I am to judge him harshly. Veal had been a hard man who cared little for the means he used, only for the ends they achieved. Yet he was honest in his way. He believed he was doing God's work, but sometimes it had given him little pleasure.

Williamson laid down his pen with a sigh. 'What's this about Durrell? Is he causing mischief again?'

There are exceptions to every rule, and my maxim did not apply to Durrell. The better I knew him, the more I hated and feared him.

I avoided the question. 'Does he still do the Duke's bidding in everything, sir?'

'He has no other master now that Veal's dead. Only the Duke. And His Grace pays him well, so he has no need to look elsewhere.' Williamson's voice rose. 'Now answer my question.'

I hesitated only a moment. 'I think he has a connection with the Chard Lane affair.'

'The almshouse murder? Was that his work?'

'Perhaps. I don't know for certain. But he assaulted me last night to encourage me to keep my distance.'

'What's the Duke's interest?' Williamson said.

'I wish I knew.'

'Have a care, Marwood. I doubt the Duke realizes how dangerous Durrell is. I'm told that when he was little more than a lad, he saw his mother raped by royalist troopers before his eyes, and his father disembowelled. Such things sour a man's soul. Since he lost his master as well as his hand, they say he's become more vicious than ever. Veal was a treasonous devil but he kept Durrell on a leash most of the time. If you have any choice in the matter, keep as far away from him as you can.'

'Do you know if the Duke has some particular business on hand at present?'

'I heard a whisper that he's undertaken an intrigue which has some bearing on the French. Our new allies.' Williamson shrugged. 'But I can see nothing to link that with Chard Lane. That's all I can tell you.'

I laid a hand on the latch. 'Thank you for seeing me, sir.'

'Keep away from Durrell. This is all your fault, of course.'

I blinked. 'What? I—'

'You were there when that madman chopped off Durrell's hand. You should have let him bleed to death. It would have saved us all a deal of trouble. Instead I'm told you saved his life. What were you thinking?'

I wondered how Williamson had learned that. It was never wise to underestimate the range and depth of his intelligence-gathering.

He took up his pen again and scowled at me in his old, familiar way. 'By the way, I don't give information for nothing. You know that.'

I felt strangely cheerful. 'I'll tell you what I can, sir. When I know myself.'

He snorted in disgust or derision or even amusement. 'Go away. I have work to do.'

* * *

At Goring House I found a letter from Arlington waiting for me. My lord had at last found time to respond to the one I had sent him on Wednesday. His reply was brief and to the point.

News of the Chard Lane almshouse murder had reached him from more than one source. He commanded me to discover the identity of the corpse and to provide him with further information about Iredale, the copyist at the Council for Foreign Plantations, and about the masked foreigner who had visited him. He declined to trouble Mr Rush on Cat's behalf until he knew more about all aspects of the matter.

So that was that. Cat would have to wait until the bishop's coroner arrived.

I took pen and ink and replied at once. The foreigner, I wrote, was almost certainly Monsieur Pharamond, a French tutor who had not been seen since the night of the murder. I told my lord about the purse I had found concealed at Iredale's lodging, my visit to the house of Iredale's parents, and the box I had discovered there. I mentioned that the purse might possibly have some connection with one of the Queen's ladies. I dealt with Buckingham and Durrell. I did not dwell too long on their behaviour to Cat and myself, but I passed on the information I had just gained from Mr Williamson about the rumour of a new intrigue on the part of the Duke.

Last of all, there were the two samples of handwriting. Arlington already knew about the scrap of paper with a fragment of Iredale's address, which Cat had found in the French shoe from Chard Lane. But now there was another: the list of figures headed *Dieppe, le 15° Septembre 1670* in Iredale's box, with a bookplate on the other side bearing the arms of the Duke of Orleans.

That was interesting enough in itself. But it was equally significant that the two pieces of handwriting had almost certainly been written by the same person. I had already made a copy of the papers, so I enclosed the originals with my reply.

I was lucky. I caught the courier as he was leaving. I added the letter to his pouch before it was sealed.

Afterwards I walked across St James's Park in the sunshine and looked at the antics of the ducks in the canal. I had a whimsical notion that the ducks might amuse Grace Hadgraft as much as they amused me. I had met the young lady only once but I could not rid my thoughts of her. My fancies bred among themselves: one day, perhaps, I might bring her here and we would disport ourselves among the King's birds and the King's animals like Adam and Eve newborn from the shadows of London.

CHAPTER FOURTEEN

'YOU'LL HAVE TO pay for that,' Mother Gribbin said as the lock gave up the unequal struggle.

The door flew open with a shriek of splintering wood. I let my eyes rove around Pharamond's garret under the eaves of the Three Crowns. The room was barely adequate to house a large dog. Even at the highest point the ceiling was no more than five feet high. A tiny window of cracked glass looked out on the blank wall of the tavern's neighbour.

Behind me, in the larger attic beyond, Mother Gribbin raised her voice. 'On my oath you'll pay for that. And what about my seven shillings? If there's anything worth having in there, it's mine.'

There was nothing she could do to hinder me. I had shown her my warrant as a matter of form, though she couldn't read it. More usefully, I had brought one of Lord Arlington's footmen with me, an enormous, red-headed fellow named Job who often acted as a sort of bodyguard to my lady when she went out.

'I'll send for the justice, you carrot-topped squittershins,'

I heard her say. 'You see if I don't. He'll put you in the stocks soon as look at you.'

'Hold your clack,' I said without turning round.

The ceiling was so low I had to stoop. The Frenchman's bed was a mattress covered with an old cloak. Clothes hung on wooden pegs hammered into the wall. The only furniture was a press cupboard beside the bed and a shelf on which stood an unframed fragment of mirrored glass and an earthenware bowl and pitcher.

I stripped the mattress and discovered nothing apart from the fact that the sheets should have been changed some time ago. The press cupboard contained clean linen, much mended but neatly folded, a well-thumbed pack of cards, a dice box, writing materials and a book sumptuously bound in leather.

I opened the volume at its title page. It was the *Oeuvres meslées* of Monsieur de Saint-Évremond. I examined the blank pages at the front of the book. One of the pages had been ripped out, almost certainly the one with the bookplate with the arms of the Duke of Orleans.

I set the book aside. I was going through the clothes on the pegs when I became aware of a commotion below, followed by footsteps ascending the narrow staircase to the attics.

'There, sir,' screeched Mother Gribbin, 'there they are, the thieving devils.'

'Out of my way, fellow,' commanded a familiar voice.

Job glanced over his shoulder. 'Shall I knock him down, sir?' he said as casually as if he were asking if I wanted him to find us a hackney.

'No,' I said. 'Let the gentleman in.'

Job stood aside. Rush appeared with Mistress Gribbin twitching malevolently at his elbow.

'It's the hand of providence,' she hissed in his ear. 'There you were, master, passing through Newgate just when I needed you.'

He ignored her. 'Mr Marwood. And what are you doing now?'

'Here is my warrant, sir,' I said.

He skimmed the contents and handed it back. 'My Lord Arlington reposes much trust in you. Let us hope it's deserved. What's all this?'

'I'm on the same business as before.'

Rush began to say something but stopped and looked at Mother Gribbin: 'Stand by the farther door, mistress. I must be confidential with this gentleman.'

'The mounseer owes me seven—'

'Be off, woman!' he roared in a voice that must have been audible in the street below.

She scuttled away. Rush turned back to me.

'You mean the Chard Lane murder?' he said in a lower voice as he glanced over my shoulder at the garret. He wrinkled his nose. 'Who lives in this kennel?'

'One Pharamond, sir. A Frenchman. Until lately he was tutor to Mistress Grace Hadgraft.'

'I might have known Hadgraft would be mixed up in this.'

I let that pass without asking why. 'Do you know the man, sir?'

'Not as far as I'm aware.' He fixed me with his hard blue eyes. 'What have you found? Letters? Papers?'

'Nothing of significance.'

We stared at each other. I knew that Rush wanted to search

the garret himself. But he couldn't, not with Lord Arlington's warrant in my pocket to lend me authority and Job ready to follow whatever orders I gave him.

'The bishop's coroner will soon be here, sir,' I said, playing Rush at his own game. 'If I find anything material to the inquest, you may be sure I shall give it to him.'

He scowled. Almost immediately, though, his face cleared, and he said in an oddly jaunty voice: 'Do you think this Frenchman could be the wretch I've got rotting in my cellar? Faith, he smells even worse now.'

By the time I finished at the Three Crowns it was after midday. I had the door of the garret sealed up. I took away the book, probably the most valuable item in the room, leaving a receipt with Mother Gribbin.

All the while, Rush had remained at the doorway, watching me while Job stood like a man mountain at his shoulder. I could have ordered him to leave but I wasn't sure he would obey, or even that the terms of my warrant gave me such authority over one of the King's justices.

Afterwards the three of us went downstairs and into the street. I sent Job back to Goring House with the book and set off down Snow Hill. To my surprise, Rush fell into step beside me.

'Why do you walk with me?' I demanded.

'I find you are going my way, sir,' he said blandly. 'A fine opportunity to extend our acquaintance, don't you think?'

'If you say so.'

Not a whit rebuffed, he talked incessantly as we went, pointing out the places we passed or telling me snippets of information about the people we saw. He had previously struck me as a taciturn man, but now I found it hard to slip a word in edgeways.

'Tell me, sir,' I said in a brief lull when he paused to draw breath, 'do you know a man named Iredale?'

'Never heard of him. Who's he?'

'A copyist at the Council for Foreign Plantations.'

'Why do you ask?'

'He had a list of names in his possession,' I said. 'Yours among them. But your name had been crossed out. Any idea what that list could be?'

'No.' He threw me a glance. 'Why don't you ask the fellow himself?'

'Because I can't find him.'

He raised bushy eyebrows. 'Then I suppose you must look for him.'

I had assumed that Rush was going back to his house in Hatton Garden. Once we were over Holborn Bridge, however, he showed no sign of leaving me.

'I intend to call on Mr Hadgraft, sir,' I said, interrupting him in mid-sentence. 'I can't think you want to come with me.'

'Why ever not? I fancy you want to talk to him about this Frenchman of his. I think I should be there too.' Rush inclined his head towards me. 'It is no more than my duty. Until the bishop's man arrives, I have a responsibility in this matter.' He looked innocently at me, widening his eyes like an astonished child. 'By the King's authority.'

Perhaps I should have quarrelled with him. But I couldn't help smiling instead. I was learning that Rush was a man for all seasons: abrupt, hard and overbearing; yet also witty in both senses of the word, his quick intelligence leavened with sparks of dry humour.

Hadgraft received us in his study, the room I had seen on my previous visit. He acted as if he and I were quite alone in the room. Rush did not appear disconcerted. He stood with his back to the wall, looking first at me and then at our host. It was as if he were at the play: the curtain had risen, and he was waiting for the actors to speak their lines. I glanced out of the window at the summerhouse in the garden. It was empty.

'A pleasure to see you again,' Hadgraft said to me. 'You're come about the same tiresome matter, I expect?'

'Yes, sir. In particular, though, I should like to ask you about your former tutor. I went to Monsieur Pharamond's lodging this morning. He hasn't been seen there since Saturday. May I ask when you saw him last? And where?'

'Here. It was on Saturday evening. He gave my daughter a lesson in the afternoon, and the foolish girl asked him to supper. Afterwards I caught him stealing the spoon.' Frowning, Hadgraft chewed his lip. 'We'd left the dining room and went up to the drawing room. Pharamond left us for a moment. I followed – I had my suspicions, you understand. He went back to the dining room. The servants hadn't yet cleared the table. I saw him slip the spoon in his pocket with my own eyes. When he heard me outside, he made some excuse – he said he'd left his handkerchief on the chair. What nonsense.'

'What did you do?'

'I called for my man, and I told Pharamond to empty his pockets. He blustered, of course, pretended to stand on his honour. But I ordered the servant to knock him down if he didn't obey. He soon changed his mind.'

'But why didn't you summon the constable and have him committed for trial?'

'I should have done. But he begged for mercy. I'm a just man, I hope, but not a hard one. And I had to think of my daughter's reputation, and indeed my own.'

Ah, I thought, there's the real reason.

'I had him thrown out of the house instead,' he went on. 'And that was the last I saw of him.'

'What time was that?' I asked.

'After eleven . . . I can't be sure. My daughter might know. Would you like me to call her in?'

'I'd be obliged, sir.'

My mouth was suddenly dry, making me wish I had accepted the offer of refreshment. Rush cleared his throat, a harsh, rasping sound.

The study seemed to brighten as Grace Hadgraft entered it. She lowered her face modestly and curtsied to me, followed by a token bob in the direction of Rush. She had clearly taken her father's quarrel with the magistrate for her own.

Her father asked his question, and she replied in a low voice that Pharamond had left the house nearer midnight than half past eleven, for she had heard the clocks striking a short time afterwards. She looked at me as she spoke. I felt I could listen to that sweet voice and stare at that perfect face until the last trump sounded. I was not alone. Rush was looking at her as well.

Hadgraft noticed too. For the first time he addressed Rush. 'Have you seen and heard enough? I believe your business here is finished. Indeed, I don't understand why you needed to come here in the first place. In a day or two, the bishop's coroner will arrive and your connection with this sorry affair will be entirely over.'

Rush changed colour, and his hand dropped to the hilt of

125

his sword. But he restrained himself. He bowed stiffly and marched from the room. The three of us listened to his footsteps in the hall, the murmur of the servant's voice and the sound of the street door opening and closing.

'At last,' Hadgraft said, his restless eyes moving from my face to his daughter's. 'Now let us take a glass of wine and a biscuit, and be pleasant together.'

CHAPTER FIFTEEN

CAT CALLED AT Mr Hadgraft's house in the hope of finding him at home. She wanted to discuss the rescheduling of work on the site after the inquest and, with luck, extract a payment on account from him.

On previous visits she had been shown into the study. This afternoon, however, the servant led her upstairs. The sound of voices grew louder at every step. When Cat entered the drawing room, she was greeted by Grace Hadgraft's laughter. It was an affected, tinkling laugh that Cat found particularly disagreeable.

To her dismay, Marwood was there. He rose hastily from the sofa on which he had been sitting with Hadgraft's daughter. Biscuit in hand, he came forward to greet her.

'Mistress Hakesby.' He bowed. The biscuit made him look ridiculous. So did the hangdog expression on his face. 'How do you do?'

Grace Hadgraft had also risen to her feet, though far more gracefully than Marwood. Only then did Cat realize that there was a third woman in the room, Grace's waiting woman, who had been sewing by the window.

'My father will be back directly,' Grace said. 'Pray take this chair — it's nearer the fire. Susannah, bring Mistress Hakesby some wine.'

Cat refused the wine but accepted the chair, for to remain standing would have been awkward. 'Will he be long?'

'I'm sure he won't. Mr Marwood was telling me that he believes you and my father will soon be able to begin work at the almshouse again. I'm sure that will be a great relief.'

It was not so much the words themselves that grated on Cat as the way they emerged so sweetly from those perfect lips, while Grace herself inclined her body towards Marwood as if drawn into an invisible alliance with him; an alliance bounded in the material world by the sofa, which enclosed their two bodies so snugly that there was barely an inch or two between them.

'Has the bishop's coroner set a day for the inquest?' Cat said.

'I'm afraid not,' Marwood replied. 'There may be further delays.'

'Ah, sir, but you were just saying that you will write again to my Lord Arlington.' Grace turned her head towards him and smiled. 'I'm sure that will lend wings to the coroner. My lord can do all things if he wishes, and Mr Marwood has his ear.'

Marwood himself looked embarrassed at this generous assessment of his influence, but he did not deny it. To Cat's relief, and perhaps everyone else's, there were footsteps on the landing. Hadgraft opened the door and bustled into the room.

He was in a good humour and he greeted Cat with warmth. She soon realized that he wanted nothing to do with business this afternoon. Moreover, she thought, if she really pressed the point, he would take her down to his study, leaving Marwood to all intents and purposes alone with Grace Hadgraft. The poor fool would be defenceless against her armoury of melting glances and sweet words, not to mention the gentle sighs that made her breasts rise and fall in the way that men tended to find curiously fascinating.

'I'll call again at a more convenient time,' Cat said, rising to her feet. Hadgraft's presence in the drawing room would surely reduce the opportunities for billing and cooing.

To her surprise, Marwood also stood up. 'I must go as well. My lord's business won't wait.' He looked down at Grace, whose face was turned up to his. 'I wish it were otherwise, madam.'

'You must come to supper in compensation!' Hadgraft cried. 'Why delay? Shall we say Monday, sir? We'll not take no for an answer, will we, my dear?'

Grace transferred the gaze of her wide brown eyes from Marwood to her father. 'No indeed, sir.'

'You can find a hackney in Holborn,' Cat said coldly once they were out of the house. 'Since my lord needs your invaluable services so urgently.'

'Permit me to escort you back to Chard Lane, madam,' Marwood said. 'My lord can wait.'

Cat gave an inelegant snort of laughter. It was one thing for him to be courtly with Grace Hadgraft, but quite another with herself. 'I think I can find the way to the site office on my own.'

'I want to talk to you.'

'I think you'd prefer to talk to Grace Hadgraft.'

'I was making conversation with the lady. I could do no less. You wouldn't have me be unmannerly.'

'I know all about that sort of conversation,' Cat said. 'And I admired your display of manners immensely.'

'She confided a secret in me,' Marwood said.

'I suspect that's her way with all the gentlemen. It helps to make a man believe he's won her heart. Can't you see, it's nothing but a stratagem? You're an innocent, sir.'

To her secret satisfaction, Marwood changed colour, a pale pink blush that faded almost at once from his cheek. He didn't reply. On the other side of the bridge, he took her arm and guided her towards the paved way along the east side of the newly canalized Fleet River. It was quieter there than in the street.

'Grace told me why there's bad blood between Rush and the Hadgrafts,' he said.

'I thought they fell out over business.'

'No. Rush was Grace's lover. He asked for her hand.'

'He must be almost old enough to be her grandfather.'

'So? He is a gentleman of far higher rank than her father. He stands well at court, he's more than rich enough to support a wife and family.'

They stopped outside the site office. Marwood rapped on the door to summon Ledward the watchman.

'What did her father say?'

'He supported her in her refusal. Then Rush flew into a passion and withdrew his capital from your almshouse. Hadgraft couldn't abandon the project because he had already signed the agreement with the trustees.'

That explained it, Cat thought; that explained why Rush was causing every difficulty he could about the inquest. Cat was reluctant to exonerate Grace from all blame in the matter. No doubt she was the sort of woman who enjoyed exercising the twin powers of her beauty and her father's fortune over men, and men were stupid enough to rush towards her like lambs to the slaughter.

'Did you ask him about his name being on Iredale's list?' she said.

'No. I didn't want to do it in front of Rush, and then Mistress Grace was there. It'll keep.'

'You can ask him when you go to supper there. How convenient.'

Cat knew she was acting the shrew, but she didn't care. Marwood knocked again. There was still no sign of life on the other side of the door.

'I forgot,' she said. 'I gave Ledward leave to go out for an hour today. But I have a key.'

Marwood took it from her and unlocked the door. 'I'll come in with you for a moment,' he said.

'Why?'

'To make sure all's well.'

'There's no need.'

It was too late. He had already opened the door and preceded her into the house. Cat followed him inside. To tell the truth, she was glad of his company. They were greeted by the familiar smells of damp, ashes and freshly sawn timber. They went quickly from room to room. Everything was in order. Last of all, he unbarred the door to the yard.

'The idle knave,' she said. 'I told Ledward to move those sails and hang them to dry before he went out.'

A heap of canvas sails were piled at the foot of the wall separating the yard from the almshouse site. Cat had bought a job lot from the Navy Office. Patched and faded, they were useless for the purpose for which they had been made. But they served to keep off the worst of the weather from new-laid mortar and stacks of timber.

In a fit of irritation – with Ledward, Marwood and above all Grace Hadgraft – she took one corner of the nearest sail and dragged it towards the overhang of the shed where someone had once kept fowls.

'Let me do that,' Marwood said; he sounded irritated himself, which didn't improve Cat's temper.

She ignored him and continued to pull the sail. He threw down his stick with a clatter and took another corner.

She glanced at him. 'There's no need for you to—'

'Stop. Stop now.'

She let fall her corner of the sail. 'Why?'

'What's that?' he said.

Marwood was pointing at the ground. Moving the sail away from the pile had exposed both the one beneath and part of the ground beside it. Both were dry, because the sail on top had protected them from rain. There were rust-coloured stains on the fabric, with smaller spots around them and darker smudges on the bare beaten earth.

She cleared her throat. 'It . . . it could be anything.'

He squatted, moistened the tip of a finger and rubbed it on one of the stains. He examined the finger. 'No, it couldn't. It's blood.'

* * *

Like God, I rested on the seventh day.

The body of the man with no face had been discovered at the almshouse site on Monday morning. Now it was Sunday and the first day of October. When I woke up, I was thinking of the blood that Cat and I had found yesterday in the yard of the site office. There was no actual proof that it had come from the veins of the murdered man, no proof that he had been stabbed and bludgeoned to death there. But I had little doubt that it was so. For some reason the blood made the murder more real to me, more horrific, than even the body in Rush's cellar had done.

With an effort of will, I pushed the memory of it away from me. For a few precious hours, I tried to give myself a holiday from the dreary and inconclusive affair of the Chard Lane murder. The contradictory results of my investigations lay about my mind with no more logic or order to them than a heap of dead leaves twitching and shifting in the wind. I used all my powers of concentration to exclude them, along with Durrell's threats and the devious malice of his master Buckingham.

I stayed in bed past eleven o'clock, listening to the jangle of London's ill-tuned bells and the sounds of the house below. There was sawing and hammering downstairs. Yesterday, after Durrell's visit the previous evening, I had set Sam to work strengthening the bars and bolts that protected the house from intruders.

Instead of the murder, I thought of Grace Hadgraft: her soft voice, the lustrous, well-shaped eyes that had darted glances at me yesterday and the way her breathing quickened as we talked; I thought of her father's wealth, and how pleasant it would be to have a wife to order my possessions in a neat, new-built house, to command my meals, and to sit at my table while I ate, and to lie in my bed and, if God willed it, bear my children.

Was it, I wondered, such an impossible dream? After all, I was young, I was ambitious, I worked in Lord Arlington's private office. Mr Hadgraft had even been impressed when he discovered that I was the great-nephew of the late and not at all regretted Alderman Marwood.

For a while these thoughts made me almost happy. Except I couldn't repress the memory of Cat yesterday afternoon: her scornful glance when she accused me of being an innocent; and something else, something worse – the expression on her face when she came into Hadgraft's drawing room and found me sitting on the sofa with Grace.

For an instant she had looked like a wounded animal. And it was I who had wielded the knife.

Cat kept a pew at St Paul's in Covent Garden, as the late Mr Hakesby had done. It was useful to see others there, and to be seen in one's turn. It was a modest church designed by Inigo Jones before the Civil War as part of his piazza for Lord Bedford. Cat went there two or three times a month and also contributed carefully calculated sums to the relief of the parish poor.

Sometimes she sat alone, attended only by Jane Ash. Sometimes the newly minted Mr and Mrs Brennan kept her company. Occasionally James Marwood would join her if they were engaged to dine together afterwards or had a Sunday outing in mind. But Marwood's mind was elsewhere these days, so perhaps those occasions were over.

On the first day of October, Cat sat in her pew with Jane

Ash. When the service was over, she glimpsed a familiar face among the crowd at the back of the church. Margaret Witherdine often came to St Paul's on a Sunday: not for the sermon, but to be near the tablet commemorating Stephen, the boy to whom she and her husband had given their surname after his death.

Outside it was raining. Cat returned to the sign of the Rose, leaving Jane to fetch Margaret. Later, when the two servants arrived in the parlour, Cat sent for wine and persuaded Margaret to take a glass to warm herself. She drank it standing up, unwilling to sit, made uneasy by this mark of condescension.

'I can't stay,' Margaret said. 'Sam needs someone to keep an eye on him. Yesterday morning, master told him to make the house more secure. He was fitting new bolts to the shutters when I left.' The wine had brought a rush of extra colour to her cheeks. 'And Master said he should see to the weapons too. I haven't got the marks out of the kitchen table from last time.'

Roger Durrell, Cat thought with a chill of apprehension. Buckingham. They were the reason for Marwood's orders. She knew that Margaret was more concerned for Sam's safety than her kitchen table.

Aloud she said, 'It's sensible to take precautions. I'm sure your master is wise.'

There was a knock at the door, and the porter's boy brought a letter. Cat broke the seal and signalled to Jane to refill Margaret's glass.

The letter was from Mr Hadgraft, and within the same cover was another with her name written in an unfamiliar hand.

At last we have a date. The Bishop's Coroner, Mr Osmund,
is anxious to complete the business as soon as may be. He
has appointed tomorrow morning at eleven o'clock in the
public room at the Three Crowns in Snow Hill. I enclose
your summons as a witness.

'Will you give your master a note?' Cat said to Margaret.
'I'll have it written in a moment.'

She scribbled a few words to Marwood, telling him the
time and the place of the inquest. She was tempted to add a
sardonic postscript expressing the hope that he would enjoy
his supper with the Hadgrafts, but she managed to resist. He
was making his own bed, she told herself, and he would soon
have to lie on it, very probably with that pert hussy Grace
Hadgraft by his side.

After Margaret left, Cat sent Jane to fetch their dinner from
the cookshop. As the minutes passed, unease crept gradually
over her like a fog, becoming steadily thicker. Jane was taking
longer than expected. At this time of day, the streets should
be safe enough for a servant girl who was well-known in the
area, particularly on a Sunday; but one could never be sure,
not in London.

Marwood feared there might be trouble. Cat knew that she
should take precautions as well. All she had to keep Durrell
away was the street door guarded by a corrupt porter and
his half-grown boy. But she didn't want to ask Marwood for
help. She didn't want to ask him for anything.

A quarter of an hour later, Jane's footsteps came pattering
up the stairs. But the fog of unease did not lift.

CHAPTER SIXTEEN

T HE INQUEST WAS packed. In the past week, the murder of the unknown man with no face had achieved notoriety throughout London. The coroner and his clerk were given chairs; so were Mr Rush, Mr Hadgraft and Cat; and at the last moment a chair was brought in for the younger son of an earl, who spent the proceedings sucking the head of his stick and staring about him with huge brown eyes like a calf's. For everyone else it was standing room only. The hastily empanelled jury was penned into a corner of the public room behind a row of benches.

'Mr Osmund seems a sensible man,' Hadgraft murmured in Cat's ear. 'He has other business to transact in London, and with luck he won't delay things any longer than necessary. It's been as clear as day from the start what the verdict must be – murder by person or persons unknown.'

Osmund was younger than Cat had expected, a slim, dark-haired man with piercing blue eyes that gave him a possibly misleading air of intelligence. He conducted the inquest briskly, hearing evidence about the discovery of the body, the nature of the wounds sustained by the victim, the blood-stains under the sails in the yard, and the continuing failure to identify the corpse. He cut short witnesses who showed a tendency to wander from the point and was cruel to those who stumbled over their words or were confused in their testimony. He was particularly harsh with Thomas Ledward, who fumbled his evidence.

'Then you saw nothing, heard nothing and know nothing, eh?' Osmund said. 'Is that what you're trying to say?'

'Yes, your honour.'

'But it's clear to me that you should have seen and heard something if you were awake and doing your duty. You were the watchman, after all, weren't you? Where were you that night? Asleep in your own bed? Next witness.'

Once Cat had given her own evidence, she relaxed and looked about the court. Most of the crowd were men. She had half-expected to see Marwood among the spectators, but he wasn't there. She wasn't sure whether to be relieved or pleased.

Apart from herself, the few women in attendance were clustered about the doorway, as if to show that they were not really in the room at all but happened to be passing and chanced to glance inside at the men going about their business. Susannah, Grace Hadgraft's waiting woman, was among them. She avoided meeting Cat's eye. At the back, towering over the rest of the group, was Mistress Farage's maid from Swan Yard. She was a tall, shabbily dressed woman whose head was too small for the rest of her. It poked forward from her shoulders, like that of a tortoise with a fit of the sullens.

Rush noticed her too. 'That's Patience Noone by the door,' he said to Osmund during a lull in the proceedings. 'The tall one. Do you remember I told you about her? She's the maid at the house where one of the missing men lodges. A Mr Iredale, employed at the Council for Foreign Plantations.'

Osmund nodded. He was updating his notes.

'Will you call her?' Rush asked.

The coroner glanced at him. 'I don't see any need. You said she was shown the body but she couldn't identify it.'

It was barely half past eleven when Osmund delivered his summing up. He told the jury that they had no alternative but to return a verdict of murder by person or persons unknown. The jury obediently followed his direction. Before dismissing them, he ordered that the body be interred at the cost of the parish. Mr Hadgraft whispered something in his ear, at which the coroner added that work could resume on the almshouse site at once. Rush stared at the floor.

Afterwards, Osmund declined Hadgraft's invitation to dine with him and left the inn. Rush followed, his face expressionless. Perversely, Cat was left with a sense of anticlimax.

'Well,' Hadgraft said as they left the Three Crowns, 'there's nothing to stop us from carrying on. At last. What a waste of time this has been. He'll have to go, by the way.'

'Who will?' Cat said.

'Ledward. We can't leave a man like that in charge of the site at night. You heard what Mr Osmund said. He seems well enough but he's clearly either a knave or a fool.'

The common people streamed into the Snow Hill with Patience Noone among them. On impulse, Cat called her name. The maid must have heard her. But she turned her back and strode away on her long legs as if she were trying to outwalk the Devil himself.

* * *

After he had dined in the City, Mr Hadgraft called at the site office. He stood at the window, looking over the yard wall at the spoil heaps and trenches, where three men were already at work again.

'Rush's nose is out of joint, I warrant,' he said, his pleasure bubbling out of him. 'How all this must annoy him.'

'It will take us a day or two to get fully under way,' Cat said. 'We've lost over half of our labourers. Mr Brennan's out hiring this morning. We're better off for the skilled men, but we can't use most of them yet.'

'Oh we'll manage, Mistress Hakesby – I'm sure of it.' Hadgraft turned. 'I've every confidence in you and Mr Brennan; you know that.'

'Thank you, sir. It would help greatly if we could put down a payment in advance for the lime we shall need to bond the foundations. And if you could see your way to—'

'All in good time. We'll discuss that later when I've had leisure to go through the figures.' He slipped adroitly to another subject. 'By the way, it was a pleasure to meet Mr Marwood. A most interesting gentleman. Well placed at court through my Lord Arlington, no doubt, and also in the City perhaps, through his late uncle the alderman. Who knows how far he will rise? I would have thought a knighthood is not completely out of the question in ten or twenty years' time. Have you known him long?'

'Five years or so,' Cat said, turning away to roll up a plan on the table.

'Is he a man of substance? I know he doesn't flaunt his wealth, like so many of our foolish young men do, but I imagine he has some fortune of his own?'

'Not that I know of.' Cat knotted the ribbon with unnecessary force around the plan. 'But you must ask him yourself.'

It was as plain as the perfectly shaped nose on Grace Hadgraft's face that her father was thinking seriously of Marwood as a possible suitor for his daughter. Cat gave the knot an extra tug, half-wishing it were Grace's neck. The roll of paper buckled and creased under the pressure.

'He has a house in the Savoy, he tells me,' her client continued, unaware of the murderous thoughts coursing through Cat's mind. 'Those cramped old lodgings can't be convenient for a man in his position, particularly if he wants to enlarge his establishment. Perhaps he thinks of taking a lease on a modern house. We might even propose one of ours to him—'

He broke off at the sound of shouting below. He and Cat exchanged glances. Cat pushed past him and threw open the window. As she did so, two labourers shouldered their way through the gateway in the wall between the yard and the main site.

'What is it?' she said.

'We found the dog, mistress,' one of them shouted. 'Tom Ledward's dog. What's left of it.'

CHAPTER SEVENTEEN

L EFT TO MYSELF on Monday morning, I would have
gone to the inquest at the Three Crowns. Instead I
went to the Council for Foreign Plantations. Arlington's
commands had been brief but clear. He wanted information
about the corpse's identity and about Iredale. It was unlikely
the inquest would tell us much more about the former, and
if it did I would soon hear. But Iredale was a different
matter.

At Lord Bristol's house, I went through the gateway and
across the courtyard to the offices of the council, where I
asked for Mr Davis. To my surprise, the porter was expecting
me.

'They sent word down, sir. You're to see Mr Evelyn first.'

The porter's boy took me upstairs. Evelyn was talking to
some other gentlemen in the long gallery. When he saw me,
he broke away and came to greet me. As the others were still
within earshot, I made a civil enquiry about the fate of his
Madeira and his Cheshire cheese, the subject that had exercised him so greatly at our last meeting.

'No news on that score.' A flash of annoyance passed over his face. 'I continue to make enquiries.'

He led me through the door to the council chamber, and then into a square room furnished as a library. Some of the shelves held books but at least half of the space was given over to rows of neatly labelled boxes. He closed the door behind us.

'I won't keep you long from Mr Davis,' he said, 'but I thought I should have a private word with you first.'

'Has there been a development?'

Evelyn gave the ghost of a shrug. 'Since you called here last week, Davis and I have been making our own enquiries. Much of our work here is confidential, as I'm sure you understand. Some of the intelligence that passes through our hands could have considerable commercial value if it fell into the wrong hands. We have our suspicions that someone here is selling information.'

I cut in as he paused to draw breath: 'Do you think it's Iredale?'

'In a word, yes,' he said. 'Or at least it's more than possible that it's him.'

'How does such corruption work?'

He winced at the word. 'Let me give you an illustration: we had decided to abandon one of our West African forts and switch its trade to a new site further south. Only the council was aware of this. When it was too late to turn back, we discovered that a group of English merchants had recently taken a lease on our chosen location from the native chief. Of course they claimed it was purely coincidental. Unfortunately for us, it was the only practical spot on that part of the coast, both in terms of defence and the security of the harbour. We were forced to acquire the lease from them at an inflated price and grant them certain trading privileges as well.'

It would be hard to prove corruption in such cases, I thought, unless you could discover the source of the information. Aloud I said: 'How long has this been going on for?'

'Months. The first case we know of was in February this year. It concerned a projected expansion of a branch of our joint import and export trade that requires a ship to make three distinct voyages.' I must have looked puzzled because Evelyn proceeded to explain. 'It's very simple, sir, in essence. For example, a ship exports our manufactures – beads, weapons, cloth and so forth – to the Gold Coast, where we trade them for slaves. Then the same ship takes the slaves to the West Indies or perhaps to our North American colonies, where the slaves are sold to the plantation owners. And the ship brings back a cargo – usually sugar – to England. Thus, you see, the trade creates a virtuous circle to the benefit of all parties.' He gave me a prim smile. 'Or rather should I say a virtuous triangle?'

While he was speaking, my own slave, my poor dead Stephen came into my mind. In a fit of drunken generosity, I had given him his freedom; not that he had shown me any gratitude; but perhaps I had deserved none for returning what should not have been taken in the first place.

'Apart from the slaves, that is,' I said.

'What?'

'I fancy this virtuous triangle cannot be much to their benefit.'

Evelyn frowned. 'That's hardly our affair. Their fellow

savages enslaved them. Besides, slavery is common to all ages – it's part of God's plan. And bear in mind, sir, these people are not Christians.'

I thought of the grieving Witherdines and the plain tablet set high on the wall of St Paul's, Covent Garden. Was that part of God's plan too? Simultaneously a distant clock struck the hour.

'But time and tide wait for no one,' Evelyn continued. 'We mustn't allow ourselves to wander in the byways of theology, however tempting that may be. The important thing is that we must discover whether Iredale was responsible for this unauthorized disclosure of intelligence. But everything must be done in strictest confidence.'

'When I searched the house of Iredale's parents,' I said, 'I discovered a box containing a large sum of money, most of it in gold. It was hidden away.'

Evelyn brightened. 'That's surely evidence of guilt.'

I took out my pocketbook and found the list of names. 'There was also this.'

He glanced at it. 'Some of those are familiar. Davis will know. Mr Rush was a member of Parliament at one time; a fine soldier, I believe. What was the list?'

'I don't know yet. Is it in Iredale's hand? Could it be something he copied here?'

'Again, we must ask Davis.' Evelyn led me towards the door. He paused and turned back to me. 'Apart from Davis, by the way, the only people who know about this here are myself and the secretary to the council. And now you. I should be most grateful if you kept it to yourself.'

'Is there a particular reason for discretion? Beyond the usual?'

Evelyn inclined his head towards me and said quietly, 'Did Davis tell you how Iredale got his place here?'

'Yes. He was put forward by one of the Duke of Buckingham's people. He had done the Duke some service in France.'

'Exactly. The Duke is a member of the council, not that he troubles to attend our meetings. The Secretary feels that if we move against Iredale without sufficient evidence, the Duke may take it as a personal slight: it would be as if we were questioning his judgement. As you may know, he is — ah — touchy on the subject of his own honour.'

'I know,' I said.

'When it suits him, that is,' Evelyn murmured, his tone unexpectedly waspish. 'His Grace's honour is a most curious organ of remarkable flexibility.'

Mr Davis slid off his stool and came to greet me.

'How do you do, sir.' He ushered me away from the clerks' room. He said nothing apart from a few words about the weather until we were alone in a closet overlooking the pleasure ground, with the door closed. 'Any news of Iredale?'

'He seems to have disappeared into thin air.'

'Then the body at the Chard Lane almshouse . . . ?'

'We can't be sure whose it is. The inquest is this morning, but I doubt it will get us much further.'

'Poor fellow,' Davis said, his small features twisting into a grimace. 'I hope it's not him. Now what can I do for you? I'd no idea you were coming today until Mr Evelyn told me.'

Once again, I took my pocketbook and extracted the list of names I had found on the other side of the Orleans bookplate in Iredale's box. 'I'd be glad if you could tell me whether this is Iredale's handwriting.'

Davis glanced at it and then looked more closely. 'Those loops on the initial capitals – see? – they are a little more rounded at the top than is customary. Yes, almost certainly his. His copying can be erratic in its accuracy, but he writes as neat a hand as any man.' He looked up at me, frowning. 'Rush – the name here that's scratched out – isn't that the magistrate in your Chard Lane business? And Mr Hadgraft's here too. The lawyer who's the principal investor in the alms-house project – yes?'

I nodded. I was impressed that Davis was so well informed. 'And the other names?'

'Some are City men. You should ask at the Exchange – they'll know more about them than I do. Others I don't know: they may be gentlemen of means like Mr Rush.'

'Why would Iredale list them together?'

'Who knows? It may have nothing to do with the council's work.'

'Indeed. But for the sake of argument, say it has.'

'The council's remit is broad. It has to be, for everyone's sake. We deal with many legal issues here. Disputes within or between our colonies – that sort of thing. Plantation boundaries, port privileges and so on. But I somehow doubt these names have to do with one of those. More likely they're shareholders in a particular venture that touches on our business here. Investors often approach us for advice or information about trading conditions or the government's intentions.'

'As Mr Evelyn was telling me.'

'There's a good deal of money at stake. Trading voyages

can bring great profits. But the risks are substantial too, and so is the necessary investment. That's why any ship and its cargo will usually be owned by a number of men. Otherwise, the potential loss would be unthinkable. Even the richest man in London would hesitate to be the sole proprietor of a vessel that could founder thousands of miles away or be seized by pirates within two or three days' sail of London or Bristol.'

'Then the council exists to lessen these risks in whatever way it can?'

'Yes, you could say that. It's bad enough even if a voyage goes well. There are always losses to be set against the profits. Why, if they're shipping slaves to the West Indies, for instance, they allow as a matter of course for at least a third of the cargo to die while they are at sea.'

Again the uncomfortable memory of Stephen stirred in my mind. 'And these names.' I touched the list which lay beside us on a table. 'Let's say they are shareholders in some enterprise that touches on your work here. Could you hazard a guess which one?'

'You'd have to ask Iredale when you find him.' He tapped the list with his finger. 'Or one of these gentlemen.'

I had already asked Rush, who denied all knowledge of both the list and Iredale. I would see Hadgraft this evening, though I had no desire to raise the matter with him in his daughter's company. Perhaps I would find an opportunity to speak to him alone.

'I'd dearly like to find out what's happened to Iredale,' Davis said when I rose to leave. 'Pray keep me informed if you learn anything.'

'Of course.'

'Or tell Mr Evelyn if that's more convenient. He'll pass it on.'

'He is much concerned about this, I think?'

'Yes.' Davis lowered his voice. 'He's an honest man, and he wants our work to be beyond reproach. I can't say that about everyone who sits at the council table.' For an instant there was a note of emotion, almost anger, in his voice. 'It's important that our business here is above board and that it is seen to be so. Otherwise, what's the point of it?'

'Indeed, sir.'

Our eyes met. He opened the door and we walked in silence through the chamber with the turkey-work chairs. There were men's voices in the lobby below, one of them loud, confident and uncomfortably familiar to me.

Then another voice in reply, quieter, lower-pitched. 'As Your Grace wishes. We . . . we had not expected to have the honour of seeing you here.'

I ducked back into the chamber. I didn't want a confrontation with Buckingham here. 'Is there another way to leave?'

Davis looked surprised but he gave a quick nod. Without saying anything he led me back into the long gallery. At the end he paused beside the tapestry nearest to the door to the council chamber. Half concealed by the hanging was a much smaller door. I heard the Duke's strident tones in the room we had just left.

Davis opened the door. 'This way.'

He followed me through and shut the door behind us. A dimly lit staircase spiralled both up and down. Servants' stairs. The only light came from a narrow window above us.

'We go down,' he said. 'There's a handrail. Better let me go first.'

149

We descended into the gloom and emerged into a flagged hallway furnished only with a roughly made trestle table.

'Is there another way to reach the street?' I said.

'If we go through the old kitchens, there's a yard beyond. You can reach the alley along the side of the house from there.'

We passed a set of empty butteries and pantries and came to a vaulted kitchen where it looked as if nothing had been cooked for decades. The dressers, benches and two vast tables were thick with a coating of grey dust spotted with the droppings of rats and birds. Next came sculleries, from which a door opened into a long yard bounded by high brick walls topped with spikes. On one side was a line of outbuildings, some roofless. Weeds sprouted among the cobbles.

Davis glanced back. 'No one uses this side of the house at present. We have permission to come and go by the gate to the alley at the back. It's convenient if the weather is bad. Or if a man has creditors waiting at the front.'

We walked the length of the yard to double gates set in an archway. They were barred and bolted. Beside it was a smaller door secured with a bolt and a lock. Davis drew back the bolt. Then he stretched up to the lintel and removed a key from the ledge above.

'Go through and turn right,' he said, turning the key in the lock. 'At the end, go left. A few steps along Duke Street will bring you through the archway to Lincoln's Inn Fields.'

'I'm in your debt.'

'You want to avoid the Duke of Buckingham, eh?'

'Yes.' I owed Davis an answer in return for his kindness. 'It might have caused unpleasantness. Particularly if a man of his was with him. A bulky fellow missing a hand.'

'It's possible the porter mentioned you were here.'

I thought it equally possible that one of Durrell's people had followed me. 'Especially if someone asked him.'

'Mind you, we don't often see the Duke.' Davis hesitated a split second. 'May I ask why you don't wish to meet him?'

'Better not.' I softened the refusal with what I hoped was a rueful smile. 'He doesn't wish me well. Let's leave it at that.'

CHAPTER EIGHTEEN

A FTER THEY HAD dined, a party of ladies took the air in the Privy Garden. The younger ones hung back, grumbling quietly among themselves. The sky was heavy with clouds, and the chill in the air announced that autumn was fully upon them. That was why they were in the garden, which was nearer the Queen's apartments than the Park. It was also more private. There were no gentlemen in the party, apart from three elderly courtiers attached to her household. The poor men were too old, too poor and too uninteresting to be wanted at Euston or Newmarket.

Louise de Keroualle walked by herself. She did not have intimate friends among the ladies of Whitehall, who treated her with a degree of suspicion unless they hoped to gain something by her. She was French, which was bad enough, but almost from the first there had been a sense that she was not the same as the rest of them, particularly where gentlemen were concerned; and what marked her apart most of all was the attention that the King paid her.

This afternoon she had pains in her belly again. It could

not be *those* again, so soon after the end of the last monthly bleeding, and she prayed it was not some foul canker growing beneath the skin. More likely, she thought, it was the endless worry, and that was bad enough, a sort of canker of the heart.

Mr Williamson, the Under Secretary, and Monsieur Colbert were approaching. Louise hadn't expected to see them in the Privy Garden, not at this time. The two men strolled through the archway by the King Street gate and zigzagged slowly along the paths between the low hedges, their legs invisible below the knee and their heads nodding close together.

Williamson sheered away as they drew near and walked briskly to the doorway in the corner between the Vane Room and Matted Gallery. Colbert, however, wreathed in smiles, sauntered down the gravel walk, bestowing a greeting on each lady with punctilious courtesy. He exchanged a few words with one of the gentlemen. At last, he came to Louise. Bowing, he turned to face her, penning her as if by chance against one of the low hedges.

'Mademoiselle,' the ambassador said, 'you look enchanting. The cool air has brought a most charming blush to your cheeks.'

Rising from her curtsy, she looked modestly at the ground.

'My wife sends her compliments. I'm the bearer of a thousand good wishes from her.'

'How kind of her. Pray thank her.'

'She had a letter from my Lady Arlington this morning. Her ladyship confided that she could hardly tear herself away from London, did she not nurse so strong a hope of seeing you soon again.'

Louise murmured that she was not worthy to be the recipient of her ladyship's kindness, and that she was truly sensible of the honour that her ladyship did her.

'The Queen writes that she has most graciously given her permission for you to come to Euston with us. Madame Colbert and I hope to go down with you in a day or two, so we shan't have long to wait. You'll enjoy the races, I'm sure. Newmarket is only twenty miles away or so, and most of the court is already there if it is not at Euston. The whole town will be *en fête*.'

The rest of the party had moved on – not far, but enough to leave Louise alone with the ambassador.

'I have had a word with Madame des Bordes,' he went on in a more businesslike tone. 'She will help you to find whatever you need to make yourself look as well as possible. We are not so formal at Euston and Newmarket as we are here.' He chuckled. 'And you must let art improve nature. Why not? *All* your clothes should aim to please, remember. Think of yourself almost as a maiden as her wedding approaches, one who desires above all to please her future master.' He paused long enough for the implication to sink in. 'Take Madame des Bordes' advice on such matters,' he went on in a more practical voice. 'She knows her business. I have told her to send the bills to me.'

Louise inclined her head to show she had heard. She didn't speak. After all, what would be the point? Nothing she could say would alter anything.

'There's no time to be lost,' Colbert continued. 'We'll go together in my coach, along with my wife. In the meantime, avoid the Duke of Buckingham. He makes trouble wherever he goes and he's not a suitable friend for you.' He smiled unexpectedly. 'Don't look so frightened, my child,' he said. 'Enjoy what's yours for the taking. While you can.'

The watchman's dog was an ungainly beast with long, discoloured teeth and a mottled coat.

In life, he had been an ugly creature, but in death the unfortunate animal was worse than ugly: he was a decaying abomination. He had been stabbed several times, perhaps with the same weapon that killed the faceless man. He stank far worse than the corpse in Rush's cellar. Maggots and flies had gathered to feast on him: they shimmered in clouds over his wounds, his mouth, his nostrils, his genitals, his anus and his eyes.

The labourers had uncovered the dog in the spoil heap, not far from where the unknown man had been found. The body was wedged between a fragment of brick wall and a broken beam and then covered with a layer of rubble. The smell would have been noticed sooner if Rush hadn't ordered the closure of the entire site.

Hadgraft glanced at the corpse and then turned away, pulling a fold of his cloak over his mouth and nose. Cat followed him through the doorway into the site yard.

'The foul thing,' he said. 'Have the men dispose of it at once.'

'Shouldn't we send word to Mr Osmund? Or even Mr Rush?'

'Why? It doesn't change the verdict. It doesn't change anything. And it's nothing to do with Rush.'

'As you wish. We'll have to pay the men extra, by the way. They're already saying the place is cursed. This will make it worse.'

'Superstitious fools.' Hadgraft spat on the ground. His face twitched and he gave a grunt of frustration, unexpectedly high-pitched like a dog's yelp when someone treads on its paw. 'This on top of everything else.'

'It's no bad thing, sir. The missing dog was a loose end. I suppose we should tell Ledward that it's been found.'

'If he'd done his job properly, none of this would have happened. But that reminds me: we need a new watchman now he's gone. I'll cast about for one. My coachman will do for tonight. He's a stout fellow and not afraid of the dark.'

After Hadgraft left, Cat spent most of the afternoon making sure the labourers did their work and trying to forget how James Marwood would be spending his evening. She stood over the men while they buried the dog, which gave her more than enough opportunity to observe what death had done to it. Once the corpse was safely stowed four feet under the far corner of the waste ground, she set them to moving the spoil heap.

They didn't like her standing over them while they worked. She heard one of them saying it was unnatural to have a woman set above them, so she sacked him on the spot, despite the shortage of labour. Things were better after that.

She sent the men away when the light began to fade. Brennan was waiting for her at the site office. She quickly brought him up to date.

'Are the men right?' her partner said. 'Is this place cursed?'

'Of course not,' Cat said irritably, though in truth she was beginning to wonder herself. She forced herself to speak more calmly. 'Looked at rightly, this is good news. The murderer killed the dog, which is why it didn't rouse Ledward. The blood under that heap of sails was probably the dog's, not the man's.'

'Or both,' Brennan pointed out with ghoulish relish. 'No way of knowing, is there?' He went to the office window and looked at the yard below. 'To think they could have been killed down there. The pair of them.'

'We must get on,' Cat said wearily. 'God willing, we can make up for lost time if this weather holds for a few more weeks.'

'Did you get any money out of Hadgraft?'

'Not yet.'

Brennan sucked air through his teeth. 'Something's amiss with that man. I feel it in my bones.'

They walked around the site, discussing the day's progress and planning the week's work. Hadgraft's coachman arrived, not best pleased to play the part of nightwatchman. Once he was settled, Cat and Brennan left for the day, agreeing to share a hackney.

'Let's pick one up in Holborn,' Cat said.

Brennan frowned. 'Why? We could find one nearer by Newgate.'

'I want to call on someone in Swan Yard by the bridge. It won't take us five minutes out of the way.'

It took them considerably longer to reach Mistress Farage's house. Brennan knocked on the door. It was opened by a small girl, a child of no more than ten wearing a filthy apron too big for her.

'Yes?' she muttered.

'If your mistress would permit me, I'd like to talk to Patience Noone.'

'Betsy?' The croaking voice came from the room beyond an open doorway. 'Who is it?'

'They're asking for Patience,' the girl screamed back.

Something fell with a clatter on the other side of the doorway. There was a shuffling sound, mingled with the occasional grunt, and Mistress Farage appeared in the doorway, leaning on a stick and supporting herself on the other side by clinging to the doorjamb. Her lips were closed but they moved restlessly against each other as if she were masticating a mouthful of flies.

'Mistress Farage,' Cat said, 'forgive me for calling unannounced, but is Patience—'

'That strumpet!' Spittle flew into the air. 'You'll not find her here.'

'Where is she then?'

'Gone to the devil for all I care. I'll not shelter a whore under my roof. Betsy! Close the door.'

'The insolence of that woman,' Brennan said, when the door was safely closed and there was no chance of Mistress Farage hearing him. 'I've a good mind to tell her how she should talk to her betters.'

'A *whore*?' Cat said. 'Patience Noone?'

There was a chuckle from a hunched figure sitting on the mounting block of the neighbouring house.

'She's in a passion today, ain't she?'

'Hold your tongue, fellow,' Brennan snapped.

'No, stay.' Cat turned to face the old man. He had not been there a moment ago. 'Where did you come from?'

'Saw you when you come in the yard, mistress. You was here before, eh? Asking questions.' If he had any teeth, there was no sign of them, and their absence blurred his words as if he were speaking through a mouthful of watery mud. 'Master Iredale . . . is he the dead man up Chard Lane?'

It took Cat a moment to interpret what he was saying.

'We're looking for the maidservant this time.' She fumbled for her purse; in the shadows of this city, everything was for sale, nothing was free. 'Patience Noone.'

The coin vanished into the folds of the cloak. 'Bless you, mistress. The old witch threw her out last night.'

'Last *night*?' Patience had been at the inquest this morning.

He gestured at the ground by the mounting block. 'She left her box here. Took some things out, wrapped them in a bundle and then off she went.'

'Any idea where she's gone?' Cat asked, without much hope of learning anything.

'Maybe.' After another coin had vanished into his cloak, the old man said, 'I heard she got a lift with the Chester carrier this morning.'

'*Chester*?'

'Aye. He always puts up in Swan Yard when he's in London. He left a little before midday.'

By now Patience would be miles away, even at a carrier's pace. 'Has she family there?'

'If she hasn't now, she will soon.'

'What do you mean?'

The old man squinted up at Cat and grinned. 'She's with child, mistress. That's why the old bitch threw her out.'

In the afternoon, I went across the Park and up to Lord Arlington's office off the Privy Gallery, where I had papers to file. Afterwards I planned to escape from Whitehall earlier than usual and return to the Savoy.

Dudley Gorvin was at his desk. As the senior clerk, he presided over the outer office in my lord's absence and reported to Mr Williamson. I drew him aside.

'Was a letter for me from my lord misdirected here?'

He frowned. 'You haven't heard?'

'What? I've been away from Goring House all morning.'

'The courier was caught in a fire at Bishops Stortford. His pouch went up in flames. He was lucky to escape with his life.'

'That explains it,' I said. 'I was expecting to hear from him.'

'To order you down to Euston?'

'I hope not. I'd rather stay in London.'

'I can guess the reason why,' Gorvin said. 'You sly dog.'

'What do you mean?'

'I've been hearing things. The fair Hadgraft, eh? I warrant that's why you'd rather stay in town.'

'Nonsense,' I said, feeling myself grow hot.

'Is it? I'm told the father has been asking questions about you.'

'I've been obliged to wait on him once or twice about this Chard Lane business. Naturally – he's the developer of the site.'

Gorvin wagged his finger under my nose. 'Wait on him, eh? And then on her?'

'What does he want to know about me?'

'What do you think? All the things a father wishes to know about a suitor for his only daughter: viz, the man's fortune, his birth, his prospects.' He lowered his voice. 'Is she very lovely?'

I ignored the question. 'I'm sure what he learned about me came as a disappointment.'

'I don't know. You may not be rich as he is rich, but he's mighty taken with your Mr Alderman Marwood. As of course am I.'

'By all accounts my uncle was a worthless fool,' I said.

Gorvin was baiting me, and I was as helpless before his goads as a bull in a pen. But he was not a cruel man and he sensed it was time to show me mercy. 'Faith, that doesn't matter a jot. Hadgraft simply likes the idea of your having an alderman uncle. And what's wrong with that? Anyway, what really impresses him is your place here. He has gold enough for two. But he doesn't have my lord's ear.'

'Lord Arlington listens to no one unless he wants to hear what they have to say. You know that as well as I do.'

'But Hadgraft doesn't.' Gorvin's tone became serious. 'A man with his way to make in the world could do worse than marry his daughter. There's money there if not breeding. And he has only the one child so it must all come to her. I'm told that Mistress Hadgraft is all that a lady should be. And is she truly as lovely as they say?'

'Yes,' I said helplessly, abandoning my defences. 'Yes, she is.'

He patted my arm, then jerked his head towards the window. Movement on the path below had caught his eye. 'Look,' he said. 'There's another beauty. You'll be able to feast your eyes upon her at Euston.'

Below us, two ladies were walking with a footman and a maid behind them.

'Who are they?' I said.

'Maids of honour. The one on the left is Mademoiselle Louise de Keroualle.'

Cat had mentioned the lady to me on Saturday. I stared at the King's favourite, the woman he meant to make his mistress. She had been in Dieppe at the same time as Iredale, and I had found a purse which might have been hers concealed in his lodging.

I leant out of the window to have a better view of her. Her cloak hid her figure. The brim of her hat tilted, and for an instant I caught a glimpse of a rounded cheek and a delicate nose.

'She travels down to Euston with Monsieur and Madame Colbert in a day or two,' Gorvin said drily. 'So you'll soon be seeing more of her. But I doubt she'll be a maid by the time she comes back to London.'

CHAPTER NINETEEN

M Y COLLAR, CUFFS and shirt were as clean as
Margaret could make them. My wig was freshly curled,
and I had summoned the barber to shave me during the
afternoon. I wore a new suit of dark-green broadcloth, more
than twice as expensive as any suit I had owned before.

I debated with myself at some length whether to wear my
sword or take my silver-headed stick. In the end I decided
against the sword on the grounds that it would make me look
as if I were laying a fraudulent claim to a gentility I did not
possess. Better to give the Hadgrafts the impression that I
was a man of quiet substance, solid achievements and prudent
ambitions: all in all, the worthy great-nephew of an alderman.

Sam hobbled across the hall and opened the door for me.
He made a great to-do of removing a speck of dust from my
sleeve. 'There, master,' he said. 'I warrant there's no finer
gentleman in the whole of London.'

He kept a straight face as he spoke, but I knew that he and
Margaret would make merry at my expense after I was gone.
I resisted the temptation to box the saucy fellow's ear, because

that would let him know that I felt the barb concealed within his words.

'Have a care, sir,' he said in a lower voice.

I looked sharply at him. 'What do you mean?'

'If I was you, master, I wouldn't walk about after dark. Not by yourself.'

It was impertinent of him to speak to me like that, but it was good advice. I gave him a nod and said, 'Mind you lock up well.'

He grinned at me. 'Aye, sir.'

I walked up to the Strand and along to the hackney stand, where I hired a coach to take me to Holborn. I told the man to set me down where the road bellies out to the west of St Andrew's church. I wanted a few minutes to compose myself before knocking at Mr Hadgraft's door.

The afternoon had been cloudy, but the sky had now cleared; and the red ball of the sun was sinking slowly towards the horizon, as if intending to incinerate Oxford forty miles away. I stood aside to allow a gaggle of drunken law students to pass.

As I did so, I glanced over the road at the corner of Hatton Garden. From where I stood, I couldn't see Rush's house. But further along Holborn to the west was the narrow mouth of a court. I guessed it led to the cluster of buildings at the bottom of Rush's garden. I wondered if the body of the faceless man had been removed from his cellar.

As I was watching, a sturdy man came out of the court and turned to his right along the street. He was dressed as a labourer, and there was something faintly familiar about him, or rather about the way he walked: marching swiftly, swinging his long arms like a soldier.

I turned down Fetter Lane and forgot him. My mind was full of what might lie ahead. With a studied absence of haste, I walked down to the Hadgrafts' house, swinging my stick. When I reached the house, the servant showed me into a richly furnished drawing room on the first floor. I glanced about me, registering with a slump of disappointment that the only person there was my host.

Smiling broadly, Hadgraft came forward to meet me. 'My dear sir, welcome. What a pleasure to see you. At last, we can put aside this tiresome business that's wasted so much of our time.'

We exchanged bows and he ushered me towards a sofa that looked so elegantly delicate that I feared it might collapse under my weight.

'My daughter will be with us directly. You know what the ladies are – such endless debates about the precise disposition of a piece of lace or the proper arrangement of hair . . . it's a wonder we gentlemen are ever permitted to see them at all.'

I murmured something in reply and his flow of remarks continued in the same strained and artificially genteel mode. For the past year or two I had been much in the company of gentlemen, and I knew instinctively that Hadgraft was trying too hard to be what he was not.

'Sir,' I interrupted when he paused for breath, 'while we're by ourselves, may I ask how the inquest went this morning? Did all go well?'

His eyes gleamed. 'It could not have gone better. The bishop's coroner saw the matter entirely as I did – as I believe any man of sense must. Work has already resumed on the almshouse.'

'And the verdict?'

'Murder by person or persons unknown. What else could it be? That fool Rush looked as sick as a dog. I discharged Ledward afterwards – the fellow is clearly either corrupt or incompetent. And that reminds me . . .' he lowered his voice '. . . one of my labourers found the missing dog this morning. The beast had been stabbed – that must be why it didn't sound the alarm on the night of the murder.'

There was a noise above our heads, as if something had fallen heavily on the floor.

'What are they doing up there?' Hadgraft said tetchily. He forced a smile. 'Grace's woman has probably knocked something over – Susannah is a clumsy creature at the best of times. She's a cousin of my late wife's with not a farthing to her name. I took her in as an act of charity or else she would have starved.'

'I wonder, sir, as we have a moment or two by ourselves, may we deal with a small matter of business?'

His Adam's apple bobbed. 'Of course.'

'It's in connection with this unhappy murder. A list of names has been brought to my attention, one of which is yours. It probably has nothing to do with the dead man, but I'm obliged to check.'

'How very curious,' Hadgraft said warily. 'May I ask how you came across this list?'

'It was in the possession of a copyist at the Council for Foreign Plantations. A man named Iredale.' I took out my pocketbook and removed the list. 'I'm told that the handwriting is his.'

Hadgraft took the paper without comment. He scanned the column of names and then looked up at me. 'There's no mystery here. We are all shareholders in a trading venture. Between us we've raised the capital to charter and provision a ship, the *Princess Mary*, and lade it with cargo. She's at sea now. God willing, she's nearing the Gold Coast.'

'First the Africa run and then the West Indies?'

'I see you know something of the business.'

'Enough to know that it's risky at the best of times, and particularly now, with the autumn gales not far away.'

'Indeed, sir, that worries me as well.' He moved uneasily in his chair. 'We were late in the year as it was, and then one of our investors withdrew his capital at the last moment. You won't think the worse of me if I speak plainly, I hope? It was Rush. Hence the line through his name. The others wanted me to find a replacement. Easier said than done. In the end I was forced to take over his share myself.'

'Perhaps it will be all for the good, sir,' I said. 'If the voyage prospers, you will profit doubly. But why should Iredale have a list of your investors in his possession?'

Hadgraft sighed. 'I see I must tell you the whole. I wrote to the council to enquire about current conditions in the West Indies – there have been rumours at the Exchange of changes in the market this last year. A few days later Iredale came to me with a suggestion for spreading the risk of such a venture as mine. He had done his research, and he knew who our shareholders were – as you see by that list. He told me a plantation owner of his acquaintance had asked him whether it would be possible to earmark promising slaves on the voyage. In other words, to take out an option to buy before they reached the West Indies. Well-set-up, lusty young males are at a premium on the plantations, as you may imagine. It was an interesting idea – both parties, the seller and the buyer, would bypass the slave market, and therefore avoid the extortionate commissions that the slave dealers charge, as well as the auctioneer's fees. Healthier for the chosen slaves too.'

'But how would such a system work?'

'Iredale's idea was that the plantation owner would pay a small but non-returnable advance to the ship's shareholders. That would help defray their costs and also secure them a guaranteed sale at a fixed price, with an allowance made for wastage on voyage. The planter would be sure of receiving prime slaves. Indeed, he could have the pick of those available.'

I kept my voice studiously neutral. 'And what did Iredale achieve for himself by this arrangement?'

'A modest fee from each of the parties.' Hadgraft smiled blandly at me but his eyes were straying towards the door. 'He gave me to understand that the transaction was entirely under the aegis of the council, and that the fees were to cover the costs of arranging the matter. Given the complexity and the risks of this business, I considered the sums involved were reasonable. I gave him six pounds, and no doubt he had something from the planter as well.'

It was more than I had expected. 'Would you be surprised to hear that Iredale was making these arrangements on his own account? The council knew nothing of them, and I believe they would not have endorsed them if they had.'

'God's truth, sir, I had no idea!' The Adam's apple gave a convulsive jerk. 'Do you mean to tell me that Iredale was acting corruptly?'

I kept a straight face, though I knew Hadgraft was lying, and he knew that I knew. 'I fear so, sir. He was selling confidential information that he gained from his work at the council.'

'The devil he was. He seemed so . . . so respectable. A most worthy man.'

'No doubt.' I remembered the shimmer of gold in Iredale's box. 'I'm sure you were not the only one he – ah – misled.'

'I blame Rush, you know,' Hadgraft said, returning to his grudge like a dog to his bone. 'If he had not withdrawn his capital – and with no notice given, mark you – it would not have been so urgent for us to spread the risk in whatever way we could.'

'Well, the harm is done now, sir. There's no help for it.'

'But our particular arrangement will hold, I fancy.' Hadgraft paused for a moment, no doubt to run over the ramifications in his mind. He brightened. 'I can't see why not. After all, both the planter and ourselves stand to gain. Besides, there's no convenient way to cancel it even if we wanted to . . .'

His voice trailed away, and he looked sharply at me. Finally, I thought, he has made the connection.

'Is it possible . . . ? Do you mean . . . ?' Hadgraft took a deep breath and went on in a low voice: 'Was Iredale the man with no face? Did someone kill him because of this?'

The door opened, and Grace Hadgraft was on the threshold. I rose and bowed, first to her and then to the waiting woman who slipped like a shadow behind her mistress into the drawing room. Hadgraft was saying something, but his words were a minor irritation, like the buzzing of a bluebottle.

Grace curtsied low to me. 'Your servant, sir.' She peeped through long, lustrous lashes. 'Pray forgive us for keeping you waiting.' Her lips, which were wide and full, parted in a hint of a smile. 'But if we let it, time runs away with us all, sir, don't you agree?'

'Oh indeed, madam,' I said, thinking the remark both witty

and profound, though afterwards I was hard-pressed to remember quite why.

She turned to her father. 'Forgive me for keeping you waiting, sir.'

Hadgraft was all geniality now. 'Mr Marwood and I kept each other company well enough,' he said. 'We had a trifle of business to dispose of in any case. And now you've whetted our appetites, shall we go down to supper?'

I scarcely noticed what the four of us ate and drank that evening. The fire and the candles lent a softness and a glow to the dining room and its rich furniture; one wall was masked with a tapestry where the figures of gods and nymphs danced with borrowed life; the glasses glittered, and there were sparks of fire in our wine and blurred reflections in the polished wood.

The light was kind to us too: Hadgraft's features looked less ugly than usual; Mistress Susannah's thin, tight-lipped face was transformed into an austere, almost-beautiful mask; and Grace acquired a loveliness that belonged to the world of angels. I was drunk that night, but not on wine.

Hadgraft did the lion's share of the talking. He described the houses he planned to build on the waste ground once the almshouse was done. 'You must permit me to show you the plans. If all goes well, we shall start next summer, and they should be ready for occupation by the spring of seventy-three.' He gave me a glance over the top of his glass. 'Why, one of them might be the very thing for a man in your position. Or perhaps you are content with your present lodging?'

By accident or design, he had touched on my growing dissatisfaction with the damp, crumbling house in Infirmary Close. It held too many memories of Stephen. The stink of the Thames poisoned the air. The generations of the dead were restless neighbours in the overstuffed graveyard at the back. I allowed myself to be drawn into a discussion about a house that would precisely suit my needs and desires. Hadgraft encouraged me to ask Grace for her advice on the arrangement of the rooms, the furniture and the decoration, and even the disposition of my kitchen, scullery and pantry.

'You may rely on her,' he said. 'Young though she is, my daughter manages this household for me, and she knows to a nicety how such things should be done.'

Mistress Susannah stirred in her chair beside me.

Soon we were talking about the size of house I would need. 'After all,' Hadgraft reminded me, 'man was not born to live a solitary life, and it is not impossible that one day you will need a larger establishment than you have now.'

I heard a soft snort to my left, where Mistress Susannah was sitting. I glanced at her, but her pale profile revealed nothing. She was staring at her plate.

'Did you say something, Susannah?' Grace said sharply.

'No,' she said. 'A crumb caught in my throat.'

'Grace, my dear,' Hadgraft said, 'will you play something for us, and perhaps sing?'

'Sir, I have nothing fit for Mr Marwood's ears.'

He smiled across the table at me. 'My daughter is too modest. Why, her singing master told me she could make her living by her voice if she wished. And as for her lute teacher – ah, but I shall spare her blushes. Shall I ask her for a song? There is a pretty Italian piece that always enchants me.'

'Pray do,' I said, looking at Grace. She returned my glance. 'If Mistress Hadgraft is agreeable, of course.'

'There you are, my dear,' her father said. 'You won't refuse Mr Marwood, will you?'

There was an instant of silence, which to me was crowded with delightful possibilities.

'No, sir.' She gave me a shy smile. 'I would not do that.'

CHAPTER TWENTY

AFTER SUPPER ON Monday evening, Louise touched Madame des Bordes' arm. 'May I speak to you in private?'

The candlelight yellowed the skin of the older woman's face and threw deep, shadowed cracks across her cheeks. 'I hear you're going to Lord Arlington's house near Newmarket?'

'Yes . . . Everyone tells me that it is very beautiful. A treasure house of fine things.'

It was a gamble, Louise thought, but then everything was a gamble. At Euston, she would place the only thing she had of any value on the turn of a single card. Not that she had wanted to play this particular game in the first place. But she had another card in her hand, one that belonged to another game altogether. It was probably already lost. But if she did not play the card now, she never could, and she would never know whether perhaps she might have won after all.

'Has Monsieur Colbert spoken to you about me? He said he would. I'm to travel down in his coach.'

'Yes. He's asked me to advise you on what you will need

and help you to buy it. It's all arranged. He told me to send the bills to him.'

'When shall we do it?' Louise asked. 'And how?'

'Let's start tomorrow morning. We'll need to spread it over two days. I would advise that we send for a selection, and then you may choose at your leisure.'

'Not here, madame. I don't want to do it here. Everyone would see. I would find it . . .'

'Ah. Yes.'

Louise groped for a few more words to cover her weakness. 'The other ladies would be a distraction. You know what they're like. Everyone would want to look, to touch. To talk.'

'Indeed they would.' Madame des Bordes fell in with the suggestion with unexpected enthusiasm. 'But you're right. If we take a coach into the City, we shall be undisturbed, and we shall have a far wider choice. We'll go to the New Exchange, and then to Cheapside. After that—'

'May I ask you something in strictest confidence, madame?' Louise said hesitantly.

'Of course.'

'May we also call on someone when we go to the City? A friend from Paris. It's to say farewell, or at least to leave a message.'

Madame des Bordes' eyes narrowed, and the shadowed cracks deepened in her skin. 'Perhaps. If it's convenient.'

The clocks of London were striking in all their jumbled, jangling confusion. Ten o'clock, Pheebs thought, and a dry night, if a trifle on the cold side. But there would be a good fire at the alehouse in Half Moon Passage, and mulled ale if a man felt the need of a little warmth within.

He kicked Josh's leg to wake him. The boy was dozing on a bench by the door. He sprang to his feet, rubbing his eyes.

'I'm going out,' Pheebs said. 'I need a walk to settle the stomach.'

Josh nodded, knowing what such walks meant.

'They're all in.' The porter's thumb jabbed upwards, indicating the inhabitants of the house at the sign of the Rose. 'Even her.'

'Her' meant Mistress Hakesby. Josh was aware that Pheebs was afraid of her. She had a tongue in her head that could slice a man's ear off.

'If anyone asks, say I've gone to the necessary house. Terrible griping pains. I won't be long.'

He wrapped his cloak around him and took his stick. Josh let him out of the house. The wind was getting up. The freshly painted rose on the signboard was creaking on its hinges above the door.

Pheebs walked down Henrietta Street. The nightlife of the city flowed around him, in and out of the shadows between the dull glow of lanterns and the flickering flares of torchlight. Covent Garden and its neighbourhood were rarely completely dark or completely silent.

He quickened his pace as he turned the corner in Bedford Street. Half Moon Passage lay ahead, with the Strand beyond. He glimpsed its sign, briefly illuminated by the torch of a passing linkman.

Mulled, he thought as he crossed the mouth of Maiden Lane, and it must be the stronger ale from Southwark way, the one they brewed every autumn to keep out the chill.

He heard footsteps accelerating behind him and rapid

breathing. Before he could even draw breath, there was a man on either side of him and something sharp digging into his neck.

'Hold your tongue. Or I'll cut it out.'

The voice was a low rumble in his ear. In a parody of good fellowship, the men linked arms with him and steered him into Maiden Lane, which was unlit. To the right was a ragged string of mean houses and outbuildings, punctuated by the openings of the crooked alleys that ran down to the Strand. The lane was a cul de sac ending in my Lord Bedford's garden wall.

'I'll give you my purse,' Pheebs whispered. 'Take anything. But spare my life, I beg you, masters.'

His captors ignored him. He stumbled in the mud and would have fallen if the two men had not dragged him onwards. They hustled him deeper and deeper into the shadows of the lane. A big man to the right, Pheebs thought, a giant. He was the one with the dagger. A smaller one on the left had a grip like a pair of pincers.

'This'll do,' said the deep voice. 'Put him here.'

He made no resistance as they rammed him against the wall of someone's garden.

'Pheebs, ain't it?' The giant's voice was a low rumble, like distant thunder. 'I know you.'

'Who are you?' Pheebs whispered. There was blood or perhaps sweat trickling down the side of his neck and under the collar of his shirt. 'What do you want?'

'Cover his mouth.'

A fold of coarse cloth was clamped over Pheebs's lips. A cloak. The pressure eased on his neck. Durrell, he thought, the man who killed old Hakesby. An instant later, a fiery pain shot through his arm. He screamed and thrashed, but could not free himself.

'We got a squealer,' Durrell said. 'Send him to sleep.'

Pain filled Pheebs's head like sheet lightning in the sky. Then there was nothing.

It was almost midnight when I left the Hadgrafts' house. My host sent his manservant to fetch a hackney. The roads were clearer at this time of the evening and I was soon set down in the Strand near the lane to the Savoy.

My condition was somewhere between drunkenness and euphoria. But I had not forgotten Sam's warning. I hired two linkmen to light me home, though it was only a few hundred yards.

While I walked between my two companions, my thoughts executed one of those unexpected turns that characterize the ramblings of a weary mind. I remembered the man I had glimpsed in Holborn, emerging from the alley at the back of Rush's house. All of a sudden, I knew why he had seemed familiar, despite the fact I had not seen his face. It was Ledward, the former watchman at Chard Lane, though he had been better dressed than he was at the almshouse.

The porter let us into the Savoy. I would usually have paid off the linkmen at the gate, but tonight I told them to light me to my door. The place was a crumbling labyrinth of buildings, old and new. It was meant to be secure at night, but there were a dozen ways to gain entry if you knew where to look or whom to bribe.

No one disturbed us. Nothing was out of the ordinary. Infirmary Close was quiet. The only lights came from my house at the end of the narrow alley.

I knocked on the door, my mind still full of Grace Hadgraft. The shutter slid back. To my surprise, I saw Margaret's face, not Sam's.

'Master?'

'Who else would it be?'

I paid off the linkmen while listening to the familiar music of rattled chains and grating bars on the other side of the door. Once inside, I shrugged myself out of my cloak and let it fall on the chest. Margaret secured the door.

'Where's Sam?' I demanded. 'He's not drunk again, is he?'

'He's below, master. You'd best come and see him.'

My mood sobered instantly. I followed her down the steps to the kitchen. The fire was burning brightly, which was unusual at this time of night, and half a dozen candles were burning. I noted automatically that they were my best tallow ones, reserved for my own apartments. On the table was a small armoury of weapons: Sam's pistol, dagger and cutlass, and also my own rarely used sword.

He was sitting beside them, his good leg up on a stool. He had a bandage around his head and another half-wrapped around his right arm. In front of him was a bottle of my brandy. He didn't have the key for the cupboard where I kept it, but Margaret knew where it was.

'What the devil do you think you're doing?' I said.

'It's his own fault,' Margaret said, taking up the loose end of the bandage. 'I told the numskull not to. But would he listen?'

'I had a fancy for a drop of Mistress Fawley's ale,' Sam said. 'So I took a jug up to the Silver Crescent. They got me afterwards, once I was back in the Savoy. A couple of bullies.'

'Anyone you know?' I knew he would recognize Durrell again if he saw or heard him.

'No. I didn't know them from the Holy Ghost and the Virgin Mary. Mind you, it was dark.'

Thieving bullies were two a penny in Alsatia, only a few hundred yards away. But I needed to make sure. 'Were they after your purse?'

'Maybe. But they didn't get it. Anyways, I reckon they wanted me more than me purse.'

'You're such a fool,' Margaret muttered, yanking the bandage tighter. 'I could kill you.'

'I went down,' Sam said, licking lips that I noticed only now were swollen. 'Took me off guard.' He patted his amputated leg. 'That didn't help. And the jug broke. All that ale went to waste.'

'I see you've made up for your loss with my brandy.' I was trying to mask my relief that he was still alive. 'What happened then?'

'I gave one of them a poke in the eye with my crutch.' Sam touched his dagger. 'And I put that in the other one's belly or thereabouts.' He grinned at me. 'Then they went away.'

'You'd better have some more brandy.'

'He's had enough,' Margaret said. 'And he knows it.'

'Are you sure they were after you in particular?' I went on. 'After Sam Witherdine? They might have marked you down as a target in the street or in the Silver Crescent. Just another drunken fool asking to have his purse lifted.'

'Oh no, sir. They knew exactly who I was. I heard the villain say, "Is that him? Marwood's cripple?"'

CHAPTER TWENTY-ONE

CAT SLEPT BADLY and woke on Tuesday morning with a headache. She sent Jane to fetch rolls partly to get the unfortunate girl out of the way of her mistress's ill humour. The strain of the Chard Lane business had left its mark. Now they were able to resume work, she was paying the price.

She had almost finished breakfast when she heard steps on the stairs, followed by a knock on the parlour door. It was Marwood. She dismissed the maid and said coldly to her visitor: 'Pheebs should send up to see if it's convenient before he permits a visitor to come upstairs.'

'It was Josh who let me in,' Marwood said. 'There was no sign of Pheebs. Anyway, they know me well enough by now.'

Cat scowled at him. 'They're afraid you'll have them turned off if they refuse you anything. Besides, you grease their palms to keep them sweet.'

He didn't bother denying it, but she felt ashamed of her ill humour. There were good reasons why Marwood kept his eye on the porter and his boy, and she was grateful. Pheebs had shown himself untrustworthy in the past; had he been less venal, Cat's late husband might still be alive.

She was honest enough to know that what really irked her was the thought that Marwood had spent yesterday evening as an honoured guest at Hadgraft's house, with Mistress Grace making sheep's eyes at him. Cat had taken him for a man of sense. How could he risk making a fool of himself over a spoilt girl with no more brains than a peahen and nothing to recommend but a pretty face and a rich father?

'I won't stay long,' he said, not looking at her. 'I need to be at Whitehall in less than an hour. But I thought you should know that I learned a little more about Iredale yesterday. And about Hadgraft.'

Her attention sharpened. 'In what way?'

'You remember the list of names we found in Iredale's box? They were the investors in a slaving venture. Iredale was using the knowledge he got at the Council for Foreign Plantations to broker a deal with Hadgraft on the one hand and a planter in the Caribbean on the other. Judging by the amount of gold we found in his box, it wasn't the first time he'd done it.'

'Rush's name was crossed out,' Cat said.

'He withdrew his capital from the venture at the last moment. As he did from the Chard Lane project.'

'After Grace refused him?'

'Perhaps.' Marwood still wouldn't meet her eye. 'Not that Hadgraft said as much.'

It occurred to Cat that Hadgraft must have had to take over Rush's share in the ship, as well as in the almshouse, if he hadn't been able to find a replacement at the last moment. That would explain why he was so short of ready money.

'He told me that work on the almshouse has started again,' Marwood was saying. 'And that you've found the watchman's dog.'

'It had been stabbed,' Cat said, wrinkling her nose at the memory of the putrefying corpse. 'Like the man with no face.'

'The murderer had to keep the brute quiet, I suppose, and that must have been the easiest way. But that reminds me: I saw your old watchman yesterday evening. He was coming out of an alley at the back of Rush's house.'

'What was Ledward doing there?'

Marwood shrugged. He looked bored, Cat thought, and probably eager to be elsewhere; no doubt with Grace Hadgraft. Cat's irritation with him steadily mounted.

'Patience Noone is with child,' she said, hoping to disconcert him. 'Her mistress threw her out of the house.'

'How do you know?'

'Brennan and I went to Swan Yard to talk to her yesterday evening. But she'd gone. I'd seen her at the inquest. I tried to speak to her afterwards, but she ran off. A beggar in Swan Yard said she found a ride with a carrier bound for Chester.'

'*Chester?* Is that where she comes from? And who put the child in her belly?'

'I don't know. But I do know that Hadgraft's hiding something. He keeps delaying our stage payments. He's short of money. Not that you'd guess it from the way he lives.' She was unable to resist adding, 'I do hope he can still give his daughter a proper dowry.'

While she was speaking, Marwood had walked to the window. He stared down at the street. 'There's something I should tell you.'

About Grace? Cat felt something turn sour inside her like curdling milk. 'What?'

He turned to face her. 'Sam was attacked on the way home last night.'

She caught her breath. The relief was almost painful. 'Is he hurt?'

'He'll mend. By all accounts, he gave the rogues worse than he got. But he didn't think they were thieves. They went for him because he was my man. I wager Durrell sent them. I told Sam and Margaret to be on their guard against him. I think he's trying to frighten me by attacking my servants.'

'And did he succeed? In frightening you, I mean?'

'What do you think?'

In the silence that followed, they heard a commotion in the street below. Marwood threw open the window and looked out.

'Oh, devil take it.' He withdrew his head. 'There's some men carrying Pheebs on a door. He's in a pool of blood.'

If anything, Sam Witherdine's adventure yesterday evening seemed to have raised his spirits.

When Cat called at Marwood's house in Infirmary Close later that morning, secure in the knowledge that Marwood himself would be in Whitehall, Sam opened the street door for her as usual and gave her his notion of a bow. His face was bruised and grazed. He wore a bandage at a rakish angle around the crown of his head. He was not wearing a coat or jerkin, only a waistcoat above a shirt whose left sleeve had been ripped to the shoulder to allow room for another bandage, this one on the upper arm.

He beamed at her. 'Good day to you, mistress.'

'What have you been doing to yourself?' she said sternly, and then spoiled it by adding, 'I was worried. Your master gave me the idea you were sorely wounded last night.'

'So I was. But I can't lie abed all day, can I?'

While he was speaking, Margaret appeared in the doorway to the kitchen stairs. 'I tried to make the fool rest, mistress,' she said, 'but it's like trying to get a puppy to make water outside. It's going to do it inside anyway so you might as well give up.'

'Pheebs was attacked last night as well,' Cat said.

'Serves him right,' Sam said. There was no love lost in that quarter. 'Always leering at Margaret.'

'Hush now,' she said, though she was smiling. 'That's nonsense.'

'You know it ain't.'

'What happened to him?' Margaret asked.

Cat drew off her gloves. 'Josh says he went to the alehouse in Half Moon Passage around ten o'clock. He never got there. They found him this morning in Maiden Lane.'

'Who did it?' Sam said. 'What does Pheebs say?'

'He doesn't say anything,' Cat said. 'Or at least he hadn't when I left the house to come here. He's unconscious. They beat him about the head and stabbed him in his legs and arms. They took his purse but left his clothes.'

'Poor devil,' said Margaret, her face creasing with concern.

Sam touched the bandage on his arm. A deep crease appeared between his eyebrows. 'Did you say they just stabbed him in his limbs?'

Cat nodded.

'So me and him was set upon the same evening?'

'Yes,' she said.

'They went for me because I was Mr Marwood's man. They weren't after my purse.'

'What are you saying?'

'If you want to kill someone,' he said, 'you put a knife in his belly or his heart. Or maybe his throat. If you just want to knock him out, you give him a bang on the head. But why stab him in his limbs?'

'You need to sit down.' Margaret peered into her husband's face. 'Your wits are wandering. We need to have you bled.'

Sam ignored her. He was still staring at Cat. '*Why?*'

'Because the attack wasn't meant to kill him. It was meant as a warning aimed at me. And probably the attack on you was designed to scare off your master.' She hesitated. 'There's something else you should know about Pheebs. They cut the letter D on his forehead. Sliced through the skin.'

'D? What's that about?'

Margaret, whose grasp of letters was better than Sam's, let out her breath in a rush. 'The devil signed his name, didn't he? D for Durrell.'

CHAPTER TWENTY-TWO

AFTER I HAD left Cat in Henrietta Street, I walked along to the Park and across to Goring House. On the way I mulled over Cat's sullen mood and the attacks on Sam and Pheebs, in the intervals of daydreaming about Grace Hadgraft.

At my desk I wrote a report to bring Lord Arlington up to date. I spent the remainder of the morning working my way through some of the tasks that had piled up in my absence. My lord had commanded me to investigate the Chard Lane affair, yet he still sent me the usual papers to deal with; they formed an ever-larger heap in the box on my desk.

It was approaching half past eleven o'clock when I heard a disturbance outside. A footman came to inform me that the courier had arrived and desired to wait on me with his pouch. At last, I thought, a reply to my letters from my lord.

The courier brought in the pouch. I broke the seal and shook out the contents on my desk. Among them was a letter for me in my lord's own hand. I tore it open. The contents were brief to the point of brutality. He ordered me to continue my enquiry into the murder, the two missing men, and the corruption on a government committee. But he forbade me to investigate further anything to do with the court or with the two handwriting samples.

That was surprising enough. But it was the final sentence that took my breath away and burned itself instantly into my memory.

The matter touches by chance on a state secret. If you breathe a word of it to anyone, I shall have you ruined.

It was wholly unlike Arlington to make such a crude threat. But the letter was written in his own hand, and with his signature below. Perhaps the tone of the final sentence was not angry exactly, but desperately urgent to make his meaning clear beyond any possible doubt.

As the shock subsided, I tried to work out what might have made him write the words. Had the reason nothing to do with me? Or had it been something in my last letter?

The site office was empty, but I found Brennan directing workmen laying the foundations of the roadside facade of the new almshouse. He looked up when he heard me approaching and bared his long, yellow teeth in a scowl. We didn't much care for each other but we both wished Cat well, and that made a bond of a sort. He wished me a civil good afternoon.

'I'm looking for Mistress Hakesby,' I said.

'I wish I knew where she is myself, sir. I was expecting

her this morning. She sent Josh with a note saying that she'd be here tomorrow.'

That was a disappointment. I was aware that Cat and I had parted on a sour note, and I had hoped to mend matters between us.

Brennan glanced at the labourers, who were beginning to whisper among themselves. 'There's nothing to gossip about. Get on with it.'

'You may be able to help me just as well as she could, sir,' I said. 'I'm interested in Ledward. Is he about?'

'The watchman?' He turned back to me. 'Our former watchman, I should say.'

'Has he been discharged?'

'Aye, Mr Hadgraft turned him off yesterday. It's a pity. He was a good man, taken all in all. Mr Hadgraft's sent his coachman to do duty for the time being, and I wager the fellow spends most of the night snoring his head off.'

'Do you know anything about Ledward? Where he lodges? Or how he came to work here?'

Brennan shook his head. 'All I know is that nothing was stolen while he was here, and we had no reports of break-ins. He was civil enough in his way. His dog was an evil beast but that's what you need in a watchman's dog.'

'You give him a good character, sir.'

Brennan shrugged. 'No more than his due. But as to where he lives – well, I've no idea.'

'Who put him forward for the job?'

'Ledward was here before we were. I assume Mr Hadgraft hired him when he took out the lease on the site. I'll ask him if you like. I must call at his house later.'

'No matter. I may look in there myself.'

The foreman approached Brennan and was waiting hat in hand for a break in our conversation. He was the oldest of the labourers, a squat, weatherbeaten fellow.

'Well, what is it?' Brennan snapped.

'Begging your pardon, sir, it's time for the men's break. Asking your permission.'

'Very well,' Brennan said. 'Five minutes. No more.'

'Beg your pardon, sir,' the man said again, for he had clearly discovered that a show of respect was the best way to handle Brennan, 'I couldn't help hearing some of what you and the gentleman were saying. About Ledward.'

Brennan frowned, but I motioned to the man to go on.

'Well, sir. I happened to see him in the Three Crowns. It was back in June or maybe July. We shared a jug of ale, just to be friendly, and we talked a while. He said Mr Rush put him forward for the job.'

'You shall have something to buy another jug of ale with,' I said, taking out my purse. 'Drink Mr Brennan's health as well as mine.'

I walked over Holborn Bridge and a few minutes later knocked on Mr Rush's door in Hatton Garden. He was at home, though he made a great business of sparing even a moment for me, claiming to be much occupied with business. I found him sitting at a table in a parlour with little in evidence to support his claim of having business. The air was thick with tobacco smoke, and his pipe smouldered on a dish before him, along with a glass and a bottle.

There was no pretence at offering hospitality or even

exchanging the usual compliments. His manner was markedly more hostile than before, and I thought I knew the reason for it. Grace Hadgraft.

I wasted no time, either his or mine. 'Lord Arlington has desired me to enquire further into this matter of the unknown man.'

'Why, in heaven's name?' He pushed aside the dish with the pipe. 'The coroner has given his verdict.'

'Because his lordship wishes to know more.'

Rush shrugged and glanced at the ceiling, as if to say he could not be held responsible for other men's folly and did not want to be associated with it.

'Pray tell me what you know of the former watchman at the almshouse,' I said. 'Ledward.'

'What about him?'

'I'm told you found him the position. And that was before the building work had even got under way, while you were still in partnership with Mr Hadgraft.'

'True enough,' Rush said. 'He petitioned me for work. He's a well-set-up fellow, and I knew nothing to his discredit. Hadgraft was in need of a watchman for the site, so I put him forward.'

'Did you know him before?'

'What's it to you, sir?' Rush's colour was mounting. 'Your curiosity is unmannerly. Gentlemen have ways of dealing with that.'

The violence of his reaction took me by surprise. 'I wouldn't inconvenience you with the matter if my lord hadn't insisted that I should.' I was stretching the limits of Arlington's instructions, but Rush couldn't know that. 'If you can't answer me, I shall be obliged to tell him. But the choice is yours, of course.'

'You won't frighten me with idle threats, sir. You'll find that Willoughby Rush has friends enough at court when he needs them. I sailed with Prince Rupert himself in that rogue Cromwell's time, and His Highness would support me against any man. And the Duke of Buckingham told me only the other—'

'Sir, I have no doubt you have friends,' I interrupted.

I remembered my lord's unwillingness to antagonize Rush. He was a man with powerful allies. No doubt Arlington could outmanoeuvre them all if he had to, but he would not willingly put himself to so much trouble for such a trifling cause.

'On the other hand,' I went on swiftly, 'where's the harm in answering me? No one dreams of imputing any irregularity to you. And pray forgive me if my manner seemed unduly brusque when I came in. I confess this business is weighing heavily on me.'

He subsided in his chair, apparently mollified. 'As a matter of fact, I did have some small acquaintance with the man. Ledward sailed with me for a voyage or two. And I know that later he served in the Duke of York's regiment during the Flanders campaign.'

'I chanced to see him yesterday,' I said.

'Where?'

'Holborn. He came out of the court that your garden backs on to. Does he lodge there?'

Rush nodded curtly.

'May I see him?'

He considered for a moment. 'I don't see why not. I've

nothing to hide, and I doubt that he has, either. Have the goodness to pull that bell rope.'

I obeyed, though I did not care for the fact that he was treating me scarcely better than a servant. When the footman came, Rush sent him to fetch Ledward, saying to me that the fellow was lodging in the house where he had kept the body of the man with no face.

'Wait here, sir,' Rush said to me a moment later. It sounded like an order.

He stood up and left the parlour, closing the door behind him. I heard his footsteps in the passage, then silence. When he returned a few minutes later, Ledward followed him into the room. I knew that Rush would have told him why I was here; I had lost any element of surprise I might have had.

Ledward stood before me, head bowed, his hat clasped in his hands. I took him over the events of the night of the murder, but he added nothing I did not already know. I mentioned the discovery of the dog yesterday afternoon. He said carelessly that he had supposed that the brute must be somewhere or other and finding him now didn't much signify one way or the other.

I had questioned many people over the last five years, and I had acquired tricks to uncover the truth. But Ledward was proof against them all. Truth to tell, he impressed me. He reminded me of some of my father's puritan friends, men who had a perfect confidence in their own being, which armoured them against the misfortunes and snares of this world.

When we were done, Rush sent Ledward away. 'Well, you've had a wasted journey, I fear.' He led me into the passage, where his manservant unbarred the street door for us. He added, too quietly for his man to hear the words, 'Take care how you deal with Hadgraft.'

I looked sharply at him. 'Why?'

'Because he's as cunning as the serpent, and he serves no one but himself.'

The servant opened the door and stood back to let me pass.

On the step I turned to face my host. Rush was smiling. It was not a friendly smile, it seemed to me, but one that expressed mockery and disdain. All of a sudden, my self-control slipped away from me.

'And Mistress Grace? Is she cut from the same cloth?'

The smile vanished. Rush's features twisted into a glare. He lunged forward, knocking his servant against the wall, and slammed the door in my face.

CHAPTER TWENTY-THREE

AFTER MY UNSATISFACTORY visit to Hatton Garden, I could not resist the temptation to call at Mr Hadgraft's house. I manufactured two reasons to explain my visit: I wanted to ask him whether the Duke of Buckingham was in any way connected with his trading venture and his dealings with the Council for Foreign Plantations; and it would be churlish not to thank him and Mistress Grace for their hospitality yesterday evening. In truth, all I wanted was to see Grace again, and I did not care if I had to make a fool of myself to achieve this end.

The doorkeeper let me into the house. The first thing I heard was the sound of raised voices coming from the study. Mistress Susannah, Grace's woman, was coming down the stairs. When she saw me, a flicker of curiosity passed over her thin face. She curtsied civilly enough and asked how she might serve me.

'I called to see Mr Hadgraft,' I said. It was impossible to ignore the raised voices within. 'But it sounds as if he is engaged.'

'Yes, sir, he is. May I take a message?'

'I wonder . . . is Mistress Grace at home? Perhaps I might have a word with her instead if she's at leisure.'

But at that moment a door opened and Hadgraft himself appeared. He was still facing into the room he had left. 'In that case, the devil can drag you away and roast you in hell.'

To my surprise, Brennan followed him through the doorway: 'You're a ruined man,' he said, showing his teeth and looking more than ever like a disgruntled fox. 'Faith, I warrant you'd drag us down to join you in the gutter if you could.'

'Get out of my house,' Hadgraft snarled.

'Willingly!'

I had not thought Brennan capable of such rage, such language to a client. My respect for him increased. He stormed down the passage. Simultaneously, he and Hadgraft realized that I was standing there, making an audience of three with Susannah and the doorkeeper.

Brennan said to me in the same snarling tone: 'The fool's ship miscarried before it even reached Africa. Foundered with all hands and took the whole of his fortune with it. He can't pay what he owes us, and the almshouse will never be built. I wish the devil would fly away from him.'

He pushed past us in his hurry to leave the house.

There were footsteps on the stairs. Grace was running down at breakneck speed. Her hair was undressed, her clothing disordered, and her face red and swollen; her cheeks shone with tears.

'Sir,' she cried, 'is it true? I heard all – are we ruined?'

'Hush,' barked Hadgraft. 'Hold your tongue, girl.'

Grace saw me and stopped abruptly. She forced a smile

like a rictus of the dead and sank into a curtsy. 'Why, sir, I didn't see you there in the shadows. How do you do?'

'Very well, madam. But I fear I've called at an inconvenient time.' I turned to her father. 'Forgive me for disturbing you, sir. I'll call again later if I may.'

Out of the corner of my eye I glimpsed Susannah's avid, excited face. She was turning her head this way and that, as if anxious to miss no detail of the scene unfolding before her.

With a palpable effort, Hadgraft controlled his agitation. His Adam's apple executed its usual manoeuvres. 'You mustn't pay attention to that man's ravings, sir. I'm sorry you had to hear them.' He grimaced. 'It's true enough that the *Princess Mary* is lost. I don't deny it's a blow, both for myself and for my fellow venturers. But I'm not such a fool as to chance my all upon a single throw of the dice.'

'Allow me to condole with you, sir. But I must go. I . . . I merely called to thank you for your hospitality. And to thank Mistress Hadgraft for her song and her company yesterday.'

Grace had mysteriously contrived to become beautiful again. True, her face was still flooded with colour, and her eyes still shone with tears. But the way she now smiled at me made her lovely. The disorder of her dress and her loose hair seemed alluring, not slatternly. After all, what did it matter if one of her father's investments had failed? Wealth was merely love's handmaiden, not the lady herself.

'You are courtesy itself, sir,' Hadgraft said in a high, uncertain voice. 'But pray come again tomorrow if it is at all possible. I know my dear daughter will count the moments until you return.'

I was looking at Grace as her father was speaking. Her

smile vanished. She winced. For an instant, it was as if a curtain had been whisked aside. I saw revulsion in her face. She did not love me. She did not even like me. My house of cards collapsed.

She lunged forward and appeared to trip. Automatically I moved to break her fall. She flung her arms around my neck and nuzzled her tear-stained face against my shoulder. Her closeness was unsettling, but in a way I would not have anticipated. I was aware of the unexpected solidity of her body, the moist skin and the hot, unsweet breath. Above all, I sensed her desperation.

'Well, sir,' Hadgraft cried, for all the world like a Drury Lane pimp, 'ah, she cannot wait to press you to her bosom. See how she burns for you.'

At the far end of the hall, the tip of Susannah's tongue moistened her lips. She was looking at me.

I unclasped Grace's hands and pushed her away. She sank down against the wall and covered her face with her hands.

'Madam, I must go.' I hardly knew what I was saying. 'Forgive me, I'm awaited – pray excuse . . .'

Hadgraft lost what remained of his self-control. He rounded on his daughter and overrode my stumbling words: 'Go to your chamber. At once.'

I looked from father to daughter. 'I don't understand.'

'Of course you don't.' Hadgraft snarled. His face was red and his features were twisted almost beyond recognition. But when he spoke next, his voice was low and exhausted.

'Go, sir,' he said. 'There's nothing for you here.'

CHAPTER TWENTY-FOUR

WHEN CAT REACHED Henrietta Street, it was past six o'clock. She cast a wary eye up and down the road before walking the few steps to the sign of the Rose. It was Josh, the porter's boy, not poor Pheebs himself, who answered her knock.

'Is there news?' Cat asked once she was inside the house.

'They say he'll live, mistress. He's at his aunt's. She said she'd take him in if he pays his way.'

'Can he?' Cat asked.

'Oh yes.' The boy's eyes were wide with wonder. 'They found silver and even a piece of gold under his mattress.'

Cat wasn't surprised. Pheebs was as corrupt as they came. But once you accepted his many failings, he could be managed with a policy of alternating bribes and threats.

She climbed the stairs with slow, weary steps. Nothing about the day had been good. She had been in the City, attempting to find a former client who still owed them money for work done last year.

Her maid was waiting in the parlour. 'There's a letter, mistress,' Jane said. 'Will you open it directly?'

'Yes. By the fire.'

Cat's first thought was that the letter might be from Marwood, though there was no reason why it should be since they had met this morning. But when Jane brought it to her, Cat saw with a pang of disappointment that it was from Madame des Bordes. She sat down and broke the seal.

You told me on Friday that you would be glad to meet Mademoiselle de Keroualle. She and I will be at the New Exchange tomorrow morning at about eleven o'clock. I will encourage her to call at the establishment of Monsieur Georges. You will find it easier to talk privately there than at court. If you are able to join us, I will introduce you. The young lady goes to Lord Arlington's mansion at the end of the week and may not return for some time. She has many demands on her at present.

'Bring me the writing box,' Cat said to Jane.

It was too good an opportunity to miss, though there was the delicate matter of Monsieur Georges' unpaid bill for the new shoes. But the underlined final sentence of the letter told its own story. Madame des Bordes, discretion herself after a lifetime at court, was adept at hinting at her meaning: here was a reminder that the most important demands on Mademoiselle de Keroualle were likely to come from the King himself.

Cat began to write. Halfway through the first sentence, there was a loud knocking downstairs. Jane gave a squeak.

'Hush, girl,' Cat said. 'There's nothing to frighten you.'

Nevertheless, she felt in her pocket for the little knife she kept there. She laid it on her lap in case of need.

They listened to the slow, dragging footsteps climbing the stairs. After half a minute it became clear that the caller was coming up to their floor of the house. Then came a tap at the parlour door. Cat nodded to Jane. If it were Durrell or one of his kind, he would come inside whatever they said or did; a lock would not deter him.

When Jane opened the door, Brennan pushed past her. 'Bad news,' he said to Cat. 'The worst imaginable.'

In that instant before apprehension took shape in her mind, Cat thought *Not him, please God, not him*. Brennan was speaking, the words spilling in a jumbled rush from his mouth, and as their meaning reached her, she forgot Marwood.

'Everything?' she said. 'Hadgraft's lost *everything*?'

'That's what they're saying on the Exchange. His ship is lost, and now he hasn't a penny to call his own. He's already mortgaged what he can. All he has left are debts.'

'Go to the closet,' Cat told Jane. When she heard the door close, she said in a low voice, 'Including the money he owes us, I suppose?'

'Yes. And we'll be liable for what we've bought in his name. All of it, bricks, nails, wages. It goes without saying the almshouse project won't go ahead unless the trustees can find someone to underwrite it. And that's about as likely as the Man in the Moon coming down to sup with us.'

'I need time to think,' Cat said.

'Why?' Brennan stared at her, his eyes round with misery. 'There's no point. We're ruined too.'

* * *

200

That evening I wandered aimlessly through the streets, letting my feet bear me where they would. In the event they carried me away from Holborn and took me in a sluggish, south-westerly zigzag in the general direction of the Savoy. Every few hundred yards, I staggered into an alehouse or a tavern and quenched my thirst.

All the while, my mind was occupied with what I had heard and seen and felt at Hadgraft's house. I measured the length and breadth and weight of what had happened. I probed it for meanings beneath the surface. I rehearsed the memory again and again, speculating about causes and consequences. What a fool I had made of myself over the girl. I couldn't blame her for that, or her father. I had done it all myself.

By now, the evening was well advanced, and the shadows of the city increasingly oppressed me. It occurred to me that I needed drink in the light and laughter of an alehouse. I patted my pocket and discovered that someone had stolen my purse. In my present condition this was a minor misfortune, significant only insofar as it delayed my quest for oblivion at the bottom of a mug or a glass.

I looked about me. I was approaching Lincoln's Inn Fields. A few more yards would bring me to the Duke's Theatre at the back of Portugal Row. A crack appeared in my misery, and I wondered hazily whether Gorvin were there tonight, loyally applauding whenever his mistress appeared on stage. He was a good fellow, I reminded myself, and he would willingly lend me more than enough money to achieve my goal.

At the theatre, I asked after Meg Daunt, Gorvin's mistress. The doorman told me she was not in the house tonight, so I went in the direction of her lodging in Vere Street, where

Gorvin had recently set her up at vast expense. Even if Gorvin himself wasn't there, I told myself, Meg knew me well enough to take pity on my plight.

I reached the corner of Portugal Row and glanced up Arch Rows. I had been there only yesterday after leaving the Council for Foreign Plantations. The new houses lining the west side of the roadway were brightly lit, and there was much traffic of people coming and going.

A tall woman lumbered down the pavement with a basket on her arm. She came to the archway and paused, as if to get her bearings.

Torches burned in iron brackets on either side. I saw the shape of her by their light. There was something familiar about her posture: about the narrow, slouching shoulders above the broad hips, and the head poking forward in a manner that reminded me of a tortoise. She went under the arch and, just before she vanished into the street beyond, her profile was caught in the light from the torches.

The glimpse was only fleeting. But I recognized her: Patience Noone, the missing maid from Iredale's lodgings. But hadn't Cat told me this morning that she was not only pregnant but on her way to Chester?

The surprise had a mildly sobering effect on me. I set out after her, walking more purposefully than I had done for some time. I followed her under the arch into Duke Street, where I paused and leant against a wall to steady myself.

The street was poorly lit compared to Arch Row, but there was enough light to see that Patience was still there, walking ahead. Then, suddenly, she wasn't there.

It took me a moment to realize that she must have turned into the alley that led to the service entrance of my Lord

Bristol's house and the Council for Foreign Plantations. I hastened after her.

The fumes of wine and strong ale entangled me. I turned into the alley. I stumbled and almost fell on the corner. She was still ahead, reduced to a shadow and a set of rapid footsteps. She had almost reached the back gate, the one that Davis had shown me yesterday morning.

'Stop at once!' I called. 'I command you!'

I was aware of sudden movement to my right. I felt a shattering blow to my head. I dropped my stick and fell forward. But by a miracle I regained my balance. I was conscious that I had lost my hat and wig, and that the night air was cold on my newly naked scalp.

Then I stopped being conscious of anything at all.

CHAPTER TWENTY-FIVE

ON WEDNESDAY MORNING, Cat rose shortly after dawn. She pushed her feet through the gap in the bed curtains and felt for her slippers on the floor. She pulled on her gown and padded across the room to the window, shouting for Jane as she went.

Early morning sunlight slanted into the street below. Wisps of smoke from newly lit fires rose into the clear sky above the chimneys of the houses over the road. The day was clean and fresh, still full of possibility and promise. She had faced far worse things than this crisis at the almshouse, she reminded herself, and she had not only survived but prospered.

If she were ruined, Marwood wouldn't let her starve; he owed her that at least, and he was a man who paid his debts. But that might now depend on whether he was shortly to be a married man with an expensive wife and a ruined father-in-law.

Jane Ash came in with the bowl and a jug of warm water. Her face was drawn and unsmiling, and her eyelids were puffy with weeping.

'What ails you?' Cat asked.

'I couldn't sleep, mistress.'

'You'll make up for it tonight.'

Cat washed her face and hands with the cloth. It would be both foolish and cowardly to wait passively for whatever providence had in store for her. But she couldn't spare the time to meet Madame des Bordes this morning, she decided – there were other, more urgent matters that demanded her attention. Despite Hadgraft's losses, it was possible that he still had a sufficient fortune at his command to continue with the Chard Lane project. His word couldn't be trusted, so it would also be wise to take soundings on the Exchange.

If he were truly ruined, the next question was whether she and Brennan could find another developer to underwrite the rebuilding of the almshouse in return for the profits that could be made from the attached waste ground. Otherwise, they must move out the materials they had stored there, and hope that their suppliers would take at least some of them back.

When Cat went into the parlour for breakfast, the first thing she noticed was that a chest and two chairs were piled against the door to the stairs. 'What's this about?' she demanded.

Jane was looking more haggard than ever. 'Faith, I'm scared, mistress. They might come up here.'

'Who might?'

'Them that half killed Pheebs. There's no one to protect us now.'

'Nonsense,' Cat said, though she privately thought that Jane had a point. The sooner they found someone to replace the porter the better.

The girl's eyes were very large in her face. 'Couldn't you ask Mr Marwood to help find someone? He'd deal with it.'

Cat suppressed a spurt of irritation. 'There's no need to trouble Mr Marwood. We shall manage perfectly well by ourselves.'

She ate her breakfast in silence. Perhaps, she thought, it would be wise for her to meet Madame des Bordes this morning after all. Because it was all connected somehow, and everything sooner or later led back to Roger Durrell and the Duke of Buckingham, including the attacks on Pheebs and Sam Witherdine.

Whatever the Duke was up to, it probably had something to do with Louise de Keroualle, as well as with the faceless corpse at Chard Lane. The inquest was over and done with, but the murder was still unsolved, and the threat of more violence hung over the sign of the Rose.

Until that was settled, none of them would rest easy in their beds.

'We must visit Monsieur Georges while we're there,' Madame des Bordes said as Monsieur Colbert's coach carried them in splendour into the Strand. 'You won't find a better shoemaker in London. I saw a most delightful pair of his last week.'

'There's no time to have something made for me,' Louise pointed out.

'Sometimes he has stock for display or in his workshop. Believe me, he's worth every penny he charges. It's not just the workmanship: it's the designs: he's in constant communication with Paris, and he has all the latest fashions. These poor English shoemakers simply can't compete. You must

206

think ahead, my dear. If you order a pair now, they will be ready by the time you return from Euston.'

'But the expense,' Louise said. 'We've spent so much already.'

'Mademoiselle, you need not worry about that.' Madame des Bordes gave Louise a look that Louise did not altogether like. 'You'll not always be poor, I dare say. You heard what Monsieur Colbert said. Send the bills to him.'

The conversation lapsed for a few minutes. There were three of them inside the coach, for Louise's English maid had come with them. The girl was an oaf who had no French.

Louise said hesitantly: 'You have not forgotten my friend, madame?'

Madame des Bordes glanced sharply at her. 'The friend you would like to bid adieu to before you go to Euston? It will be better if we go after dinner, I think. On our way back. And not with your maid in tow.'

Since they were speaking in French, the gender of the friend could not be concealed. For once, Louise envied the English their uncouth language, which allowed a certain ambiguity in such matters.

They were drawing up outside the New Exchange, their coachman expertly forcing his way among the crowd of coaches that clustered there. When they came to a halt, the footmen, who had been sitting up behind, jumped down. One let down the steps and waited to help the ladies descend. The other cleared a space for them to walk unimpeded, cuffing aside an importunate beggar and forcing a respectable citizen's wife to step off the pavement into the mud.

The two ladies entered the building, with the maid behind them. The shops were arranged on two floors. In the main, they catered for the wealthy. One went elsewhere for the necessities of life: here one found life's refinements.

Louise allowed herself to be guided upstairs to the first floor. The two footmen were close behind, partly bodyguards, partly outward symbols of the importance of the ladies they attended.

'You will need other things than shoes, my dear,' Madame des Bordes said. 'You'll find it all here. Gowns, lace, fans. Cloaks, hats, gloves and muffs. Even a pretty purse for when you sit at table to play. These little things matter, don't they?'

Despite her worries, Louise's spirits were rising. It was agreeable to be free of the routines and iron conventions of the Queen's apartments if only for a few hours, and she relished the consequence that Monsieur Colbert's footmen gave them in this place.

Monsieur Georges himself was behind the counter at the back of the shop. He welcomed Madame des Bordes as an old friend, for they had had many dealings in Paris during her years as *femme de chambre* to Madame, the Duchess of Orleans. Louise wondered whether he paid Madame des Bordes a commission when she introduced a new client to him. Why not? It was the way the world turned.

After he had been introduced to Louise, the three of them were soon deep in conversation with pattern books open on the counter before them. Apprentices fluttered to and fro, bringing samples of materials, colours and finished shoes for the ladies to examine.

They were so absorbed in discussion that Louise was at first unaware that another lady had entered the shop. It was only when Monsieur Georges looked up and said, '*Un moment, madame, si vous plaît*,' that she glanced over her shoulder to see who it was. A plainly dressed woman, her face obscured by a veil, was standing by the door – a citizen's wife or some such, Louise thought, a person of no importance.

To Louise's surprise, however, Madame des Bordes curtsied to the newcomer and said, 'Madame Hakesby! What a surprise to see you here.'

The Englishwoman replied in fluent, if stilted, French and turned politely aside to examine some samples of dyed kid leather. Madame des Bordes turned back to Monsieur Georges.

'Mademoiselle will also need slippers,' she said. 'This is a matter of very great urgency. In a day or two she will be visiting the chateau of a great nobleman, and she must appear elegant even in her hours of leisure.'

'Ah.' The muscles at the corners of his mouth twitched. 'I understand perfectly. I have a pair next door that might suit you very well, mademoiselle. The uppers are of course covered in silk, dyed to the deepest midnight blue, with a pattern of cherry blossom in pink. They are lined with pink to match, also silk.' His long fingers fluttered gracefully. 'And also with ribbons. So.'

He excused himself and went through the doorway to the workroom behind. Louise turned over another page in the pattern book. The newcomer removed her veil.

'I believe Madame Hakesby has something to ask you,' Madame des Bordes said quietly.

Louise frowned. Surprise made her rude. 'Why?'

The widow was a nobody. Elegant enough in her way, and in fact almost pretty, but a mere nobody. It surprised her that Madame des Bordes even acknowledged the acquaintance.

The Englishwoman had undoubtedly been eavesdropping, for she had appeared at Louise's side. 'Mademoiselle,' she said. She laid a small, embroidered purse on the counter. 'Have you seen this before?'

Louise stared at it. 'Where . . .' she broke off, for her mouth and lips were dry, and the words would not come as they should. She swallowed, moistened her lips and stiffened her spine.

'Where did you find this?' Frowning, she stared at the Englishwoman, studying her face more carefully than she had before. 'Do I know you? Your face is familiar.'

'Madame Hakesby is an architect,' Madame des Bordes explained. 'She came to France last year to advise Madame about a poultry house, and later in Dover. And she was in the Queen's apartments the other evening.'

'I don't understand,' Louise said, summoning up all the haughtiness at her command. 'Is this a trap?'

Madame Hakesby smiled at her. 'Not at all. But pray tell me about the purse.'

'Why should I say anything to you, madame?'

'Why, it's practically midday,' Madame des Bordes said simultaneously. 'Why don't we dine together?'

The Blue Dolphin was on the south side of Piccadilly at the eastern end. According to Madame des Bordes, it was an agreeable tavern where the private rooms really were private, and the food was at least tolerable. That was because it came from the eating house next door, which had a French cook.

In the coach, Madame des Bordes whispered that they would send the bill for dinner to Monsieur Colbert, as for everything else, so there was no reason to economize. She smacked her lips in anticipation.

Cat was aware how uninteresting in ordinary circumstances

her society must be to a well-born French maid of honour to the Queen. But Mademoiselle de Keroualle had at least agreed to the proposal that the three of them should dine together. It was hard to know what she was really thinking but clearly she was made of sterner stuff than the doll-like face suggested. Only for a moment, when she had seen the purse lying on the counter, had her self-control slipped, revealing something altogether more vulnerable beneath.

Their room at the tavern was pleasantly furnished and well lit. After much discussion with the servant, Madame des Bordes ordered the dishes for their dinner and sent the man away. Louise withdrew to the necessary house. Her maid and one of the footmen escorted her; they would stand guard at the door to prevent any annoyance.

'She's terrified,' Madame des Bordes whispered. 'The King will have her when she's at Euston. The whole world knows it, and so does she.'

'The poor woman.'

'What can she do? She must live, eh? She must seize the chance while she can. The King's middle-aged now, and they say he has a fancy for a little virgin half his age.'

'A virgin? In God's name, why?'

'To make him feel young.' Madame des Bordes glanced at Cat. 'That's the rumour among the Queen's women, and they are often right about these matters. Men past their own youth hunger for a maid in their bed. They have the means to pay for the pleasure too.'

'But a virgin . . . ?' Cat said.

Madame des Bordes gave a weary smile. 'To take a woman's maidenhead gives a special pleasure because it makes them feel powerful. You know that.'

Cat felt herself blushing. She lowered her head to conceal her face.

'Besides,' the other woman went on in the authoritative tone of a good cook discussing the proper ingredients for a sauce, 'for a man of the King's type, virginity in a mistress is practical. To lie with a courtesan – or a courtier's wife, for that matter – there is always the risk of the pox. But with a virgin he knows he will be safe.'

'Is there no way out for her?'

'Can you see her as a poor little mouse in a convent for the rest of her days? I can't, and nor can she.' Madame des Bordes leant closer. 'I think she may have a tenderness for a Frenchman who is in London at present. But either he's unsuitable or his intentions aren't honourable. Or surely he would have acted by now?'

'Has that purse something to do with him?'

'Very possibly. But I hope she won't be a fool about him. If she doesn't take her opportunity now, the King will find another young maid in her place. So our little Mademoiselle—'

She broke off and lifted a finger to her lips. There were footsteps outside. Louise came in. The door closed, shutting out the servants.

Madame des Bordes smiled at her. 'You must forgive my little stratagem with Madame Hakesby, but—'

But Louise was looking at Cat. 'Where did you get it?' she demanded, abandoning the pretence that the purse was unimportant.

'Is it yours?' Cat said.

Louise lifted her chin, a small gesture of defiance. 'Why won't you answer me?'

'Is it?'

Their eyes locked. Then Louise said. 'Perhaps it is. Or was.'

'How did you part with it?'

'I – I gave it to someone.'

'A gentleman named Monsieur Pharamond, perhaps? Who lodges at the Three Crowns by St Sepulchre.'s on Snow Hill.'

Louise caught her breath. She gave a curt nod. Then her self-control slipped away from her. 'Have you seen him?'

'No one's seen him for ten days or more,' Cat said. 'He's disappeared. This purse was among the possessions of an English clerk, who has also disappeared.'

'How did *he* get it?'

No one answered her. In the street below their window, two men were having a drunken quarrel, and a woman was singing a ballad in a cracked voice.

Madame des Bordes stirred. 'Who is this Pharamond? I don't recall a man of that name.'

'It is a *nom de guerre*,' Louise said without looking at her.

'And his real name? Do I know the gentleman?'

Louise clamped her lips together.

Cat said, 'Monsieur Pharamond and this Englishman appear to have something in common. The Duke of Buckingham sent his bullies to find them. And now they are both missing.'

'Buckingham. That devil.' Louise's voice was barely audible. She covered her face with her hands. 'It's my fault. But they were . . . they were making trouble for me. They have papers of mine, and they wanted money for them. It was Iredale's doing, I'm sure of it. My – Monsieur Pharamond – he would do nothing like that for himself, Iredale must have forced him to it, he must have had him in his power.'

There was confirmation: Louise knew the clerk was Iredale. Cat said softly, 'And Buckingham?'

'He said he would help. He would see that they were warned off. If necessary, he told me, he himself would pay them what I owed. Whatever happened, he would make sure that my papers were returned to me. Truly I didn't want Monsieur Pharamond harmed, I swear. I *told* the Duke that.'

'Harming people is what his bullies do,' Cat said. 'They have no other purpose in life than to serve the Duke, and that is the way they do it. Believe me, I've seen them at work, mademoiselle. One of them killed my husband a few years ago. And the night before last they maimed the porter at my house, quite possibly for life.'

'Oh good God.' Louise's shock was unfeigned. 'I should never have trusted Buckingham after Dieppe.' Her lips drooped. 'All this wouldn't have happened if he hadn't abandoned me there, week after week. It's his fault.'

'Is that where it began?' Cat said gently. 'While you were waiting for Buckingham to send his yacht to bring you to England?'

'Yes. He promised the yacht would be there when we arrived. But it wasn't. We waited day after day. There was no word from him, no word from Paris. I had nothing to do, and the bills were mounting. I had to find money to pay them. I hoped to win what I needed at cards. What other choice had I? This Iredale, he arranged it. And – and – the other one, the gentleman, he had come to Dieppe . . . to follow me and because he wanted to find a passage to England. I was already acquainted with him, and he needed money as much as I did. The Chev— that is, he played cards with us and – and, well, he was *kind* to me. He is always kind to me.'

'Ah.' Madame des Bordes smiled. 'I begin to understand. This Frenchman: was he by any chance the Chevalier de Vire? I saw you talking together more than once when Madame was alive.'

Louise said nothing, but the colour in her face was all the confirmation they needed.

'The Chevalier was sometimes with us at St-Cloud or the Palais Royal,' Madame des Bordes murmured to Cat. 'A gentleman of very good family.'

'Indeed he is,' Louise put in eagerly.

'But the Chevalier belongs to a cadet branch of a cadet branch,' Madame des Bordes continued remorselessly, 'and he has no fortune, no friends at court, nothing but the clothes on his back. He is always in want of funds, always with debtors at his heels, always willing to make a fool of himself with a dice box or a pack of cards. But he has considerable address, I'll say that for him. Particularly with the ladies.'

'You are too harsh,' Louise said. 'The Chevalier has a generous, manly spirit. But it's true that he has been cursed with misfortune. He has had so many false friends . . . He had to leave France because of his debts. And because he wanted to follow me. He told me so himself.'

'Did you lose money to both of them?' Cat asked.

'Yes, but especially to Iredale. He kept winning, you see. And he also lent me what I needed to pay my bills at the inn when we left Dieppe. Monsieur de Vire said he would forgive his part of my debt. But in England, both he and Iredale wanted payment. I'm sure it was only Iredale really. But they still have certain papers . . .'

'Papers?' Madame des Bordes said quickly.

'Some letters of mine.'

Cat stirred in her chair. 'Why did you ask Buckingham of all people for help?'

'Because he offered it. Since we came to England, he has wanted to be my friend.'

'Mademoiselle de Keroualle has made quite an impression at Whitehall,' Madame des Bordes said. 'And Monsieur the Duke now realizes that she is not the little nobody he took her for, and so he wishes to oblige her in any way he can. Previously he didn't much care, one way or the other.'

'He was good to me at Whitehall when no one else was,' Louise said simply. 'One evening I confided my troubles to him, and he said he would make them go away. I told him it wasn't Monsieur de Vire's fault, that he couldn't have realized what that wicked Iredale was doing. I expect he is in Iredale's debt, just as I am.'

'The Duke of Buckingham serves no one but himself,' Cat said. 'He isn't kind to people. He uses them. If he gets his hands on those letters, do you really think he'll give them to you if they have any value to him?'

Louise whimpered. 'If only I could see the Chevalier. If I could but talk to him, he would understand and perhaps between us we might find a way to solve everything.' Her cheeks were flushed, as if she had drunk too much wine, too fast. 'I believe he . . . he loves me, you see.'

A strange way to show it, Cat thought. 'You gave him the purse.'

'Yes. In Dieppe. It was a . . . a token of friendship. But why would Iredale have it? Did he steal it?'

'Possibly.' Or perhaps the Chevalier had given it to him to settle part of a debt. A purse of such workmanship was worth a few shillings.

'The dead man,' Louise whispered. 'The man with no face. Is it . . . ?'

'It could be the Chevalier or it could be Iredale,' Cat said bluntly.

Louise gave a little scream, instantly hushed.

'But no one knows for sure except the murderer,' Cat went on. 'We can't find either of them. And until we do, we don't know which of them may be still alive.'

There was a tap on the door. The beaming face of the landlord appeared.

'Shall we serve dinner, my ladies?' he said.

CHAPTER TWENTY-SIX

'BUT WE MUST do something,' a woman said, her voice low and obstinate. 'We can't leave things be.'

Another dream. For countless hours I had drifted in and out of sleep. Apart from the pains in my head, there was a dryness in my mouth. My eyes hurt. Someone was trying to drive a spike into my head, pushing harder and harder, sinking its point further and further into my brain.

'What if he dies?'

No one replied. The voice receded as the dream faded. There was something sour in my nostrils. I sniffed. Someone had vomited nearby.

I forced open my eyelids, and the pain increased. There was a rectangle of brightness a yard or two away from where I was lying. Gradually I made out a small, shuttered window through which cracks of light entered the place where I lay. They formed a senseless and unpleasantly bright pattern on the ground. As my eyes grew further accustomed to the gloom, I saw an empty wine bottle on the flagged floor, and something beside it that might have been a curl of cheese rind. Had I drunk it last night and passed out?

Something stirred in the memory and then went to sleep again.

I took stock of myself. I felt a draught on the skin of my scalp, which told me that my wig and hat were missing. At this point, my memory gave another useless twitch. There were pains inside my head. But there were also exquisitely sore places on the outside, one above the left ear and the other at the back of my skull.

My eyes focused again on the wine bottle lying on its side on the floor, with the cheese rind beside it. Why, I wondered, were they somehow familiar? For an instant I almost had the answer, but then with a rush of shame and anger a far more powerful memory elbowed it aside.

Go, sir. There's nothing for you here.

I heard those words in my head and I remembered Hadgraft's red, twisted features and the huddled figure of his daughter crouching against the wall. I saw the expression on Grace's face when she looked at me and winced at what she saw.

It came back to me then: the shipwreck of Hadgraft's venture and the shipwreck of my hopes. Even my desire for Grace had fled, leaving scraps of pity behind like the lees in a bottle of wine. Had my love for her had such shallow roots? What must Cat think now she knew me for such a fool?

I remembered walking aimlessly through the streets, pausing only to drink. For some reason I found myself thinking of Patience Noone, Iredale's maid, but I could not for the life of me work out why.

Afterwards there was a blank: a dark wall that I did not wish to penetrate. Slowly, though, this blank, this absence, enveloped me completely, and I passed into a place of shadow between sleeping and waking. My thoughts moved sluggishly through a dry, painful world I did not recognize.

In the end, I ceased to pay attention to them.

When I next became aware of myself, the light had changed. Sunshine was now pouring through the cracks in the window shutter, making golden stripes on the floor. One of them passed over the wine bottle and sparked green fire in its depths.

My head still ached abominably, though less than before. My mouth was as parched as the Arabian sands.

The image of Grace Hadgraft slipped unbidden into my mind. To distract myself, I rolled cautiously on to my side. I grunted with pain. My vision blurred, then slowly cleared. I lay there a moment to recruit my strength.

'Awake now?'

The whisper was so close, the man might have been inches away from my ear. I writhed like a landed fish and tried to stand up. The pain in my head made me cry out. I fell back. I was lying on a straw mattress. I took a deep, painful breath and struggled into a sitting position.

'Who are you? Where am I?'

The man advanced across the lines of sunlight. His face was in shadow. 'How do you do, Mr Marwood?'

'You know my name.'

'I searched you while you slept.'

He must have found my pocketbook. In which case he would have discovered the warrant with Lord Arlington's signature. I touched the breast of my coat, trying surreptitiously to establish whether the pocketbook was still there.

'Don't worry, sir. I put your papers back. You're a lucky dog, though it may not feel like it. Your guardian angel had you tucked under his wing last night.'

I licked dry lips with a dry tongue. 'I'm thirsty.'

He moved away. I heard the rustle of liquid. When he returned, he crouched beside the mattress and handed me a mug. I drank and drank. The effort left me exhausted, incapable of speech. He had given me small beer, sour and old, but it tasted like nectar. I was so thirsty I would have drunk the water from the Fleet Ditch.

He was still there, hunched at my elbow. There was enough light to see that he had a scrubby beard and a broad, low-crowned hat, like those that Cat's labourers wore.

I cleared my throat. 'Who did this to me?'

'You don't remember?' He paused, and I had the sense that he was deliberating how much to tell me. 'You were in your cups. Some rogues attacked you and had you senseless on the ground. I frightened them off and gave you shelter before another villain came along and picked you clean.'

A patch of fog cleared in my memory. 'Patience Noone,' I said. 'I remember. I was following Patience Noone.'

He pounced on me and gripped my neck. 'Why?'

I tried to tear his hand away but it was no use. I was too weak. When at last he released me, I could not speak for a moment. I lay there without speaking. But the shock acted as a stimulant to my mental faculties.

'I asked you a question,' he said.

'Where is she?'

'That's no business of yours.'

'But are you John Iredale?'

He pushed me backwards. My head collided with the wall, and I cried out. But this time I was half prepared for the attack and better equipped to deal with the pain.

'I'd have left you where you were,' he said. The anger had left his voice, perhaps purged by the brief show of violence. 'But the wench said otherwise. Her kind heart will be the death of me.'

'It was you who attacked me, wasn't it? Because I was following her.'

He didn't deny it. 'She said you searched my lodgings.'

'And your parents' house in Paddington. I wasn't the first to go there, by the way.'

'What does that mean?' Iredale demanded, bringing his face closer to mine.

'Some men rode up by night and tried to get in. But your father fired his gun at them, and they went away.'

'You lie. He's blind.'

'He's also a man of spirit who owns a fowling piece.'

I drew up my legs, the better to prop myself against the wall behind me. In doing so, I dislodged the empty wine bottle and thereby dislodged another memory.

'Is that Mr Evelyn's wine bottle by any chance? And is the rind beside it all that's left of his Cheshire cheese?'

'Faith, how could you know that?' Iredale sounded fearful. 'Are you a necromancer?'

'Hardly. I assume we're in one of Lord Bristol's outbuildings at the back of the Council for Foreign Plantations.'

'Have you talked to Mr Evelyn?'

'That gentleman has told the whole world about his losses, not just me.'

Iredale grunted. 'I had to eat and drink something. At the beginning I had nothing.'

'Why are you hiding?'

'Why do you think?' He drew breath sharply. 'That blackguard Durrell threatened to kill me.'

'You know him?' I said, surprised.

'Aye. He was sometimes about when I was in the Duke of Buckingham's service.'

'When did he threaten you?'

'Saturday before last. Look.'

Iredale tore open his coat and lifted his shirt. He angled his body this way and that until one of the shafts of sunlight caught it. There were two angry red cuts in the skin, intersecting at right angles, the longer almost a foot in height. Together they looked like a cross, the mark they chalked on the doors of afflicted households in times of plague.

'What is it?' I asked.

'A warning.' He touched the wound gingerly. 'The devil did it with that damned spike of his. It's not healing properly. Anyway, that's why I'm here. Best thing to lie low until the business blows over.'

'And which business might that be?'

Iredale turned away, declining to answer.

I ignored Lord Arlington's prohibition. 'Dieppe.'

He swung round. 'What do you know of that?'

'Enough. You might as well tell me the whole. I can't help you unless you do.'

'*Help* me?'

'Why not? I've no interest in harming you or Patience Noone. Quite the reverse. We have a common enemy. Durrell hates me too.'

Iredale turned this over in his mind. Weak and feeble though I was, I realized that he needed help as much as I did. He had seen my pocketbook and its contents. He knew that I was, God help me, a respected member of Lord Arlington's household. He would credit me with resources I did not possess. Whereas Iredale was a fugitive with no one to turn to but a maidservant who had lost both her reputation and her position.

Whatever else he was, Iredale wasn't a fool. 'It's not just Durrell,' he said in a voice that trembled. 'They'll all think it's me who killed the man at the almshouse.'

'Pharamond?'

'How do I know who he is?' he said sharply. 'Are you trying to trick a confession out of me? But faith, who else could it be? Is anyone else missing? It has to be him. Patience says he's vanished. I know why he was killed, too, because Durrell found me first. He was warning us away from a little bit of business we had with someone who owes us money. I went to the Three Crowns on Saturday evening looking for Pharamond. He wasn't there, but when I came out Durrell and his friend pushed me in a doorway and got me on the ground. They gave me a kicking and told me what's what. They also left me with this.' Iredale touched his chest. 'Me, I like an easy life, I didn't try to argue. Best lie low, I thought, so I was off within the hour. But Pharamond's different. He's a gent, see? Prickly about his honour. And a hot-tempered fellow too, like all these Frenchmen. If Durrell found him, he'd have put up a fight, I'd wager my life on it. Which is why he'd end up dead and buried. And why they'd beat his face in so no one would know him.'

It made sense, as far as it went. But I wanted more. 'When did Durrell find you?'

'In the evening . . . about nine or ten o' the clock. He looked for me in Swan Yard first, then came on to the Crowns. He wanted to know where Pharamond was.'

'What did you tell him?'

'That he was probably at old Hadgraft's house. You know the man? The lawyer who's rebuilding the almshouse? Rich as sin. Pharamond was the daughter's French tutor. Quite the gallant. He had hopes of winning the girl's hand and fortune. By his account, she was more than willing.'

His words brought the taste of bile to my throat. But the answers dovetailed with what I knew already. Durrell had certainly called at Swan Yard on Saturday, looking for Iredale. It was perfectly plausible that he had found Iredale afterwards and then waylaid Pharamond after he left the Hadgrafts' house.

'It's true, sir,' Iredale pleaded, taking my silence for disbelief. 'Ask anyone. I wouldn't hurt a fly.'

I rested my aching head against the cold wall and tried to marshal my thoughts into some degree of order. Clearly the connection between Pharamond and Iredale had something to do with Buckingham and Dieppe. But what of Hadgraft and the box I had found in the attic of the cottage in Paddington?

'I ain't a murderer,' Iredale burst out, as if the words had been dammed inside him until at last the force of his desperation had blown away the obstruction. 'I didn't kill the Frenchman or anyone else. I swear it.'

'Listen,' I said, keeping my voice low and gentle. 'I'm grateful to you for giving me shelter. I'll help you if I can. But you must understand: the case against you looks black. You knew the murdered man and you went into hiding on the night of his death. You have marks of violence on your person.'

There was silence. Iredale was breathing hard as if he had run a race.

'And remember this,' I went on. 'Durrell is Buckingham's man, and it's the Duke who wants you warned off. If they don't hang you at Tyburn for Pharamond's murder, you'll be dead by Durrell's hand. They won't want you talking, will they?'

'Why should I believe a word you say?'

'Because you have to,' I said. 'Because the Duke of Buckingham is my enemy too. But I can't help you unless I know the whole of the matter.' Iredale started to speak, but I overrode him. 'That means you must tell me all about you and Pharamond.' I hesitated, with Arlington's threat in my mind, but only for a moment. 'And about Mademoiselle de Keroualle and Dieppe.'

He made no reply, or not in words. His footsteps retreated into the shadows at the far end of the building. A door opened and closed. A bolt shot home. Then there was only silence.

CHAPTER TWENTY-SEVEN

A FTER THEY HAD dined at the Blue Dolphin, the three women went their separate ways. Mademoiselle de Keroualle had barely picked at her food, and Cat had done little better.

Madame des Bordes, on the other hand, had made a hearty meal, though she was critical of the sauces. 'Not all French cooks are good cooks,' she said. 'This one is only good enough to impress the English. No doubt that's why he came to London.'

But she was not insensitive, murmuring to Cat that she would take Mademoiselle de Keroualle back to her own apartments, for there would be no more shopping today. She looked sharply at Cat as she finished speaking.

'How are you yourself?' she asked sternly. 'You have been very quiet.'

'Forgive me, I've much on my mind. But I'm perfectly well, I assure you.'

Madame des Bordes looked dissatisfied, but she did not probe further. Shortly afterwards the elder of the two footmen announced that the ambassador's coach was at the door of the tavern. The two Frenchwomen departed in the direction of Whitehall with a gaggle of ragged boys running after the gilded equipage in the hope of pennies.

Cat took a coach to Chard Lane. She found Brennan in the site office, making arrangements to remove materials before the bailiffs claimed them as Hadgraft's. He was in a better temper than Cat had expected, for he was in his element: the task before him called for precise measurement and orderly arrangement, activities he excelled at.

Hadgraft hadn't dared show his face, Brennan said, and when Cat asked him if Marwood had called, he gave her a surprised look and said no, why should he have?

Cat pretended not to have heard. There was no reason why Marwood might have come here other than the strength of her own desire to know whether his passion for the pert baggage had outlived the loss of the pert baggage's dowry and her father's ruin. Knowing Marwood as she did, she feared that the numskull was quite capable of declaring the world well lost for love.

Dear God, she thought, her mind running on in a most unruly way, he needs someone to look after him, to stop him making such a fool of himself.

'Are you well?' Brennan asked tactlessly. 'Your face is grown quite flushed.'

'I'm perfectly well,' Cat snapped. 'Thank you.'

I heard breathing.

'Who's there?'

There was no answer. Only the breathing.

'Iredale?'

'I brought you something to drink.'

It was a woman's voice, flat and harsh. Patience Noone came closer, and I was able to see her, or at least her outline. 'Are you hungry?' she said. 'There's bread as well. You should eat something.'

There was something different about her voice: her tone lacked even the trace of subservience she had shown before. I had only encountered her in Mistress Farage's house in Swan Yard, when I gave orders she was obliged to obey. Now our roles were different.

I sat up. The movement made my head swim, though not as much as before. Judging by the light, such as it was, the afternoon was shading into evening. I had been dozing restlessly for at least an hour, dreaming, drifting in and out of my surroundings.

'Where's Iredale?'

Patience didn't answer. She put the beer and bread within my reach. I took a gulp of beer to moisten my mouth.

'I want to help you,' I said. 'But I can't do that here. You must let me go.'

'Stand up,' she commanded. 'Sir.'

The 'sir' was almost insolent in its timing. But I tried to obey, only to find that my knees gave way and I fell back on the mattress.

'Thought so. You ain't going nowhere on your own two legs. Not today.'

'Then let me send a message,' I said. 'My servants will fetch me. And . . . and they will bring you food, clothes, money, whatever you need.'

'What's to stop you betraying us instead?' For the first time she sounded uncertain of herself.

'Why would I do that? Hasn't Iredale told you? We have a common enemy.'

Patience was already walking away from me.

'I'm your only hope, woman,' I called after her.

She stopped at the door. 'Eat something. Sir.'

The door opened and closed. The bolt slammed home. I was alone again with the shadows.

The light faded, and gradually the colours of the city grew paler and paler until its corners filled with shadows. The dull glow of oil lamps made pools of dirty yellow in the dusk. Torches flared and sputtered. Candle flames swayed on windowsills.

As the light retreated and the shadows gathered, Cat moved from window to fire, from chair to window again. The room was too small to contain her restlessness.

Jane, hovering by the door, asked if she should light the candles. Cat bit back an angry retort. Blameless Jane Ash had done nothing wrong whatsoever. It was not her fault that Cat found her presence an irritant.

'I'll be upstairs,' Cat said. 'You may send Mr Marwood to me if he calls, but otherwise I don't want to be disturbed. Stay here by the fire. Light yourself a candle to sew by.'

There was always sewing to be done and, thanks to Margaret's instruction, Jane was slowly becoming more skilled at it.

Cat left the parlour and climbed the last flight of stairs to the Drawing Office at the top of the house. She made a circuit of the long attic, recklessly lighting one candle after another and damning the expense. If she was ruined, she thought defiantly, what did it matter if she lit as many candles as she wanted? Wax too, not stinking, penny-pinching tallow: she would live as well as she could while she had the means.

The room was now blazing with light. Cat paced up and down, wondering why Marwood did not come to see her. She had thought he would at least enquire how she did after the attack on Pheebs. Did he not trust her any more? Had that little minx not only cast a spell over him but poisoned his mind against Cat?

She had so much to tell him, and it was information that he would want to know. That made his absence doubly irritating. The sooner he learned the identity of Monsieur Pharamond, the better. She could now lay the entire intrigue before him and reveal how, thanks to the interference of Durrell and Buckingham, it had taken a fatal turn: either for the Chevalier or Iredale.

At the heart of it, of course, was that forlorn young Frenchwoman with her baby face and her inexplicable allure for men, together with her taste for games of chance and her infatuation with the Chevalier de Vire. If Mademoiselle de Keroualle hadn't had the misfortune to catch the eye of the King, neither Buckingham nor Arlington would have had any interest in her, and the man with no face would have still been alive.

What was it about men and the pretty young women who knew how to please and tease them to the edge of insanity? She was thinking of Marwood and Grace Hadgraft again. She pushed them aside. She should be making plans for her own future. Despite Hadgraft's ruin, something might yet be salvaged for herself, Brennan and their dependants. There were fees unpaid, past clients who might be encouraged to commission more work, new clients who might be worth approaching. But every time she turned her mind towards the problem, it shied like a horse refusing a fence, and cantered away in the opposite direction.

Meanwhile the evening sounds of the house and the street formed a backdrop to her thoughts, a backdrop so familiar that she was barely conscious of it. Within the Drawing Office, the only noises were her own breathing and the soft, slippered tread of her feet as she paced up and down the room.

Four storeys below, a rapping on the street door cut through the comfortable monotony. Cat unlatched the door to the landing and stood listening. Time passed inexplicably slowly. Then she heard the sound of someone climbing the stairs.

She knew almost at once who it was by the irregular pattern of thumps, grunts and scrapes that rose up the stairwell. Sam Witherdine lacked a foot and part of a leg, but he employed his hands, his crutch and his one remaining foot so effectively that he swarmed up a flight of stairs with the agility if not the speed of a sailor swarming up the shrouds.

Not Marwood then: but at least his servant, perhaps with a letter. Cat took up a candle, gathered up her skirts with the other hand, and ran down the stairs to meet him. She and Sam reached the landing place below the parlour at the same time.

'Do you bring a—?'

Sam was speaking, his words overriding hers, falling out of his mouth in a torrent. 'Have you seen master? Is he here?'

'No,' she said. 'Come with me.'

He followed. The parlour was nearer, but Jane Ash was in there, and Cat climbed further up the stairs to the Drawing Office. Once inside, Sam stood in a daze, blinking in the light.

He was wearing a cloak, with the outline of a cutlass visible beneath it. The bruises on his face had turned a fine mulberry colour, but the swelling had diminished.

'Well?' she demanded. 'Has he not been home?'

'No, mistress. He didn't come back at all last night. Didn't send word, either.'

'I've not seen him since yesterday morning.'

'There's a letter waiting for him. Margaret says it's from my lord, an express.' Sam lowered his voice, though there was no one to hear. 'I tell you, mistress, she's worrying herself to death. You know – after what happened to me and Pheebs the other night.'

'There's probably a simple explanation,' Cat said, which sounded unconvincing even to herself.

'The only other thing it could be . . .' He broke off, avoiding Cat's eyes. 'No, it's nothing.'

'Tell me,' she said sternly.

He stared at the floor. 'Margaret said – but you know what women are like, adding two and two and making seven . . . Oh, faith, mistress, not you, I swear I didn't mean you . . .'

'What did she say?'

'She reckons master has a desire . . .'

'For what?' Cat was pleased that her voice sounded perfectly normal, if a little stern. 'A desire for what?'

Sam was still avoiding her eyes. 'A lady.'

He put a slight emphasis on the last word, which suggested to Cat that, in Margaret's judgement at least, this was not a sudden passion for an actress or waiting-maid, likely to burn itself out once its object was gained. This, Margaret thought, was the sort of woman her master might marry.

'She's worried,' Sam said, his weathered face creasing in

misery. 'If master finds himself a wife, what will become of us? *She* won't want us, will she? She'll want her own servants about her.'

'Enough of that,' Cat commanded. 'Your master won't turn you into the street, whatever happens; you may be sure of that. Besides, if he marries, it doesn't mean you will lose your positions.'

Privately she understood Margaret's concern. A new mistress might well feel that the Witherdines were not appropriate servants for the household of one of Lord Arlington's private secretaries. Sam in particular would not find it easy to get a new place. Marwood grumbled about him and occasionally threw shoes at him, but he was an indulgent master in everything that mattered, and the shoes usually missed their target.

'Why does she think that he has a . . . a desire for someone?'

'He's grown particular about his dress. His wig. He gets himself shaved more than usual.' He smiled grimly. 'If Margaret says he's found himself a young woman, I believe her.'

Cat said, 'Do you believe your master might be with her now?'

'What do I know? He's been acting strange, though, and maybe it's because of her that we've had no word from him.'

'Go back to Margaret,' Cat said. 'Let me know at once if you hear from him. And if I have news of him, I'll send word to you. In the meantime, worrying won't help. How did you come here?'

'What?'

'Don't stand there gaping, Sam. Answer me?'

'I walked, mistress. Up to the Strand, and—'

'You walked, did you? I thought so. It's only two days since you were attacked. You'll go back in a chair, do you hear? Come down to the parlour and I'll give you the fare.'

'No need, mistress, it's only a step or two to the Savoy.'

'You'll do as I say. Think – if you were attacked again, who would look after Margaret?'

He stared at her in silence, his face changing as her words had the desired effect.

Four storeys below them, there was a frantic knocking on the street door.

When she reached the lodgings of the maids of honour, Louise ignored all questions and fled to her chamber.

Her maid was there, sewing by the window to catch the evening light, her stupid English face bent over her needle-work and her tongue peeping wetly from the corner of her mouth. Louise shouted at her to leave. The girl fumbled over her belongings and dropped her mistress's second-best veil in the hearth. Louise flung an empty chamber pot at her. The girl shrieked and scuttled from the room.

Heads or tails. Even or odds. Living or dead. The Chevalier de Vire was one or the other. Perhaps it no longer mattered. Nothing mattered after that terrible dinner at the Blue Dolphin.

Louise wasn't sure whether it was the doing of the strange, freakish Englishwoman or the effect of Madame des Bordes' calmly brutal common sense. Whatever the reason, something had broken. Something had finished. And there was no longer even the slightest hope.

She slumped on the window seat. Time passed, and there came a tap on the door. She ignored it. But the latch lifted anyway, and Madame des Bordes came into the room without asking permission. She closed the door and peered at Louise's face.

'You've been crying.'

'What's it to you, madame?'

'A sadness.' The older woman sat down uninvited in a chair by the window. 'Too many tears in this world. But what can one do? Do you think any of us has a choice in these matters?'

'It's not fair,' Louise burst out. 'If only things had been different. If the Chevalier had a patron, or—'

'Things will never be different, my child. For you or Monsieur de Vire.'

'I think I love him.' It was a relief to say those words aloud, a relief streaked with despair. 'Whether he still lives or not. Whether his motives are noble or base. Despite everything. It doesn't matter. I *burn* for him.'

'Love is not enough,' Madame des Bordes said crisply. 'You can't eat love. It won't keep out the rain or put clothes on your back. Or, for that matter, shoes from Monsieur Georges on your feet.' She turned her head and spat with elegant accuracy into the back of the fireplace. 'Me, I spit on such love.'

Four knocks on the door.

Josh glanced at the old man who had been enlisted as a temporary replacement for the hall porter at the sign of the Rose. He claimed to be an old soldier – more old than soldier, in Josh's private opinion – with a weak bladder and shaking hands.

He nodded to Josh, who slid back the shutter in the outer

236

door. To his relief the boy made out a familiar hat and cloak, caught in the light of the lantern above the doorway.

'It's Mr Marwood,' he said over his shoulder to the old pisspot, who was still slumped on the stool with his chin resting on the head of a weighted stick and his unshaven jowls drooping on either side like a pair of dewlaps.

'Who?'

'Marwood.' The boy jabbed a thumb in the air. 'He visits them upstairs regular.'

Josh set to work on the bolts and bars. When he had opened the door, the visitor pushed past him into the house.

The man wore Marwood's hat, Marwood's wig and Marwood's cloak with the brass clasp in the shape of a lion's head. All of them looked the worse for wear. He was about Marwood's height and breadth too.

But he didn't have Marwood's face.

CHAPTER TWENTY-EIGHT

THE CANDLES WERE still burning brightly. There was more than enough light to see that the stranger was trembling.

The grubby sheet of paper had been clumsily folded several times. It was unsealed. Written on the outside were the words *To Mistress Hakesby at the sign of the Rose, Henrietta Street*. The handwriting looked like Marwood's, Cat thought, though it was less neat than usual. Either it was his or a very good copy.

First came relief that he was alive, then a spurt of anger with him, followed by anxiety for his safety. Cat tugged at the letter and smoothed it out on her drawing slope.

Meanwhile the stranger stood with his back to the wall near the door, now closed and bolted. Sam was beside him, his dagger drawn. On the floor was a huddled mass of clothing: Marwood's cloak with the lion's head on the fastening, his beaver hat and his best wig. All of them looked as if they had been dragged through the mud.

Cat looked down at the letter.

Madam,
I met with an Accident last Night and was
rudely assaulted by Lincoln's Inn Fields by two rogues
  and left for
dead. This man rescued me
and has tended me ever since. Pray send a coach and a
  man with the Bearer of this
Letter (whose name is Brown) to fetch me hence, together
  with a purse to
enable me to reward him as he deserves.
JM

Why did the letter contain so little information? Was it a trap? It was hard to see how or why. She reread it more slowly. Something was odd about it. The language? The handwriting?

She looked up. 'Is he badly hurt?'

'A little bruised about the head. He can't walk steadily, or without pain.' The stranger's voice was pleasant enough to the ears, though no one would mistake him for a man of breeding. 'At first I thought his wits were astray but probably that was the wine.'

'He's drunk?' Cat's concern for Marwood veered back towards irritation.

'He was last night. Even now he stinks like a brewer's dray. He—'

'And why are you wearing his clothes?'

'He lent them to me, mistress. You see, I have a trifle or two of debt about the town. I don't want to wear my own clothes abroad. And Mr Marwood said wearing his cloak would prove I came from him.'

239

Cat's eyes dropped to the letter again. This time she was struck by the jaggedness of the right-hand margin, which was not only unsightly but a waste of paper. Paper was expensive. Marwood was not a man who wasted it, whether it was his own or anyone else's. She glanced at Sam, who was chewing his lower lip.

whose name is Brown . . .

Suddenly she saw what Marwood was telling her.

'Tell me, Iredale,' she said. 'Where exactly are you hiding?'

'Who?'

'Don't play the innocent,' she snapped.

'You mistake me. I—'

'Your name's John Iredale,' Cat went on. 'You've been missing from your lodgings ever since the body of a murdered man was found at the Chard Lane almshouse ten days ago. You're certainly a rogue and quite possibly a murderer.'

His resistance crumbled. 'I know it looks black against me, mistress, but on my honour—'

'Honour? What right have you to prate of honour? Mistress Farage turned off the maid at your lodging because you got her with child.'

'Patience is a good woman. I swear I shall look after her. Faith, I am already doing so. I've provided her with a roof over her head and—'

'She's with you?'

'Aye, she is. She was bringing me food and news when she could.' Iredale was gabbling now, his former fluency abandoned. 'It's only the watchman and his dog at the place where I am. The mastiff knows me, and the watchman's a sot. But now she's homeless, and we make shift together.'

'Where?'

'A stable at the place where I work. No one uses it now.'

'At the Council for Foreign Plantations?'

Iredale nodded, his eyes straining towards Sam at his side.

'Sam?' Cat said.

He raised the dagger's blade in both a salute to her and a threat to Iredale. 'Mistress.'

'I'll send the boy for a hackney. Then we will fetch your master. You know what to do if this knave shows fight or leads us into a trap. Save the hangman a job and kill him.'

It was now fully dark, with a wind blowing upriver, rattling the casements and making the fire smoke.

'Truly,' Cat said to Marwood, 'I believe you do this on purpose to plague me.' After the briefest of pauses, she added, 'And Margaret, of course,' in case Margaret felt slighted or interpreted the remark as meaning more than Cat intended.

She stared at him. He was lying in his own bed at last. Margaret was bending over him on the other side, her face red and wrinkled with worry. There were candles burning around them. Cat had the unsettling sensation that to a stranger the scene would resemble a deathbed.

At least he was safe for now. The Savoy's gates might offer only limited protection from intruders, but the old walls in Infirmary Close were much thicker than those in Henrietta Street. Moreover, Marwood had installed heavy bars and stout shutters on the windows. He had also replaced the bolts and locks on the outer doors. And Sam was below with his weapons.

Marwood's head moved restlessly on the pillow. His breathing was rapid and shallow, his cheeks pale, and his eyes black and glassy. Cat had given him laudanum, perhaps more than was wise. But she had wanted to make him comfortable. On the way here, he had cried out when the coach jolted over ruts and cried out again when they were carrying him through the narrow passages and alleys of the Savoy to his own house. Sam had put it about that his master had been set upon by thieves up St Giles' way.

'What's he been up to now, mistress?' Margaret stared at Marwood, who stared blankly back. 'That's his best suit. It's ruined.'

It wasn't the suit that mattered. They both knew that.

Marwood's clothes were on the chest opposite the bed. The two women had stripped him, ignoring his weak protests. They exchanged few words as they worked. They had nursed Marwood before. His body was scarred with old wounds and marked with new bruises and grazes. They eased a nightgown over his head and half-carried, half-dragged him to the bed.

The sight of him moved Cat, though she did her best to pretend to herself and everyone else that she was perfectly indifferent to his damaged nakedness. Marwood was a clerk, for God's sake, not a soldier, and yet time and again he found himself in situations he was shockingly ill-equipped to deal with.

His head turned slowly towards her. 'Madam,' he said weakly. He cleared his throat and tried to moisten his lips. 'You must know I suffer myself to be bruised and bloodied solely to vex you and Margaret.'

Relief poured over her. He might be wounded but he was still himself, despite the laudanum.

'But I can't lie here for long. I must—'

'You'll lie there until Margaret and I decide otherwise,' she interrupted. 'I'm by no means persuaded that the blows to your head haven't addled your wits.'

'Where's Iredale?'

'Safe and where you can find him. Sam's standing guard. You're not to trouble yourself about that now.'

Marwood licked his lips. Margaret cradled his head in one hand and brought the mug to his mouth.

'Patience?' he said afterwards. 'The maidservant?'

'I left her where she was. She didn't like it, but there wasn't anything she could do. I gave her a shilling and told her that you had to talk to Iredale, and that he would come back soon. I said we wished neither of them any ill, though I'm not sure she believed me. I hope I did right?'

There was no reply. Marwood's eyes were closed. He was breathing more slowly now.

Margaret looked across the bed at Cat. 'Will you be staying, mistress? I can make up a bed if you like.'

Cat shook her head. 'I'll come in the morning.'

Marwood's eyelids fluttered. 'You saw the acrostic in my letter. I thought you would.'

'Just as well I did.'

'I had the devil of a job to make it spell Iredale.'

'You left out an "e". Go to sleep.'

Five minutes later, he didn't stir when Cat rose to leave. Margaret came downstairs with her.

'You won't go back to Henrietta Street by yourself.'

'I'll do as I please.'

By the street door, Sam rose from his stool, and looked from one woman to the other.

Margaret folded her arms. 'He'll fetch you a chair with two stout bearers,' she said. 'He drinks with them all so he knows who can be trusted. He'll find you a link boy too.'

Cat looked from Margaret to Sam, who was already fastening his cloak. She recognized defeat when she saw it.

'And there's a fire in the parlour. You can wait there.'

When Sam was gone and the door safely barred, Margaret settled Cat by the fire and brought her biscuits and a glass of wine to recruit her strength.

Cat closed her eyes. She was very tired. Marwood's best suit, Margaret had said. He had been dressed for wooing. Brennan had told her that Marwood arrived at the Hadgrafts' house as he himself was storming out. Did that mean that Marwood's desire for Grace was as hot as ever, despite her father's folly? He was fool enough to ruin himself for love.

She heard a cough and opened her eyes. Margaret was hovering near the door. 'Mistress,' she said, 'a man in my lord's livery brought a letter today. Did Sam tell you? I don't know what to do. It might be important, but I don't want to trouble master with it, not now.'

In this house, my lord meant Lord Arlington. Margaret wouldn't break the seal on a letter to Marwood. Besides, she probably wouldn't be able to read much of it, even if she did, for anything much longer than a row of simple words was difficult for her to decipher, especially if the writing was hurried or slovenly. Cat also knew that Margaret, who was given to flaunting her skill with reading and writing to Sam, did not care to have her limitations in this area widely advertised.

'Give it to me,' she said. 'I'll make it right with your master. If need be, I can write to my lord to explain he's been attacked in the street.'

Cat broke the seal and unfolded the letter. It contained a few lines from Mr Gorvin, the principal clerk in Arlington's office at Whitehall. My lord had sent word of the change of plan. Rather than delay any longer in London, Marwood should immediately assemble any papers relating to his current business and bring them down to Euston.

'It can wait,' Cat said. 'We'll show him in the morning.'

In the absence of Their Majesties and so much of the court, the excitement had drained away from Whitehall. It was as if the sun and the moon had removed themselves from the sky, and the stars had followed suit, leaving only a handful of insignificant clouds.

On Wednesday, after supper in the Queen's apartments, there were the usual entertainments: dancing, music and games of cards, together with a dish or two of tea, the insipid drink that Her Majesty had insisted was now served. Time dragged: the amusements did not amuse, and the tea did nothing much at all.

For Louise, though, it was at first a comfortable and bless-edly familiar evening. She clung to its diversions as a child clings to home on the evening before he is sent away to live elsewhere. The absence of so many gentlemen came as a relief.

Perhaps, Louise thought, a nunnery might not be so very bad; at least life would be simpler, though considerably more tedious. Then prudence reminded her that hell itself must surely include a chamber where impoverished, well-born virgins were trapped together with nothing to do but gossip among themselves and tell their rosaries.

Monsieur Colbert came in and made himself agreeable to

the company. By and by, he worked his way to Louise, who was at cards, playing for sixpences not gold. For once she was winning.

The ambassador bowed. 'Mademoiselle, I rejoice to tell you that we go down to Euston on Friday. Everything is in train. My lord is already there with Lady Arlington.'

Louise rose from the table in a flutter of panic. 'But monsieur, I have so much to do, so much to pack . . .'

'You mustn't trouble yourself. It's you they want, my dear, not your clothes. And don't worry about the journey. It's a trifle over eighty miles, but the roads are good at this time of year and my flying coach is a miracle of comfort. We shall put up for the night on the road, for we don't want you and Madame Colbert to arrive at Euston fatigued and jolted to death, do we? Are you looking forward to it? I know we are, after the noise and stink of London.'

'Oh indeed,' Louise said mechanically, knowing what politeness required, the meaningless response rising effortlessly to her lips. 'What a joy it will be to breathe the sweet air of the country again.'

Colbert smiled at her. 'And not merely the air will be sweet, eh? I'm sure you'll find sweetness of all sorts to enchant you there.'

Louise felt her colour rising. The ambassador moved away, leaving the insinuation trailing behind him.

Before she could turn back to the card table, a tall and splendidly dressed figure cut his way through the crowd to her side. He bowed absurdly low, his wig glinting golden in the candlelight.

'Mademoiselle,' said the Duke of Buckingham, 'you look enchanting this evening.'

'I heard you were in Newmarket, Your Grace.'

'How could I linger there when you were here? Truly, you are God's most lovely angel sent by divine benevolence to walk among us humble mortals and show us the path to heaven.'

She did not reply. What could one say to such a tedious, overblown compliment?

'Oh cruel one to show me such a stony face,' he murmured. 'How have I earned your displeasure?'

'What did your creature do to the Chevalier?'

Buckingham spread his hands wide. 'Nothing in the world. My man looked for him, as you wished, but he couldn't find him. He seems to have vanished from the face of the earth. Perhaps he has gone back to France.'

Louise lowered her voice to a whisper. 'Are you sure your man didn't kill him?'

The Duke's face became a mask of mock horror. 'Of course not. How could you even ask such a thing?'

'Then he's still alive?'

'That I cannot tell you.'

Louise looked at the Duke's blotched face, at the network of veins that criss-crossed the flushed skin, at the blackened teeth and the nose like a chicken's beak, at the bright, watery eyes and the falsely youthful curls.

'I don't believe you,' she said, and turned away.

CHAPTER TWENTY-NINE

WHEN I AWOKE, my head was clear. Someone was
snoring.

I tugged back the bed curtain. Gradually I made out a
huddled shape in the chair by the empty fireplace.

'Margaret?' I said. Then again, louder: 'Margaret.'

The poor woman struggled to her feet. The blanket that
covered her fell to the floor. She stumbled towards the bed
and stared down at me.

'You're alive,' she said hoarsely. 'God be praised.'

'Of course I'm alive. And I need the pot.'

'Who attacked you?'

'Iredale, of course. I was following Patience.'

My head hurt and my body was feeble, but my mind was
sharp enough. Margaret helped me use the pot. She insisted
I went back to bed, and I made only token resistance.

'Where's Sam?' I asked.

'Downstairs,' she said. 'By the street door.' She noticed
my expression and explained: 'In case we had visitors. Also,
he couldn't sleep in our bed, could he? Not unless he wanted

to share with that stinking knave you brought back with you.'

Margaret went away, and I heard her calling to Sam. When she returned, she brought a foul-tasting drink of her own concoction, which she assured me was an infallible specific for such injuries as mine. Whatever the truth, I was soon asleep again.

The murmur of voices roused me. The bed curtains were still open, and I knew from the light that the morning was considerably advanced. Cat and Margaret were conferring by the window. They turned as they heard me stir.

'How are you?' Cat said.

'Better, I think.'

Margaret bustled to the bed and gave me more of her medicine. 'Mistress Hakesby's brought more laudanum.'

'I don't need it.'

'Yes, you do,' Cat said. 'Open your mouth. Lean forward and drink this.'

I was in no condition to resist. Afterwards I sank back on the pillows, and willed the soothing draught to do its work quickly. Margaret gathered up my filthy clothes from the top of the chest.

Cat said in a voice too low for Margaret to hear, 'Iredale and Pharamond met Mademoiselle de Keroualle in Dieppe. Do you understand what I'm saying?'

'Yes. But . . .'

'Hush. Pharamond's real name is the Chevalier de Vire. He is a nobleman by birth, but he's also a penniless rogue living on his wits and making love to any woman who's fool enough to let him. Mademoiselle is half in love with him and half afraid of him.'

Margaret glanced in our direction and went away, leaving me alone with Cat. She perched on the side of the bed.

'The Frenchman and Iredale preyed on her when they were all at Dieppe and waiting for a passage across the Channel. She lost a fortune she doesn't have by playing cards with them. Once they reached London, they started dunning her. Are you still listening?'

'Go on,' I said. Iredale had not told me Pharamond's true identity or the unsavoury details of what happened in Dieppe.

'She foolishly confided her troubles to Buckingham, who sent Durrell to warn them off. That must have been on the Saturday evening, the twenty-third of September. Iredale's alive, you say. Which means that Pharamond must have been the man with no face at Chard Lane.'

Though my body was weak, my mind seemed to be working remarkably well. Sometimes, I had noticed, laudanum clarified mental faculties rather than clouded them. 'Buckingham set this in train. And Durrell went too far.'

'Durrell always goes too far,' Cat said, her voice hardening. 'You know that.'

Neither of us spoke. We were both thinking about her late husband, old Hakesby. He had been ailing and cantankerous towards the end of his life, though he had died at Durrell's hand as gallantly as any man could.

'You had a letter from Mr Gorvin yesterday,' Cat said in a strained voice, a little more loudly than necessary. 'I took the liberty of opening it.'

'Where is it?' I tried to sit up and failed. 'Let me see.'

She fetched the letter from the mantelpiece and handed it to me.

I read the note in a moment. 'I must go to Euston directly.' I began to drag myself out of bed.

'Not today,' Cat said, pushing me back against the pillows and pulling up the covers. 'Probably not tomorrow either. I'll come back later today and write a reply for you. And there's something else we must discuss. There's more to this matter than you might think.'

'Now,' I said like a petulant child. 'Tell me now.'

'Later. It will keep.'

'But where are you going?' I said, unwilling for her to leave me to my own company.

'I'm awaited – I'm pressed for time.' She was moving towards the door as she spoke but, when she reached it, she paused and glanced back. 'Besides, you have other business to deal with here. Have they told you?'

'Business? What business?'

Cat ignored the question. I listened to her footsteps almost running down the stairs, as if glad to be free of me. Neither of us had mentioned Grace Hadgraft but her invisible presence lay between us.

Cat found Brennan in the part of the site facing Chard Lane, which was where the principal range of the old almshouse had stood. The trenches for the new foundations were already crumbling, and puddles of rainwater had formed in the mud. Her partner was conferring with the foreman, who had been kept on when the other labourers were dismissed, though he now insisted on receiving his wages daily and at a higher rate than before.

Brennan looked up as Cat approached and came to meet her. 'You found time to pay us a visit.'

'I was detained.'

'I noticed. We've done most of the work now.'

She bowed her head, as if in submission. He had every right to feel deserted, and there was no point in quarrelling with him. 'How goes it here?'

'We'll be ready to move out by tomorrow afternoon, Saturday at the latest.' There was a hint of pride in his voice. 'All the materials are in the yard now, and most of it accounted for. It's only the site office to sort out.'

'You've done well,' Cat said, meaning it.

'Someone had to do the work.'

'We need to discuss where we go from here, how we can raise money. Shall we find somewhere to dine?'

'If you think it's worth it. And if you can pay for it. I can't.'

Brennan trailed after her as she went into the yard beside the site office. Everything was stacked and covered; and she knew that his pocketbook would contain neatly written lists of the materials stored there, along with their various quantities, values and other measurements as appropriate, and all as accurately recorded as the motions of the stars by an astronomer.

'Let me see the figures,' she said as they went upstairs, knowing that showing her the neatly tabulated evidence of his industry would raise his spirits if anything could.

'Very well.' He already sounded slightly mollified. 'But I warn you, it doesn't—'

A hammering on the street door interrupted him. They exchanged glances. Brennan went to answer the knocking, which continued even while he was unbarring the door.

Willoughby Rush was on the doorstep. 'Ha.' He lowered

his stick. 'I feared you might have gone already.' He bustled into the house, forcing Brennan to step aside. 'Good day to you.' He nodded at Cat, who was coming down the stairs. 'Is there somewhere we can talk privately?'

She led him up to the office and offered him the only chair the room contained. She sat on a stool.

Rush gestured with the stick towards Brennan, who was standing in the doorway, half in, half out of the office. 'Do we need him?'

'Yes,' Cat said. 'Mr Brennan and I are partners, and we carry on the business together.'

Rush grunted, and Brennan took the remaining stool.

The magistrate's chair was by the window. He glanced outside at the yard below, and at the almshouse site beyond. 'You're almost done here by the look of it.'

'We should be out by the end of the week,' Brennan said.

Rush ignored him. 'It can't be easy for you, madam. A project this size, it sucks up credit like a sponge, eh? I doubt it left you with much time for other business either.'

'We manage, sir. Thank you.'

'I'm glad to hear it.' His face was redder than usual, and the pockmarks seemed deeper. 'Still, this is a sorry affair. The project itself is sound enough. That's why I was willing to put money into it at the start. But I should have realized that nothing under Hadgraft's direction could prosper.'

'Do you know what will happen to the site now, sir?' Brennan said.

Rush looked mildly startled, as though the door handle had demonstrated an ability to speak. 'Well, not to mince the matter, that's what I want to talk about today.'

'I assume the lease will be sold to help satisfy Mr Hadgraft's creditors,' Cat said. 'With the rest of his possessions.'

'He's not been declared as bankrupt,' Rush said. The corners of his little mouth turned up with amusement at the thought. 'Yet.'

'It won't be long,' Cat said.

'True. A day or two at best. I warrant there are at least half a dozen lawyers sniffing around the carcass of his estate already. But they will find that the lease on this site does not form part of it.'

The magistrate's words so surprised Brennan that he wobbled on his stool and had to put out a hand to steady himself. Cat drew in her breath sharply.

'You weren't expecting that, I see,' Rush said smugly.

'Then who does have the lease now?'

'It formed part of Mistress Hadgraft's dowry.'

'*Formed?*'

'Just so. Mistress Hadgraft was married yesterday afternoon and, under the terms of the settlement, the lease and any profits deriving from it go to her husband, to be held in trust and to pass after his death to the heirs of her body. In the meantime, her husband has the unconditional use of her estate.' He grinned, revealing his three remaining teeth, two above and one below. 'It's all mine now, madam. And so is she.'

It had been a Fleet wedding conducted according to the forms of the Established Church. By a neat irony, the clergyman had been driven to take sanctuary there by his debts. He was now drinking himself to oblivion, but he was still an ordained clergyman, and he had been tolerably sober,

Rush said, when he conducted the ceremony. Any court in the land, whether lay or ecclesiastical, would uphold the legality of the marriage.

The ceremony had been paid for by the groom, and duly witnessed by gentlemen of unimpeachable veracity who had the honour to be intimate with Mr Rush. Afterwards, while the wedding party was dining at the Devil Tavern nearby, several legal documents were signed and witnessed by these same gentlemen. The papers concerned the bride's dowry and the precise terms of the marriage settlement. All parties professed themselves delighted by the arrangements.

'So you see,' Mr Rush said to Cat and Brennan, 'all's well that ends well. Faith, it's like a comedy at the theatre. I also have the lease on Hadgraft's house, and the contents, including his plate, as well as a few other trifles. There's one thing to be said for having a lawyer as your father-in-law. You can trust him to make sure everything's watertight and wind-tight. Mark you, I had my own man go over the papers with a toothcomb before I put my signature to them. Poor Hadgraft won't have a pot to call his own by the time his creditors have finished with him.' Rush threw back his head and gave a bark of laughter. 'We'll have to find a place for him in our new almshouse.'

He drained his glass and called for another bottle to drink Mr Hadgraft's health. He had invited Cat and Brennan to dine with him while they discussed the terms of the new arrangement. They were in a private room at the Three Crowns on Snow Hill.

Rush's proposal was straightforward. The three of them would renew the agreement that Cat and Brennan had previously had with Mr Hadgraft, but with Rush himself as the client. He proposed only one other variation to the contract, which concerned the new houses to be built on the waste ground after the almshouse had been erected. He offered Cat and Brennan the option of purchasing at a preferential rate the thirty-year lease on the last house to be completed, provided the entire work was finished within the twelve months. If they failed in this, their fee would be reduced by a fifth.

'That leaves us very little leeway,' Cat pointed out. 'And winter lasts so long these days that we couldn't resume work until next year is well advanced. But if you allowed us fifteen months . . .'

'I fear I cannot oblige you,' Rush said with a sigh he did not pretend was sorrowful. 'I shall have to look elsewhere.'

Brennan, whose expression had grown increasingly anguished, tried to speak, but Cat interrupted him. 'Another of our difficulties is this. You saw the yard at the site office this morning. You saw the materials stored there. We ordered them for this project in good faith. They were delivered in good faith. And now we have to pay for them. Our suppliers won't wait twelve months for their money.'

Rush raised the wine bottle. 'We all have our crosses, madam. But I'm—'

'Mr Brennan has the facts and figures at his fingertips. He will show the papers to you now if you wish. But we have bought goods for this project on credit and the payments are falling due. In order to meet them, we would need to look elsewhere for smaller commissions to bring in the necessary funds, for these would bring us a swifter return. We would regret it greatly, sir, but if we ourselves are to avoid insolvency, you understand that we have little choice in the matter. Moreover, you might also consider that it may well take you months to find another builder who is both capable and willing to do the work, whereas we have done all the preliminaries and could start tomorrow if we can but agree terms today.'

Rush held up his hand. 'Enough, madam, enough. I catch your meaning perfectly. My good fortune in love has made me generous. Let us say that I pay at once for these materials as an advance on your fees. That's on condition that the total is not absurd, and your figures and your stock match the bills. In return, you complete the almshouse and my houses within the twelvemonth. And if you fail, your fee will be reduced by a quarter, diminishing by a further three per centum with each month's delay after that.'

'Fourteen months,' Cat said. 'We cannot do it in less. Nor could anyone else.'

He scowled at her. 'Very well. It goes against the grain, but let us shake hands on fourteen.'

The terms were hard but, if all went well, not impossible. Cat looked at Brennan, who took a deep breath and gave her a scarcely perceptible nod.

'But if we agree to this,' she went on, 'we shall also need to agree a schedule of stage payments. We cannot live on air while we build the almshouse and your houses.'

'You drive a hard bargain.'

'Not as hard as yours.'

Rush stared at her. She held his gaze. His sharp, irregular features rearranged themselves into an unexpectedly charming smile.

'Well, madam. You have vanquished me. Here's my hand on it. Let's drink to my almshouse. And my street of houses.'

'And to your marriage, sir,' Cat said politely.

For an instant her imagination conjured up an unwelcome image of the pretty young bride in the arms of this ugly brute more than twice her age. At least, she thought at the same time, James Marwood can't have the vain bitch now.

'Indeed.' Rush grinned, revealing his three teeth again. 'I am a fortunate man.'

CHAPTER THIRTY

'I'LL BE MASTER in my own house,' I said. 'Bring me my breeches.'

Margaret glowered at me. I was sitting up in bed. I felt as weak as a newborn calf, but anger gave me strength to glower back at her. She gave way and helped me dress, grumbling all the while. Between us we hauled up the breeches, tucked my shirt into them and fastened a belt around my waist. She pushed my arms into my gown and knelt to put the slippers on my feet.

'Thank you,' I said.

'You're mad, master.'

'That's as may be. But I'm going downstairs and you will help me.'

As we descended, Margaret's face grew redder and shinier from the effort of supporting much of my weight. Halfway down, I was obliged to sit on a stair to restore my strength. Sam was waiting in the hall below. He brought a stool for me to sit on.

I gripped Sam's arm. 'Help me up. We'll go on now.'

Between the three of us, we managed to negotiate the short but steep flight of steps down to the kitchen, which lay partly beneath the level of the ground outside. One of the doors it contained led to the narrow closet where Sam and Margaret slept. The space therein was barely large enough for their pallet bed. There was one small window, giving a partial prospect of the overflowing Savoy graveyard, which was still digesting the influx of corpses from the exceptionally calamitous outbreak of plague six years earlier.

The door was bolted on the outside. Cat had ordered Iredale to be shut in there in case he tried to escape. Despite the loss of their own bedchamber, I was willing to wager twenty pounds that the Witherdines had obeyed her without a question or even a grumble, at least to her face.

'He's been as quiet as a mouse,' Sam whispered hoarsely.

'He's got water,' Margaret said, as if defending herself from an accusation of inhumanity that only she had heard. 'And a bit of bread to eat. And a pot to piss in.'

'And our bed,' Sam said, aggrieved.

I lowered myself on to the bench by the table. Sam laid his pistol down and murmured to me that it was loaded. Margaret picked up the poker. Cutlass in hand, Sam advanced to the door and cautiously drew back the bolt. Their precautions struck me as ridiculously overblown, and I had to repress a smile.

Iredale had been sitting on the low bed and leaning back against the wall by the window. As the door opened, he scrambled to his feet. In the gloom of his hiding place in my Lord Bristol's outhouse, he had been little more than a shadowy outline. Now I saw him clearly for the first time.

He was a well-set-up fellow in the prime of life, in

appearance not unlike the man whose body had been found at the almshouse. His eyes were large and expressive. His features were regular and in other circumstances might even have been accounted handsome. But what I noticed most of all was how filthy he was. If I had met him in the street, I would have put him down as a vagrant, and a villainous one at that. His coat and breeches were muddy and torn. The shirt was closer to brown in colour than white. His neck was bare and his stockings had puddled around his ankles. Lice crawled busily among the short hairs on his scalp.

He stepped forward and tried to bow. But when Sam growled and raised the cutlass, he jerked back and stumbled against the bed. 'Truly,' he said in a rush, 'I mean no harm.' He lifted his hands, palms towards us, in a gesture of submission. 'Where am I?'

'At my house. You're safe here.'

'May God bless you, sir. I—'

'As long as you give me no trouble and tell me freely everything I want to know.'

'Anything, sir, anything.'

'The gold you stored at Paddington.' I saw him stiffen. 'How did you come by so much money? Not honestly, I'll be bound.'

'I was lucky at cards and at dice, sir. I played a good deal in France, you see, to pass the time. Everyone did.'

'And more recently you sold private intelligence from the council to Mr Hadgraft. Did you have other customers as well? I fancy you did.'

Iredale tried to smile. 'I'm a poor man, sir. If a gentleman makes me a small present of money for some little service I do for him, what's the harm? No one suffers by it.'

'Only the council's reputation and the government's revenues.' I was beginning to dislike the man and his plausible manner. 'And also any individuals who lost money as a result of your corruption.'

He held up his palms again in a gesture I suspected was habitual, along with the rueful, insinuating smile that accompanied it. My dislike hardened, and it was that as much as anything else that made me decide to ignore the prohibition in Lord Arlington's letter.

'Your box of gold contained something else,' I went on. 'A schedule of debts. Sums owed by a certain lady to you and Monsieur de Vire.'

'Ah, the cards.' He waved his hand, dismissing them. 'I forgive the lady her debts. She was young and foolish.'

'It seems to me that you and the Chevalier were foolish when you set out to fleece a lady with powerful friends.'

He cleared his throat. 'Fleece, sir? That's a hard word.'

It struck me as interesting that he had so easily forgiven the debts of Mademoiselle de Keroualle. When all's said and done, a debt is a debt to a greedy man like Iredale, however come by. I remembered the embroidered purse that he had concealed in his lodging. A love token to the Chevalier from the poor foolish girl? I also recalled the scrap of paper that we found in the dead man's shoe, with a fragment of Iredale's address in the same childish handwriting as the schedule of debts in Iredale's box.

I drew a bow at a venture. 'There's more,' I said, 'isn't there? The lady was in love with Monsieur de Vire. She wrote to him, here in England. She sent him your address in Swan Yard, hoping he'd deal with you on her behalf. Tell me, where are those letters now?'

262

'Letters?' Iredale's eyes flickered, and I knew my words had sparked a response. 'What letters?'

Weariness rolled over me. 'Remember,' I said. 'A word from me to Lord Arlington, and you will be taken up and tried for the murder of Monsieur de Vire. As well as the assault on me.' He tried to protest but I waved him into silence. 'Then you will be hanged, as surely as the sun will rise tomorrow. Is that really what you want?'

The rogue had the impertinence to smile, even now trying to cozen me into liking him. 'You are too sharp for me, sir. Yes, there were letters, *billets doux* as the French call them. Monsieur de Vire kept them on his person. If anyone has them now, it will be whoever killed him.'

It occurred to me that perhaps the letters might not be important now. The Chevalier was dead, and he belonged to a time before the King had set his heart on Mademoiselle de Keroualle.

But Iredale was ahead of me. 'If they were just *billets doux*, they wouldn't matter now, if de Vire is in his grave. She can't hanker after him, and he can't pester her for money. But you see, sir, she was so hot for him that she lay with him in Dieppe. At least two or three times. The Chevalier told me that those letters make it clear as God's heaven that she's no more a maid than I am. Does the King want a virgin in his bed? If the answer be yes, he must look elsewhere.'

Before the King went to Newmarket, he had commanded that a small drawing room should be set aside for the use of Mademoiselle de Keroualle. What the Queen had thought of this, no one knew or dared enquire. She was a wise woman and she kept her own counsel. Her manner towards her maid of honour did not perceptibly alter, and for this Louise was grateful.

On her last day at Whitehall, Thursday, Louise sat reading in this salon, with her lumpen English maid and one of the Queen's seamstresses at work with their needles, adding lace to the hems of new shifts and altering two petticoats. She was in low spirits.

After a while, Madame des Bordes came in to keep Louise company. The visitor talked comfortably of the past, of the days when Madame the Duchess of Orleans had been alive, and she and her ladies had shuttled between Saint-Cloud and the Palais Royal and Saint Germain.

'Pray don't talk of those times,' Louise said, interrupting the older woman in mid-sentence. 'The past is past.'

Madame des Bordes glanced at her. 'You prefer to talk of the future?'

Louise opened her mouth to speak and then stopped. She wanted to ask the older woman if there was news of the Chevalier de Vire. She could not believe he was dead. He told her more than once that he was a lucky man. Surely there was still the faintest possibility that he would appear at the last moment and make everything right for her?

But she had told Madame des Bordes too much about her confidential affairs already. Suppose confiding in her in the first place had been a terrible mistake, yet another in a catalogue of errors? Perhaps that plain, motherly face was the mask of a spy.

The more Louise thought about it, the more obvious it seemed. After all, Madame des Bordes was the Queen's *femme de chambre*, and probably Colbert was paying her something as well. Thanks to Arlington, she had an English pension now. She must know where her own best interests lay, and they did not lie in serving a penniless maid of honour. But Louise might not be penniless much longer. She shivered.

'Are you cold, my dear? Shall we ring for coals?'

'No, thank you. I do very well as I am.'

It seemed to Louise that suspicion had crept like smoke into the air of the room. Would it always be like this now, never trusting anyone? From now on, would kindness always be a mask for self-interest?

The two women sat in silence until it was time to go down to dinner with the rest of Her Majesty's household.

I refused to go back to bed.

Once Iredale had been returned to his temporary prison, I sat by the parlour fire with a blanket over my knees and writing materials beside me on the table.

What the devil was I to do with the man? If I set him free, he would be at the mercy of Durrell. The only scheme I had was to send him back to his hiding place in my Lord Bristol's outhouse, where Patience Noone was waiting for him. But they might be discovered there, whether by Durrell or someone else. Or they might run away.

In any case, I had no faith in Iredale. He had already tacitly admitted that it was he who attacked me when I was following Patience on Tuesday night, not some nameless rogues.

I pushed the problem aside. I was ferociously hungry. I could not remember when I had last eaten. I rang the bell and ordered the Witherdines to bring me a roll and a bowl of broth, more laudanum, Gorvin's letter from my bedchamber, and a scuttle of coals.

The food refreshed me. My head still ached, but the pain was less acute than it had been. I took another dose of laudanum and replied to Gorvin. My language was guarded – I did not know how far my lord had taken him into his confidence about the details of the Chard Lane matter and its ramifications – and I said merely that I had been attacked and robbed on my way home the previous evening.

I had no alternative but to recruit my strength at home, I wrote, but, God willing, I would be well enough to leave for Euston tomorrow. I begged him to bespeak a place on my behalf on the daily coach reserved for my lord's business. Once the letter was sealed, I sent Sam to dispatch it by one of the boys who lingered outside the porter's lodge at the Savoy's Strand gateway.

Afterwards I dozed in the chair. I slipped by degrees into the familiar but strangely disturbing dream in which my house was burning down, and the dead were rising from the Savoy graveyard for the Second Coming of Our Lord. Soon I was surrounded by their skeletal figures, and the heat of the flames lapped at my face, and the stones of my house were cracking and crumbling in the heat.

Death had come for me at last.

'Wake up. You're on fire.'

I opened my eyes. A strange woman was shaking me. The fire in the hearth was burning high and bright. One of my slippers was smouldering. The woman stamped on it, smothering the flame in its infancy. Before I had a notion of saying anything at all, two words passed unbidden from my lips.

'Dear heart,' I said.

The words came from nowhere. I did not mean to say them or indeed say anything. It was as if my mind were not in my control, as if it were frozen in the vast, blank space that lay between the horror of my dream and my relief at being awake: as if a stranger had usurped the command of my organs of speech. And then I heard myself saying those words again.

'Dear heart.'

CHAPTER THIRTY-ONE

'*W*HAT DID YOU say?'

'Nothing,' Marwood said. He moistened his lips. 'I was dreaming.'

Dreaming of Grace Hadgraft, Cat thought, you poor fool. *Dear heart*, indeed. 'You should be more careful. You nearly set yourself on fire.'

He drew his legs away from the flames. 'I hate this house. Too many ghosts. I must find me another.'

Cat wondered whether the opium had addled his wits.

He cleared his throat. 'What time is it?'

'Near four o'clock. Sam said you've been snoring like a hog.'

'Sam's an impudent rascal.' To her relief, his voice sounded stronger and clearer.

'You're looking better,' she said.

'I am, I think.' He sat up straighter in the chair. 'I wrote to Gorvin myself. I fear I've given you a wasted journey.'

'Not wasted. I rejoice to see you revived.'

'I go to Euston tomorrow.'

'You should rest another day or two first.'

Marwood shook his head, which made him wince. 'My lord wants me. You know what he's like. He doesn't care to be denied.'

Cat sat down on the bench on the other side of the table. 'You may see me as well.'

'Where?'

'Euston. Lord Arlington wants me to advise with Mr Evelyn. My lady said she would send word when I should come, though she hasn't yet. Perhaps she's forgotten.'

'You at Euston . . .' he said softly, considering the possibility.

'Sam told me you talked to Iredale,' she went on, returning to a safely neutral topic. 'Did you learn anything new?'

'That he's a cunning rogue with a clever tongue in his head.'

Marwood fell silent. He seemed abstracted, as if his mind were a hundred miles away. Cat didn't try to break the silence. She knew that she should tell him about Grace Hadgraft and Willoughby Rush. The idea of causing him yet more pain held her back, though this coexisted in her mind with a desire to hurt him.

He glanced at her and smiled. He looked surprised but glad to see her there. 'Iredale told me something new,' he said. 'Mademoiselle de Keroualle was so mad for the Chevalier that she lay with him. And then she wrote letters of love that made quite clear what had passed between them. When Durrell killed the Chevalier, he must have searched the body when he stripped him. Which means that Buckingham probably has those letters now. He knows she's lost her maidenhead.'

Her eyes met his. 'If that's true, does it mean he has the

power to destroy her chances with the King? Unless he wants to influence her when she becomes the King's mistress.'

She watched him weighing her words. He looked up, about to speak, but she held up a hand to stop him.

'But there's more to this than meets the eye, isn't there? It's not just a matter of a pretty young woman catching the King's eye, and Buckingham trying to squeeze advantage from the situation. There's also the point that the French ambassador is encouraging the liaison by every means in his power. Which means that his master has ordered him to do so. And Lord Arlington and his lady are also cultivating her as if she were an heiress.'

There was a spark of understanding in Marwood's eyes. 'Arlington told me this affair touched on a state secret. He's now forbidden me to investigate anything further concerning the court or those two pieces of paper. And now we know why. The King of France, and indeed Arlington himself, want the King to have a French Catholic mistress in his bed. A pliant girl who will do what they tell her in the interests of France. Someone to whisper in his ear whatever they want to say. Because the King will listen to words that come with her caresses. And no doubt the French will soon hear what the King says to her as well. A man doesn't put a guard on his tongue when he talks idly to his mistress.'

'To put it plainly,' Cat said, 'they want a spy in the King's bed. And—'

There was a mighty clattering and shouting below.

Marwood swore. He struggled to his feet.

There was the sound of a shot.

* * *

I was so weak that I couldn't prevent Cat from running ahead of me. My head swimming, I staggered down the stairs to the kitchen.

The room was dimly lit at the best of times, and by now the daylight was retreating and the shadows were on the march. There was a thrashing, grunting, swearing mass of bodies on the floor. The air was dense with acrid smoke from the discharge of the pistol. The gunpowder failed to mask the stench of tallow. The candles had been overturned in the commotion.

Most of the illumination came from the fire, which cast a red, baleful glow across the flagged floor. Over the coals hung an iron pot whose unregarded contents were spitting and spilling on to the coals below.

Despite the gloom, I saw at a glance that the door to the Witherdines' closet was open. As my eyes adjusted, the mass on the floor resolved itself into three bodies. Poor Margaret was somewhere underneath. Sam was on top of the pile, beating Iredale about the head with his fists.

'Sam,' I shouted from the doorway. 'Enough.'

He ignored me. Cat snatched his cutlass from the table and slid the blade past his neck until the tip rested against the collar of Iredale's coat. Sam felt the touch of the steel sliding against his skin. He froze, his right fist poised in mid-air.

'Sam. Get Margaret up.' I snatched a stick from the table. 'Iredale – stay on the floor, face down, arms out flat, or by God you're a dead man.'

I sat on the bench and leant forward on the table, resting on my elbows. The spurt of energy had drained me of life. Little by little, a semblance of order returned to the kitchen. Cat gave Sam the cutlass and told him to stand over Iredale and stab him between the shoulder blades if he made mischief. She took a taper from the fire and relit the two candles, placing one on the dresser and the other on the table.

Margaret was bruised and breathless but otherwise unhurt. She went into the scullery to tidy herself and wash her face in cold water. On the way back, she kicked Iredale on the side of his knee, making him yelp with pain. In the years I had known her, it was almost the only occasion I had seen her exhibit malice towards another living creature.

'What happened?' I said when all was calm.

'I was out in the yard,' Sam said. 'Margaret was in here, and—'

'He cried out,' Margaret interrupted. 'Said he had a pain in his belly, and a terrible thirst, and he was dying. Begging me for water. I brought a jug but when I opened the door, he sprang up and knocked me down and seized the pistol, and—'

'Villain,' Sam snarled, leaning more heavily on the cutlass and eliciting a scream from Iredale. 'Coward. I'll cut your liver out, so help me God.'

'Enough,' I said. 'Let Margaret go on.'

'He cocked the pistol,' she went on, 'and said I had to let him out of the house or he'd kill me. Then I rammed my knee up his manhood, and the gun went off, and Sam came in.'

Iredale was whimpering quietly. Had he not put my people in danger, and Cat and myself as well, I might almost have felt sorry for him. As it was, I felt anger, cold and implacable. 'Put him back in the closet,' I said. 'But first make sure it's secure.'

Margaret picked up the candle from the table and went into

the little room. I had caused bars to be set on the window to the graveyard, and the glass to be fixed in place so the casement could not be opened. She poked and prodded the mattress and examined the door and walls.

She turned back to me. 'A mouse couldn't get out.'

'Sam,' I said, 'I want the dog in his kennel. Lash his wrists and tie him to the window bar. Iredale, if you give us more trouble, Sam can do as he pleases with you.'

Iredale turned his head to look at me. 'I helped you,' he said thickly. 'I saved your life.'

'You lie,' I said. 'It was you who attacked me when I was following Patience. And for that you can slither into your kennel on your belly.'

Marwood refused to be put to bed. Instead, they helped him back to his chair in the parlour. He asked for brandy and gave Margaret the key to the cupboard where it was kept. Cat poured it herself, wondering if it would revive him or send him to sleep.

'You were hard on Iredale,' she said when the servants had left them alone. 'He gave you shelter, and he brought your letter to me.'

Marwood looked at her. His eyes seemed feverishly bright and unusually blue. 'He attacked my people in my own house. I can't let that pass.'

It was a fair point. Loyalty worked both ways. Cat said, 'What will you do with him? You can't leave him in there to rot. And what will happen when you go to Euston? Would you turn Sam and Margaret into your gaolers?'

'I've a notion how to manage that. Let me think on it a little.'

She went on in a lower voice, 'There's something I must tell you. Something about the Hadgrafts.'

He turned to face her again. 'What?'

'Mr Brennan said he saw you at their house on Tuesday evening. Then you must know that Hadgraft's ship miscarried and he is ruined.'

Marwood nodded and looked away. If only, she thought, there were an art to read the heart's desires in a man's face.

'Mr Rush has taken over the lease on the almshouse site,' she said.

'He bought it from Hadgraft?'

'He didn't buy it. He acquired it as part of Grace's dowry. They were married yesterday afternoon.'

Marwood tossed off the rest of his brandy and set down the glass on the table. He stared at the fire. She watched him uneasily. After a moment, he glanced at her.

'Pray,' he said, 'would you bring me pen and ink and paper? But first a little more brandy.'

CHAPTER THIRTY-TWO

M Y LETTER SOON brought an answer, though not one I had expected.

When I heard the knock at the door, I was alone in the parlour. Cat had returned to Henrietta Street, prudently locking away the brandy before she went.

I heard the scrape of Sam's crutch as he came down the passage to the door, and the sound of the shutter sliding back. There was an exchange of words, but I couldn't distinguish what was being said. Then came the familiar racket of bolts and bars and chains, followed by heavy footsteps outside the parlour. The door opened, and there was Mr Under Secretary Williamson, with Sam hovering awkwardly at his shoulder. I struggled to rise.

'Sit, Marwood.'

My old master advanced into the room. With unusual tact, Sam withdrew, closing the door behind him. Williamson took the other chair and sat facing me. He peered at my face, moving the candle to see it better.

'What have you been doing to yourself this time?'

'I was attacked on the street the other night.'

He looked disapprovingly but said nothing.

'Sir, I had not dreamed that my letter would bring you in person. I am most—'

'I have an engagement in the City in half an hour,' Williamson interrupted in a harsh voice. 'I merely pause for a moment on my journey. It doesn't inconvenience me in the slightest, or I should not be here. It saves me the trouble of writing to you.'

'May I hope you will be able to grant my request?' I asked.

'If you want my help, you must tell me a good deal more.'

I hesitated only a second. 'I've a man in custody in a closet off my kitchen. He has enemies searching for him. He's also untrustworthy, and he will flee if he can find an opportunity. But my lord has commanded me to wait on him at Euston. I must keep the man safe until my return – and also prevent him from escaping while I'm gone.'

'You wrote that he's connected to the Chard Lane matter you mentioned to me.'

'Yes. Which my lord has desired me to enquire into.'

'Name?'

'Iredale. John Iredale.'

Williamson grunted. 'He has some small employment at the Council for Foreign Plantations, I think? And he had his place there through the good offices of the Duke of Buckingham.'

'Yes, sir.' It was never wise to underestimate Williamson's grasp of detail.

'And he's now in danger from Roger Durrell?'

'Yes, sir.'

'Is he a rogue?'

'Without a doubt.'

'Could you make out a case against him that would stand up in a court of law?'

'I believe so. I don't think he was responsible for the alms-house murder, but the evidence against him looks black and would probably convince a jury. He's also been selling the council's confidential information. If you would be so good as to issue a warrant authorizing me to lodge him in the Scotland Yard gaol during my absence, it would ease my mind greatly. When my lord returns, he will decide how to resolve the matter.'

'Lord Arlington has not seen fit to mention any of this to me. You ask me to take your word.'

'Yes, sir.'

Williamson considered. In Lord Arlington's absence from Whitehall, he was empowered as my lord's Under Secretary to wield many of the powers my lord usually reserved for himself. One of them was the authority to sign the warrant necessary to confine a prisoner to the gaol.

The prison building was near the Scotland Yard dock, a discreet and convenient place to hold captives under interrogation without the glare of public attention that shone on prisoners placed in Newgate or for that matter the Tower. It was as secure and private as anywhere in the land, and those who administered it in the King's name were not overtroubled by Habeas Corpus or other legal niceties. Over the years I had had several dealings with the chief turnkey, a gross, venal fellow who was nonetheless efficient in the discharge of his office.

'Very well,' Williamson said. 'I'm minded to oblige you.' When I began to express my gratitude, he cut me short. 'But one condition: that you uncover this whole business to me, so far as you know it yourself. I shall make no written memorial of what you tell me, nor will I tell a living soul what I have heard. But if you wish for my signature on this warrant, I must know what I sign my name to.'

Grim-faced, he stared at me with his pale eyes. The temporary disposal of Iredale was what lay on the surface of this discourse between us. Beneath it lay something far more profound and far-reaching, whose consequences were unknowable.

Sometimes in this life a man must decide to place his trust in another. It is always a decision fraught with danger. I trusted few people, and I suspected that Mr Williamson trusted fewer still. He was now offering to trust me, despite the fact I no longer served him. But in return I must trust him.

My head swam with tiredness, laudanum and brandy. My eyelids were heavy. But I made my decision without fuss or delay.

'In truth, sir. I hardly know where to begin. But I will try.'

I felt a curious sense of release, a sense that a load was about to be lightened; perhaps the sensation was akin to the relief a Papist must feel as he kneels in the confessional to unburden his soul to a Jesuit.

'I'm awaited elsewhere,' Williamson said in his grimly practical manner. 'I'd be obliged if you don't delay me any more than you have done already.'

'My difficulty is this, sir,' I went on. 'This strange business has as many malign aspects as the Hydra has heads. It is hard to know which one to cut off first. And I fear another will presently appear in its place.'

* * *

I discovered afterwards that Williamson had brought four soldiers with him. They had been waiting outside the house while we talked. He had intended from the first to grant my request.

The little file of Redcoats clumped down to the kitchen, where Margaret scowled at them and looked at their boots. Williamson hung back in the parlour with the door half-open so he could see but not be seen.

At a word from me, the sergeant unfastened the closet door. Iredale twisted his head and blinked at us. His face was bewildered and terrified.

'On your feet,' the sergeant said.

Iredale scrambled up as far as he could, for his wrists were still tied to the window bar.

'Cut him loose and cuff him,' the sergeant ordered.

'Sir,' Iredale said, 'where are they taking me? For the love of God, don't abandon me.'

'It's for your own safety,' I said, suppressing a twinge of pity. 'The less you struggle, the better it will be.'

While they were cuffing him, I drew the sergeant aside. 'You have Mr Williamson's warrant?'

'Yes, sir.'

I took a sixpence from the pocket of my gown. I gave it to the sergeant. 'Treat him gently if he gives you no trouble.'

'Like a babe in arms, sir.'

'And tell the turnkey at Scotland Yard he will oblige me if he keeps the fellow close. Tell him not to let the prisoner starve, and he'll find me generous.'

Iredale had fallen silent. He suffered himself to be led upstairs and out of the house. There was no help for it: this was the wisest course for all of us, and in any case he deserved it for what he'd done to me and my servants. But the thought of Patience Noone alone in that noisome outbuilding worried me. She had given me only hard words, but her actions had been kind. She was with child. Iredale was her only protector in this hard world. My conscience twitched and scratched like a dog with fleas, and it would not obey when I bid it lie still.

Margaret let out her breath in a rush. 'Look what they brought in with them,' she muttered. 'All that mud. I swept the floor but an hour ago.'

There was no animosity to the words. Her eyes were on the empty closet where Iredale had been. She looked troubled.

Despite her protests, I ordered Margaret to rouse me at five o'clock on Friday morning. I couldn't afford to try Lord Arlington's patience by lingering in London for another day. I slept soundly and I felt much refreshed. My head was clear, and though it still ached, I was the master of myself and my limbs.

One of my lord's coaches left London every day of the week except Sunday, bearing his people, his less important guests and their servants to Suffolk; and every day except Sunday another coach departed from Euston. Gorvin had reserved a place for me on Friday's departure. Dosed with yet more laudanum, I took a hackney from the Strand. Sam attended me, with a variety of weapons distributed about his person in case of trouble from the Duke of Buckingham's people.

We came without incident to Scotland Yard, where the coach and four was waiting to take me up in the courtyard. I squeezed myself into a corner. I found myself facing a young clergyman, a newly minted Master of Arts from

Cambridge who introduced himself as John Banks. Beside me was a perspiring peruke-man taking up two-thirds of the seat, whose name I did not trouble to discover or he to share. Our party was made up with a maidservant wrapped like a parcel in her cloak. She was sitting bolt upright in the far corner, clutching her bundle to her chest as if she feared that the Reverend Mr Banks might try to steal it.

When at last our driver was ready, the coach rumbled under the archway towards the street. Here we were forced to wait. Another, far more splendid equipage was approaching from the direction of the Court Gate. It was a flying coach drawn by six horses, with gilded paintwork and glass windows, and an unfamiliar coat of arms on the door. Half a dozen horsemen, all armed, formed its escort.

'That's the way to travel, sir,' the peruke-man said, his jowls trembling. 'Lucky devils. Why, they'll travel at twice the speed we can, and in thrice the comfort.'

'Whose arms are those?' the clergyman said.

'That's the ambassador's coach, sir,' the maid said.

The two men looked disconcerted as though they had not expected her to be in the possession of a tongue.

'Which ambassador?' I asked.

'The French mounseer and his lady, sir,' she said. 'They're taking my mistress to Euston.'

'And who is your mistress, girl?' the peruke-maker demanded.

'Mamzelle Carwell, sir. Her Majesty's maid of honour.'

CHAPTER THIRTY-THREE

A T TEN O'CLOCK on Friday morning, Cat and Brennan arrived on the doorstep of Mr Rush's house in Hatton Garden. Rush had sent word the previous evening that he wanted to discuss various matters concerning the resumption of work at the almshouse.

'I hope we'll get some money out of him too,' Brennan said.

They found the magistrate toying with a plate of rolls and a jug of cocoa in the dining room. He was also toying with his wife, whom he had set upon his knee for the purpose. The lady was in déshabillé, and he was still in his nightgown. Susannah, the cousin and waiting woman of the new Mrs Rush, was sitting at the other end of the table with her eyes cast down and her lips compressed.

'Mistress Hakesby,' Rush said. 'A very good day to you. And to you . . .' he waved his hand limply towards Brennan. 'Brown?'

'Brennan, sir.'

'Pray allow me to introduce my wife, Mistress Rush. My

love, this is Mistress Hakesby, my surveyor and architect, and her assistant.'

Cat curtsied. 'I've already had the pleasure of meeting Mistress Rush, sir. And Mr Brennan and I are in partnership.'

Grace, held in place by her husband's restraining arm, bobbed her head.

'You must forgive me for receiving you like this,' Rush said smugly. He pinched his wife's cheek, making her gasp. 'You find me still warm from my bed. I charge this lady here with the responsibility for that. Newlyweds, eh? What say you, my dear?'

She forced a smile. 'You're always in the right of it, sir.'

He patted her thigh and whispered in her ear, loudly enough to be heard by everyone in the room. 'That's my little honey-bird.'

'Perhaps, sir,' Cat said, 'we should call again later in the day? We wouldn't wish to inconvenience you for the world.'

Rush stood up abruptly, dislodging his wife, who clutched at the table to retain her balance. 'Nonsense,' he said, knotting the belt of his gown. 'No time like the present. I shan't be long, my dear.' He brushed crumbs from himself to the floor and threw a glance at Susannah. 'And you can make my wife look pretty for me while I'm gone.'

He led the way to his counting house, the sparsely furnished apartment where he conducted his duties as a justice as well as his business affairs. In those few yards, his manner changed, the doting husband becoming the grim-faced man of business. When the door was closed, he turned to Cat.

'You want money from me, no doubt,' he said without any preamble. 'And you shall have it.' He took a bunch of keys from his pocket and unlocked a cupboard, from which he removed a canvas bag. He dropped it on the table. There was a metallic clunk on impact. 'Thirty pounds.'

Brennan suppressed a gasp. It was much more than either he or Cat had hoped for.

'That should keep your creditors at bay,' Rush went on, 'and cover your expenses at the almshouse for a while.' He gestured to one of the stools at the table. 'Count it. I want a receipt.'

He brought pen, ink and paper from the same cupboard. Brennan sat down and untied the strings that secured the bag. Cautiously he shook out the contents. A shining shower of silver and gold scattered across the table and came to rest.

'I'll need an exact account of how you spend it,' Rush went on, 'and I'll inspect your progress at Chard Lane when I return. If it's satisfactory, there will be more.' He looked at Cat and raised his ill-disciplined eyebrows. 'Do you understand, madam? I keep my word, and I expect others to keep theirs. I also expect those I employ to work as diligently in my absence as they do when they are under my eye.'

'You intend to make a journey, sir?' she said, ignoring the warning.

'I shall take my wife to Newmarket for a few days. The world is there now. We leave on Monday. Will you be at your house on Sunday evening?'

'Why?'

'I'd like to call on you. Shall we say five o'clock, if it would not be inconvenient? I desire to familiarize myself with your most recent plans for the site in case I wish to make modifications. And it would be useful to inspect the accounts you kept for Hadgraft. It's important that we both know what we're about as soon as possible.'

'Very well, sir.' Rush's way of doing business was brusque, Cat thought, but at least he was direct and to the point. 'When do you leave on Monday?'

'As early as possible. God willing, I hope to be at Newmarket on the same day.'

'For the races?'

His eyes narrowed momentarily. 'Why else? But I've also a trifle of business to discuss with His Grace of Buckingham. He was in London for a day or two, but I missed him. He's never still for long.'

'Thirty pounds exactly,' Brennan said, and dipped the quill into the inkwell.

The ambassador's coach and six made short work of the miles. Wrapped in her travelling cloak, Louise sat back among the cushions. She was opposite her host and his wife, with her back to the horses. The freshly perfumed interior of the coach was lined with silk, and the seats were upholstered with fine leather. She was agreeably warm despite the chill of the early morning. The servants had provided her with furs and heated bricks to supplement her own cloak and gloves, newly delivered by Monsieur Georges.

At first they had little conversation. Madame Colbert closed her eyes and appeared to fall sleep. Her husband took a rosary and a small volume from his pocket and read for ten minutes or so, despite the jolting of the road. Louise watched him surreptitiously. He held the book very close to his eyes, and as he read his lips moved, and his thumb pushed the rosary beads one after the other over the forefinger of his hand. The beads were coral of a particularly dark red shade like drops of blood on a string.

Afterwards he removed a packet of papers from a leather case and studied them, while his wife began to snuffle in her sleep. The miles passed. Louise drew back the curtain and watched the country stream away from her like an endlessly dreary tapestry unfurling outside the window. Villages and towns were a blessed relief, breaking the monotony if only for a few minutes. The novelty of the journey had long since worn away when at last the ambassador looked up and enquired how she did.

'Very well, monsieur. The coach is most . . . elegant.'

'We're making good speed.' He slid the papers back into the case and took up his rosary again. 'Lord Arlington's palace is about eighty miles from London, perhaps a trifle more. If the road remains as good as this, we should be there during the evening. Barring accidents.'

There was a silence inside the coach, apart from Madame Colbert's increasingly stertorous breathing. The beads slid slowly through Monsieur Colbert's fingers. He continued looking at her with a half-smile on his lips. He should have been a handsome man, but his nose was a little too long and his chin tapered to a point. He had a way of staring very hard at the person he was talking to, as if trying to peer into that person's innermost soul, where only God or the Devil should see.

He leant forward, bringing his head closer to hers. 'This is, I think, as good a moment as any for us to advise together about certain matters. We are as private here as in the middle of a desert. You know why we are going to Euston, don't you?'

She kept her eyes downcast and did not reply. But he went on as if she had agreed with him.

286

'It is wise to make sure we both know precisely where we stand, eh? Forgive me – I must speak bluntly. But where affairs of state are concerned, mademoiselle, we cannot afford false modesty and we must be frank with each other. Our duty to His Most Christian Majesty demands no less.'

Louise looked up quickly. 'His Majesty must never doubt my loyalty.'

'I'm sure he doesn't. Your conduct towards the King of England will strengthen his belief in your loyalty and his desire to be your friend.' Colbert gave her an insinuating smile. 'And no one but God can be a better friend than the King of France.'

She nodded, not trusting herself to speak.

'Between ourselves, Lord Arlington has told me with his own lips that he and his colleagues are concerned that their own master demeans himself by associating so freely with actresses and orange girls and whores. Even at court, he favoured Lady Castlemaine above all others for many years. As I'm sure you know, my lady is a shrewish, ill-tempered woman. She's scarcely better in either birth or manners than a common whore. No decent man should associate his person with such mean people. Let alone a king chosen by God to be the father of his subjects. It cannot be right, eh?'

The coach rolled on, swaying and bumping over the ruts. Outside, the world was full of drumming hooves and jingling harness. Inside the coach, Louise watched the beads of the rosary rising and falling with the mysterious inevitability of divine providence.

'No, indeed,' Monsieur Colbert said, answering his own question. 'For his hours of private recreation, a king should find a lady of the best family possible; a lady whose public conduct is good, and one who will delight him with her private discourse without diminishing his dignity or distressing his friends.' He lowered his voice to a caressing murmur. 'No person of breeding would object to associate with such a lady. One might almost say that she would become a sort of queen at court, a queen without the inconvenience of a crown.'

The coach slowed. Louise turned her head to look out of the window. They were passing through the outskirts of a town, perhaps Bishop's Stortford. Soon, God willing, they would stop. Yet she wanted to stay, to hear more.

The murmuring flowed on. 'In a case of this nature, mademoiselle, such a paragon would be in a position to serve two kings at once: for, should she carry herself judiciously, she would help bring together two kingdoms in the blessings of peace and harmony. All this must surely be pleasing in the eyes of God.' He smiled at her. 'And in doing so, she would also earn the profound gratitude of two earthly kings.'

Louise thought with the cold, merciless clarity of a trapped animal that the ambassador would have made a fine preacher had he not chosen instead to be a pander.

Colbert leant even closer. He skewered her with those uncomfortable eyes. His voice hardened. 'Kings are not like other men. They are chosen of God, and to serve them is a great blessing. To serve two would be doubly blessed. Do you agree?'

'I seek to serve God and my king, sir,' she said in a voice that was barely audible above the noises outside. 'Always.'

He sat back and gave her a thin smile. 'Of course. I had expected no less of you.'

CHAPTER THIRTY-FOUR

T HE TRACES OF one of the horses snapped, occa-
sioning the first delay, and another horse lost a shoe,
which cost us yet more time. We came at last to Chesterford,
where we passed the night after a cold and unappetizing
supper. I shared a bed with the peruke-man and the parson,
both of whom snored as if in conversation with each other.

The following morning, we travelled on without further
mishap and reached Euston at eleven o'clock. Our coach filed
behind a line of others into a large courtyard enclosed by the
three wings of the mansion. It was a vast place, bustling with
enough people to provide the inhabitants of a small town.
There was an air of excitement, which was soon explained.
The King had arrived shortly before us, having ridden over
from Newmarket with a small escort.

A servant greeted us civilly and conducted us to an office
in one of the side wings, where the steward of the household
was greeting visitors and dispatching them to their various
destinations. When he heard my name, he beckoned me to
one side, ignoring my companions.

'Mr Marwood? Your servant, sir. You're to wait on my lord directly.'

I was dismayed. I had hoped to have time to wash away the grime of the journey and snatch some food before I saw him. 'What about my luggage?'

'We'll take care of that, never fear.' He summoned a footboy and sent him scurrying towards the coach. 'You've a bed to yourself, you'll be pleased to hear, indeed an entire chamber will be yours alone, though I'm afraid it's little more than a closet.' He smiled apologetically. 'Also, I regret that we couldn't find space for you in the main house. We've never had such a party here, and we have more to come.'

He directed me to a doorway that led to the principal block of the house and told me I would find my lord on the first floor. I mounted a great staircase of noble proportions, far more magnificent than that at Goring House. In my travel-stained clothes I was out of place, a scar on perfection.

In the anteroom at the head of the stairs I encountered a courtier who was much in Lord Arlington's company at Goring House. He was an agreeable, rattle-pated gentleman.

'Mr Marwood,' he cried in the affected tones of Whitehall. 'I fear you've had a wasted journey.'

'You mean I could have stayed in London?'

'No – only that the King is here, so my lord will not see you until this evening at the earliest. Come back when His Majesty's gone.' He looked more closely at me and frowned. 'What *have* you been doing with yourself?'

'I had a difference of opinion with a blackguard,' I said.

'I hope you gave the fellow as good as you got.'

There was a flurry of movement in one of the doorways, and Lady Arlington came into the antechamber. She had her arm around the waist of a small lady with the face of the prettiest child a man could wish to see. It was the young woman whom Gorvin had pointed out to me in the Privy Garden. The two of them had a perfumed escort of young gallants. They passed through the antechamber among a bowing and curtsying crowd and vanished through another doorway.

'They're going into my lord's drawing room,' the courtier murmured. 'The King's in there.' He lowered his voice still further. 'Do you know that young lady?' Without waiting for an answer, he gave a knowing chuckle. 'Mark her well. We'll be seeing a good deal more of her.'

'Mademoiselle de Keroualle,' I said. 'The French maid of honour.'

'Plump little partridge, ain't she?' He smacked his lips. 'Ready to be plucked and cooked to a turn on His Majesty's spit.'

My lodging was in a mean-looking building of some antiquity, perhaps a wing or outbuilding of an old house that had formerly stood on this site. It was separate from the mansion, screened from view by a walled garden and a line of trees.

The chambers were small and low, and many had been subdivided with partitions. Those on the ground floor, where I was to sleep, were reserved for men. My cell-like room was dark, for there was a yew bush growing close to the window that blocked much of the light. But it was set apart from the rest, its door opening off a short passage leading to a side door.

I washed my face and hands, changed my shirt and went to dine at the common table for the lodging. In the hall set apart for the purpose, I encountered both the young clergy-man and peruke-man from the coach. Afterwards I went out to walk off the stiffness in my limbs from the journey. I had taken a dose of laudanum at the Chesterford inn. Since then, I had managed without it.

I strolled through the gardens, making a wide circuit of the house and stables. A gentle drizzle began to seep from the grey sky. I reached the great courtyard, where I was in time to see the horses brought round for the King and his party. Soon he and my lord emerged, escorted by many other gentlemen of quality and a crowd of servants. They stood uncovered and watched the King and his party gallop down the drive.

I felt oddly detached from the spectacle, as if I were sitting alone in a box at the theatre, and the scene unfolding before me had been staged for my sole benefit. I shook my head vigorously to rid it of these foolish notions as a dog shakes itself to fling the raindrops from its coat.

Now the King was gone, my little holiday was over. I fetched my packet of papers from Goring House and found a servant to take me to my lord's closet. Arlington wasn't there, but I sat in the chamber beside it along with half a dozen others who were waiting on his pleasure. A tall, stern-faced footman stood by the closet door, staring impassively into the distance. In the corner, an austerely splendid longcase clock in an ebony case ticked time and my life away.

As I sat there, my eyes half-closed, my thoughts wandered into a strange wilderness of ideas. Power, I reflected, is a most terrible thing. Here we all were, waiting on Lord Arlington's whim. Power makes fools and puppets of those who lack it, turning us into poor, needy creatures, desperate to win favour from our master. And when we taste a little power ourselves, we place our dependants in the same position that we were in, as if to exact a vicarious revenge for past humiliations; and thus power works its slow corruption on those who do not have it as well as those who do.

Truly, I thought, the laudanum must be still clouding my mind, for how else could such unnatural thoughts come into my head? Both the Bible and our own reason tell us that some men must have power over others, that rank and hierarchy are ordained by heaven and revealed in nature. Otherwise, anarchy follows as surely as night follows day.

I steered my thoughts into safer channels. I wondered what Cat was doing now, whether she and Brennan had resumed work on the Chard Lane almshouse. I had a sudden, fierce hunger to see her, here and now, standing in front of me. No doubt that was the laudanum too.

I had almost fallen into a doze when my lord walked into the chamber and glanced around at its occupants. He ignored the others and crooked his forefinger at me, which gave me an unworthy pleasure. I followed him into his closet and closed the door. He sat down heavily in an elbow chair and looked towards the bundles of papers that had accumulated on his desk.

'Where have you been?' he said abruptly. 'You haven't deigned to report for days.'

'Forgive me, my lord, but I was attacked and beaten about the head on Tuesday night. I wrote to Mr Gorvin—'

'Quickly. The ambassador awaits me.'

'I was set upon by the missing copyist in the Chard Lane murder. John Iredale. On Mr Williamson's authority, I have placed him in the gaol at Scotland Yard to wait your lordship's pleasure, and also to keep him safe from the Duke of

Buckingham's people. I think we may conclude that the man with no face at the almshouse was the French tutor who went under the name of Monsieur Pharamond.'

'Have you found out his true identity?'

'According to Iredale, he was the Chevalier de Vire. A gentleman of good family, forced to flee from France last year. His creditors were pursuing him.'

'I wanted you to go no further in that business,' he said coldly. 'I thought I had made myself entirely clear on that point. You have disobeyed me.'

'On my oath, my lord, I have not.' I felt unjustly accused, but I was on treacherous ground. 'Your letter reached me too late, and the knowledge was forced upon me. It was not my doing that I was attacked, or that I was forced to take Iredale into custody.'

'Who killed the Frenchman then? Iredale?'

'He says it was Durrell.' I hesitated, and a sense of fairness forced me to qualify this: 'Though not perhaps intentionally. The Duke has been seeking to curry favour with Mademoiselle de Keroualle. Both Iredale and the Chevalier had become annoyances to her, and—'

'Why the Duke of all people?'

'He's been paying court to her since she came into England. Since . . . since her prospects have altered. And Iredale was in his service when they were in France.'

'How were he and Chevalier annoying her?' Arlington demanded.

'The lady chanced to fall in their way last year, when all three were in Dieppe, waiting for a passage to England. She was greatly embarrassed for money, and she sought to remedy the situation at cards. She lost large sums to the Chevalier

294

and Iredale. The paper I sent you is evidence of that, with its list of figures below that heading.'

'The one you found in Iredale's box?'

'Indeed. And it appears that the Chevalier also took advantage of her in other ways. In fact it's possible they had met each other before Dieppe. In any event, Iredale said there were passages of love between them.'

'*Love?*' He glared at me. 'What does that mean? Billing and cooing? Or did they . . .'

'Iredale claims they lay together, and more than once. He also told me there was written evidence – the lady wrote *billets doux* to her lover that leave no room for doubt about their intimacy. He believes that the Chevalier had them in his possession, and that was part of his hold over her.'

'But who has them now? His murderer?'

'More likely his murderer's master.'

'Unless they were overlooked at the time of the murder.'

I shook my head. 'It's possible of course, my lord. But if Mademoiselle de Keroualle wanted those letters back, would she not have mentioned them to the Duke? In which case, His Grace would have ordered Durrell to search the Chevalier and bring him any papers he found.'

Lord Arlington leant back in his chair, his eyes half-closed. 'In summary, then: you believe that the Duke sent Durrell to threaten Iredale and de Vire, to persuade them to keep away from her, and to retrieve these letters?'

'Durrell certainly succeeded in persuading Iredale. He cut a cross in the poor man's chest to make his point. Iredale was terrified – he immediately hid himself away at Lord Bristol's house – that is, in an outhouse attached to the office of the Council for Foreign Plantations.'

'Do you believe his story?'

'I think it must be true. For what it's worth, I've seen the cross on Iredale's chest. Durrell marked Mistress Hakesby's porter in a similar way – he cut a D on the man's forehead. And now the Frenchman's body has been found, Iredale is doubly scared: he fears he may be taken up for the murder himself. But Monsieur de Vire, I suspect, would not have been so easily frightened by Durrell. He usually wore a sword. If Durrell attacked him, he would have fought back.'

Arlington nodded. 'Of course. As a gentleman would.'

'And Durrell would have killed him,' I said. 'As Durrell would.'

He shot me a furious look. 'Do you grow pert with me, sir?'

'I beg your pardon, my lord. I meant only to signify that viciousness is part of Durrell's nature. But having killed de Vire, Durrell would then have the problem of disposing of him. That would explain the mutilation of the features and the removal of the clothes.'

To my relief, Arlington's face reverted to normal, in other words, to being as expressive as a moderately lively stone. 'Where do you think all this took place?'

'By or even inside the almshouse site. The Chevalier was walking back from Mr Hadgraft's house by Holborn, where he was employed as a tutor in French to Mistress Hadgraft. He took the shortest way from there to his lodging off Snow Hill.'

'Do you know all this for certain?'

'No, my lord. But there is no other sequence of events that fits the known facts.'

'You talk like a natural philosopher, Marwood, not an intelligencer.'

I bowed my head, taking this remark as a reproof rather than as a compliment. 'There's circumstantial evidence to support it. It looks as if Durrell and his man seized him and dragged him into the yard beside the site office. We found blood on the ground under a pile of old canvas sails. That was probably where they killed him and destroyed his face. They killed the watchman's dog too, lest it rouse the neighbourhood. Then they hid both bodies in a heap of spoil to delay discovery.'

The clock in the neighbouring room began to strike the hour.

'Five o'clock.' My lord stood up. 'I must go. You've done well so far as it goes,' he added grudgingly. 'Of course, much of what you say is speculation, but it has a thread of sense to it. There remains this matter of the letters and what they may contain. It's all for nothing unless they can be found.'

'If Durrell took them, the Duke has them. Or Durrell overlooked them.' Suddenly weary, I swayed on my feet. 'It's also possible that Pharamond hid them somewhere.'

'*Possible*.' Arlington put a world of disgust into the word. 'But I want to be *certain*. The Duke is in Newmarket. If you can, find out where those letters are. If he has them, I must know of it. Bribe his servants if you must – anything.' He took a paper from the desk, scanned the contents and stuffed it in his pocket. 'I'll see you tomorrow morning, Marwood, seven o'clock. Report to me here. Look at that desk – you're behind with your other work. See the steward before then and have him find you a closet to work in.' He straightened up. 'The door. The door.'

I hurried to open it. In the chamber beyond, everyone scrambled to their feet. When my lord reached the doorway, he glanced back at me.

'One more thing. Mr Evelyn comes in a day or two. Send for Mistress Hakesby directly. I want her down here as soon as possible for a night or two. If you write to her now, you can give the letter to the evening courier.'

CHAPTER THIRTY-FIVE

'EUSTON?' SAID MR Rush as he prowled about the Drawing Office. 'What's this?'

'I had an express this afternoon,' Cat said. 'My Lord Arlington desires to advise with me about his stables. It's only for a day or two. I agreed to visit him some time ago, though I didn't know precisely when he would need me.'

'But what about my almshouse? It won't build itself. And we're almost halfway through October already.'

'I've already sent word to Mr Brennan. He's more than competent to oversee the work for a day or two. At this stage there's little for us to discuss.'

Rush digested this in silence – almost literally, Cat thought, for his mouth and jaw moved as though he were chewing a piece of gristly meat, and occasionally he swallowed. As arranged, he had called at Henrietta Street promptly at five o'clock on Sunday. Cat had brought him up to the Drawing Office, where she had already laid out the Chard Lane plans for his inspection.

'How long will you be gone?'

'It depends how soon I can find a coach to take me. Mr Marwood said that my lord has a daily coach from Whitehall to Euston. But all the places are taken for tomorrow and Tuesday.'

'Everyone's going to Newmarket at present. You'll be lucky to find a place anywhere.' Rush drummed his fingers on the arm of his chair. 'As it happens, I'm going myself. You had better come with me, I suppose.'

'What do you mean?'

'I mean what I say, madam. Come with me. I can't put it plainer than that, can I? I've a friend's coach at my disposal. My wife, her waiting woman and me – that's three of us. There's room for a fourth. I don't mean to spend longer on the road than we need. Barring accidents, we should be at Newmarket by tomorrow night.'

'But Euston is—'

He waved her objection aside. 'No point in your going on to Euston, even if you could find someone to take you at that hour. You can lodge with us in Newmarket if you don't mind sharing a bed with my wife's woman. You'll be with my lord before midday on Tuesday – Euston's only a few miles further on. And if fortune favours us, you could be on your way back to London by Thursday morning by the latest.'

'You're very kind, sir . . .'

'I'm not kind. I don't believe in kindness. I'm being practical, madam. I don't share your confidence in that fellow Brown.'

'His name is Brennan.'

'And second, the sooner you go, the sooner you return. And the sooner you return, the sooner you build my almshouse.' He cocked his head. There were steps on the stairs. 'And there's Brown by the sound of it.'

'Brennan, sir,' Cat said. Without warning she lost patience with Rush. 'How many times must I say it? His name's Brennan.'

He burst out laughing. 'I like a woman of spirit.'

Louise had been given apartments in one of the four pavilions at the corners of Euston Hall. It was a mark of honour to have not only a spacious bedchamber to herself, but also a closet and an anteroom, together with a page to wait outside and receive any commands she might be pleased to give.

On Sunday, when she returned to prepare for the evening ahead, she found a strange maidservant in her bedchamber. She was a small, fair woman with projecting teeth and muddy green eyes fringed with sandy lashes. The fire was burning brightly, and the clothes for the evening had already been laid out on the bed.

'Who are you?' Louise demanded, in English.

'Your new maid, mademoiselle. My Lady Arlington sent me to wait on you. The English woman had to go away.'

She spoke in French, the French of Paris. Without waiting to be told, she came to Louise's side and helped remove her cloak, hat and gloves.

'What's your name?'

'Marie, mademoiselle. But you are chilled. Would you care to sit by the fire for a moment and warm yourself? Shall I ring for an infusion of herbs?'

Before Louise could reply, there was a tap at the door, and

Lady Arlington entered. 'My dear,' she said, 'you must forgive me. I've been trying to find you all afternoon.'

'I was walking in the garden . . . but why did you want to see me?'

'That English maid you brought – I had to send her away. The girl had the most dreadful cold, and she shouldn't be allowed within a mile of a lady of quality. But I have been so distracted,' my lady went on in her usual composed manner. 'I should have told you at dinner, but it quite slipped my mind. What a giddy-brained creature I am.'

'It doesn't signify at all,' Louise said. 'I didn't care for her.'

'Yes – my housekeeper said she's a dull, clumsy thing, so I dare say it's all for the best. I'm sure you will do much better with Marie. She came to me from Madame de La Fayette, and she knows how things are done.'

While they were talking, Marie herself stood by the bed, head bowed and hands clasped. Lady Arlington, by contrast, moved about the room like a restless butterfly, examining ornaments, exclaiming over the lace on the bed and talking gracefully of nothing in particular. Then, without a change of tone, she began talking of something quite different, something that mattered.

'Do you know what His Majesty whispered when he took his leave of me? He could hardly tear himself away, he said, but he was expected at Newmarket this evening and he had no choice in the matter. But he told me his heart would remain in Euston. Is that not charming?'

Louise knew she was blushing. She turned her head towards the fire. But the flow of soft, insinuating words continued.

'He wouldn't leave before I promised to make up a party and come over to see him on Tuesday. There is to be a great race, and the King himself is to ride in it. The whole court will be there, but I believe he will have eyes for only one person among the crowd. Marie will help you look your best, I'm sure – and if there's anything you lack, send her to my apartments and one of my waiting women will find it for her. After all, the honour of France is at stake.'

Lady Arlington departed in a cloud of compliments. Marie closed the door softly, curtsied to Louise, and enquired whether Mademoiselle wished to begin her toilette.

In the morning, I was at my desk from seven o'clock until the midday bell. Lord Arlington's correspondence had mounted up in my absence, and it would take me the better part of two days to bring it under control. I felt refreshed and clear-headed. I was still not entirely free from pain but, with some regret, I left the laudanum alone.

Much of the work was mechanical, requiring only part of my attention. My uneasy thoughts roamed elsewhere. The knowledge that I might soon encounter Cat unsettled me. Last year, after we had shared a time of great danger, there had been passages of love between us. I had offered her my hand and heart, but she rejected me out of hand. Yet I had hoped that she was not wholly indifferent for all that she gave me so little encouragement. But in my brief madness when I burned for Grace Hadgraft, she had given me sour looks and harsh words, and even now there was a distance between us, a gap I did not know how to bridge.

I was between the devil and the deep sea. Lord Arlington wanted me to find those cursed letters at all costs, which meant I must find a way to approach the Duke. But that would be rank folly for he, insofar as he condescended to think about me at all, would be happy to see me hanged, drawn and quartered if it could be contrived without putting himself to too much trouble. I would be a fool to try his patience further by enquiring openly after Mademoiselle's letters. I had some protection from his hostility because I was in Arlington's service and because the King had shown me kindness in the past. But I would be a double fool to rely on either man to preserve me from the malice of Buckingham and Durrell.

How was I to find those letters? How was I to stay alive?

CHAPTER THIRTY-SIX

WILLOUGHBY RUSH WAS as good as his word. His party left London before dawn. They were accompanied by Thomas Ledward, the man whom Rush had put forward for the watchman's job at the almshouse before his quarrel with Hadgraft. He rode beside or in front of the coach, leading his master's riding horse.

Cat hadn't seen Ledward since the inquest exactly a week ago. In some barely definable way, he had changed since then. He stood more erect; he was better dressed, more confident in bearing and clearer in speech. His manner towards Cat was distant but entirely respectful, as befitted a manservant towards one of his master's guests; he might never have seen her before in his life.

Mr Rush had brought a case of papers which engrossed his attention in the early part of the journey. Occasionally, without raising his eyes, he would pat his wife's leg as if she were a dog in need of reassurance. Later, when wearied of sitting in the coach, he called for his horse and galloped in front of them, raising a cloud of dust.

It was a fine day, and they made good speed. The coachman was expert at his business, deft with the reins and ready to use his whip if other travellers inconvenienced him. They had no trouble on the way. Rush carried a sword and two horse pistols, and both Ledward and the coachman were also armed.

The interior of the coach was stuffy. There was little conversation. All three women were veiled against the dust of the road, but once or twice the vizard slipped from Grace's face. Her eyes were mere slits, for the lids were pink and swollen.

Susannah sat beside her mistress with a book held close to her face. She was wrapped in a red cloak, an unexpected change from the drab colours she usually wore. The wool was good broadcloth, but it had been mended with a large patch near the neck; the dye had faded irregularly, creating a piebald effect, and the hem was stained with what looked like tar. A cast-off from Grace, Cat thought, a symbol of the poor woman's dependency on her mistress for all the world to see.

Occasionally Susannah's eyes would lift from her reading and flick towards her mistress and then to Cat, as if making a routine inspection. When they stopped, she left her book behind. The last to leave the coach, Cat glanced at it, finding it was a volume of sermons. The light altered on the page. She looked up. Susannah was standing by the coach, staring at her.

Embarrassed, Cat dropped the book on the seat. 'How . . . how pleasant it must be to read on the road. I find it doesn't agree with me after a while.'

Susannah turned away, saying nothing. There had been a

306

shift in the waiting woman's behaviour since Hadgraft's ruin. Cat could not define it, beyond sensing a new assurance behind her taciturn manner.

When the light faded, Ledward lit the coach lamps and they continued on their way, albeit more slowly than before. Rush and Grace began a whispered conversation, while Cat and Susannah pretended not to listen. Cat caught only one word in four, but she gathered that they were arguing about Grace's father. The conversation ended with Rush losing patience and saying loudly, 'He can live in my pigsty for all I care.' Grace began to cry softly. Rush took her hand and called her his little sweetheart and dearest honeybird, whereupon Grace wept harder than before, while peeping at her husband through her long lashes, after which Rush promised that they would settle everything to her satisfaction on their return to London. The weeping stopped.

Night had fallen by the time they reached Newmarket. The streets of the town bustled with people. Torches swooped and flared. Somewhere nearby a group of fiddlers was playing a discordant jig, the notes shrieking and scraping as they rose and fell.

Grace peered through the window with her nose against the glass like an excited child. 'Pray, sir – look – is that Lord Rochester over there?'

'During the races,' Rush said sourly, 'half London comes here. The worst half.'

They stopped outside a large inn with the sign of the White Lion swinging above the door. Twenty yards up the street, another coach had drawn up to allow two gentlemen to disembark. Rush's party joined them on the pavement. To Cat's surprise, one of the newcomers gave a start and bowed to her.

'Mistress Hakesby,' he said. 'I hadn't thought to meet you here. Do you stay long?'

She belatedly recognized Mr Evelyn, who had shielded her from the unwanted attentions of the Duke of Buckingham on the evening of the Queen's Drawing Room. She sank into a curtsy, aware she was not looking her best after the long journey; on the other hand, nor was he.

'Only one night, sir. I go to Euston tomorrow.'

'Ah – to advise with my lord? In that case I may have the honour of seeing you there.'

He said goodnight and strolled away with the other gentleman.

Rush touched her arm. 'Let's go in,' he said. 'Was that Mr Evelyn?'

'Yes, sir.'

'You have a surprisingly wide acquaintance at court.' He led her inside, where the other two ladies were warming their hands at the common fire. His grip tightened on her arm. 'Then again, madam, perhaps I shouldn't be surprised. The better we are acquainted, the more I discover how little I know about you.'

That night the four of them lay in a modest chamber on the second floor of the inn.

They were, the landlord assured them, particularly fortunate to have the room to themselves, and to have the use of two entire beds between the four of them. He tapped his nose and said His Grace's man had given him to understand that the Duke would esteem it a particular favour if Mr Willoughby Rush and his party could be housed in comfort.

Rush grunted in reply, as if he took the Duke of

Buckingham's good offices for granted. He ordered their supper to be sent up to a private room. They lingered over the meal until he had drunk his fill.

Grace asked whether they would have the honour of meeting the Duke while they were at Newmarket.

'I shall, madam,' Rush said. 'But I doubt that you will. He has an eye for a beautiful woman, and I have no intention of letting him ogle you.'

She pouted at him. 'Oh sir. I'm sure he would not be so ill-mannered. And I have a particular fancy to meet him.'

Red-faced with wine, he glared at her. 'Why? Have you forgotten you're my wife?'

'Of course not, sir.' Grace shrank from his rage. 'It's only that I've never met a duke.'

'And I hope you never do. When all's said and done, they're but mortal men like the rest of us.' He turned his head away, dismissing the subject. 'Susannah! Make sure they warm the bed, and my night shirt as well. I cannot abide cold, damp sheets.'

The squall of anger subsided as swiftly as it had arisen. An uncomfortable silence spread around the table. Rush refilled his glass again and again. Cat glanced at Grace, who was sitting with her face averted from her husband and her mouth compressed. Rush hadn't cowed her. But he had certainly made her angry.

When the second bottle was empty, he decided abruptly that they should all retire for the night.

Cat lay with Susannah in a bed too narrow for comfort. Meanwhile, from behind the curtains of the larger bed, there came a series of rhythmic murmurs and rustles and grunts and moans, together with the occasional squeak of pain, as

Mrs Rush's husband exercised his conjugal rights with boyish enthusiasm. The sounds built to a crescendo and then rapidly diminished. Afterwards there was silence for a few blessed minutes until Rush began to snore and Susannah muttered something that sounded like 'little prick'.

The waiting woman had sharp elbows and knees, a fact that forced itself on to Cat's attention as Susannah tossed and turned before at last falling into a heavy sleep. She also had a disconcerting habit of murmuring incomprehensible words with strange urgency, as if talking to someone in her dreams.

Meanwhile, the sounds of revelry from the street below continued unabated. The wailing of the fiddles ebbed and flowed, as grating to the ear as a nocturnal orchestra of cats charged with the duty of murdering sleep.

Supper on Monday night was an informal affair. Lord Arlington did Louise the honour of sitting beside her. He helped her to all the dishes on the table and talked incessantly in a low, confidential voice.

Every now and then, Louise glanced about her. On one occasion, she caught Lady Arlington looking at her, her face rosy in the candlelight; and when their eyes met, she smiled at Louise. On another occasion when she looked up, it was to find Monsieur Colbert staring at her, his fleshy features gleaming with patches of perspiration as if imperfectly varnished.

The Arlingtons' servants were attentive to a fault. Louise drank more than was wise. But how could she avoid it, when so many people wanted to toast her? Then she was obliged to toast them back; and her glass was always refilled as soon as it was empty.

All the while, my lord was talking in the soft, persuasive voice he could so easily summon up when he wished. He spoke a little of the Queen, and how she endured so nobly the various ailments that beset her, and how sad it was that she had not yet been able to present His Majesty with an heir.

Then, little by little, he encouraged Louise to confide in him about her years as a maid of honour to the King's late sister, poor Madame, the Duchess of Orleans. This somehow led to the subject of Louise's family, and in particular to the precise line of her descent, through her grandmother, from the French royal house.

'Ah,' Lord Arlington said, smiling pleasantly, 'then you may address His Most Catholic Majesty as *mon cousin.*'

'No indeed, my lord,' she blurted, shocked he should joke about so serious a matter. 'I should not dare, even in my dreams.'

He lowered his voice. 'Even with royal blood in your veins? What a privilege. Why, mademoiselle, you might marry whomsoever you chose.'

Louise looked down at her plate. Only now did she dimly perceive the purpose of this laboured conversation, though she hardly dared articulate it even to herself.

The Queen of England was barren and ill. The King of England was in need of an heir. If the Queen should die, he must marry again, and naturally he would desire his new queen to have royal blood in her veins, even if her connection with royalty was so remote as to be barely discernible.

'His Majesty will be with us in a day or two,' her host was saying in a changed voice as if marking the introduction of a different subject. 'As he was leaving yesterday, he told me that he may do us the honour of passing a night or two here.'

But it was not a change of subject, Louise thought, it was the same subject as before. It was always the same subject.

In the morning, Mr Rush rose early and left the inn, saying he would be back by midday, unless he sent word to the contrary.

The curtains of the bed he shared with his wife were still closed. Susannah parted them an inch and asked if her mistress would like her pot or some hot water. Grace snapped at her to go away and let her sleep.

Cat, who had returned to the chamber to fetch her cloak and gloves, was an unwilling eavesdropper. She and Susannah left the room together.

'When she wakes, will you tell Mistress Rush that I'm gone to Lord Arlington's Newmarket lodging?' Cat said on the stairs. 'I must find out how I am to go to Euston.'

'No doubt it will be more agreeable there.' Susannah's voice was colourless.

Cat glanced at her. 'The sooner I manage my business,' she said, stressing the word 'business', 'the sooner I can leave. Mr Rush wants me in London, at the almshouse.'

'Will you see Mr Hadgraft when you return?' Susannah said, as she followed Cat down the stairs.

The question took Cat by surprise. 'I've no reason to seek him out. I don't even know where he's living.'

'His house is shut up. The lease is to be sold. Mr Rush put him in the cottages behind his own house for the time being.' Her face expressionless, Susannah stared at Cat. 'With one of his servants.'

It sounded almost as if the man were Hadgraft's gaoler. Or as if he himself had been reduced to the level of Rush's servants. The cottage must be the one where the murdered man had lain, waiting for the coroner.

'Why did you ask if I'd see him?'

'Because I wonder how he does. If you see him, pray tell him I asked after him.'

They reached the landing place. It was the nearest approach to a conversation that they had ever had. Susannah dropped a curtsy and walked swiftly down the passage to the common parlour of the inn.

Cat descended the final flight of stairs to the street. Susannah's words had something under their surface, she thought, something hard and uncompromising like hidden rocks in placid waters.

CHAPTER THIRTY-SEVEN

ON TUESDAY MORNING Lady Arlington assembled a party of pleasure to spend the day at Newmarket. There was great excitement, even among those of us who were not invited.

'What a spectacle it will be,' the young clergyman, Mr Banks, said wistfully. I had encountered my companion from the coach as we left our lodging. 'The whole world will be there.'

'No it won't,' I said. 'Only the fools who care to waste their time and money on such amusements.' The poor man looked so crestfallen that I felt guilty. 'On the other hand,' I went on, 'no doubt it will be a most interesting spectacle, one that will afford many useful reflections to a man of sense.'

Mr Banks had heard the details of the excursion from the peruke-man, our fellow traveller, who had been summoned just after dawn to make an urgent repair to Lord Arlington's wig. He had had his information directly from my lord's valet. The party was to dine in Newmarket, Banks told me, and His Majesty might well join them. Afterwards, they would watch the great race on the Heath. This year it was believed that the prize would go either to the King himself, who was riding one of his own horses, by the name of Woodcock, or to a Gentleman of the Bedchamber who was riding Flatman.

'And in the meantime,' the clergyman said, 'we shall be left to our dull devices here.' He glanced at me, his expression a mixture of pride and trepidation. 'Mind you, I shall not be idle. I am to preach before the whole party on Sunday. I must lay the groundwork for my sermon. I shall take as my text "A divine sentence is in the lips of the king: his mouth transgresseth not in judgement." Proverbs, chapter sixteen, verse ten. I hope it will please His Majesty. But . . . well, I do wish I could go to Newmarket today.'

We parted amiably enough. When I reached the apartments set aside for my lord's business, I found a message waiting for me. I was to go to Newmarket with him, riding in his own coach so that he could dictate as we went.

We assembled in the forecourt – three coaches for the ladies, a pair of elderly gentlemen and their attendants, together with a cavalcade of gentlemen to escort them. Mademoiselle de Keroualle rode with Lady Arlington.

There was also a fourth coach, lighter and smaller than the others, for Lord Arlington and myself alone. On the road to Newmarket, he dictated letters and memoranda to me, rattling through them as if a pack of hounds were on his tail.

During the previous year, I had followed Cat's example and taught myself shorthand according to the system outlined in Mr Shelton's *Tachygraphy*. To this I had added convenient abbreviations and adaptations of my own. My lord had several secretaries at his disposal, but I was the only one who could keep pace with his dictation, which kept my services in demand; sometimes my skill seemed more a curse than an advantage.

Dictation kept us busy until we were entering the outskirts of Newmarket. The road grew mighty congested and our progress slowed to little better than a walking pace. My lord's party forced its way through the throng.

'Write those up for my signature when we get to the lodging,' Lord Arlington said to me, raising his voice to be heard above the noises of the street. 'The Duke of Buckingham is in town, by the way. See if you can find out whether he has the letters and if that rogue Durrell is with him. But be discreet.'

I felt an abrupt sinking of the spirits. I resolved to take as long as possible over the transcripts.

'If Durrell's breaking the law, by the way,' my lord went on, 'so much the better. I'd dearly like to lay the fellow by the heels for some trifling matter. If we had him in custody, perhaps we might get the truth out of him about the letters.'

The coach drew up outside the house in the High Street that Lord Arlington had taken for the season. My lord emerged slowly from the coach while his servants beat back the beggars and supplicants who pressed towards him. Fiddlers were playing in the street, and a drum was beating; the din they made was loud enough to rise above the noises of the road.

Arlington walked towards the doorway of the house. As I was climbing down from the coach I heard him saying, 'No, no, let the lady pass. You've made good time. I had not thought to see you until later in the week.'

I stood for a second, blinking in the sunshine and dazed by the hubbub of the town. A few yards away Lord Arlington and Cat Hakesby were walking into the house.

At that moment the drummer and the fiddlers drew level with the coach. They were marching up the roadway, to the great inconvenience of the traffic. Behind them rode the Duke of Buckingham, splendidly dressed and splendidly mounted. Talk of the devil. It was as if the very mention of his name had conjured him up. There was another rider with him, but the tall figure of the Duke blocked his face from my view.

To my dismay, Buckingham caught sight of me by the door of the house. 'Why, God's bones, sir, what have we here?' he called out. 'Can it really be the Marworm?'

His companion slowed and turned his head to look. I recognized the craggy, unsmiling face of Willoughby Rush.

Cat encountered Mr Evelyn in the parlour on the first floor of Lord Arlington's lodging. He acknowledged their acquaintance at once.

'I go on to Euston later today, madam, and will no doubt see you there. What are you to do for my lord?'

'He's considering alterations to his stables, sir.'

'I hope we shall find time to continue our conversation. It's always agreeable to discuss the merits of architecture with someone who has a knowledge of the subject. At my request, by the way, Lord Arlington showed me the poultry house you designed for him. An elegant little building.'

There was a hint of benign condescension in Evelyn's tone, together with a sense that he was consciously making an allowance for her work on the grounds of her sex; in just such a way had an aunt once praised the needlework of Cat's sampler, in that case making an allowance on the grounds of age.

'And what will you do now?' he asked.

317

'The coach will take me to Euston at half-past twelve. In the meantime, I suppose I shall have my luggage sent over from the inn and wait here.'

There was a brief silence. She would have liked to have seen the sights. But she could not properly walk out unattended, particularly in a strange town crammed with court gallants and every sort of rogue bent on mischief. She had been subject to catcalls and other nuisances even on the short walk from the inn.

Mr Evelyn cleared his throat. 'Would it amuse you to look over the palace?' His face was long and his expression disapproving, as if to ward off any suggestion of impropriety. 'I intend to walk over there myself this morning, and I will happily escort you.'

Nothing could have pleased Cat more. A few minutes later they were strolling along the High Street. Evelyn paused in front of the street facade of the palace. It was set back only a yard or two from the roadway, shielded by a whitewashed wooden railing.

'Alas,' he said, 'the palace scarcely deserves so dignified a name. The new work is Mr Samwell's – a man who usually knows his business – but to my mind the building is low and mean, as well as small. Indeed, it's little better than a hunting house. And it fronts the street, like a common citizen's. There's nothing kingly about it whatsoever; no avenue before it or anything to mark it out from the rest of the street.'

'It's a curious mixture,' Cat said. 'How unfortunate they kept the older range beside the new.'

'Indeed. A most unhappy conjunction. Lack of money, I suppose, as at Whitehall. Everything comes down to money in these sad times.'

There was no difficulty about their entering the palace: Mr Evelyn's face was well known at court. The principal range of the new building ran back from the road. The state rooms, such as they were, and the royal bedchambers and closets were on the first floor.

'As you see,' Evelyn said, 'the Queen has her pavilion at right angles to the range, and His Majesty's is at the end. Quite in the French style. I have no quarrel with the plan, only the execution.'

They walked slowly through the rooms, with Mr Evelyn telling Cat what she was seeing and the opinions she ought to have about what she saw. He spoke gravely as if to a daughter, and in a tone that brooked no discussion, let alone disagreement. At first Cat was irritated by his manner; then she became mildly interested in what he was saying, for he was well informed if not always in the right of it. Also, though Evelyn was scarcely the gayest of companions, she felt safe in his company: a pleasant luxury for a young widow who lacked the protection of a family.

He paused outside the King's bedchamber to point out a fireplace in an adjacent closet. 'Look, madam. A fireplace in the corner of the room! Mr Samwell has a lamentable taste for the à la mode in his detailing – can you imagine anything so inconvenient? Some Dutch crotchet of his, no doubt, like the double rows of dormers at Bushey House. And mark that window: it's what they call a *sash* window, which opens vertically without hinges: the upper and lower halves slide over each other, suspended by an invisible system of pulleys and weights. A foolish novelty – far too complicated to last. What is wrong with simple casements? They were good enough for our forebears, and surely they are good enough for us and our posterity?'

They passed through the King's Withdrawing Room to the Privy Chamber and came at last to the King's Presence Chamber, the largest of the rooms, which had windows looking out on the street. All three rooms had corner fireplaces, each of which earned Mr Evelyn's disapproval.

'One can almost pardon a man for installing a corner fireplace in a closet. But in a state room?' He clicked his tongue against the roof of his mouth. 'No, no, no, no, no.'

Cat was growing weary of this, and moved to the window, as if to study the view, though it was not very different from the one from their bedchamber at the inn. The street below was a river of noise, with people and vehicles moving to and fro. Directly opposite the windows of the Presence Chamber was another inn. To its right was a large house with a saddler's establishment on the ground floor, the shutters open to the street. Between them was the entrance to a passage leading to the yards and gardens behind the buildings.

A tall man was standing just inside the passage. There was something familiar about his posture. She rubbed the glass to see him more clearly. He was leaning against the wall as if for additional support for his large belly. He wore a sword hanging by his right leg, and a low, broad-brimmed hat.

'When we go back downstairs,' Evelyn was saying behind her, 'I will show you the chambers beneath this range. I inspected them while the work was in progress last year . . .'

The man was Roger Durrell, the Duke's hireling. Cat would have recognized him anywhere, whether in her nightmares or in broad daylight.

'. . . There at least I can find no fault with Mr Samwell's work. The arches that support the floor above are admirably well-wrought.'

A woman came scurrying along the pavement, swathed in a cloak and keeping close to the wall. The cloak caught the eye, for it was a faded red colour. It was also teasingly familiar. An instant later, Cat recognized Susannah.

Durrell turned his face towards the waiting woman. His lips moved. Susannah stopped abruptly. A man walking behind almost knocked into her. His irritation was obvious, even at this distance. Then he saw Durrell, his hand resting on the hilt of his sword, and quickly went on.

Susannah joined him in the passage. They faced each other, presenting their profiles to Cat. Durrell bent over the woman's small, hunched figure like a parent over a child.

'You'll see more of Mr Samwell's work at Euston,' Evelyn was saying. 'There's less to offend the eye there, but I cannot entirely subscribe to the general admiration of it, particularly the exterior. But some of the interior is very fine.'

Durrell pointed his spike at Susannah and made stabbing motions, as if to drive home a point he was making.

Evelyn was at her elbow. 'Would you care to see the gardens as well, such as they are?'

Susannah nodded. Durrell handed her something small, which she pushed inside her cloak. The meeting ended as abruptly as it had begun. Durrell turned his back on the street and walked down the passage. Susannah slipped into the street and continued on her way.

'The gardens?' Cat smiled at Evelyn. 'If you can spare the time, sir, I should be delighted.'

Arlington's lodging in Newmarket was in the charge of a grave fellow with a hesitant, sideways mode of walking, as if he feared he might upset someone by proceeding in a more direct manner. It took me several minutes to explain who I was and what I wanted, but once he had grasped these facts, he found me a closet at the back of the house where I could transcribe my shorthand notes without interruption.

He lingered in the doorway for a moment, watching me unpack the writing materials I had brought with me. He had long, crooked fingers, and he massaged them as if they pained him.

'If you need anything, sir,' he said, 'come to the head of the stairs and shout for the boy.'

'I'm obliged,' I said, angling the table so it would catch the light from the window.

'I hope you don't find the sounds below a distraction from your labours. When my lord and his party come to town there is always a great deal of noise and bustle within doors.'

He looked so anxious as he said this that my heart went out to the poor man. 'You mustn't trouble yourself,' I said. 'I'm accustomed to it.'

'I wish I could say as much myself.' He rubbed his forehead. 'I have headaches, you see, and when the house is full, it seems to bring them on.'

He edged out of the room, leaving me to my work. I wrote steadily for over an hour, pausing occasionally to take a turn about the room to stretch my limbs. Footsteps came and went on the other side of the closet door, but no one disturbed me. There was a good deal of commotion below, both inside and outside the house. I don't know why it should be, but court gallants regard it almost as a point of honour to make as much noise as possible.

As midday approached, I was nearing the end of my labours

when there was a tap on the door, and the servant sidled into the closet.

'Forgive me for disturbing you, sir,' he said, 'but there's a gentleman below. He – he wishes to see my lord, but he has no letter of introduction. When I tried to send him away, he mentioned your name, and he said you would vouch for him. He's very pressing, but it's quite impossible for him to see my lord at present. He's with the King all day. Besides, as you know, his lordship sees no one without an appointment.'

'What's his name?'

'Rush. A Mr Willoughby Rush.' He fell to massaging his fingers again. 'A most choleric gentleman.'

I frowned, puzzled by the news. The servant mistook my expression and began to apologize again. I interrupted him. 'I'm slightly acquainted with the gentleman. But you're in the right of it, it's out of the question for him to see my lord today. Indeed, it's possible my lord will have no desire to see Mr Rush at all.'

'There's something else, sir . . . I chanced to look out of the window an hour or so ago, and I saw this gentleman in the street, though I didn't then know who he was. He was discoursing with His Grace of Buckingham – ah, their conversation became quite heated – indeed they attracted unseemly attention from passers-by. I almost feared it would end in a challenge . . .'

This was stranger still. I had seen the two men riding together only an hour or so earlier, and they had seemed the best of friends. I asked whether it would be of use if I came down and enquired more particularly into Mr Rush's business.

'Oh sir, I should be much obliged.'

I followed the servant's shambling figure downstairs, where Rush was pacing up and down in a crowded waiting room by the street door. The scabbard of his sword swung from side to side as he walked, obliging the other men there to give him a wide berth.

He glanced at the doorway as we entered. 'Ah, Mr Marwood. At last! I thought they'd keep me waiting here all day. It's of the utmost importance that I see my lord, and this . . . this man here tells me it simply cannot be done. Nonsense! Pray take me to him directly.'

I had not seen Rush like this before. His colour was higher than usual, and his voice sounded clipped and hard. I marked a strange energy about his movements. All in all, I judged it prudent to take him aside into the garden that lay behind the house, where we could be more private.

'I may have some intelligence for Lord Arlington,' he told me as we paced down one of the paths. 'Intelligence he will consider of the highest importance. That's why I must talk to him. And at once.'

'What's the nature of it?'

'I prefer not to say. My business is for my lord's private ear.' He scowled at me. 'Believe me, he would wish it so.'

There was an element of bluster about this speech that made me wonder whether Rush was less confident than he wanted to appear. On the other hand, everything I knew of him suggested that he was not a man to make idle claims.

'You can't see him today,' I said. 'But—'

'Can't? Nonsense.'

I continued as if he had not spoken. 'I'll mention your request if he's at leisure this evening. If he agrees to see you, I'll write and tell you when and where to wait on him. It will probably be at Euston, and it won't be before tomorrow at the earliest.'

'It's most inconvenient,' Rush said. 'And he will regret the delay.'

'I can't help that,' I said, losing patience. 'Where do you lodge?'

'The White Lion. Write to me there.'

'I saw you with His Grace of Buckingham this morning.'

'Aye. And I saw you by the door of this house. What of it?'

'Could your intelligence have some connection with the Duke?'

'Good day to you, sir,' Rush snapped.

He stormed into the house. I followed him inside. At the other end of the passage, the footman opened the street door for him. Rush looked back at me.

'His lordship will regret it if he doesn't see me soon,' he said. 'Perhaps you will too.'

CHAPTER THIRTY-EIGHT

SHORTLY AFTER MIDDAY, two coaches drew up outside Arlington's Newmarket lodging, greatly inconveniencing the other traffic in the street. The old servant was in a pother, wringing his hands while trying to decide who should go in which coach according to the dictates of rank and propriety, which unfortunately were not at all the same thing.

Cat was placed in the second coach. She had hoped she might encounter Marwood in Newmarket, but there had been no sign of him, and she had not liked to advertise their acquaintance by enquiring where he was.

It was late afternoon by the time they turned into a drive leading to the hall. As the coach jolted along, Cat pulled aside the curtain and surveyed their surroundings. She had heard so much about the splendours of Euston that the reality came almost inevitably as a disappointment. The country was flat and unadorned. There was an attempt at a park. They passed a dilapidated church marooned like a stranded galleon blown off course from the village it had been built to serve.

Nearer the house, a cluster of walled enclosures and a substantial stable block came into view. The mansion itself was large but plain. Its three wings were arranged like the outline of a square lacking one of its sides. At each of the four corners was a stubby pavilion in the French style, as Mr Evelyn had promised, but they were less elegant than the King's at Newmarket. Two pilasters framed the front door, adding the sole touch of ornamentation to the entrance front. Evelyn said that, buried invisibly within Mr Samwell's new work, were remains of the old house that had stood on this site before Lord Arlington acquired Euston.

My lord should have found himself a more adventurous architect, Cat thought: Webb or Pratt or Wren or even me.

The coach clattered through a gateway set in a railing and entered the forecourt. The front door stood open, its mouth sucking at a stream of visitors and vomiting out others. Servants scurried to and fro, while three small boys with shovels and buckets darted from one pile of horse shit to another.

Cat and the other passengers stiffly disembarked. Two menservants appeared at a trot to deal with their luggage. The Arlingtons were efficient in everything that was theirs, and her ladyship kept her servants on a tight rein.

They were directed towards a smaller doorway set in one of the wings, for the servants knew by the strange alchemy of their kind that the passengers in this coach did not merit the front door.

A youthful clergyman was standing by, watching the scene with his mouth agape like a small boy at a Punch and Judy booth at Bartholomew Fair. As Cat approached, he blushed and sketched an awkward bow in her direction.

'Oh madam,' he blurted out, 'you've dropped your glove.'

He darted forward, scooped up the glove and presented it to her with another bow.

'Thank you, sir,' she said with a smile; and before she passed into the house, she was in time to see his blush deepen even further.

The visitors who were housed in the separate lodging took their meals in a hall used by the servants when there were fewer guests at Euston. Cat went into supper on her first evening. Before she had eaten a mouthful, the youthful clergyman insinuated himself into a vacant place beside her on the bench. He introduced himself as Mr Banks of Cambridge and tried without much success to engage Cat in conversation.

She was facing the door. When Marwood came in, she felt a lift in her spirits at the sight of his familiar face. That was natural enough, she told herself, for there was hardly a soul she knew in this place. He didn't see her. At the far end of the hall, a man wearing a drab coat and an enormously elaborate wig signalled to Marwood that there was a place beside him.

Afterwards, however, when supper was over, he looked about him and caught sight of Cat. When he came over, she interrupted Mr Banks in mid-sentence.

'Pray, sir,' she said to the clergyman, 'allow me to introduce Mr Marwood, one of Lord Arlington's secretaries.'

'The gentleman and I have already met, madam,' he said stiffly, with the immense dignity of youth.

'I believe he may have my lord's instructions for me. Would you excuse me?'

Outside, Marwood steered her away from the lodging and

towards an orchard beside a vegetable garden. The sky was clear, and the moon had risen. The grass was wet with dew. Their steps made little sound on the grassy path. As Cat's eyes adjusted, she made out the shape of the trees and the lines of the walls.

'This is a surprise,' Marwood said. 'I thought it would take you longer to get here.'

'Mr Rush brought me to Newmarket yesterday, together with his wife. Someone lent him a flying coach.'

'How convenient,' he said in a carefully neutral voice, as if Mistress Rush were neither here nor there to him.

'Thank you for rescuing me. Mr Banks is a very good young man, I'm sure, but I find a little goes a long way.'

'I can't understand why he's here,' Marwood said, showing a willingness to pursue the subject that surprised her. 'He's perfectly agreeable, I suppose. But he's as awkward as a fish on land and he's nobody of importance.'

'Who is he?'

'A connection of a local squire. He tells me he's just taken orders and been given a fellowship at his college.'

'This is a house of strangers,' she said. 'Only God and Lord Arlington know why we are all gathered together.'

But Marwood wouldn't leave Mr Banks alone. 'He says he's to preach on Sunday. In that case it may very well be that he will preach before the King himself. But to give such an honour to—'

'Durrell's come,' Cat interrupted.

'Here? At Euston?'

'No. Newmarket. I saw him this morning, but he didn't see me.'

'Where does he lodge?'

'I don't know.'

'Lord Arlington wants me to find him. And have him arrested if at all possible. Because Durrell must know what happened to those letters.'

'I saw him talking to Mistress Grace's waiting woman. You remember her – Mistress Susannah? And she seemed willing to listen.'

It was too dark under the trees to see Marwood's face, but she thought he shivered. 'Why's Rush come here?' he said. 'Did he say?'

'He has business with Buckingham. We had our bedchamber in the inn last night thanks to the Duke's good offices.'

'When Rush had a seat in Parliament, he was of the Duke's party.' There was a silence, broken only by their soft, slow footsteps on the path, and distant voices and snatches of music. 'I saw them together today,' he went on. 'The two of them were riding down the street with a band of fiddlers clearing the way. His Grace saw me too.' Another pause, and then he added hesitantly: 'Did I tell you he calls me the Marworm?'

'Then the Duke's even more of a fool than I thought,' Cat said tartly. 'And you're a fool too if you let a fool's words prey on you.'

They walked on and reached the end wall of the orchard. Marwood said, 'Later on, Rush called at Lord Arlington's lodging in Newmarket. He wants to talk privately with my lord. But he won't say why. He was most pressing.'

'Will my lord see him?'

'I haven't had a chance to ask.'

'It's strange,' Cat said. 'Rush is newly married. Yet he comes to Newmarket a day or two later. And not for pleasure, either, or not entirely.'

'First he sees Buckingham. And now he's urgent to see Arlington. Why both of them? He can't serve two masters.'

'Rush only serves himself.'

The evening was growing chillier. Cat shivered. There was a whirr of wings, more a current of air than a sound, and a sense of something pale and ghostly passing over their heads. It was followed by a faint, high scream, cut brutally short.

'Barn owl,' Cat said. 'The night killer.'

Louise's closet was snug and pleasant, hung with tapestries to shut away the chill and the damp. She often sat in there: it was warmer than the bedchamber. As Marie remarked, persons of breeding felt the cold more acutely than common people. She suggested that Mademoiselle should make her toilette in there too. There was even a prie-dieu for her devotions, a thoughtful touch from a Protestant hostess like Lady Arlington.

On Tuesday, Louise retired early. The excursion to the Newmarket races had been tiring for everyone, and cracks were appearing even in Lady Arlington's habitual veneer of good humour. During the afternoon, the wind had risen. It was now blowing hard and cold from the east, making the windows rattle and the candle flames dance like fiery maenads.

As they were making their good nights, her ladyship put aside her crotchets. She murmured to Louise that there was no need for her always to dress so formally at supper. If they were private, as they had been tonight, with only themselves and their intimate friends at table, she might appear in her undress if she wished, quite as if she were in her own home and among her own family. It was a great compliment, Louise knew, an invitation that implied that she was considered as an intimate friend herself. But there was something about the suggestion that left a sour taste behind it.

In the bedchamber, the fire was sulking in the grate. Louise had gone beyond tiredness and was now restless and disgruntled. She ordered Marie to bring her a posset to settle her stomach. Usually the maid would have sent the page downstairs with the order, but it was growing late and there was no one waiting by the door of the anteroom. Marie hinted that such tasks were below her dignity, but Louise stamped her foot and ordered her to obey.

When she was alone, she went into the closet. Candles were burning on the brackets beside the mirror on the dressing table and in the candelabra on the desk. To her surprise, a dark-green bedgown with an ermine collar was warming by the fire. She had never seen it before. She ran her fingers over the fur and the silk, testing the quality and finding it good.

Where had it come from? A present from my lady? Or from someone else? Louise sat at the dressing table and stared at her wan face in the mirror. The green gown was all of a piece with Lady Arlington's suggestion that she dress informally when they were among themselves.

Suddenly she was aware of a brief flicker of movement at the very edge of her range of vision, near the corner of the room furthest from the fire. With a gasp, she swung round, nudging the candelabra with her elbow and almost oversetting it in her haste.

Nothing was moving, nothing she could see. A rat, she thought with a shiver of distaste, or perhaps a mouse. She was turning back to the mirror when it happened again: a faint swell of movement where the tapestry met the floor, as if the woven figures were rippling into life.

Her alarm subsided. Clearly the tapestry had not been fixed properly at the bottom. She took up the candelabra and crossed the room to the corner. The draught was stronger here, the air cold and fresh.

She set the candelabra on the floor. The heavy material hung loosely from the ceiling. She peeled it back, exposing the corner of a panelled door. She ran a finger up the vertical edge until she found the latch. She raised it. But the door wouldn't budge. She let the tapestry drop to the floor and went back to her chair.

There were footsteps. A bubble of panic rose inside her. Her breath came hard and quick as if she had an obstruction within her throat. She glanced at the corner with the draught and then at the closed door to the bedchamber. There was a knock, and Marie came in with the posset on a tray.

'It's draughty in here.' Louise stared at her reflection in the mirror. 'The tapestry in that corner is loose. Have someone nail it down in the morning. And where did this gown come from?'

'It is a present for you, mademoiselle. It came this afternoon, but there was nothing to say who sent it.'

CHAPTER THIRTY-NINE

'DID YOU FIND Durrell yesterday?'

Arlington threw the question at me before I had time to close the door.

'No, my lord. I searched after dinner, but there was no sign of him. There was such a press of people in town. I couldn't make my interest too obvious.'

He drummed his fingers on the desk. I stared over his shoulder through the window behind him. Low autumn sunlight gleamed on the parkland, which was still silvery with the night's ground frost. It was shortly after dawn. Arlington had summoned me earlier than usual. He wanted to transact the business of the day before they arrived. The King and his party were dining at Euston and might well pass the evening here as well.

'But I do have news of him,' I went on. 'Mistress Hakesby was at supper last night. She came to Newmarket yesterday in Mr Rush's coach, along with his wife and her waiting woman. She told me that she saw their waiting woman – one Mistress

Susannah – talking privately with Durrell in Newmarket. That was yesterday morning. They were in an alley opposite the palace.'

'What business could he have with her? To pass a message from the Duke to Mr Rush? Or vice versa?'

'I think not, my lord. The Duke makes no secret of the connection, and nor does Mr Rush. I saw them riding together earlier in the morning.'

'Then why?'

'Perhaps His Grace does not altogether trust Mr Rush, and he wishes to have a spy in his family. Which of course begs the question . . .'

Arlington grunted. 'Of why the Duke should be interested in Mr Rush in the first place.'

'There's more. Mr Rush called at your lodging in town later in the forenoon. I saw him myself. He begs you to grant him the honour of an interview.'

'Then this was after you saw him riding with the Duke?'

'Yes, my lord. And he was most urgent to see you.'

'What does he want?'

'He wouldn't say. He told me it was for your private ear alone.' I cleared my throat. 'He also said you would regret it if you did not let him speak to you.'

Arlington frowned at me. 'He presumes too much.'

'Indeed, my lord.'

'On the other hand, perhaps there's a way to turn this to advantage. Tell him I will grant him a brief interview at eleven o'clock tomorrow. Here. Where does he lodge?'

'At the White Lion. A letter should reach him this morning before midday.'

335

'No.' Arlington's lips twisted into a thin smile. 'It will be a verbal message. And you will be the one who takes it.'

Cat once told me that I looked like a sack of flour on horseback. It was true enough that I had no taste for riding, and no skill at it either, but sometimes it could not be avoided.

On my way to the stables, as it happened, I chanced to see her. She was in company with two of my lord's servants. They were examining the ground between the house and the stable block. The men were taking measurements, while she made notes in a pocketbook. She did not see me, and I judged it best not to advertise our connection by approaching her unnecessarily.

One of the grooms found me a quiet, good-tempered mare, and I set off. To my inexpressible relief, the day was fine, the road good and the mare kind. Nevertheless, Newmarket was over twenty miles away, and I was stiff and saddle-sore by the time I reached Lord Arlington's lodging.

First, I had to deliver my lord's message to Rush. I had two other commissions while I was here: to find Durrell and, if possible, have him arrested, using the blank warrant that Arlington had given me for the purpose. Both tasks were unwelcome, but also, I hoped, likely to prove impossible to carry out.

I walked over to the White Lion, only to find that Mr Rush was not in the way. The porter added that Mr Rush's lady was in her chamber. Would I like him to send up to enquire whether she was at liberty? Reluctantly I agreed to the proposal and dropped a penny in his waiting palm.

In truth, the very idea of seeing Grace made me clench my guts with distaste. Perhaps that was unfair to her. She could not help that her father was a rogue, and it was hardly her fault that he had ruined both himself and her; nor could I blame her for falling victim to so sophisticated and ruthless a lover as the Chevalier de Vire. Who was I to judge her, let alone condemn her? She had been desperate. Despair has its own rules of conduct. As for marrying Rush, what other choice had she but penury? But for all that, I did not want to see her again.

I waited below while the porter's boy went up with my message. I heard footsteps descending, first the light, rapid patter of the boy's feet, followed by a slower tread.

'Looks like you're in luck, master,' the porter said.

The boy appeared at the turn of the stairs, taking the last few steps two at a time. After him came the figure of a woman: Susannah, not Grace. I felt relief like a breath of warm air passing over my skin. She did not look directly at me. She seemed even paler and slighter than before, more a ghost than a woman of flesh and blood.

'My mistress isn't at home,' she said in a rapid, monotonous voice like a child reciting by rote.

'As it happens, I'm looking for your master. Your new master.'

'He went out. I don't know where.'

'Will he dine here?'

'He didn't say.'

I beckoned her to one side of the passage, out of the porter's earshot. 'Is Mistress Rush resting?'

'I don't know, sir.' She looked sideways at me. 'She's not upstairs.'

If Grace had gone shopping, I thought, or to see the sights

of the town, surely she would have taken her waiting woman?' 'Where is she?' I demanded. 'And who's she with?'

Susannah smiled and gave me another of those sly, sideways glances. 'I'm sure I don't know that either. She went away about half an hour ago. She said she wouldn't be long.'

'Could she be somewhere here – in the inn?'

'She took her cloak and pattens.'

'You didn't think to ask where she was going?'

'It's not my place to do that, sir.'

'You may go,' I said curtly. I waited until Susannah was out of sight on the stairs. Then I went back to the porter. 'It seems that the lady went out about half an hour ago. You're sure she didn't go by the street door? You would have seen her?'

'Aye, sir.' He stuck out his lower lip like a child falsely accused of wrongdoing. 'I'd have known. Especially a fine-looking lady like that.'

'Is there another way out?'

'Only the back, sir, into the yard. But a lady wouldn't want to go there.'

'Wouldn't she?' I said. 'We'll see.'

The porter's boy showed the way, escorting me past storerooms, larders, a kitchen, and into a lobby with a brick floor. From here a flight of stone steps led down to the yard with a necessary house, a laundry, a hen coop and various outbuildings for coal and wood. Two pigs were rooting in the muck with violent enthusiasm.

The only sign of human life was an old man chopping kindling very slowly with a small axe. He looked up when he saw the boy and me on the steps. I stepped gingerly through the refuse towards him. He removed his hat in a leisurely way and bobbed his head.

'Have you seen a lady pass by this morning?' I asked.

'Yes, master.' He stared at me with watery eyes. 'Don't see many of those down here. She was in a hurry.'

'Which way did she go?'

He gestured towards the gate at the back of the yard. 'Through there. The lane.'

I opened the gate. A crooked alley stretched away between two walls of flint and brick. A one-eyed cat sat at an open window in a cottage by the gate. The animal was staring at me with its singular fixity. There was no other sign of life.

The old man followed me into the gateway, the axe dangling in his hand. 'But she ain't there now,' he said helpfully.

There were dozens of doves pecking at the ground. It was midday and the stable clock at Euston was tolling to signify that the dinner hour was here. Cat walked past the front of the house, hurrying a little because she was late. A party of ladies and gentlemen was walking towards the wrought-iron gateway into the courtyard. Cat drew aside to allow them to cross her path. To her surprise, one of the ladies broke away from the rest and hurried towards her.

Cat recognized the face beneath the broad brim of the hat. She curtsied. 'Mademoiselle de Keroualle. Good day.'

'Mistress Hakesby. I didn't know you would be here.'

'Nor did I until a few days ago,' Cat said.

Exercise had brought colour to Louise's cheeks. She looked very pretty and very young. Though their previous meeting with Madame des Bordes at the Blue Dolphin had not been a happy occasion, she seemed pleased to see Cat.

'Why have you come?'

'To advise with my lord about the design of his stables.'

Louise laid a hand on Cat's arm. 'Tell me – is there news?' she whispered. 'Of *him*?'

'The Chevalier? I'm afraid he still hasn't been found, but . . .'

'Mademoiselle?' one of the ladies called.

'Then there's hope,' Louise whispered. 'He may be alive.'

Cat opened her mouth to speak, to say that despite the absence of absolute proof, there was very good reason to think that the Chevalier de Vire was dead. But she was too late.

'Pray hurry. We're late. My lady will scold us terribly.'

Louise skimmed across the gravel to join them, her cloak fluttering behind her. In her wake, a dozen doves took to the air in a panic-stricken whirl of white feathers.

By the middle of the afternoon, I had had enough of Newmarket. My limbs ached grievously from the unaccustomed horse exercise and my spirits were low. I had achieved almost nothing.

Both Grace and Rush himself appeared to have vanished from the face of the earth. I spent a couple of hours among the crowds on the Heath and going from tavern to alehouse in search of Durrell. I even made discreet enquiries about the pair of them at the Duke's lodgings and at those of his mistress, Lady Shrewsbury. I drew a blank everywhere. Both houses were full of people coming and going. It seemed unlikely that Grace could be kept unnoticed in either place.

The one thing I learned that afternoon came by chance and might well be of no importance. I fell into conversation with the landlord of a tavern near the church. I mentioned that Durrell was Buckingham's man and that he had a spike in place of a hand.

'A *spike*? No, sir, I ain't seen him in here. A spike's a thing you'd notice.'

'He's not a man you'd miss in any case.'

'Trouble is, the town's so crowded, looking for anyone's like looking for a needle in a bundle of hay. Besides, your fellow might not be here at all, if he's one of the Duke's people. He could be lodged outside Newmarket at His Grace's other place.'

'Where's that?'

'Elveden way. Do you know it?'

'I know where Elveden is,' I said. 'But nothing more about it.'

'The Duke's taken a hunting lodge near the village. I wager he left it too late to get somewhere nearer town. We're more crowded than ever this year.'

'He lives there himself?'

'No, sir – a gentleman wouldn't want to live in that house if he had any choice in the matter. It was sacked in the late wars and it's still half ruinous. But it does very well for His Grace's horses and some of his servants.'

I thanked him, finished my drink and took my leave. I had ridden through Elveden on my way here. At a guess the village was no more than five or six miles from Euston.

Before leaving Newmarket, I called at the White Lion. Rush had still not returned, and nor had his wife. I scribbled a few lines, passing on my lord's message, and left the letter with the porter, with orders to give it to Rush as soon as he returned: into his hands only, I emphasized, not into those of his wife or her waiting woman.

'Heard about his servant, sir?' the doorman said as I was about to leave. 'Terrible business.'

I stopped on the threshold and looked back. 'Mistress Susannah?'

'No, the manservant. Tom something.'

'Ledward. What's happened to him?'

'His master gave him leave to go to the races. I don't know the ins and outs of it, but he got into a fight with someone. They found him senseless in a ditch about an hour ago.'

'Is he badly hurt?'

'Stabbed. I heard he's bleeding from the head, and he stinks of strong waters. His arm's broken too.'

'Where's he now?' I asked.

'In an alehouse. They don't want to move him far, and they can't find Mr Rush. It's up to him to decide what to do.'

I considered this. I didn't believe in coincidence. The attack on Thomas Ledward sounded like Durrell's work, like those on Sam Witherdine and Pheebs in London. That was how Buckingham put pressure on people: by attacking their servants. If Durrell had assaulted Rush or Cat or me directly, there would have been too many questions asked.

'Is Mistress Susannah in the house?' I asked.

The porter nodded. I sent for her. After a few minutes, she glided slowly down the stairs, with her hands clasped together, her eyes on the ground; she looked demure as a nun.

I beckoned her into an alcove near the street door where we could speak confidentially. 'Now,' I said, 'I would like you to tell me the whole truth.'

She raised her eyes to mine. 'About what, sir.'

'About where your mistress is.'

'I told you, sir. I don't know.' There was no insolence in her voice. There wasn't much of anything at all. She might have been reciting a lesson that held no interest for her whatsoever.

'Where were you yesterday morning?'

That threw her. I saw her eyes flicker. But she recovered herself instantly. 'I was here, sir.'

'All the time?'

'Mostly.'

'So you did go out,' I said. 'Where?'

'Mistress Rush sent me to buy puppy water from the apothecary.'

'And who was the man you talked to on the way?'

'What man?'

'Don't lie to me. You were seen.'

She lowered her eyes again. It struck me how remarkably self-possessed she was.

'Well?' I prompted.

'Oh . . .' she said dreamily. 'Perhaps you mean that old broken-down soldier? Poor man. He was selling broadsheet ballads. I felt sorry for him and I bought one.'

'Show it to me.'

'I threw it on the fire, sir. It was a foolish thing. I only bought it to save his pride and give him charity.'

It was a clever lie. I couldn't disprove it and I couldn't force her to tell me the truth. I sent her away and walked back to Lord Arlington's lodging. At the stables that served the house, they gave me a different horse from this morning's. It was another mare, but I soon learned that her temperament was less placid than her predecessor's. It took all my work to manage her on the way out of town. It was a relief to find myself at last on the open road where there were fewer distractions.

I rode steadily and painfully for what seemed like a small eternity. Controlling the horse required all my attention. To my left, the sun dropped lower in the sky, and gradually the shadows of the trees lengthened across the fields.

I guessed that I must now be not far from the village of Elveden. I looked about me for signs of a substantial house or at least a range of buildings in the distance: anything that might be the Duke's establishment. There was nothing in sight, though I glimpsed something that might have been a chimney behind a belt of trees to the west of the road.

At that moment I heard hooves drumming on the road behind me. A single horse was coming at a gallop, and the sounds of its approach drew rapidly closer. The rider was blocked from view by a high, untrimmed hedge between me and the bend in the road.

The hooves grew louder and louder. The hedge dipped and I saw the rider. Or rather I glimpsed a man's hat bobbing up and down over the top of the hedge, while the curls of his wig danced behind him in a complex counter rhythm of their own.

My own horse meanwhile was moving restlessly beneath me, her head snapping to and fro and her body twisting in her agitation. I tried to guide her to the side of the road, but she resisted my tugs on the reins.

The horseman burst round the bend not twenty paces away, throwing the mare into an intense paroxysm of panic. She reared.

For a split second, time stopped. I was suspended between now and then, between here and there. I landed with a bone-jolting shock on the grassy verge by the road. My mind went blank.

After an interval, I opened my eyes. Above me was the blue, uncaring blank of the sky. The horse was placidly cropping the grass on the verge as if nothing had happened. My shoulder throbbed, and my head felt like a violently shaken egg. I was strangely undisturbed by this. It occurred to me that I must still be alive. Either that or I had entered an anteroom of heaven. Assuming, of course, that heaven was my ultimate destination.

A shadow moved across my blank, blue sky. Above me a voice spoke, and the voice was neither God's nor the Devil's.

'Faith, you fool,' said Willoughby Rush, 'are you trying to get yourself killed?'

CHAPTER FORTY

TOWARDS THE END of the afternoon, Cat finished in the stables and sent away the two servants who had assisted her. It had been a good day's work. She had surveyed the buildings and the neighbouring ground. She had even sketched out an idea or two in her notebook.

On her way back to the lodging, she encountered the head groom and learned from him that Mr Marwood had not yet returned. She felt disappointed, a disproportionate reaction. It was only that she wanted to tell him about her meeting with Mademoiselle de Keroualle before dinner and to discover what he had learned in Newmarket. But she hoped he had not met with an accident. Horsemanship was not his strong point.

She was passing the courtyard at the front of the house when Mr Banks appeared in the doorway leading to the steward's office. He saw her on the other side of the railings and waved like a man trying to summon a hackney. He broke into a run, his gown ballooning behind him and his clerical bands dancing around his neck. She stopped by the gateway to wait for him.

'Madam,' he said, his face reddening with embarrassment, 'would you – might I – that is, would you allow me to speak with you in private? I have something most particular to ask.'

Oh the devil, Cat thought, the numskull's not going to whisper words of love to me, is he?

He lowered his voice though no one was within ten yards of them. 'It's just that – if you permit – I wish to ask your advice on a most delicate matter.'

That sounded safer. In his agitation, Mr Banks was twining and untwining his hands. They were good hands, Cat noticed, shapely and long-fingered.

'Of course, sir. But I scarcely think I can—'

'Pray, madam, not here,' he interrupted. 'Let's find a place where we can talk discreetly.'

'Very well.'

'You – you're kindness itself. Perhaps the garden?'

The gardens were large, with many secluded corners. Cat had no desire to risk being alone with him. Instead, she led him into the yard in front of their lodging. It was spacious enough for them to talk privately there while people passed to and fro. They found a quiet spot beside a horse trough on the furthest side from the doorway. The air already had a chill to it, and no one was lingering nearby.

'What is it then?' Cat said, drawing her cloak more tightly around her.

'Madam, I had the most extraordinary interview this afternoon. My Lady Arlington sent word she wanted to advise with me.'

'About Sunday?' Cat wondered whether Lady Arlington wanted to give Mr Banks a friendly hint about his sermon before it was too late.

'No, not that at all; she didn't even mention it. She was most civil, most condescending – she saw me in her own closet with only her maid standing by. It appears that she wants me to play a part in an entertainment she has devised. A . . . a sort of masque, perhaps – in fact, I'm a trifle unclear about its precise nature.'

Cat suppressed an urge to laugh. 'Are you to act or sing or dance?'

'To act, I suppose. Though I have no skill in the dramatic art. To tell the truth, it was a little hard to ascertain exactly what my lady does want me to do.'

'But you're to play a part in this entertainment, whatever it is?'

'Yes, yes. One might almost say I am to play myself.'

Cat shivered. The wind was in the east, and she was becoming colder by the minute. 'You grow paradoxical, sir,' she said tartly. 'Your meaning?'

'Forgive me . . . I'm to play a clergyman. Which is why, in a manner of speaking, I am to play myself. You see, her ladyship intends the entertainment to have a pastoral theme. It will portray a country wedding. A swain will wed his sweetheart. No doubt there will be rustic dancing and a song or two.'

'When is this?'

'She was a little unsure. Soon, though. Tomorrow evening, perhaps, or Friday. I am to hold myself in readiness. It will only be a small private party, she said, a little innocent merriment among friends, and she will tell me exactly what to do.'

'You're to play a clergyman,' Cat said slowly. 'At a wedding. Which means, I suppose, that you are to conduct the ceremony?'

'Yes, I cannot think what else it could be. But what worries me is whether I should have agreed so readily to the proposal. At the time I was flattered by such kind attention from her ladyship. Who could not be? It was only afterwards that I wondered what the master of my college would say if he heard I had allowed myself to be drawn into such a sportive diversion, however innocent its nature. Or worse still, if the Bishop had word of it. I am in holy orders, after all. I should think of the dignity of my office.'

Surely, Cat thought, this cannot mean what I think it does? 'You could still refuse if it troubles your conscience.'

'But I would not disoblige Lady Arlington, madam, not for the world.' The blush returned. 'There is a living that will soon be vacant which is in his lordship's gift. It's quite eighty pounds a year, and a good house to go with it. She as good as said it should be mine as soon as the present incumbent is dead. I can't afford to turn away from such a generous and obliging offer. I'm the sole support of my poor mother, and I have three young sisters as well. They look to me to put bread in their mouths.'

Cat felt immense pity for Mr Banks. 'I suspect the Bishop will never hear of this. And even if he does, I doubt he would find grounds to censure you, given the company you would be keeping.'

Banks let out a sigh. 'Oh, madam. Your words take a weight off my mind. It is an inexpressible relief.'

'Be careful, though,' Cat said. 'The entertainment may not be quite as you expect.'

When I had my breath back, I struggled up into a sitting position beside the road. I was dizzy and bruised but, as far as I could tell, nothing was broken.

Rush was still on his horse, towering above me and looking about him. 'Where's Elveden?' he demanded. 'Is this Elveden?'

'If it isn't, it can't be far. Would you fetch my mare?'

The cursed animal had moved further away along the verge to another patch of grass. Rush glanced at her and then back to me. 'I'm looking for a place called Prior's Holt. Where is it? Quickly, man.'

'I don't know,' I said, which strictly speaking was true enough. 'Why?'

'Because that rogue's holding my wife there against her will.'

'Which rogue?'

'The Duke, of course. Or that villain of his. The one with the spike.'

Rush rose in his stirrups and turned his head this way and that.

I raised my voice. 'Mistress Susannah said your wife went out this morning without saying where she was going.'

He glanced down at me. 'I know.'

'Why do you think the Duke has something to do with this?'

'For the love of God,' Rush bellowed. 'Must you pester me so? Because when I got back the chambermaid had just told Susannah that she saw my wife being taken up by a coach. This morning, it was, on the corner behind the White Lion. The coach had the Duke's arms on the door. I went straight to his lodging. They know me there. The steward said his master took a coach to Cambridge today, and my Lady Shrewsbury with him. The Duke only has one other coach in Newmarket, and it took that vicious ape of his to

Prior's Holt this morning. That's an old lodge where he keeps most of his horses. In Elveden. Is that clear enough for you?'

'As far as it goes,' I said. 'But why?'

'Oh, hold your tongue, will you?'

'Did the porter give you my note?'

Rush nodded.

'We must go to Euston,' I said. 'If we lay all this before Lord Arlington—'

'No time. God knows what they're doing to her.' He looked past me. A farm labourer had rounded the corner and was trudging slowly and unsteadily down the road 'Ah – at last.'

He clicked his tongue and trotted off towards the new arrival. My horse looked up as they passed her and ambled after them. Rush had a moment's conversation with the fellow and tossed him a coin. The labourer dropped it, scooped it up from the road, and retreated out of sight. Meanwhile I scrambled with some difficulty to my feet. My vision blurred for a moment and then cleared.

'He says the Duke's place is over there,' Rush shouted to me. He pointed with his whip towards the belt of trees to our right. 'A lane goes off to it round the corner. Beyond that oak tree.'

That was the direction where I had glimpsed what might have been a chimney. 'Come to Euston first,' I said again. 'We'll manage the business much better with help.'

'You're worried about your precious skin, aren't you?'

That galled me, not least because it was true. 'If your wife is truly there, it's the safest way to rescue her.'

'You damned clerks are all the same. A lady's in danger, and you show the courage of a louse and no more honour than the slut in my kitchen.' He sneered down at me. 'And I thought you claimed to have a tenderness for her, though God knows you're not worthy to sweep the ground she walks on.'

'Sir, if we go to Euston, we—'

'Go to the devil for all I care,' Rush said, his face the colour of beetroot. 'I'm going to Prior's Holt.'

He ripped out his sword, tugged at his reins and wheeled his horse towards the oak tree. In a few seconds he was out of sight. My own horse tossed her fickle head and went after him without so much as a backward glance.

I swore. There was no one in sight. It would take me at least an hour or two to reach Euston on foot, and probably longer to find help worth having in the village.

I walked slowly towards the oak tree. The exercise eased some of the stiffness from my limbs. The hoofbeats of Rush's horse already sounded distant. I couldn't hear a second set of hooves now. Did that mean my horse had lingered to graze again? In that case, I might be able to retrieve the wretched animal.

I stopped at the mouth of the lane, which was bounded by two high hedges of hawthorn and hazel. No one was in sight. After thirty yards the rutted track turned sharply to the right. I advanced cautiously to the bend. Beyond it another short stretch was followed by a second bend, this time to the left. By the sound of his hooves, Rush was now far ahead, still galloping at full tilt.

I turned the next corner. The lane ran straight ahead for at least a hundred yards. It was empty. The dark mass of trees was nearer now. The sun was low in the sky, and my shadow lay like a giant's before me.

A sound made me look over my shoulder. Two men were

standing in the lane behind me, blocking my retreat. They wore heavy leather jerkins belted at the waist. Both were armed with heavy staves, and one carried a sword.

'Looking for your friend, master?' the older one said, advancing towards me. 'Reckon you'll find him with Mr Durrell by now.'

I glanced about me. The thickset hedges were impassable. I was trapped. The two men were now close enough for me to smell the ale on their sour breath. They had Buckingham's stag badge on their jerkins. I didn't flatter myself that I would have a chance if it came to a fight. I had no weapons – even my stick was gone, still attached to the horse's saddle.

'Come along with us, master. We'll help you find him.'

There was no help for it. I turned around and walked slowly up the lane towards the woodland ahead. They fell into step beside me.

'You made Isaac very happy, sir.'

'Who?'

'The man your friend spoke to on the road. Our pigman. He came straight back to the alehouse and found us. He'll get a pot of ale or two for his trouble.'

The hedges came to an end as the lane entered the wood. My horse was waiting for me there, the picture of equine innocence. The younger man took her bridle and she walked placidly along with us.

The trees closed around us in a cool, damp embrace like a foretaste of the grave. My captors were now so close to me that our shoulders brushed together. I was silently praying. The very thought of meeting Durrell made me nauseous with fear.

After a hundred paces or so we emerged from the wood

into the early evening sunshine: above our heads was the vast dome of the heavens, decorated by trailing clouds tinged with flame by the setting sun; and there before us, framed by a gateway, was Prior's Holt.

In that first instant, I had a confused impression of a jumble of buildings with low, jagged walls, of dilapidation and ruin, and of an old house with horses in a paddock beside it. But all this was pushed aside almost at once by what was happening not twenty yards away.

The man on my right touched me familiarly on the arm. 'There you are, master. There's your friend.'

The house and ruins enclosed on three sides an expanse of grass and mud. Rush had his back to the house and was facing a semicircle of half a dozen men. Two dogs, ugly brutes with shaggy coats and spiked collars, were snapping and snarling at his ankles. He was bareheaded, and his sword was out, its tip flickering this way and that. The riderless horses had sidled away towards their brethren in the paddock.

The fellow on my left nudged me. 'Good as a play, eh?'

'More like bear-baiting,' his friend said.

'Here comes the keeper.'

The door to the house stood open. Durrell walked ponderously into the yard. He carried a cocked pistol in his left hand. Rush must have realized someone was behind him, because he was in the act of turning when Durrell put the muzzle of the pistol to his head, and the point of his spike to Rush's neck, just below the ear.

For a second or two no one moved, even the dogs. Rush dropped the sword, and the men were upon him. They threw him down on his belly, and two of them straddled him.

Durrell looked about him in a leisurely way. I had not seen

354

him by daylight for more than three years. He looked older than I remembered. His hair was thickly streaked with grey. There was a long, pale scar on his cheek that had not been there before.

He caught sight of me standing with my guardians at the gateway between the lodge and the lane. He came towards us, the pistol lowered but still cocked. His heavy body swayed like water in a barrel as his weight shifted from leg to leg. He stopped when he was close enough for me to see the unshaven hairs and broken veins on his face. He looked me up and down as if appraising my value to him. It can't have been high, for he spat on the ground between us as he had done before when he waylaid me that night by the Savoy.

'Marworm,' he growled in his gurgling voice. 'I didn't think you were such a fool.'

CHAPTER FORTY-ONE

MARWOOD WAS NOT at supper. Cat looked everywhere for him.

Even Mr Banks noticed she was distracted. He enquired if he might have the honour of being of service to her in any way whatsoever.

'No,' she said curtly, barely registering the question, and sat down in her usual place. Banks settled himself beside her. He too was preoccupied. Tomorrow evening was weighing on his spirits.

'It's not only the dignity of my office,' he confided, 'the fact that I'm in holy orders. Quite apart from that, to mix with the King and the great ones of the world, and on such confidential, such intimate terms – why, the honour is too much. I fear I shall make a spectacle of myself or commit some gross impropriety. And yet my mother and my sisters will be so proud when I tell them.'

After supper, Banks insisted on escorting her back to their lodging. At first this irritated Cat, but as they were approaching the door, it occurred to her that she could turn it to her advantage. Marwood's chamber was with those of the other gentlemen on the ground floor, and it would not be fitting to go there herself. Instead, she asked her companion if he would be so kind as to knock on Marwood's door and tell him she desired to speak to him. Possibly scenting a rival, Banks was disconcerted by the request. Cat hastily made up a tale about Marwood's promising to find her the surveyor's plan for the stables in the Muniment Room.

Five minutes later, Banks returned to her with the news that Marwood's door was locked and there was no light showing through the keyhole. The servant assigned to the men's floor had not seen him since early this morning.

Cat said goodnight to the young clergyman and went up to her own room. She did not light her candle. Wrapped in her cloak, she sat by the window. Dusk was deepening into darkness over the kitchen gardens and pleasure grounds that stretched away as far as she could see.

No doubt Marwood had been delayed in Newmarket. Or perhaps his horse had thrown a shoe. True, he was a poor horseman, but that was no reason to fear an accident had befallen him on the way.

No other harm could have come to him. No one would dare touch him. He was known in Newmarket as Lord Arlington's clerk; the harness of his horse bore Arlington's badges and would be recognized as his throughout the county. Surely even Buckingham and Durrell would hesitate to assault him in broad daylight?

Surely that was so? Surely. Then why was she so afraid?

'Why didn't you fetch help?'

'Because you wouldn't listen to sense.'

Rush snorted. 'You didn't have to run after me like a . . . like a dog after his master.'

'If you'd had the kindness to bring me my horse, we wouldn't be in this plight.'

We glared at each other as best we could through the gloom. If looks could kill, we would both have been long dead. But neither of us was in a position to kill anyone by any method whatsoever. We had been placed in a stone chamber within a ruined portion of the building attached to the back of the house. Stone floor, stone walls, stone vault: stone everything, apart from the door, which was oak, grey as stone with age and bound with iron. There were two windows high above our heads near the ceiling. They were filled with tracery, which acted as stone bars. On the far side of the tracery was the darkening blue of the evening sky and the silver pinprick of a star.

My shoulder was hurting from my fall from the horse. My bladder was full to bursting. Rush had already voided his own bladder into his breeches, glaring at me all the while in case I dared to mock him. But the pains in my body were as nothing compared to those in my troubled mind.

I had thought that I was to some extent protected from the violence of Buckingham and Durrell. It was one thing to intrigue against Lord Arlington, quite another to murder his confidential secretary. They must also know that the King himself had once been pleased to show me favour, though not the reason for his gratitude. But no one knew I was here. And perhaps I was less important to Arlington than I thought. I had learned long ago that the gratitude of princes and their ministers is not something to be relied on.

'They set upon your servant this morning,' I said. 'Did you know?'

'What? Tom?'

'He was badly beaten at the races.'

'It's by the Duke's order.'

'Of course.'

It was cold and growing colder. Rush and I had been lashed to ringbolts in the walls. They hadn't bothered with gags because there was nobody to hear us. We were only five yards away from each other. We might as well have had the Atlantic Ocean between us for all the good it did.

After a while I said: 'We're wasting time.'

'What do you suggest we do with our time? Chew our way out?'

'Better that than argue with each other.'

Rush grunted. 'Faith, you've a point there.' For a moment he stared at the floor. Then in a soft, agonized voice he said: 'I wish to God I knew whether they have my wife here or not. What if they're taking turns to ravish her? And I not there to protect her?'

'His Grace would never permit a lady to be harmed. Surely?'

'You think so? You can't rely on the Duke, you know.'

'I do know.'

'Do you? You can't trust him in anything. In any way. That's why . . .' His voice petered away.

'Why you want to see Lord Arlington now? Because you can rely on him?'

There was no reply. But I knew that I had hit on the truth. Or rather on part of it.

'You've something to offer, I think? What is it? The more I know, the more likely I can help.'

There were footsteps outside. They stopped. I heard the grating of the bolts sliding from their sockets. Two men came in. One was holding a lantern and an iron bar, which he flourished before him. The other was Roger Durrell. I couldn't see his face clearly, but his bulk was unmistakable.

'Where's my wife?' Rush barked. 'If you devils have harmed her, by God I'll—'

Durrell kicked him in the knee. Rush screamed. He slumped to the ground, where he lay, moaning softly.

'Marworm. And Mister Rush.' Durrell gave the 'mister' a heavily ironic emphasis. 'A brace of fools, eh?' He stooped over Rush. 'As for you, friend, you want to be careful with that wife of yours. Pretty enough, I grant you that, but the temper of a hellcat. Nearly took out my man's eye.'

Rush was still breathing hard but he managed to say, 'What do you want of us, fellow?'

'I'm told that *Mister* Rush has something His Grace wants. And if *Mister* Rush doesn't give it to him, then *Mister* Rush's pretty young wife won't be pretty much longer. Not that it will matter much because by that time *Mister* Rush won't be able to swive her or anyone else.' Durrell turned his head towards me. 'As for you, you'll do as you're told and keep your mouth shut. If you don't, maybe the other one won't be pretty much longer either.'

'What are you talking about?' I said, though I knew the answer.

'That creature who plies her poxy trade at the sign of the

Rose in Henrietta Street. Your Covent Garden whore, eh? I'll take particular care with her, seeing we're old acquaintances. Got that? God's arse, for her sake, I hope you have.'

'Can we not come to an arrangement?' I said, trying to strike a more reasonable note. 'I saved your life once. Surely that gives us something in common?'

Durrell came closer, so close I could smell his breath. 'More fool you,' he said softly. He raised his hand and placed his forefinger and thumb on my eyelids. The tip of his spike touched the skin of my neck. 'You should have let me die. If you had, you wouldn't be here, would you?'

In a second or two he could pierce my windpipe and gouge out my eyes. Instead he sighed and turned away. As he left the chamber, the beam from the lantern briefly touched his face. He looked weary, even sad. A trick of the light, I thought. I listened to the two sets of footsteps receding into the darkness.

'The King comes here again,' Lady Arlington said. 'God willing.' She gave a theatrical shiver. 'He's riding in tomorrow's great race, and I fear for his safety. I'm sure you must, too. Why, these races can be almost as dangerous to life and limb as a cavalry charge.'

'I shall pray for His Majesty's safety,' Louise said.

The two ladies were pacing slowly up and down the big drawing room before going down to supper. The gentlemen were at cards near the fire, some of them overlooked by their ladies.

'It will only be ourselves tomorrow,' Lady Arlington went on. 'Less than a dozen. The King will prefer it if we don't stand on ceremony. He likes nothing better than the company of a few friends in the evening, and a little innocent merriment. Almost as if he were an ordinary gentleman. Though of course he can never be that.'

They walked in silence for a moment.

'Madame?' Louise said.

'What, my dear?'

'There's a door behind the tapestry in my closet. Where does it lead?'

'To a private stair,' Lady Arlington said. 'Pray don't trouble yourself about it. It's a convenience that some of our visitors like so they may come and go without rousing their servants. It's locked, and so is the door below. You will be quite safe. On my honour.'

'I found something else in my closet last night. A gown.'

Her ladyship smiled. 'Did you like it? Green suits your colouring so well.'

'I must thank you for your kindness,' Louise said.

'Oh, don't thank me, child. The King sent it. You must thank him yourself. And the best way to do that is by wearing it.'

'Madame, I can't—'

'It will be quite proper for you to do so when there is no other company apart from us. It will be just as if you were with your brothers and sisters.' She patted Louise's arm. 'Surely you can't think I would suggest you wear it if it were otherwise?'

Louise felt the blood rising in her cheeks. 'Of course not, my lady.'

That earned another pat. 'Shall I tell you a secret? I have the most delightful plan in hand. We shall make a diversion to entertain His Majesty and amuse ourselves in the doing of it. You know how he loves the theatre above everything? We

362

shall put on a sort of masque, just among ourselves, and pretend we are shepherds and shepherdesses for an hour or two. Perhaps we shall dance or tell jokes – wherever the fancy takes us.' She patted Louise's arm yet again, a little harder than before. 'Life would be a sad thing without a little innocent mirth. Don't you agree?'

Lady Arlington stopped. She turned back to Louise and smiled. She said nothing but her face made it clear that this time she was waiting for an answer.

'Yes, my lady,' Louise said.

'And think – you will make such an enchanting shepherdess. All the shepherds will lose their hearts to you. And probably the clergyman too.'

'Hush,' I said.

'Eh? Rush straightened himself. He had been slumped against the wall, breathing heavily. 'What?'

'Listen.'

There was a sound in the distance. A faint metallic scrape. A hinge in want of greasing? I strained to hear more.

An owl hooted. I remembered the barn owl that had flown over Cat and me last night in search of its prey. The night killer, she said. A sudden, desperate desire to see her welled up within me. To speak with her. To touch her before it was too late. Time was running away from me, and there was nothing I could do to stop it. The owl hooted again.

There were footsteps outside, soft and cautious. Then the sound of the bolts sliding back. The door slowly opened. A faint, wavering radiance entered our prison, along with the unpleasant smell of a rushlight. A shadowy figure materialized behind its murky flame.

'Sir . . . ?'

The whisper was so faint I could hardly hear it. But Rush tried to bound towards it as if goaded by a spur. The ropes that bound him held him back.

'Grace . . .'

'Hush.'

She stepped further into the chamber and set the light on the floor. I glimpsed a long blade in her other hand.

'Quick. Cut the cords.'

Rush held up his bound wrists, which like mine were fastened to a ring in the wall. She put the rushlight on the floor and set to work. I watched. I was by no means certain that she would free me once she had freed her husband.

While Grace was sawing the rope at his wrists, the light threw her face into profile. For an instant, and from that angle, she had an unexpected resemblance to her father: I glimpsed the sharp, hungry features she would have as an old woman when the loveliness of her youth was quite worn away.

'Christ. Careful, woman. That's my skin.'

'Someone's coming,' I whispered.

It was the same creak that had warned us of Grace's approach. She instantly pinched out the flame, and the room was plunged into darkness. Oh God, I thought, the door is open. We'll be betrayed.

There were heavy footsteps outside, mingling with the tap of a stick. The steps were irregular, as if the newcomer was staggering rather than walking.

I sensed that Grace had slipped away from Rush. A crack of light appeared along the edge of the partly open door, wavering and dancing in time with the footsteps. Then came the familiar sound of a man hawking and spitting.

The footsteps stopped. Durrell must have seen that the door was ajar. The light swooped downwards and there was a clanking sound as he set down his lantern on the floor. Then, with a suddenness that made me gasp, he kicked the door fully open. The smell of rum was added to the stink of rushlight and urine.

Durrell's massive figure filled the doorway. The spike glinted on the end of his arm. In his left hand he carried a heavy stick. He levelled the spike at us, raised the stick and took a step into the room. Then another. Then a third.

There was a blur of movement. Durrell cried out. The stick clattered heavily on the flagstones with a dull metallic ring. His arm flailed wildly. He gripped his neck with the only hand he had.

Grace pounced on the stick. Durrell was turning to face her, but he was too late. She swung the stick at the side of his head. There was a thud, and a faint cracking sound, as if someone at the other end of a kitchen were breaking open an egg. He cried out again and fell to his knees.

Grace hit him again on the top of his head. He slumped on to his side. Blood pooled around his head and neck, black not red in the faint light from the lantern in the doorway. She lifted the stick once more.

'Grace,' Rush said in a strangely tremulous voice. 'Pray stop now. There's no need for more.'

CHAPTER FORTY-TWO

WHEN I CONSIDERED the matter later, I realized that we paint the faces we expect, or the faces we want to see, on those we meet. When I first met Grace Hadgraft, I had thought of her as an angel in human form, a sweetly passive creature endowed with all the feminine virtues including a rich father and (perhaps pre-eminently) the ability to make my blood run hot. Then, after the terrible scene in her father's house, I transformed her into a weak and desperate slut, made ugly by her need.

The mistake was entirely mine. I had assumed that Grace, like all women, was essentially a plaything of fate, clay to the potter's hand, her life destined to be moulded by her father, husband or master. (I excepted Cat from the general rule on the grounds that she was always different from everyone else.)

But what of this new Grace, capable of killing another human being without remorse, and doing so even with enthusiasm? Where had she been? Where had she been hiding? She must have been there all the time, and I had simply failed to see her as she truly was, or rather as she could be. God knows, she had motive enough to kill Durrell: he had murdered her French lover, kidnapped her, and now he was threatening the life of her English husband. Grace was her father's daughter, after all. Until his ruin, old Hadgraft had shown few scruples when he set his heart on anything. Perhaps he too would have committed murder if circumstances had made it worth his while.

To my relief, Grace freed me as well as her husband. Meanwhile Rush made certain that Durrell was dead. Afterwards he and Grace held a quick, murmured conference. Then he turned to me.

'The dogs are out,' he whispered. 'But on the other side of this place, the side by the lane. If we go the other way, across the fields, we may get away. Can you walk?'

'I think so.' My body was such a mass of aches and pains it was hard to be sure what I was capable of.

'If we're lucky they won't know we've gone until morning. Most of the men are only here for the horses. Durrell had authority over them, but he had only one real confederate among them. That's the one set to guard my wife. She heard the two of them talking about where to put us, which is how she found us here.'

I cleared my throat. 'What happened to the other man?'

'Dead drunk,' Rush said, to my relief; I had wondered whether Grace had killed him as well. 'All she had to do was open a window and climb out. Come on.'

'Where are we making for?'

'How do I know?' he answered. 'Anywhere but here.'

We left Durrell alone in the stone chamber smelling of our piss and his blood and bowels. We barred the door behind us when we went. Grace explained in a whisper that our prison was off a cloister walk that ran from the kitchen end of the house to the more ruinous parts of the place. Fortunately, the moon was out, for we could not risk taking the lantern. Rush kept the weighted stick, which he had wiped on Durrell's shirt. His wife still had the long knife. She had snatched it up as she passed through the kitchen on her way to find us, and now she seemed reluctant to part with it.

We crept down the cloister towards the ruins. The moonlight played tricks with my eyes, filling the shadows with half-seen dangers. At the end of the passage, there was a ruined wall and an archway with a door set in it. The door was barred with a single length of squared oak that ran horizontally across it.

With infinite care, Rush and I lifted the bar from its brackets and laid it gently on the ground. We could not help making some sounds, but they were nothing compared to the mighty groans of the hinges when we pulled the door open.

Rush swore under his breath. We waited for a dog's bark, a footstep, a light. But there was only the silence of the night, and the call of the solitary owl.

And something else. Grace clutched her husband's arm. 'Can you hear that?'

'No. What?'

'Through there. Listen.'

I drew nearer, putting my head into the doorway itself. Then I heard it myself: the sound of snoring, low and steady, somewhere within the ruins. I edged forward and found myself in a roofless walled enclosure, brightly lit by the moon. There were two jagged holes in the wall on the left, blocked to waist height with hurdles, leaving windows to the sky. A hut had been erected in one corner of the enclosure. It was roughly walled with stones and covered with a low, sloping roof. That was where the snores were coming from.

'God be thanked,' I whispered over my shoulder. 'Pigs.'

We left the door ajar behind us. The enclosure was floored with a treacherous mixture of rubble, weeds and the pigs' excrement. I scrambled over the nearer hurdle. Rush helped Grace over the barrier as best he could. Her skirts caught on something, and she fell inelegantly into my arms.

'You oaf,' she muttered.

The pigs slumbered on. Rush joined us. We were standing on a patch of mud, which no doubt served the pigs as a run. There were ruined walls around us. The one directly opposite was lower than the rest, and broken with another gap partly filled with hurdles. Without a word, the three of us crept towards it.

Rush reached the hurdles first. He turned as I drew level with him and said in my ear: 'Fields. Woodland to the right. Better make for that.'

These hurdles were higher than the first one and they gave us more trouble, especially with Grace. I heard fabric ripping as we manhandled her over to the other side. But this time she hardly complained. We were within sight of freedom.

Fear lent us wings. We stumbled over two recently harvested fields and followed the edge of the woodland until we had put at least a mile between us and Prior's Holt. Grace held up surprisingly well. We stopped to catch our breath and take stock.

There were no signs of pursuit behind us. Now we had stopped, I realized how cold the air was. My cloak was gone. Grace still had hers, and her hat. Rush had neither. He had also lost his wig.

I heard the other two muttering to each other. Rush turned towards me.

'Any notion where we might find refuge?' he said. 'I don't know this country at all.'

'Which way's east?'

Rush looked up at the sky. 'That way.' He pointed ahead and to the right.

'Euston must be somewhere over there,' I said. 'It's the only place we'll be safe, and it can't be that far. But we'd best avoid roads.'

I have mercifully few memories of the next few hours. The three of us staggered and stumbled across fields and through woods. The moon came and went, playing tricks with us. We fell into ditches and waded through streams. We met inquisitive cows and startled foxes. Thorns caught at our clothes. Distant dogs barked and branches slapped our faces.

I lost all sense of time. Nothing existed except the cold and the wet, the pains in my body, and above all a crushing sense of weariness. I wanted to lie down, close my eyes and die. But still I drove myself on.

Later, much later, I was walking close behind the Rushes, and I chanced to hear fragments of their conversation. Rush was questioning his wife about yesterday. I drew closer.

'. . . but what the devil possessed you?'

'Susannah brought me a letter,' Grace said. 'From the Duke himself. Begging me to do him the honour of calling on him, and saying that you were coming to him at midday, and it would be a delightful surprise for you to find me there. He said he would send his coach to collect me, but that it must all be done privately, or the surprise would be spoilt.'

'You were a fool to go. A fool to believe such nonsense.'

'But he's a duke, sir, and for your sake I did not like to offend him by refusing. And it was such an obliging letter, and all done for you, to give you pleasure. Or so I thought.'

'Then what?' Rush said.

'His coach was waiting, with a running footman in livery, and others on the box. But when I got inside I found that ogre waiting for me . . .'

'Did the knave harm you?'

'No . . . but I was so frightened.' There was a catch in Grace's voice. 'He showed me his spike, sir, and . . . and then . . .'

'Oh, my little honey-bird,' said Rush, raising his voice in the emotion of the moment.

'Hush,' whispered the little honey-bird, and the conversation came to an end as we reached yet another field gate.

The stars faded, one by one. Clouds had already blanketed half the sky, and now they were invading the rest. I stared ahead, trying to will into existence the first trace of dawn on the horizon.

We came at last to a road. On the other side was a fence that stretched to infinity in both directions. It began to rain, first a few drops, then more steadily.

'We must be here,' I said with a confidence I did not feel. 'Euston.'

'Where's the nearest gate?' Rush said, wiping the rain from his face.

I had no idea. I peered this way and that. 'This way.'

I set off to the right, to the south if we had our bearings right, and the other two trailed after me. We kept to the road. It was fringed with woodland, and I reasoned that if we heard horses we would have time to take cover. Behind me, Grace was moaning quietly, and Rush was now muttering to himself. I prayed my guess was right.

Several hundred yards later, a gateway loomed up, breaking the line of the palings on our left. The iron gates themselves were closed, but there was a wicket to one side for foot passengers, and this was unbarred. I had never seen these gates before, but they bore Arlington's arms, and the drive on the other side must lead up to the hall.

'Are there dogs loose in the park?' Rush said.

'Only nearer the house, I think.'

'You'd better be right,' he growled.

'Or what?' I said, my own temper fraying. 'Or we have our throats ripped out? Would you rather stay on the road and chance it?'

The rain fell harder as we walked up the drive, splashing through the puddles. A building loomed ahead, a block of shadow against the paler night sky.

'It's the church,' I said, tilting my hat so the rainwater poured over the brim.

'In the middle of nowhere?' Rush sounded as though this were somehow a personal insult.

'It's within sight of the house.'

Cat had told me that when the park was enclosed, the villagers were moved further up the road. But the church remained where it had always been. This was a considerable annoyance to Lord Arlington because he could not keep the villagers from using the footpaths that led there across the park, one of which ran inconveniently close to the front of the house.

'I must rest,' Grace said faintly. 'And my feet are so sore I shall die.'

'My love,' Rush said, suddenly solicitous. 'Lean more heavily on my arm.'

'We'd best take cover here,' I said. 'Wait until it's light. If we go on, the dogs may find us before we reach the house and rouse someone.'

I unlatched the lych-gate and we staggered among the gravestones to the porch. The door was unlocked, and soon we were in the church itself. The air inside was dank and, if anything, even colder than outside. But at least we were out of the wind and the rain.

We felt our way about the place until we found a vestry, where there was a cupboard full of damp, musty garments. Rush heaped a pile of them on the floor, and he and his wife laid themselves down to rest.

I went back into the church and made myself a nest of cushions and curtains in what I guessed was the Arlingtons' own enclosed pew. I lay down in my sodden clothes and tried to stop shivering.

I don't remember much more until I was suddenly aware that something was trying to drag me up from the depths of sleep, much against my will, by vigorously shaking me awake. I groaned and opened my eyes. It was broad daylight. A pink, beaky face was inches away from my own.

'Mr Marwood!' said the Reverend Mr Banks. 'Oh, God be thanked, sir! You're not dead after all.'

CHAPTER FORTY-THREE

'THERE'S MUCH TO be done,' Mr Evelyn said on Thursday morning, 'as any educated eye must see at a glance.' They had reached the end of the terrace, and he and Cat stopped, while he studied the prospect before him. 'The first problem is the soil, of course. Sandy. Did you mark it yesterday afternoon when the wind was up? It was flying about in great drifts. It rained in the night, which has settled it for a while. But I fear that most of the park must be miserably dry and barren.'

'What's the answer, sir?' Cat said, her mind elsewhere. 'Is there one?'

'Trees, madam.' Evelyn struck the ground with his stick for emphasis.

She fiddled with a glove, pulling it more tightly over her fingers. Where the devil was Marwood? He still hadn't come back.

'I think trees are almost always the answer.' Evelyn gave her a grave smile. 'The roots hold down the soil, and the trees themselves act as a barrier to the wind and provide shade. All this is quite apart from their ornamental qualities and the value of the timber they produce. In my opinion there's no better investment for a nobleman's park.'

Cat had talked to the servant at their lodging earlier in the morning. He hadn't seen Marwood. He hinted that perhaps the gentleman had found a woman to delay him in Newmarket. As he was speaking, he had observed Cat carefully and maliciously to see if his words sparked a reaction.

'And the house, sir?' Cat said to Mr Evelyn as they paused at the end of the terrace. He offered her his arm as they descended the steps to the walk below, and she took it without thinking. Some men used courtesy as a preliminary for flirtation, but not him.

'It's very splendid within,' he replied, weighing his words with care. 'Everything most modern and convenient – and yet also suitable for a Secretary of State who sometimes entertains Their Majesties. But as for the outside . . . well' – he shot her a shrewd glance – 'perhaps my lord took to heart the lesson of the late Lord Chancellor's house.'

It was rumoured that the grandeur of Lord Clarendon's enormous house in Piccadilly, which stared down the hill at the relatively humble facade of St James's Palace, had not pleased the King. Cat thought it was Marwood who had told her that, but she couldn't confirm it because he wasn't here.

'The point is,' Evelyn went on, 'it doesn't do when a mere subject outshines his sovereign. It isn't pleasing in the eyes of God or man. Lord Arlington knows that as well as I do.' He gestured with his stick towards the house. 'Look. Perfectly appropriate to what my lord and his visitors need. And no more.'

'There's a lesson for us both here, sir.'

Evelyn gave her one of his rare, grave smiles. 'You remind me of my daughter, Mistress Hakesby. If I may say so, your intelligence is uncommonly quick for one of your sex. Yes, if you make a design for altering the stables, there's no need for them to be unduly showy. But they should do all that my lord requires. Meanwhile, when I advise him, I shall bear in mind that a nobleman's park is not the same as a king's.'

Above them on the terrace there was a stir of movement and the sound of voices. Through the gaps in the balustrade, Cat glimpsed Lady Arlington arm-in-arm with the small figure of Mademoiselle de Keroualle. Behind them strolled Lord Arlington with two other gentlemen.

The ladies wheeled to their right and stood at the balustrade almost directly above Cat and Evelyn. Lady Arlington was saying something about shepherds and shepherdesses.

Mademoiselle de Keroualle looked down and saw Cat and Evelyn below. She gave a squeak of recognition. 'Pray, my lady,' she said, interrupting her hostess in mid-sentence, 'permit me to exchange a word or two with Madame Hakesby. I have a question about . . . about architecture.'

Lady Arlington was too well-bred to show surprise, but she followed Louise with her eyes as she ran down the steps to the path. Evelyn bowed and instantly pleaded business elsewhere. He walked quickly away from the house.

'Thank God,' Louise murmured, turning her back to the watchers on the terrace. 'I must speak to you alone, madame.' She drew Cat further along the path. 'My affairs have come to a crisis. We talked of Monsieur de Vire yesterday. There's still hope that he lives. If so, he must be somewhere in London. I must go there. I must find him.'

'But you won't find him,' Cat said, 'he's—'

'I have jewels,' Louise interrupted, her eyes filling with tears and a rising edge of hysteria in her voice. 'I'll give them to you, and you can sell them. They will pay for everything and more. But I need your help to arrange it all. Madame des Bordes said I could trust you in everything. And it must be now. I must go today.' The tears spilled over and ran down her cheeks. She clutched Cat's arm. 'I beg you, madame. Help me. Or it will be too late.'

'There's no point,' Cat said. 'The Chevalier is dead.'

'What do you say?'

'He is dead. I'm certain of it, and so is everyone else. I tried to tell you yesterday. It was his body at the Chard Lane almshouse. The other man is still alive.'

Louise's mouth fell open. Her face lost its colour. 'Oh,' she said. 'Oh . . . I don't believe you.'

'I can't help that. But it's the truth. The Chevalier is dead.'

In the distance, the stable clock began to strike eleven.

'Then there's no hope for me,' Louise said.

She tore herself away from Cat and ran up the steps to the terrace. Lady Arlington started forward. Louise avoided her and ran into the house. Arlington broke off his conversation and looked quickly at his wife. Frowning, he turned towards Cat, who guessed that he was about to summon her to provide an explanation for Louise's sudden flight.

But there was a diversion at the far end of the terrace. Two men in filthy clothes had appeared and were arguing with the footmen who barred their way. At first she took the new arrivals for peasants who had blundered among their betters. An instant later she realized that one of them was wearing a muddy wig, which sat lopsidedly on his head. It was Marwood.

The clock finished striking the hour. Eleven o'clock.

Arlington turned in his stately way towards the newcomers. He frowned. Marwood came forward and bowed. He said a few words to Arlington and gestured towards the other man, who bowed in his turn. Cat recognized the red cheeks and the craggy, irregular features of Willoughby Rush. His bare head made him look older, sadder and unexpectedly vulnerable.

Lord Arlington stared at him. 'At least you are punctual, sir,' he said coldly. 'But I fear you have met with an accident on the way.'

By one o'clock, the three of us were back on the familiar road to Newmarket.

This time the conditions were more comfortable. Lord Arlington had given us a coach and four. He was taking no chances. We were escorted by two mounted servants, both armed. The coachman was armed as well.

Rush still looked like a vagabond, but he was in high good humour. He was dining on a hunk of cheese and a bottle of ale. Grace, however, was melancholy and withdrawn. She spent most of the journey staring at the passing countryside.

While Rush was conferring with my lord, the housekeeper had taken Grace under her wing and summoned a maid to attend her. Meanwhile I had had time to wash my face and hands and change my shirt. The steward had found me a dry suit of clothes, albeit of an antique cut. The peruke-man had done his best with the ruins of my wig, and Mr Banks had charitably lent me his only cloak. I had even had time to make an early dinner on half a cold chicken washed down with a glass or two of sherry. I had tried to find Cat, but to no avail. I had had to content myself with leaving a note for her with the long-suffering Mr Banks.

Lord Arlington told me that he had come to an arrangement with Rush. I was to return with him and his wife to Newmarket, where Rush would entrust me with something for my lord. Arlington didn't say what it was. I guessed it must be whatever Buckingham had earlier attempted to acquire by force. My lord had obviously relied on bribery instead, and bribery had won the day. That much I knew. But I was still no nearer discovering what lay behind this affair.

We made good time, covering the twenty-five miles in under three hours. The streets of Newmarket were even noisier than usual. The King had won his race, and the whole town believed it to be its loyal duty to celebrate his victory.

The coach dropped us at the door of the White Lion. The footmen escorted us across the pavement. The porter started forward to greet us.

'Is Mistress Susannah within?' Rush demanded.

'Yes, master, but what's—'

Rush brushed aside the porter and led his wife upstairs.

I hung back. 'Is there news of Tom Ledward?'

'Still lying senseless, sir. They say he's like to die of his wounds.'

I followed the others. When I caught up, Rush was rattling the latch on the door of their bedchamber. It wouldn't budge. He knocked and bellowed for Susannah.

'Who is it?' Her voice was soft. She sounded unruffled by the noise Rush was making.

'Who do you think, Susannah? Open the door or I'll knock it down.'

When the bolt was withdrawn, Rush lifted the latch, and the three of us filed into the room. Susannah retreated to the fireplace, where a small coal fire was burning brightly. A fire was an unusual luxury for one who was little better than a servant, I thought, especially on a day that was not particularly cold.

I noticed two other things in quick succession. Susannah was holding a small paper packet in her hand. And a partly dismembered coat lay on the window seat. I had seen Rush wearing it on Tuesday. One of the side seams had been cut open from the armpit to the top of the vent at the waist. There were scraps of buckram padding on the floor.

'What are you doing?' Rush said softly, his voice low and menacing. 'Give that to me.'

'I'm alone in the world, sir.' Susannah picked up the poker and stirred the fire until small flames danced among the glowing coals. She looked back at us with narrowed eyes. 'I must fend for myself.'

'You betrayed my husband's trust,' Grace said. 'My trust.'

'I do what I must. As we all do.'

Rush plunged forward. Susannah crouched and held the paper packet over the flames, turning her head to make sure we could see what she was doing. He stopped in mid-stride.

'Don't do that,' he said. He took a step backwards.

'Or what, sir?'

'Or you'll regret it. I paid you well enough to sew that inside my coat, didn't I?'

'You paid me half a crown.'

His right hand clenched into a fist. But he softened his voice: 'Perhaps you deserve another half-crown.'

'What will half a crown do for me next month? Or next year? I can't live for ever on half a crown.'

'What does that matter? You live with us. You sit at our table as one of the family.'

'Mistress Susannah,' I said gently. 'Pray tell us what you want.'

She threw me a glance. 'Only the usual things a woman wants. A husband. A house of my own. Money to live on.'

Rush gave a snort. 'Where the devil are——?'

'Let her speak,' I said.

'I want Mr Hadgraft to put a ring on my finger and wed me,' Susannah said. 'I want a house of my own to live in. I want an annuity secured on my life, and that of any children we may have. I doubt there will be children, but you never know.'

Grace's mouth gaped as the meaning of her words sank in. 'You want to *marry* my father?'

'Why not? My cousin, your mother, married him, so why not me? I'm no worse than she was, and she was better bred than your father could ever be. And I know him better than anyone does, including you. I know his ways. All of them. He's had me warm his bed for him often enough. Did you know that? He likes me to pleasure him, as far as that's possible nowadays.'

'I don't believe you.'

'Whether you believe me or not, Cousin, it's true. And you'll thank me in the end if we wed. You must do something with him. He may be bankrupt, but you can't leave him to rot in that cottage or tongues will wag even more than they are now. Someone must keep house for him and see he's fed and clothed. Unless he lives with you, of course, and you do it all yourself. But you wouldn't want that, would you?'

Grace compressed her lips. She said nothing.

Rush cleared his throat noisily. 'You may have a point. Give me that packet. Then we can talk about it.'

'No,' Susannah said. 'First, I want your written agreement

381

to settle the money on me and provide me with a house. Shall we say five-and-seventy pounds a year, not including the lease and any charges on the house?'

There was a silence. Rush and Grace looked stunned by her effrontery.

'Look on the table, sir,' Susannah said. 'I have it written out already, drawn up fairly. All you need do is sign it, and have your signature witnessed by Mr Marwood and a servant.' She glanced at me. 'I'll give the paper to Mr Marwood for safekeeping when you're done. Until everything has been arranged.'

'What a piece of moonshine nonsense,' Rush muttered. But his voice lacked conviction.

'What makes you think my father would agree?' Grace said. 'Have you thought of that?'

'You can leave him to me. Do you think he enjoys where you've put him now? Anyway, you'll back me to the hilt now you've had time to grow used to the idea.' Susannah's voice hardened. 'You of all people know it's best for everyone.'

The women exchanged glances. *You of all people know it's best for everyone.* I sensed a hidden layer of meaning beneath the words, as if Susannah and Grace were conducting a negotiation whose terms I did not understand.

Rush was entirely oblivious to this. 'I won't have mutiny in my own house, you slut,' he roared, his rage reigniting from its embers. 'I'll beat you until you bleed.'

Susannah stared at him but said nothing. She was still crouching by the fire. She turned her head and held the little packet an inch or two closer to the flames.

'Sir, there may be something in what she says,' Grace put in. 'Pray don't be hasty. I would not want it said that we have

382

been cruel to my father. Let's consult Mr Marwood. He is a man of the world. He knows the circumstances of our family.'

'I'd do as she wants,' I said to Rush.

He scowled. 'I don't need your advice.'

'But you do need my lord as your friend, not your enemy,' I said. 'And he has it in his power to be a very good friend, as long as you give him whatever is in that packet. If you fail in that, Buckingham will come after you, and your family, and you will have no one to protect you. By the way, the porter says your man Ledward was so badly beaten he still lies senseless. They say he's like to die of his wounds.'

There was a silence. Rush looked from me to Grace, then from Grace to Susannah.

'Is what she asks so very bad?' Grace said timidly. Her opposition to the plan seemed to have melted away. 'We must think of our reputation in the world. A daughter must always have a duty to her father.'

'I could have sold this to the Duke myself,' Susannah said. 'I guessed this must be what he wanted when that man of his gave me a letter to give to *her*.' She nodded towards Grace. 'But you didn't know anything about this, Cousin' – the packet twitched in her hand – 'so you weren't much use to him, however much he tried to cozen you.'

'You knew what was in that letter?' Rush said, his voice rising. 'All along?'

Susannah smiled. The warmth of the fire had reddened her cheeks and she looked almost pretty. 'A trifle, sir. We don't have time for trifles.' She held up the packet in her hand so we could all see it clearly. The paper was already darkening from the heat. 'Do you agree to my plan or not? That's the only thing that matters now.'

CHAPTER FORTY-FOUR

'SUCH SAD, SAD news,' said Lady Arlington, folding the paper and tucking it in her pocket. 'The King sends word that he remains in Newmarket this evening. But he promises that he will be here tomorrow, come rain, come shine.'

The maid who had brought the letter withdrew. Louise felt a rush of relief at the stay of execution. They were in Lady Arlington's closet, where her ladyship had been showing her some of the curiosities she had collected for her cabinet.

'Perhaps it's as well. I think you've been crying this afternoon. I can see it in your face.'

Louise stared miserably at her lap. She hadn't really been surprised when the strange architect woman had told her the Chevalier was dead. Part of her had known from the start that it must be so. Besides, even if he had been alive, how could a man like that have ever offered her what she needed? Nevertheless, she had wept for him for more than an hour. And for herself.

'Everything passes,' Lady Arlington said briskly, 'even

sorrow. No doubt you're homesick for France, for your friends. But soon you will be more settled in this country, and you'll find that all will be well again. Indeed, it will be better than before.'

Louise looked up and tried to smile. What else was there to do but make the best of it?

'There,' Lady Arlington said. 'You look better already. Now don't worry about tomorrow. Marie will put something on your face when you retire, and after a good night's sleep it will be as beautiful as ever. We can't have a sorrowful shepherdess at the revels, can we?'

Cat was at supper when Marwood returned. He hesitated in the doorway, his eyes searching for her. He looked old, shabby and exhausted, a creature at the end of his endurance. He was wearing a ridiculously old-fashioned suit of clothes that was too big for him. She would have liked to put her arms around him and make him look young again.

She waved him over. Mr Banks looked askance at Marwood, for he had been in the middle of proving (by an ingenious argument of his own device) why the Church of England's teaching on the Resurrection was wholly in accord with the precepts of reason and recent discoveries of the Royal Society.

'Madam,' Marwood said, 'may I beg the favour of a private word?' He glanced at Banks, who turned pink, opened his mouth but said nothing. 'Your pardon, sir. It's on my lord's business or I would not venture to disturb you. And I must thank you again for the loan of your cloak.'

Cat followed him out of the hall and into the lobby. 'Where have you been all this time?' she said crossly, though she knew it was none of her business, any more than the dirty pallor of his skin or the shadows under his eyes.

'Newmarket. My lord sent me there this afternoon with Mr Rush and his lady. I'm only now returned.'

He led her outside. It was dark now, and raining. He noticed her shiver, and he slipped his cloak around her shoulders. Or rather Mr Banks's cloak. Why was he wearing that?

'How's Mistress Rush?' she asked in a colourless voice. 'Has she regained her looks?'

'I don't know, and it doesn't matter. Nor does she.' He drew away from her. 'I haven't long – I must take something to Arlington. But I want you to see it first. We must find somewhere to talk. Would you allow me to take you to the closet where I sleep? It is quite private, set aside from the rest, and there should be no one about at this time.'

For answer, she took his arm. They walked back to the lodging. Marwood moved stiffly, as if his limbs pained him. The main door led to the men's quarters on the ground floor and to the staircase to the women's rooms above. A porter was permanently stationed at the foot of the stairs, partly in the interests of decorum. Marwood steered her into a dark path that veered away towards the corner of the building.

'There's a side door along here, and the steward gave me my own key.' He pointed. 'And there's my window beyond. It's quite safe. No one will see us go in.'

And if they did, she thought with a shiver, how they would gossip about us.

Marwood unlocked the door. Inside, a lamp was burning on a bracket set high on the wall. He took a candle end from the box below and lit it from the lamp. He unlocked his door and Cat followed him inside. The closet was sparsely furnished with a truckle bed, a chair and a small table. Marwood lit another candle from the flame of the first and set them both on the table.

'What happened yesterday?' she said.

'Durrell took Rush's wife by trickery to a house the Duke leases in Elveden. Rush played the hero and went to rescue her. Instead, he fell into Durrell's hands, and that dragged me there too.'

'Where's he now?'

'Durrell? He's dead.'

'By Rush's hand?' She swallowed, her mouth suddenly dry. 'Or yours?'

'Mistress Rush killed him.'

Cat stared at him. 'You cannot mean that.'

'She did. I saw her with my own eyes.' He shivered. 'She was like one possessed. She stabbed him then she tried to beat his skull to pulp. May we not talk of it now? There's something else. I need your help.'

She sat down on the chair. Marwood perched on the end of the bed and placed a folded paper before her on the table. He moved a candle nearer to her.

'What's this?' she asked.

'It's what Rush had to sell. The Duke tried to get it by force. Arlington was wise enough to use bribery instead. I'm to take it to him directly. But I wanted you to see it first. Open it.'

'You've already broken the seal. My lord will know it's been tampered with.'

'I'll do a fresh one. There was no device on Rush's seal. He used the back of a spoon to press it down, and I can do the same.'

Cat unfolded the paper. It enclosed two letters, both addressed to Monsieur Pharamond at the Three Crowns on Snow Hill, and both in the same large, clumsy handwriting. The seals on the letters had also been broken but they had originally borne a device, though it could no longer be deciphered.

'How did he get them?' she said.

'From his servant. Ledward claimed that he'd found the packet in the Chard Lane site yard after the body had been taken away. Before Hadgraft discharged him as watchman.' Marwood shrugged. 'But all this is according to Rush. We can't ask Ledward anything at present. He was beaten almost to death yesterday morning.'

'Who did it?'

'Attacked Ledward? Durrell's people probably, with the intention of frightening Rush. It's all of a piece with the attacks on Pheebs and Sam: attack the servants to intimidate their masters.' Marwood waved his hand impatiently. 'But pray – I'm pressed for time. The letters. Will you translate them?'

She held his gaze for a moment and then unfolded the letter that was uppermost. 'It's the same writing as on Iredale's address, isn't it? On the paper we found in the shoe from Chard Lane.'

'Yes. And the same as on the note of gambling debts in Iredale's box of gold. You remember? Scribbled on the back of a bookplate bearing the Orleans arms. Mademoiselle de Keroualle's debts.'

'*Dieppe*,' she recited slowly from memory, '*le 15° Septembre 1670.*'

Marwood nodded. 'During the time when she was waiting

for Buckingham's yacht, which never came. Both Iredale and the Chevalier de Vire were there too. I wrote to Arlington from London and enclosed the bookplate and the address. When he wrote back, he told me the matter touched on an affair of state, and he forbade me to investigate them any further.' In the urgency of the moment he leant forward across the table and touched her hand. 'Cat, he said he'd have me ruined if I didn't keep my mouth shut about them.'

She did not move her hand away. The skin tingled. She wondered whether he had meant to touch her. 'What do they say?'

'I tried to read them in the coach but I struggled with the language. Will you translate? They are both unsigned.'

Cat took her hand away and unfolded the first. The letter was addressed only to 'Monsieur'. *Je meurs d'amour*. 'She says she dies of love.' Her eyes met his.

'I understood that part,' Marwood said drily.

Cat read on. 'Oh, the poor stupid girl.' She looked up again. 'Here she's thanking God that she's bled this month. Which can only mean . . .'

'That she feared she might be with child.' He was speaking rapidly now, the words tumbling out in feverish haste. 'What date's that one?'

'The eighth of October last year.'

In the candlelight, his face was intent, fixed and unreadable, as if moulded in wax. 'Then that suggests that she and de Vire lay together when they were in Dieppe. Madame des Bordes told you that the King prizes Louise's virginity highly.'

Cat said, 'That aside, she must have been terrified at the thought of finding herself with child at Whitehall. The shame of it. The mockery. The ruin of everything.'

'What else is there? Quickly. Someone's probably told my lord by now that I've returned. And I've still got to reseal the packet.'

'In the first letter? She says she's desolate that she cannot send him any money, but she swears on her brother's grave that she will find some soon. She's desperate to see him. She begs him to take her away and marry her.' Cat took up the other letter. 'This one is later – the ninth of September this year. There's more mention of the debts.' She bit her lip. 'And the tone's very different. Iredale has been demanding that she pay what she owes, and if she doesn't, he's threatening to make a scandal about her and the Chevalier. But she wants the Chevalier to tell Iredale she must have more time. She also warns the Chevalier that he mustn't breathe a word about the other thing or she can't answer for the consequences. "The matter at Dover." That's what she calls it.' Cat's mouth was dry. 'That's underlined.'

Marwood looked up at her, his eyes widening. Reflected candle flames flared in his pupils. 'The secret treaty? The little fool knows about that, does she?'

Cat spoke in a whisper: 'The French pension for the King? And in return his promise to turn Catholic?'

'Yes. Mademoiselle de Keroualle was at Dover last year, attending Madame the Duchess of Orleans. And she was there later, too, at Madame's deathbed. It's possible that she overheard something.'

'And she told the Chevalier about it? Is that why someone wanted him dead?'

'It doesn't quite fit,' Marwood said. 'Besides, she can't have been stupid enough to tell Buckingham, surely? Not about Dover. Because then the Duke would have realized he'd been made a fool of all along, by the King, by Arlington, by everyone that matters. But perhaps Arlington feared she might . . .' He rubbed his forehead. 'No – I think she must have asked the Duke to prevent Iredale and de Vire from pestering her. Nothing more. By that time, her feelings for de Vire would have cooled. After all, a whole year's gone by since Dieppe, and he's done nothing for her except demand money.'

'No,' Cat said. 'You're making this too simple. For Louise, perhaps it wasn't black and white, perhaps love wasn't a game of chess.' She paused, marshalling her thoughts. 'She wanted to stop the two of them pestering her. I think she always knew that de Vire was a rogue, but she couldn't quite let herself believe it. But now she's terrified of what will happen if she surrenders to the King. She knows she can't keep him dangling for much longer. And that's made the Chevalier seem overwhelmingly desirable to her again . . .'

'The world well lost for love?' Marwood said, refolding the letters. His lips curled. 'Is that really what she wished for?'

'You don't understand,' Cat snapped. 'De Vire was the only person in the world who might possibly have helped her. Besides, sometimes people do think the world is well lost for love, and they try to act on it. Or perhaps she doesn't really know what she wants. Most people don't. But she does know that she doesn't want the King.'

'She'll do well enough with him,' Marwood said, yawning. 'He's not ungenerous to his mistresses.'

Cat stared at him. 'You are grown strangely cynical. I don't like it.'

He looked away.

She shrugged and stood up. 'I'm going now. I want to find

Mr Banks and hear the rest of what he's discovered about the Resurrection.'

'Cat,' he said, 'stay a moment.'

She glanced at him. 'I don't want to.'

She lifted the latch and went out into the passage. She walked swiftly to the side door and let herself out into the blackness of the night.

I was directed to the library. The servant outside the door told me to knock and enter directly. I found Lord Arlington with Mr Evelyn. They were either side of a large table covered with a Turkey carpet, on which a plan had been unrolled. A candlestick stood at each corner, both shedding light and preventing the paper from curling.

Mr Evelyn was in the act of pointing out a feature of the plan with a long ruler. 'And here, my lord, would be the fountain—'

He broke off as I came in. Arlington murmured an apology: something about the King's business being a hard taskmaster. He beckoned me to follow him to the neighbouring closet. I bowed awkwardly to Evelyn on the way. One of my feet was badly blistered after last night's escape from Prior's Holt, which made me limp. I was so tired I could have laid myself down on the floor and fallen asleep in a trice.

'Well?' my lord said softly as soon as the door closed.

'I have the – the papers here.'

I took the resealed packet from my pocket and gave it to him. I had almost said 'the letters', but that would be to admit that I had opened the paper that enclosed them.

Arlington sat down and drew the candle closer. He glanced up. 'Stand by the door. I don't care to be overlooked.'

I muttered an apology and obeyed.

'How did Rush come by them?'

I told him about Thomas Ledward.

He grunted. He broke the new seal on the packet and tore open the paper. He studied both letters, holding them to the light of the candle. Afterwards he folded them carefully and placed them inside his coat.

'Good,' he said and paused. He touched the black plaster he always wore on his nose as if to make sure that it was still there. 'But then there's the unfortunate matter of Prior's Holt.'

'What?' I gawped at him like a simpleton. 'Your pardon, my lord, I don't understand.'

'I had a visitor this afternoon,' he said, his voice slow and measured. 'The Duke of Buckingham's private secretary. His Grace is now back from Cambridge, and he's deeply distressed. It appears that a confidential servant of his, a Mr Durrell, was brutally murdered last night at Prior's Holt, where the Duke keeps most of his horses. He has an ample supply of witnesses who will swear that you and Mr Rush called on Durrell yesterday evening, and that you offered him violence. Indeed, Durrell and his fellow servants were obliged to restrain you both for their own safety. But you yourself broke free during the night. You attacked Durrell in a frenzy. You stabbed him and cracked open his skull. Then you freed Rush and left Durrell dead in a pool of his own blood. You absconded through the fields, leaving your horses behind as silent witnesses to your murderous deed.'

'But . . . but, my lord,' I said. 'You know this is false. It's a pack of lies.'

'Of course I do, Marwood. So does the Duke. But whether

it's true or not isn't the point, is it? The point is that the Duke can produce a murdered man, together with a number of witnesses who will swear to your guilt. He's even got your horses as material evidence, as well as some of your clothes. Mr Rush admits he had an old quarrel over a gambling debt with Durrell, but says it was you who urged him to confront the man at Prior's Holt. And you who escaped and killed Durrell in a fit of murderous rage.'

I felt like a man trying to stand on quicksand. 'You know I'm innocent, my lord.'

Arlington waved aside that trifling fact. 'Mr Rush has offered to give me and the Duke a written account of your assault on Durrell. Duly signed and witnessed. All of that combined would make a very strong case indeed against you.'

CHAPTER FORTY-FIVE

O N FRIDAY MORNING, the Euston steward sent a footboy to escort Cat to his office. When she arrived, he offered her a chair and enquired how she was. He was a plump, elderly man who modelled his stately manners on those of his master.

'You've completed your survey, I understand?'

'Yes, sir. I have also sketched out some rough proposals for my lord. I'll need to work them up before I show them to him. But that could be done in London more conveniently than here.'

'My lord knows that you are in a hurry to return.'

'I'm in the middle of a project.'

'The Chard Lane almshouse, perhaps?' he said, raising bushy eyebrows. 'What a dreadful thing that murder was. It must have come as a terrible shock to you.'

'Indeed, sir.' Cat had fended off many enquiries about the murder during her stay at Euston, and she had no wish to dwell on the subject now. 'It also caused us considerable inconvenience. We have much to do before winter comes.'

'My lord's aware of that. He commands me to tell you that he would have no objection to you leaving on tomorrow morning's coach to Goring House.'

Cat inclined her head. 'I'm most obliged to him.'

She was relieved that Arlington's permission to leave had been so freely offered. She had feared that she would have to petition him for it. But now it had been granted, she had a perverse desire to stay here longer, to find out how Marwood fared.

She was worried about him, for his ordeal at Prior's Holt had left its mark, and the business that the Chard Lane murder had started was still unfinished. But there was another reason for her concern. Since Arlington had taken him into his employment, Marwood had changed, and not altogether for the better. Sometimes he showed a streak of weary cynicism that was not to her taste. Perhaps it wasn't to his taste either. He had risen in the world, but he wasn't happy.

'But my lord begs that before you leave you would cast an eye over the church,' the steward was saying. 'You must have seen it as you passed through the park. Something of a blemish on the estate, I'm afraid.'

'What does he want me to do?'

'To survey it and make an accurate ground plan.' The steward smiled. 'The church is much decayed, and most inconvenient. He contemplates replacing the existing structure with a building more in keeping with the Hall. And also, of course, more suitable for modern forms of worship. It would have to be on the same site, which is all the more reason for it to be congruous with its surroundings.'

Cat made a swift mental calculation. That would be at least

another morning's work, probably more, depending on how detailed a survey Arlington wanted.

But the steward hadn't finished with her. 'My lord would be interested to hear your suggestions about a new church, about some of the possibilities for the site.' He sat back and stroked his paunch affectionately. 'His Lordship's patronage is not easily won, Mistress Hakesby, but, believe me, once gained it's well worth keeping.'

The steward provided Cat with the two servants who had assisted her when she surveyed the stables. The three of them walked down the drive. Cat had seen the church from afar but until now she hadn't had the opportunity to examine it. It was only about three hundred yards from the mansion.

The building had few pretensions. The walls were faced with flint, like those of most churches nearby. There was a low tower with a long crack running down from its west window. The porch was unlikely to last the winter, tiles were missing from the nave roof, and the sagging guttering was fractured in three places on this side alone. Within, the story was the same. The roof of the north aisle had a substantial leak. The plaster in the chancel was rotting away, shedding puddles of damp dust on the flagstones. The memorials were dark with dirt and age.

All in all, she agreed with Lord Arlington and his steward. The church was in no sense a proper ornament to a nobleman's park. Surely not even God could derive any satisfaction from its melancholy decay.

Cat and the men set to work. It was curious how quickly she was absorbed in the business of recording measurements and calculating angles. When that was done, she made notes about the condition of the building and the churchyard. Meanwhile the men sat smoking and gossiping on the wall by the lych-gate.

As she worked, she forgot the murderous business with Rush, Durrell and the Duke of Buckingham. She forgot Chard Lane and Brennan. She even forgot about Marwood. Instead, she was aware of a rising tide of excitement. The possibilities of this commission filled her with anticipation. To build her first church in a place like this, in the park of one of the most important noblemen in the land, would truly be an achievement. If she carried it through as she would like, if Arlington would give her a free rein, it must increase her reputation substantially. Even Dr Wren might find something to admire in her work.

She had almost finished her notes inside the church when she paused on the chancel stop. She stared up at the gable wall, where there was another damp patch, this one in the shape of a very large heart. At the apex of the gable there was a tiny triangle of stained glass. It was only visible if you looked up from this spot. The window was so small and high that the Reformers must have missed it when they smashed the rest of the church's windows. She squinted up at it, making out a crudely outlined head against a blue background, with what was perhaps a halo behind. Probably a woman's head, she thought. Perhaps she was imagining an unsettling resemblance to Grace Rush.

She heard the latch crack up on the south door. She turned, expecting to see one of the servants. But it was Mr Banks who sidled into the church, leaving the door ajar. He had a strange ability to make himself look shifty, as if he suspected that he had no right to be wherever he was and hoped that no one would notice his presence.

'Oh!' he said, as he looked down the nave and caught sight of Cat in the chancel. 'Mistress Hakesby! I – I had no idea you were here.'

Cat didn't believe him. Banks might be awkward in company but he wasn't a fool. Even if he hadn't come looking for her, he must have seen the servants outside and noted the surveying poles beside them. She hoped he wasn't about to speak words of love to her, or even tell her more about his prospects. She wasn't a vain woman, but she could recognize languishing looks when she saw them.

'Are you come to practise your sermon for Sunday, sir?'

'No – the steward tells me that they rarely use this church for services. The fabric is deemed too ruinous.'

'It's certainly that,' Cat said. 'It could fall down about their ears.'

'It appears that I am to preach at the house. Lord Arlington has a private chapel for the family.' He shivered. 'Before the King. As you know.'

'The King's but a man, sir, when all's said and done.'

He avoided her eyes. 'And I am also to see His Majesty this evening.'

'It's confirmed that he comes today? Does it mean that he will take part in this masque or whatever it is?'

'I don't know.' Banks swallowed. 'But he will be there . . . My lady tells me I must bring a prayer book and wear my gown and bands. The great folk will be dressed not as themselves but as shepherds and shepherdesses.'

Cat could not help herself. 'Will there be sheep as well, sir?'

He took the question at face value. 'That I don't know. But I'm still not easy in my mind about it. I quake with fear at the thought of preaching on Sunday, but I know God will give me strength, for I shall be doing His work, and there can be no sin in that. But this evening's party is different. It's all in jest, I know . . . innocent merriment, as my Lady Arlington says, no more than a harmless private frolic which cannot impair the dignity of the cloth . . . And who am I to question the judgement of my betters? Of the King himself? And of course it may be to my advantage to be in such company, and in such an intimate setting. But . . . but sometimes this entertainment seems — well, almost irreligious. Madam, my conscience pricks me.'

He stared at her, and Cat saw the misery in his eyes. She felt herself reproved by his sincerity.

Through the open door came the distant sound of the stable bell ringing its midday summons to dinner across the park. She found herself liking Mr Banks.

'Will you walk back with me, sir? That was the bell for dinner.'

For an instant she glimpsed a most ungodly glint in his eyes. But the spark faded at once, and he said, 'If it would not inconvenience you, I would rather stay. I . . . I came here to pray.'

While Louise was dressing, she heard the fiddlers tuning their instruments below. To her surprise, the party was to be held in a large apartment in the same pavilion as her own quarters. She asked Marie if she knew the reason for this.

'They say it will be more convenient to have it there,' her maid said with lowered eyes. 'There are closets where the ladies can withdraw if they grow fatigued, and where they can adjust their costumes. And it's nearer to the King's apartments, so he will have less far to come.'

Louise's costume for the evening was already laid out on the bed. It resembled the dress of a shepherdess in the way a gentleman's periwig resembled a peasant's greasy hair. The gown was of silk, delicately embroidered, and equipped with a multitude of ribbons and a profusion of lace. It was a little shorter than good taste considered suitable; it even allowed the occasional glimpse of ankle. When Louise had pointed this out at the fitting, Marie said shepherdesses were obliged to wear their skirts like this to avoid soiling the hems as they went about their work among the sheep.

The accompanying straw hat was decorated with flowers, also made of silk. The matching straw basket contained sweetmeats. There were white gloves with pearl buttons at the wrists and a pair of pink shoes with vertiginously high heels.

As Marie was dressing Louise's hair, Lady Arlington came into the closet. 'My child, you look quite delicious. Your sheep will worship you, and so will your swain.' She sent Marie away and sat down. 'I wanted to tell you that I have engaged a real clergyman for this evening. The one who will preach to us on Sunday.'

'I don't understand – why is there a priest?'

'He's a Protestant one, of course, but you won't mind that. You see, it occurred to my lord that it might be considered impious if a wedding – even one of this nature – were conducted by a man who is not in fact in holy orders. My lord has to be so scrupulous. He cares for his reputation above all things.'

Louise felt a shiver run down her spine like a cold fingertip. 'Whose wedding, my lady?'

'Why yours, of course, my dear. Didn't I mention it? A merry pastoral would not be complete without a wedding, would it? Our shepherds need a reason to hold their dance. Afterwards, by the way, pray change into your green gown. I'm sure the King will wish to see you in it. It would not be polite to deny him such an innocent pleasure.'

When the time came, Monsieur Colbert arrived to escort Louise downstairs. He was in costume, which included a long, grey beard and a shepherd's crook.

'You look enchanting, mademoiselle. I'm proud to play the part of your rustic father.'

On their way down, the ambassador paused at the half-landing. No one else was in earshot. 'Remember your duty to the King,' he murmured. 'To our king. It's a great honour to be able to serve him. And truly, I believe his cousin the King of England would offer you marriage if he could. There's no doubting his passion for you.'

'He can't marry me,' Louise said, made bold by despair. 'There's no more to be said.'

'Oh, but there is. This masque, this pastoral wedding – it is not entirely in play. Consider this. My lord has found a priest to perform the ceremony. A most bashful young man, by the way, newly ordained into the Church of England. He's a heretic, yes of course. But a priest nonetheless. This means something. The King will give you his hand in marriage, will he not? And under the aegis of the church of which he is the Supreme Head.'

'He's already married,' she burst out. 'It means nothing.'

402

'Hush, not so loud.' Colbert patted her hand. 'You're wrong to think it means nothing. For him it signifies a great deal. It's a sign of intent, a promise. One might almost say that, in a sense, for him it is a form of betrothal. You are already the queen of his heart. Suppose – well! No one wishes Her Majesty to die, naturally, but it can't be denied that her health is not always as good as we would like . . .'

In the apartment below, the fiddlers began to play a jig. Monsieur Colbert led her down the rest of the stairs. At the bottom, two footmen sprang forward and opened the doors to the apartment beyond. The music stopped abruptly, and there was a burst of applause as Louise appeared on the ambassador's arm.

She registered a blaze of lights and a blur of faces. Among the little crowd were Lord and Lady Arlington. Madame Colbert was smiling inanely at her. One face leapt out at her, the only one that was not looking at her. It belonged to a thin young priest in a threadbare gown. He was staring at the newly waxed boards of the floor. He looked almost exotic in this setting like a half-starved crow among the plump birds of paradise.

Directly opposite the door, Louise's swain was seated on a carved armchair. A wreath encircled his black periwig like a green crown, and his shepherd's crook was garlanded with ribbons.

Colbert gave her arm a discreet squeeze and stood aside. Louise advanced alone. She was barely aware of the people on either side. Now this was happening, she was calm and steady. There was only this path left for her to take, she thought, and all she could do now was to make the most of it.

Three yards away from her bridegroom, she sank into a low curtsy. The King rose slowly to his full height. He towered over her. She had to fight the impulse to move back, to turn and run.

He stepped forward and raised her up. 'At last,' he said softly. 'At long last.'

CHAPTER FORTY-SIX

IT WAS GROWING late. I locked away my papers in the desk, extinguished the candles and left Lord Arlington's apartments. I took the servants' stair that led down to the lobby by the side door. The main staircase was nearer, but I was in no mood to encounter company.

I emerged into the forecourt. There was a burst of music in the distance, coming from one of the pavilions on the garden in front of the house. Fiddlers were playing a merry jig. For a man who prided himself on his sophisticated tastes, Lord Arlington was unexpectedly partial to such simple measures.

Darkness had fallen. The air was cold, and the wind held the promise of rain to come. I wrapped my cloak around me and walked slowly towards the lodgings. My limbs ached from my recent exertions and I lacked the energy to hurry. I had spent all day and part of the evening confined to a closet, attending to my lord's business and worrying about my own future. My spirits were low. I knew I should eat something, but I was not hungry.

The injustice of the affair galled me. I had done everything Lord Arlington asked, and more, and received no gratitude. But if I outlived my usefulness to him, I knew that he would have no hesitation in abandoning me. Now, thanks to the Duke of Buckingham's malice, I might well find myself on trial for murder. My lord knew the charge was false as well as I did, but if it served his purpose, I suspected that he would let me go to the gallows for it.

I had other grounds for unhappiness. This business had left me dissatisfied, not least with myself. Two men had died violently, and others had had their lives uprooted and cast to the winds. And for what? To enable the King to lie with a young woman who had had the misfortune to catch his eye. To put a Frenchwoman into the King's bed, thereby advancing French interests and increasing the influence of Lord Arlington, the King's most powerful minister. I had found my way to the heart of power, only to discover that the heart was rotten to its core.

Cat was more clear-sighted than I. She had understood this long before I had. Last night she had called me cynical, and then departed before I could try to make things right between us. She had judged me and found me wanting, and she had been right to do so. The rot that infested the court had touched me as well. No wonder she had preferred the company of Mr Banks to mine.

Like a ghostly visitant, the image of my poor dead father filled my mind. Even before his wits went astray, he had been a strange mixture: fanatical yet scrupulously honourable, violent yet capable of great love. When I was a boy, he had been fond of quoting the Apocrypha when he took a strap to me to mend my ways, which was often: *He that toucheth pitch shall be defiled therewith.* Along with the bloody stripes on my back, he had given me wisdom.

I reached the lodging place. It was not yet the supper hour. There were lights in almost every window. I shied away from the door into the lobby. The porter would be in his chair at the bottom of the stairs, and he was a garrulous fellow who, knowing I was close to my lord, wished for my patronage and was overly attentive in his dealings with me. Beyond him was the long ground-floor passage where I might well be waylaid by the obliging peruke-man who had repaired my wig after my escape from Prior's Holt. Worse still, I might encounter Mr Banks, who would look at me with daggers in his eyes and right on his side.

To avoid such annoyances, I took the longer path to the side door, the path I had taken last night with Cat. Once inside the house, I lit a candle stub from the lamp in the passage, found my key in my coat, and walked quietly toward my chamber. I went inside, shut the door and shot home the bolt with a sigh of relief.

I turned to light my own candle on the table. That was when I discovered Cat sitting on the single chair with her hands clasped together on the table and her eyes fixed on me.

The flame of the second candle grew larger and larger. The growing light banished some of the shadows from Marwood's face. But not all. Cat had never seen him look quite so despondent. She began to rise but he waved her back to the chair. He sat down heavily on the bed and rubbed his eyes.

'For a moment then, I thought you were a dream,' he said. 'A vision.'

She leant across the table and gently prodded his shoulder with her forefinger. 'Mere flesh and blood.'

'How did you get in?'

'I slipped the catch on the window,' she said. 'Easy enough with a knife blade.'

'You mean you climbed in?'

'Why not? Don't sound so shocked. Some women have mastered the art of climbing. You pointed out your window to me last night. It was too dark out there for anyone to see.'

He smiled, his face unexpectedly mischievous. 'Think of the scandal if someone had. Mr Banks, say. Or the peruke-man.'

'Our reputations would be in shreds,' she said primly. 'Both of us utterly ruined.'

'A terrifying prospect. But I'm glad you did.'

The smiles faded but neither of them looked away. If only, she thought, this moment could last for ever, suspended in time, eternally full of possibility. 'I'm come to say goodbye,' she said, answering the question he hadn't asked. 'I leave early tomorrow morning on the coach to Goring House.'

'So soon? I thought you'd be here until next week.'

'I've done what I came to do, and your master has graciously given me his permission to go. I need to see what Brennan has been up to at Chard Lane.'

'I'm sorry,' he said.

'What for?'

'I'm sorry you're going away so soon. I'm also sorry about Mademoiselle de Keroualle and this whole cursed business.' His voice became bitter. 'It's like a foul canker that eats everything and everyone.'

'The King will take her tonight,' Cat said. 'Mr Banks says they intend a pastoral masque in the form of a wedding as this evening's entertainment. He's been recruited to read the marriage service to the happy couple. He doesn't know yet whom he's to marry. But it can only be Mademoiselle and the King. Poor Banks knows there's something wrong about the business, but he can't find a way to escape. He has his mother and sisters to support. He has no money, no hope of preferment except whatever crumbs he may have from Lord Arlington. They dangle rewards before him, and he can't afford not to reach for them.'

Her tongue was running away with Mr Banks, she realized, because she didn't know what to say to Marwood. But he seemed barely to register her words.

'There's something you must know,' he said. 'Lord Arlington told me last night that Rush claims that I murdered Durrell. He's offered to sign a statement to that effect, giving copies to both my lord and the Duke of Buckingham. Then, if the Duke has his way, I'll be charged with Durrell's murder.'

'He can't do that.'

'The Duke can do what he wants. You know that.'

'Then Lord Arlington must find a way to protect you,' Cat said indignantly. 'You were carrying out his orders, after all, and you've served him well. You didn't kill Durrell. Though God knows no one could blame you if you had.'

'My lord said he will see what he can do to help me. But he pointed out that Buckingham would have more than enough evidence to have me hanged. And he'll manufacture more if he needs it. If he and Rush carry this through, I can't prove my innocence.'

'Rush has betrayed you,' Cat said.

'I know. He wants to shift the blame to me, to protect his wife as well as himself.'

'Can't you tell the world what really happened?'

'Who would believe me? Not with the Duke confirming Rush's story. Unless my lord can help me.'

'What can you do if Arlington can't? Or won't?'

Marwood shrugged. 'Flee abroad, perhaps, which would confirm my guilt in the eyes of the world. Or wait to see which way the wind blows.' He looked at her and smiled. 'On the whole, I think I prefer to stay.'

'No,' she said. 'You must go.'

'I'm damned if I'll act as if I'm guilty of something I haven't done. I won't run before I have to.'

'Don't be foolish. You must look to yourself for once, not your master.'

'I am.'

'I don't want you to risk the gallows.' Cat was trembling. She wasn't sure whether it was from anger or fear, or from an unholy blend of the two. 'And for no reason but your own folly. You have warning of this. You have money. Why not go abroad until the fuss dies down? Lord Arlington will know why, and he must help you. A scandal isn't in his interests. And you're useful to him.'

Marwood shook his head. 'I don't want to play the fugitive.'

'And I don't want you to die. For a start you don't deserve it. And I don't know what—'

She stopped. They stared at each other. One of the candles was smoking and the outlines of Marwood's face shifted and rippled as if he were dissolving before her very eyes.

'What?' he said. '*What* don't you know?'

'I don't know what I'd do without you. If you must know.'

'Cat,' he said. 'The last thing I want is to leave you.' He turned towards her and stretched out his hand.

It occurred to her that she might not see him again after this evening. Ever. After a second or two, she lifted her free hand and drew his head towards hers. They kissed each other lingeringly but awkwardly, two clumsy, embarrassed people determined to master the steps of the oldest dance in the world.

Marwood was the first to break away. 'We can't do this now. It will make everything worse if—'

'Oh you fool,' she said, and gripped his hand tightly in hers. 'You obstinate blockhead.'

'You're the obstinate one,' he said. 'In any case, I thought this wasn't what you wanted.'

'Sometimes it takes time to discover what I want. That's all.'

'And now?' His mouth was moving towards hers again. 'What do you want? What do you think?'

'I think it will be much more convenient if we are both on the bed.'

It rained throughout the night. An elderly nun, a cousin of Louise's mother, had once told her that raindrops were the tears of heaven. They were God's way of showing her His distress at the sins of mankind.

The wind must be blowing in gusts, she thought, for sometimes the rain was almost inaudible, and at other times the wind threw drops of water against the window with great force, making a sound like handfuls of gravel thrown on the glass. God's grief ebbed and flowed.

Louise stretched out her hand and parted the curtains an inch. The darkness in the bedchamber was paler. It was dawn in the world beyond the windows.

She was lying on her back in the curtained dark of the bed. She had not slept, partly because of the soreness between her legs, and partly because of the long and unfamiliar shape lying beside her. He had not meant to hurt her, she thought, but he had been urgent, particularly the first time, and his weight had almost smothered her. He had held down her arms, pinning her to the bed. There would be blue bruises on her white skin this morning.

He had fallen asleep at last. She listened to his breathing for the rest of the night, noting how it speeded up and slowed down, how sometimes it hardened into snores that began quietly but gradually increased to a crescendo; the crescendo reached a crisis in the form of a strangled snuffle; after that there would be a blessed silence, akin almost to death; and then the breathing would begin again, slow and soft.

The body beside her stirred. For a moment or two, the breathing continued unchanged. The body stirred again, and suddenly the legs thrashed beside her. The curtain on the other side of the bed was torn back with a violent rattle of rings. The King swung his legs over the side of the bed and stood up.

When he had removed his wig last night, she had barely recognized him. There were grey hairs among the stubble on his scalp. The long, swarthy face had deep pouches below the eyes. Later, when he was without his shirt, she discovered that he possessed an unexpected paunch. Before he laid himself down to sleep, he pissed in a pot before her. The King was a man like any other man. An ageing man.

She listened to his footsteps stumbling across the unfamiliar room to the window. He tugged the curtains aside and scratched himself. The ghostly light before the dawn found its way into the room. She heard a scuffling sound, and she guessed that he had scooped up his clothes, or at least some of them, from the floor. She had a sudden memory from last night, of his black wig tangled with the green gown. He had torn the gown in his haste to grope and suck her breasts.

The King padded into the closet. She heard him swearing softly to himself as he dressed. The faint scrape of a lock: he was opening the door to the private stair; Arlington had given him the key yesterday evening. Two of the King's servants were stationed at the bottom of the stairs. They had been there all night, listening to the rain, waiting to escort their master back to his own apartments.

The door closed behind him with a bang. She was alone. If she wanted, she could ring for Marie, who was sleeping on a pallet across the door in the antechamber, and Marie would bring her whatever she desired. Instead she began to cry.

My bed had no curtains, and nor had my chamber, only a coarse linen square hanging from a pole above the window embrasure. On Saturday morning I watched as darkness grudgingly gave way to light. The truckle bed was so narrow that Cat's body seemed fused to mine.

My future was a strange, uncertain place but that did not seem to matter very much at present. I had been touched by joy, I thought; and those three words set off an echo in my memory. It was what my father used to say after one of his visions. Touched by joy. Touched in the head more like, I had thought at the time. But joy was joy wherever it came from. It was Cat who had touched me.

I felt her lips move against my shoulder, and there it was again, another sweet stab of joy.

She stirred. 'What are you thinking about?'

'You.'

'That's as it should be.' She caught her breath. 'But it's late. The coach goes at seven o'clock. How am I going to leave here and reach my chamber without the porter seeing me?'

'I'll go first,' I said. 'If he's asleep, well and good, you can slip upstairs. If not, I'll tell him that someone tried to force my window last night. I'll make him come outside with me and search for evidence.'

'He won't like that. Not at this hour.'

'He'll want to oblige me. He thinks I wield enormous influence over Lord Arlington's affairs.'

Cat pushed the covers aside, wriggled away from me and stood up. For an instant she looked down at me. She was beautiful in her shift, I thought, with her body unconstrained. But I wished she would take off the shift. That would be even better.

'What are we going to do?' she said.

I sat up and took her hand. She wasn't talking about this morning now. I knew I must not leap too far ahead. I had done that last year, demanded more of her than she wanted to give, and I had demanded it too soon. We had both paid the price for that.

'I think you will go back to London and deal with Chard Lane and Brennan,' I said. 'While I must stay here and find what my lord intends to do with me. As soon as I can, I'll come to London and find you.'

'Unless you're arrested first.'

I ignored that. 'And when we meet again, we shall talk about what we do next. If you wish.'

She nodded and turned aside to rummage for her stockings in the untidy pile of our clothes on the floor. I watched her.

Cat threw a glance at me. 'Are you dressing yourself today? Or will you be stark naked when you talk to the porter?'

CHAPTER FORTY-SEVEN

FOR MOST OF Saturday, I was as one in a dream, a living ghost inhabiting the shell of my own life. The events of the last few days had left their mark. So had lack of sleep and the threat of arrest. Most of all, however, and most agreeably, I was so buoyed up by what had happened with Cat that nothing else seemed very important, even my fears about the future.

During the day, Lord Arlington kept me busy in his private office. He made no reference to Durrell's death, and nor did I. I fear I did less work than usual, for I found concentration difficult; but he did not comment on it, except to say that I had better come to him on Sunday morning as soon as it was light, as there were still letters to be written and copied.

That evening I sought out Mr Banks at supper. Cat had charged me with saying her farewells to him ('but not in such a way that might encourage him to think I wish to continue our acquaintance'). I found him in a terrible state of anxiety about the sermon he was to preach on the morrow.

I tried to soothe him. 'You must not trouble yourself. Surely

416

before God, we're all equal? The King and the Duke of York are but men as we are.'

'But, sir, my future may depend on this.' He was so upset that he seized my arm. 'And . . . well – may I confide in you? It's not merely the sermon in itself that concerns me, though that is matter enough. It's whether I should preach at all. I cannot tell you more, but I have witnessed things I would rather not have seen.'

I sat down beside him. I could guess the reason for his agitation from what Cat had told me about the projected pastoral entertainment. The King's attentions to Mademoiselle de Keroualle had occasioned much lewd speculation among my fellow clerks, and it was widely believed that he had finally succeeded in bedding the lady last night. It was rumoured that there had been a blasphemous travesty of a wedding ceremony, that the company had led them to bed, and that the stocking had been flung in the manner of a married bride.

'I'm no student of divinity,' I said, 'but God sees into all our hearts. He must know your motives are pure. And consider, sir: how many sinners have sermons led to repentance? Yours may do the same.'

He peered at me with large, moist eyes. 'You believe that God would conceive it to be my duty to preach?'

'Undoubtedly He would.' I picked up the dish before me. 'Now pray let me serve you with half a pigeon. A man cannot preach on an empty stomach.'

The next morning, Sunday, Lord Arlington had me writing letters on his behalf as soon as it was fully light. He summoned me to his closet shortly before ten o'clock. I hoped that he wished to discuss this business with Buckingham.

'It's almost time for chapel,' he said. 'You'd better attend. I want a record of the sermon. Note it down in your shorthand.'

My spirits fell. My skill at shorthand writing was growing steadily, but it was still a long way from perfect. It was one thing to take down a letter or a memorandum, but quite another to make a verbatim record of a two-hour sermon.

The family's private chapel had not been designed for the purpose originally. It was a large apartment with a ceiling on which the gods of the ancients disported themselves at a banquet. I stood near the back with the steward and other upper servants of the household. A clerk's desk was brought in for me.

A makeshift closet had been constructed to one side, and it was here that the King sat with his brother, the Duke of York, beside him. A curtain shielded them from the common gaze.

When the time came for the sermon, Mr Banks stumbled as he mounted the steps to the pulpit. I feared for him. He was very pale. The papers he carried trembled in his hand.

Once he was in the pulpit, he laid the sermon on the lectern. At that moment a change came over him. He straightened his spine and squared his shoulders. He looked out over the congregation and then directly at the King.

'"A divine sentence is in the lips of the king,"' he said firmly, '"his mouth transgresseth not in judgement." Proverbs, chapter sixteen, verse ten.'

From then on, Banks preached as naturally and as unaffectedly as ever I had heard a man preach a sermon. It was as if God had touched him with His finger. He preached for two and a half hours, always addressing the King. I tried to keep up with him, but I made a sad botch of noting down some passages, particularly when he wandered among dense thickets of Old Testament names.

I dined with him afterwards and gave him my sincere congratulations. His chosen text had been both appropriate and diplomatic, for it stressed that God's mandate was the basis of the King's authority. Yet, whether by accident or design, his sternly implacable delivery, with his eyes fixed on His Majesty, had suggested that both God and Mr Banks were not convinced that this particular king was worthy of the gift bestowed on him.

Now the ordeal was over, Banks was weak-kneed with relief. We dined together. He was delighted that I wanted to look over his sermon and correct the copy I had made. That, and the wine he drank, made him forget his earlier distrust of me. After the second bottle, he waxed confidential.

'My lord says the living is as good as mine,' he said. 'And perhaps also a reversion to a perpetual curacy in the neighbouring parish. I shall ever be grateful for his kindness to me. So will my poor mother and sisters. But . . . in a nutshell, sir, and between ourselves, I have not been altogether comfortable here. The masque or whatever it was on Friday night, for example . . . it did not seem quite right to me somehow. I shall be glad to be back in my little room in Cambridge. Nevertheless, his lordship has been most kind to me. Let us toast his benevolence.'

After we had done that, and drunk the King's health once more, he grew pensive. 'These great people live in a different way from ordinary folk, and I find it's not entirely to my taste. But I suppose you must have grown used to their mode of living?'

'I thought I had,' I said. 'But I was mistaken. Let's drink another toast, this time to ordinary folk.'

Lord Arlington kept me in suspense throughout Monday. The following day, Tuesday, he went to Newmarket. He did not take me with him. But when he returned in the evening, he summoned me to his closet and told me that the Duke of Buckingham was due to leave for the north tomorrow.

'I had a private conference with him this morning,' he went on. 'I believe I have softened his anger towards you.' My face must have shown the relief I felt because he frowned at me. 'Softened, Marwood. Not removed. Nor was it easy. I was obliged to make concessions I did not wish to make. His desire to punish you remains and it must be respected. He demands that I discharge you from my service and that of the Crown. After careful consideration, I have agreed to his proposal. So there it is. Your face will no longer be welcome at Whitehall. I suppose there's a moral here, that a wise man should know his place in the world and should strive not to offend his betters.'

'And what about Rush?'

'You need not concern yourself with him. He will not make any trouble.'

For an instant I was on the verge of telling Arlington that he was a smug hypocrite and a bully, as corrupt as a man could be, and so was the Duke. I am a coward, however, so I merely bowed my head, as if in submission.

'You'll leave my employ today,' he went on, 'and leave Euston tomorrow morning. I know I can trust you to be discreet about your time with me because you're not entirely a fool. Besides, you know what will happen if you allow your tongue to run away with you.'

'You may rely on me, my lord,' I said.

'By the way, talking of Mr Rush, you had better take his horse to London. You'll find it in the stables.'

'I don't understand.'

Arlington shrugged, his expression suggesting that my lack of understanding was only to be expected. 'The horses you left behind at Prior's Holt were brought here this afternoon. I'm told that Mr Rush is no longer in Newmarket, so he cannot take it himself.'

'How does his servant do, my lord? The one who was attacked in the street.'

'He died of his wounds without regaining his senses. And talking of death, there was another piece of news today. The body of one of His Grace's servants, a man named Roger Durrell, was discovered hidden in the bushes along the high road between Elveden and Newmarket. It looks as if he was set upon and murdered by a gang of highwaymen several days ago. The coroner's verdict will confirm that. The rogues who did it have left the neighbourhood.' He drummed his fingers on the arm of his chair. 'That will be all.'

But it wasn't quite all. As I reached the door, he called me back.

'You're a fortunate man, Marwood,' he said. 'Though you may not know it. Look to the future. The Duke is not so great a man at court as he was. Perhaps we shall see you at Whitehall again. One of these days.'

I bowed and left him to it.

CHAPTER FORTY-EIGHT

O N WEDNESDAY AFTERNOON, Cat called by appointment at Mr Rush's house in Hatton Garden. Since her return from Euston, she had spent the last two days partly at Chard Lane and partly at the sign of the Rose, making fair copies and notes of her plans for Lord Arlington's stables. She had also, as a treat to herself, assembled her ideas for his new church in the park.

During her absence, Brennan had made surprisingly good progress at the almshouse. She had underestimated his abilities. Also, the weather had remained largely dry in London, and he had been able to hire more labourers than expected, thanks to a delayed project in Cheapside, one of Mr Hooke's for the City. Sometimes luck was on your side, Cat thought, though more usually it seemed to be on someone else's.

Rush and his bride had returned to London on Saturday. He wrote to Cat that he had been much engaged in business since then. He could not resist informing her that Lord Arlington had just put his name forward for a salaried vacancy on the Council for Foreign Plantations, citing Rush's varied experiences at sea with Prince Rupert during the Protectorate, his proven business acumen and his past investments in the Africa trade.

Moreover, Rush said, he had been obliged to arrange the affairs of his poor bankrupt father-in-law, which entailed his settling a modest annuity on Mistress Susannah, now Mr Hadgraft's newly betrothed wife, and finding them somewhere to live. But now at last he found himself with sufficient leisure to turn his attention to the almshouse at Chard Lane. He asked her to call on him at his house, and after she had reported her progress, they would walk to the site together.

The appointed time was three o'clock. The servant showed Cat up to the drawing room, where she found Mistress Rush and Mistress Susannah. His wife looked flushed and uncomfortable in her new role as the lady of Mr Rush's house. By contrast, Mistress Susannah seemed more assured than before, less of the waiting woman, more of the prospective mother-in-law.

'Mr Rush has been delayed at Whitehall, I fear,' Grace said listlessly. 'He will be here at any moment.'

Cat congratulated Mistress Susannah on her changed prospects in life and asked politely whether a time had been fixed for the wedding.

'After the reading of the banns. Next Sunday will be the first time, so it will be early in November. I don't want a Fleet marriage. No one shall say this hasn't been done properly.'

It was a clear dig at her future daughter-in-law, but Grace merely smiled vaguely and nodded her head. It was difficult to believe that last week this pretty, insipid-looking woman had stabbed and beaten a man to death.

As Susannah talked about the proposed furnishing of her new house, Grace rose from the sofa, holding her hand to her mouth, and almost ran behind a screen in the corner. The sound of retching followed. She emerged shakily, wiping her mouth.

'Are you feeling better now?' Susannah asked solicitously. 'You poor love. It will pass.' She turned to Cat. 'It's possible that this blessed union has already found favour with heaven. But pray keep it to yourself. Mr Rush is not yet aware of the happy news, and Mistress Grace does not want to raise his hopes only to dash them.'

I left Euston Hall early on Wednesday morning. For safety, I rode back to London with two of Lord Arlington's people. One was a groom, fortunately for me, for he helped manage Mr Rush's horse and dealt with the stabling when we spent a night on the road. They were both uncouth fellows and I had little conversation with them. But they did not know of my disgrace and so they treated me with a respect I no longer deserved from them.

The roads were muddy after the rain, which delayed us. We passed several stranded coaches and saw two accidents, one of which had been fatal. I travelled light with only a spare shirt and my folder of papers. I left my other bags to follow in one of the Arlingtons' waggons.

We reached London late on Thursday morning. I felt a lightening of my spirits when I saw the grey smudge of the city's chimneys smeared like a shadow across the sky. The city lay before me, with all its noise and foul odours, its endless greed and its bottomless poverty. I knew where I was in London. Best of all, I would find Cat there.

During the journey I had had time for reflection. There was a myriad of problems before me and a myriad of regrets in the past. My mind shied away from all of them. Instead, I picked over the bones of the Chard Lane murder, now reduced to a puzzle that was no longer my concern.

On the face of it, the matter was simple enough: Buckingham, hoping to oblige Mademoiselle de Keroualle, had sent Durrell to warn off Iredale and the Chevalier de Vire; the Chevalier had shown fight; Durrell had killed him, stripped and mutilated the corpse, and concealed the body in the spoil heap. Durrell had now been killed in his turn. The lady had at last admitted the King to her bed. It was over.

Yet something about the business did not sit comfortably with me. We see what we expect to see. If we have a notion that something must be so, we tend to give most weight to whatever supports that notion. Contrariwise, we dismiss as trifles what fails to do so.

The more I thought about the Chard Lane murder, the more uneasy I became. Perhaps I saw the whole affair more clearly now that I was no longer charged with its investigation.

What if, I thought, and the two words repeated themselves over and over again in my mind like the beating of a drum, what if.

In London, I parted from Arlington's servants in Holborn. I rode over the bridge and turned into Hatton Garden. The outer door of Rush's house stood open, and his porter was surveying the street with a proprietorial air. He recognized both me and the horse and came out to greet us. He told me that his master was at the Chard Lane site office.

I left him to deal with the horse and walked back over Holborn Bridge. My muscles ached after the long ride, but it was a relief to be on foot again, and back in London. I felt oddly detached from my surroundings. For the first time in years, I had no immediate need to do anything. I was my own man again.

I went into a coffee house in Cow Lane and ordered coffee, a slice of pie and writing materials. I wrote a letter to Cat, briefly outlining the theory I had formed on my ride to London and laying out my reasons for it. I wrote another letter to Dudley Gorvin at his lodgings, asking him in the name of friendship to apply to Mistress Hakesby if any accident should befall me.

I drank the coffee but I found I had no stomach for the pie.

A stout, capable woman was presiding over the coffee pots, taking the money and managing the establishment. I asked her to ensure the letters were delivered and gave her five shillings to make it so. She undertook the commission readily enough, though she raised her eyebrows at the size of the fee I had given her. She slipped the coins under the counter.

'Thank you, sir. God bless you.'

'It's so you don't forget,' I said. 'Either me or the letters.'

CHAPTER FORTY-NINE

I WALKED DOWN TO Chard Lane, where I knocked at the door of the site office. It was opened by the foreman, who recognized me from my visits here. He told me Mr Rush and Mr Brennan were upstairs and asked if he should announce me. I said I would announce myself.

Rush was going over the accounts with Brennan. Brennan rose to his feet when he saw me. Rush stayed where he was.

'What are you doing here?' he demanded.

'I've brought back your horse from Euston. I left it at your house.'

'I'm obliged. Good day to you.'

'Your porter told me I would find you here. I've something to discuss.'

His eyes met mine. He nodded to Brennan. 'We'll finish this later.'

'Is Mistress Hakesby here?' I asked Brennan.

'No, sir. But you'll find her at the sign of the Rose.'

'Pray give her my compliments and tell her I'm back in London. If you should see her before I do.'

Brennan bowed and left the room.

'I haven't got all day,' Rush said.

I sat down at the table. We listened to Brennan's footsteps on the stairs.

'Has his lordship sent you?' Rush asked.

'No. I'm here on my own account. I've come to ask you who really killed the Chevalier de Vire.'

He frowned. 'What nonsense is this?'

'I'm talking about the man you knew as Pharamond. Your wife's former French tutor.'

'Why do you need to ask? It was Durrell that killed him, of course.'

'I don't think so. I think you found him first.' Rush began to bluster but I overrode him. 'It puzzled me how Durrell could have got into the site, particularly because he had no reason to know it even existed. Then there's the matter of the letters that a certain French lady wrote to de Vire. Buckingham wanted those letters and he sent Durrell to find them. But if it was Durrell who killed de Vire on Saturday evening, he would have searched the body and found the letters. Instead, he went to de Vire's lodging at the Three Crowns on the Sunday evening after the murder. That was the day before the body was found. Durrell was looking for de Vire. But why would he want to do that if he had killed him on the evening before?'

Rush's jaw moved convulsively from side to side. 'This is pure moonshine.'

I ignored him. 'As for motive, sir, you had discovered that Pharamond was making love to Mistress Grace, who had previously rejected your suit. Who told you about that? Was Mistress Susannah in your pay? Like your wife, she's a resourceful woman. I don't think you acted on impulse: this was carefully planned. You had your old comrade Thomas Ledward with you. You were waiting for Pharamond when he left Hadgraft's house on the night of his death. You waylaid him near the site office and you killed him.'

'You'll find that I have my own methods for dealing with slanderers,' Rush said.

'Ledward was still the Chard Lane watchman, so he had a set of keys. You'd originally been Hadgraft's partner, so you knew your way around. You stripped de Vire's body in the yard and you mutilated the face to prevent identification. The watchdog had to be killed, because someone might have wondered why he didn't bark while all this was going on. Naturally he wouldn't have barked at Ledward, who was his master. You dragged the corpses to the nearest spoil heap and concealed them there. Was there also the advantage that when de Vire's body was found at the almshouse site, it would embarrass Hadgraft? Whatever the truth of that, you must have hoped it would be a while before the bodies were discovered. But the rainstorm on Sunday night put paid to that. Still, you did your best to delay any investigation by insisting on summoning the bishop's coroner.'

'Is that all?' Rush threw back his head and laughed. 'You have not a shred of evidence. Merely a farrago of nonsense aimed at your successful rival in love.'

I smiled at him. 'You deserve her, sir, and she deserves you. Who did kill Ledward in Newmarket, by the way? Was his death coincidental? Or was it Durrell's work? Or was it you? Was he blackmailing you? Did you want to remove the one person who could testify against you?'

'There you go again, sir. More moonshine. You should seek out physic to purge it without causing more harm to yourself.'

I felt an unwilling admiration for Rush. He was right – I could prove nothing, even if Mistress Gribbin and the little maidservant at the Three Crowns would agree to testify that Durrell had been looking for their lodger on the Sunday evening after the murder. Neither woman would impress a judge and jury, and Rush would rip their evidence to shreds.

'When you stripped the body, you found the two letters,' I went on, determined to finish what I had begun. 'You have connections at court. You saw the value of the letters, and you also saw how to make a profit by them. You've had them in your possession ever since you killed de Vire. You went to Newmarket to offer them to Buckingham. And when you could not agree terms, you offered them to Lord Arlington instead. However you look at this affair, is it not a sordid business?'

To my surprise, this last accusation pricked him. It was one thing to accuse him of murder. But quite another to suggest that he had been guided by considerations of material gain.

He leant forward, his hand dropping to the hilt of his sword. 'Be careful what you say, sir.'

'Mr Brennan has seen me here with you,' I reminded him. 'Your foreman, too. The porter at your house knows where I am. Before coming here, I took the precaution of writing two letters, ensuring that if anything happens to me, you will be held responsible.'

Rush's hand dropped away from the sword. He made a palpable effort to relax. 'Come now,' he said, softening his harsh voice as far as he was able, 'we must not grow heated. Let's consider the case hypothetically. A lady's reputation is besmirched by a foreigner. Any gentleman, and in particular one who cared about the lady's well-being, would consider it his duty to challenge the man, if the rogue were himself a gentleman, or to chastise him if he were not. This was an affair of honour. There was nothing mean or underhand about the business.'

I doubted that. Whatever account of it Rush gave to himself, this had been a duel fought without warning under cover of darkness, by two men against one, which had left the loser dead, mutilated and buried like a dog in a dunghill. Rush called it an affair of honour: I called it murder.

Cat was working in the Drawing Office when Marwood appeared. She was alone. At the sight of him, her stomach lurched with relief. He was filthy from the road, and he carried only a satchel and his stick. She laid down her pen and went to him. After a brief hesitation, they kissed each other on the lips.

'Pheebs let me in,' he said. 'I'm surprised he's back at his post so soon.'

'He spends most of his time asleep. Josh does most of the work.' She drew away from him and looked into his face. 'Are you all right? I had your letter. Did you find Rush?'

'Yes. He admitted it all. But I can't prove anything, and he knows it.' Marwood smiled wryly. 'He and Grace are well matched, aren't they?'

'And what's happening about Buckingham's murder charge against you?'

431

He took her hand. 'Over and done with. The Duke has graciously agreed to leave me alone. Lord Arlington made a bargain with him.'

'Oh thank God.'

'Have you food in the house? I'm starved.'

They went down to the parlour, where Cat sent Jane Ash to the Savoy with a message that Sam and Margaret should prepare to welcome their master home. 'Stay there for an hour or so,' she commanded. 'Tell Margaret you are to help her prepare the house for him.'

Marwood slumped into a chair and grinned at her. She brought him bread, cheese and wine. He seized the bread and tore off a piece. 'I saw Brennan today too. He was in the site office with Rush when I called at Chard Lane. How are you faring with the almshouse?'

'We're further forward than I dared hope.'

'Rush should be pleased.'

'If he is, he hasn't seen fit to mention it,' Cat said. 'But if all goes well, he'll soon be pleased with his wife. Even more so than before. Mistress Susannah thinks Grace may be pregnant.'

'So soon?'

'That depends, doesn't it?'

'On what?'

'On who's the father.' Cat watched him. 'She and Rush have barely been married a fortnight. But he'll believe whatever she tells him.'

He gave a bark of laughter, which she felt was an entirely satisfactory response. 'You mean it might be de Vire's child?' he said.

'That would explain why Hadgraft was so urgent to see

his daughter wed. And why she seems a little plumper than before.'

He took up his glass. 'Does Rush know?'

'Not yet. Perhaps he never will. I'm sure Susannah has from the start. But if she keeps her mouth shut, there's no reason why he should. Grace can always say the child was born early.'

Marwood wolfed down a slice of cheese. 'I've news too,' he said with his mouth full. 'About Arlington's bargain with the Duke. One of the conditions is that I lose my places at Whitehall. Both with him and at the Board of Red Cloth.'

'Arlington can't have agreed to that. You've served him so well.'

'It's already done. I've signed my letters of resignation.'

'But it's ingratitude beyond belief.' Cat's indignation on Marwood's behalf rose steadily. 'He should have rewarded you not thrown you aside.'

'On the other hand, he could have left me to the hangman,' Marwood said. 'But he didn't. Anyway I'm glad of it.'

'Glad?' Cat was outraged. 'But think what you lose. Your income – your position in the world – your . . . your future.'

He shook his head and reached for the wine bottle. 'I was thinking of my father when I was on the road from Euston.'

'What are you talking about now?'

'When I was a boy, and he thrashed me, he would say while he did it, *He that toucheth pitch shall be defiled therewith*. And he made the blows of his stick match the rhythm of the words.'

'*And he that hath fellowship with a proud man shall be like unto him*,' Cat said automatically. 'Ecclesiasticus, chapter thirteen, verse one. It was one of my father's favourites too.

Though he himself was as proud as the Devil. But what has that got to do with anything?'

'I'm tired of touching pitch,' Marwood said. 'That's what they do at Whitehall all day long, all night long. The court, the government, it's all the same, it's all dirty work, and it's growing dirtier. So are those who do it.'

'And now you don't want to do it any more,' she said. 'I understand.'

'I knew you would.' He raised the bottle. 'Drink with me, Cat. Drink to what is yet to come.'

CHAPTER FIFTY

B Y THE SECOND week of December, the trees in St James's Park had a slatternly, bedraggled air, their once fine clothing reduced to tatters and rags. It rained more often than not. The sun rarely put in an appearance, and when it did, its face was pale and insipid. The air grew steadily colder, and each successive wind had a keener edge.

'How I hate England,' Louise said to Madame des Bordes. They were standing on the stairs to the Park, with their maids and two footmen at a respectful distance behind them.

'They say there will be snow soon.'

'It's not only the weather.' She pouted at the Park. 'It's everything.'

'Still. There are compensations, no doubt.'

Louise stroked the fur of her collar, silently agreeing but unwilling to admit it. 'The sun's gone in. I don't want to walk today. We shall have tea in my closet instead.'

The King had given her a richly furnished set of lodgings convenient to his private apartments. It was common know-ledge that, since their return from Euston, he supped with her whenever he could and spent at least some of the night in her bed. Whatever she wanted was hers. Everyone at Whitehall wished to be her friend. But even the King could not control the vulgar people of London. Even the King could not make Whitehall what a King's palace should be. Even the King could not make the sun shine and the air warmer.

The closet was warm and brightly lit. This was the third time that she had invited Madame des Bordes to take tea with her there, quite alone, a mark of favour that had caused comment among the ladies of the court. Madame des Bordes was the Queen's dresser but scarcely a person of any importance outside Her Majesty's household.

Louise was aware of that. But she trusted the older woman as much as she trusted anybody. Madame des Bordes knew how to keep a secret, for she had told no one about Monsieur de Vire and what had happened at Dieppe. Besides, they had their shared past in France to bind them together. Sometimes, when Louise was particularly homesick, they would talk about the time when they had both served Madame, the late Duchess of Orleans, whose death had brought them both to this cold, unfriendly country.

'The common people threw stones at my coach in Charing Cross yesterday,' Louise said while they were waiting for the water to boil. 'They ran after me in the street, shouting French fireship, Papist whore, Devil's punk and worse. What do they mean by the word fireship?'

'It means a woman with the pox. You mustn't mind them.'

When the tea had been poured, Louise dismissed the maids. 'May I confide in you, madame?' she said. 'You swear you won't breathe a word to anyone?'

'Of course not. You know that.'

'If . . . if I were with child, what signs would there be? Besides the end of the monthly bleeding?'

Madame des Bordes studied Louise's face across the table. 'When did the bleeding stop?'

'I don't know. Usually I am regular, like a calendar. But it's nearly a fortnight late now.'

'Do you have sickness, especially in the mornings?'

'No. But I find I no longer have a taste for macaroons. Usually, I delight in them. But now the very thought turns my stomach. And . . . and my breasts are not exactly sore but . . .'

'They feel a little bruised, perhaps?' Madame des Bordes suggested.

'Exactly. Though that might be the King. He can be a little rough when he fondles me.' After a pause, Louise went on, 'I don't want a child.'

'Women must accept what God arranges for them.'

'But would he still want me then? And what would happen to the child if it lives?' Louise lowered her voice to a whisper. 'Are there not ways to make sure it doesn't live? Wouldn't it be better to make sure it went away? I wondered if perhaps you knew of—'

Madame des Bordes shook her head. 'You must not do that.'

'Because it's a sin?' Louise's temper flared. 'That's all very well, but God is not a woman.'

'Because if you do, whatever you drink, or eat, or have done to you might kill you as well as the child.'

'Hush. Not so loud.'

Madame des Bordes took Louise's limp white hand in hers.

437

'Tell the King. He will be pleased. He has many bastards, and he loves them all, and he spoils them too, as he spoils his dogs. Believe me, if you give him a child, it will draw him closer to you, not push him away.'

'Why?' Gorvin said. 'Why did you bother with a wastrel like Iredale? Haven't you enough to worry about?'

It was a good question, one without an easy answer. I sipped my coffee, delaying the need to reply. We had chosen to meet at Will's Coffee House on the corner of Bow Street and Russell Street, where Gorvin sometimes called on the way back to Whitehall from his mistress's lodgings.

'His family has need of him,' I said at last. 'He's a rogue, but he's been good to his parents.'

Gorvin shook his head. 'You're cracked, Marwood. With the turnkey's fees, the whole thing must have cost you the better part of five pounds.'

'But it's done now? He's free?'

'He was released yesterday morning, on Mr Williamson's signature. A woman collected him in a hackney.'

John Iredale had been in prison for two months in all, since I had petitioned Mr Williamson to commit him to Scotland Yard for his own safety. He had been moved to Newgate in November to await trial. No one had much interest in pursuing the case against him, however, and he had been left to rot in the common hold.

It seemed to me that it was best for all concerned to tidy away the loose ends of the Chard Lane affair as neatly as possible. Shortly after my return to Euston, I called at the Council for Foreign Plantations and explained as best I could to Mr Davis, the chief clerk there, that a woman was concealing herself in one of the derelict outbuildings behind the council's office. I told him that the disgraced Iredale had hidden her there, and that she was with child by him. But the woman had done nothing wrong, apart from succumbing to Iredale's advances.

Now, I said, I wanted to remove her to live with Iredale's parents in Paddington. Davis managed the business discreetly and he was wise enough not to ask questions. I took Patience Noone, now five or six months pregnant, to Paddington and placed her with Iredale's parents. She needed a refuge, and they needed someone to keep house for them. I told them that she was their son's wife, and that she was carrying their grandchild in her belly, so they welcomed her like a daughter.

'I suppose,' I said at last, 'I did it for the woman's sake, not Iredale's.'

'Pretty, is she?'

'Not at all. But everyone had forgotten her, you see, and left her to rot. She didn't deserve that.'

'As I said, you're cracked. A tragedy for your friends. You used to be a man of sense.'

We exchanged smiles. It takes adversity to know who your friends are. I had assumed that my acquaintance with Dudley Gorvin would lapse after Arlington dispensed with my services, and Whitehall was closed to me, at least for the foreseeable future. Instead we had fallen into the way of supping together once a week, sometimes after the theatre, sometimes not.

Gorvin signalled for more coffee. 'I saw an old acquaintance of yours at Whitehall yesterday,' he went on. 'Willoughby Rush. He came over from Goring House with my lord, and they seemed very intimate together. I hear that His Majesty

439

has graciously signified his intention to knight him in the New Year.'

'Think of it,' I said. 'Sir Willoughby Rush. How he will enjoy that.'

'I don't know what went on at Euston,' Gorvin said, 'and I don't want to know. But it seems to me unjust that a man like Rush should be rewarded, while you are cast into darkness.'

The servant arrived before I could reply. He made a performance of pouring the coffee, standing on tiptoe and judging the distance and the angle of the jug to a nicety. The black liquid glided from the spout in a shining arc. He filled our dishes without spilling a single drop. Gorvin tipped him and at last he left us alone.

'I've another piece of news,' he said in a lower voice. 'I fear it won't be welcome because it's another injustice. You're to lose your house at the end of the quarter.'

The Savoy belonged to the King, and I occupied my house in Infirmary Close under a grace and favour arrangement at the discretion of the Crown. The grant was automatically renewed at the end of every quarter, when I paid a modest fee supposedly earmarked for the upkeep of the fabric of the building.

The current quarter ended on Christmas Day. I was to be ejected from my lodging in less than three weeks' time. Had it not been for Gorvin's kindness, I should not have had even this much warning.

I knew this must be Buckingham's work. In the devil's bargain he had made with Lord Arlington, he had agreed to spare my life. But he had found other ways to exercise his malignity at my expense.

When we left the coffee house, Gorvin and I parted, he to Whitehall and I to the City. I had no reason to go there but my restless mind made my legs restless as well. My thoughts tumbled about my head, and I was scarcely aware of my surroundings until I found myself walking up Ludgate Hill towards the grimy hulk of St Paul's at the top.

It had begun to rain. Even the fence enclosing the ruins looked ancient and derelict. Demolition of the cathedral had begun last year, but it was a slow and perilous job. Many of the walls were still at their full height, though blackened and cracked. Five years earlier, I had first met Cat here during the Great Fire, on a night when the flames were destroying St Paul's and it had seemed that the whole world was coming to an end. When I tried to help her, she bit my hand to the bone and ran off, like the wild cat she was.

I smiled at the memory as I turned up Ave Maria Lane and then, without thinking, into Pater Noster Row. My father had carried on his printing business in the eighth house on the left. I had grown up here, and served my apprenticeship, and kissed my first girl. The house was long gone, and so was my father.

But it was here, now, in front of Mr Gellibrand's shop at the sign of the Golden Ball, that my thoughts at last grew calm. All this lay in the past. I had been living in dreams since leaving Arlington's service, taking each day as it came. Now I must rouse myself and look to the future.

I would soon be homeless, but I was not without resources. My savings amounted to almost £230, a very substantial sum, together with a few pieces of plate that were probably worth another thirty pounds on top of that. I must continue to provide for the Witherdines, for I flattered myself that they would not be easily persuaded to leave me. I must find new lodgings for us. I must find a new way to gain my bread, for we could not live for ever on my savings.

Most of all I must talk to Cat. I could do nothing until we had made up our minds about ourselves.

'Mistress?'

Cat was in the process of inking in the presentation plan for my Lord Arlington's new church at Euston Park. Even if he turned it down, her design was a beautiful thing, worth doing for its own sake and worth showing to Dr Wren when it was as perfect as she could make it. She had borne in mind Mr Evelyn's advice to avoid anything that could be construed as grandiose. If my lord followed her scheme, they would reuse the lower two stages of the tower and at least some of the walls of the existing church. (There was no need to spend the client's money for the sake of it.) The external walls could be faced in their entirety with good quality rendering and decent stone quoins and dressings; the interior would be groin-vaulted, including the transepts, and there would be delicate circular windows in the clerestory of the choir. The simplicity of the new upper stages of the tower would . . .

'Mistress?'

Cat laid down her pen. 'What is it?'

'You'll have to tell him, you know.'

Cat looked up. 'What are you talking about?'

'You need to tell master.' Margaret was even redder in the face than usual. She had an uncharacteristic frown on her forehead. 'And the sooner the better.'

They were alone in the Drawing Office. Margaret had called at Henrietta Street to oversee Jane's alteration of one

442

of Cat's gowns. She had come upstairs on the pretext that the supply of candles in the Drawing Office was running low.

Cat swivelled on her stool and faced Margaret. 'What do I have to tell him?'

'What's in your belly.'

Suddenly dizzy, Cat gripped the edge of her drawing slope.

'You do know, don't you?' Margaret went on, inexorable as the Grand Inquisitor.

'I . . . I wasn't sure.'

'Oh, you are, mistress. There's a look. But then there's the cloths.'

'Speak clearly, woman,' Cat snapped.

Margaret stood her ground. 'Jane washes out your cloths. Every month she does it, after *those*. But she didn't have to wash them at the end of October, and she didn't have to last month either. Have you felt other signs? Felt different?'

'I have not been quite myself,' Cat mumbled. 'It's hard to put a finger on it.'

'And all the time, master's going about like the cat that's found the cream pot. That's men for you. He needs to make an honest woman of you.'

Cat gathered the shreds of her dignity about her. She felt hot. She wanted to cry. A pit of fear opened inside her and threatened to swallow her, to swallow everything she was, everything she had become and everything she hoped to be.

Margaret went away, as abruptly as she had come, the only sign of her feelings the fact that she was still carrying the bundle of candles.

* * *

443

Since Euston, they had fallen into the habit of supping together whenever it could be conveniently and discreetly arranged, which was two or, if they were lucky, three times a week. They were careful not to patronize the same establishment too often, to avoid gossip. Marwood would bespeak a private room and order the dishes beforehand. After they had eaten – or sometimes before – they would linger undisturbed with the door bolted on the inside against intruders. During the last few weeks they had found pleasure together in everything, even the secrecy.

This evening was different. Cat was tempted to instruct the new porter to tell Marwood she was unwell when he called for her. But she had to talk to him sooner or later. The longer the delay, the longer the uncertainty.

He collected her in a hackney at the usual hour. With a jerk the coach pulled away. They kissed in the noisy, evil-smelling darkness of its interior but in a manner that seemed to her almost perfunctory.

'I've something to tell you,' he whispered, his breath warm and soft on her ear. It was a distraction. 'And something to ask.'

Cat drew her head away. 'So have I. You first.'

'After Christmas, my house will revert to the Crown. I must look for a new lodging.'

'Is this Buckingham's work?'

'Who else can it be?'

'Do you have enough money?' she said, her voice sounding cold in her own ears.

'Oh yes. For a while, at least.'

'And what about Sam and Margaret?'

'I'll take them with me.' Marwood cleared his throat. 'And

now to my question.' He sounded awkward, she thought, and also pompous, as though he were reading a report to a council meeting. 'Will you do me the honour to take my hand in marriage?'

She didn't reply. The coach wheels ground their way round a corner. 'I don't know,' she said at last.

'What?' His body moved against hers as he turned to face her. 'After all this, I thought—'

'I don't want to lose what I have. What I've made.'

'You mean the business?'

'Of course. God made me to build houses, not keep one for a husband.'

'Very well. Is that all?' He sounded relieved. 'Margaret will keep the house, I'm sure. There's no reason for you to stop what you do.'

'I will make my own decisions. I will spend my money as I will. Brennan will continue as my partner. I will come and go as I wish. I must have—'

'Cat. Stop.' Marwood took her hand and squeezed it. 'You shall have whatever you want. For all I care you may draw up an agreement and have me sign it before a public notary. All I want is your hand in marriage.'

'All?'

'And your presence in my bed.'

The coach jolted onwards for another hundred yards or so. And stopped.

'Very well,' she said. 'In that case we shall be pleased to accept your proposal.'

'We? What's this *we*?'

'You must ask Margaret about that, sir. She's the one who thinks it might be so. There are signs.'

'Do you mean . . . ?'

'And I believe such consequences are not uncommon when a man and a woman share a bed. Are you having second thoughts now?'

'No, madam.' He kissed her forehead and then her lips. 'If Margaret's right, it simply means you will do me double the honour.'

There was a banging on the roof of the coach. 'Hey! We're here. You mean to spend the night in there?'

HISTORICAL NOTE

THERE IS AN unhealthy connection between sex and power. Power sometimes takes as one of its rewards the right to demand sexual favours in ways not usually sanctioned by society. Human nature doesn't change much. This novel had its origins in the present as well as the past.

The ideas for *The Shadows of London* germinated over a number of years. The groundwork was laid as the unsavoury exploits of Harvey Weinstein and Jeffrey Epstein were gradually exposed to the harsh glare of public scrutiny. The catalyst, however, was when I read Dr Linda Porter's *Mistresses* (Picador, 2020), a well-researched and refreshingly down-to-earth account of the more important women who shared Charles II's bed (together with one who was eventually forced to elope with another man in order to resist the King's increasingly determined advances).

One chapter deals with the career of Louise de Keroualle, the impoverished Breton aristocrat who became Charles's chief mistress during the second half of his reign. What makes her case particularly interesting is the fact that from the start her seduction was a matter of international politics. Charles had recently agreed to a controversial alliance with his cousin, Louis XIV of France.

When Louise caught Charles's eye shortly afterwards, the French government was delighted by the possibility of installing a malleable young Frenchwoman in the King's bed. It would strengthen Charles's attachment to France. Moreover, pillow talk might be a useful source of intelligence while also providing a discreet channel for the French to influence Charles in his hours of ease.

This isn't speculation. The letters that passed between the French ambassador, Colbert de Croissy, and the French foreign ministry, are quite explicit. Louis XIV himself took an active interest in the process of seduction.

Nor were the French the only players in this game. Lord Arlington, the most powerful man in England after the King, had been one of the architects of the French alliance. It suited his purposes to work with Colbert de Croissy to bring about Louise's seduction. He and his wife assiduously cultivated her. Louise was soon installed as the Queen's new maid of honour. The ambassador worked closely with the Arlingtons to bring her to Euston Hall, the perfect setting for a carefully choreographed seduction. After its successful conclusion, Louis XIV signalled his gratitude by sending a diamond necklace to Lady Arlington.

John Evelyn witnessed this long-drawn-out ritual of sexual conquest from afar. The diarist was not only a courtier and a noted horticulturalist, but an authority on matters of taste. His advice was eagerly sought by men such as his friend Lord Arlington. Evelyn was a royalist to the bone, but his loyalty to Charles II was increasingly strained by the louche behaviour of the King and his court.

He was not impressed by his first sight of the Queen's new maid of honour at an entertainment for the young Prince of Orange. He confided to his diary on 1 November 1670: 'I now also saw that famed beauty (but in my opinion of a childish simple & baby face) Mademoiselle de Quirreval, lately maide of honour to Madame, and now to be so to the Queene.'

It is difficult to establish the precise sequence of events that led to Louise's seduction. Not only are the sources fragmentary and sometimes contradictory but, as Dr Porter crisply points out, her 'biographers, both French and English, have written a great deal of nonsense about Louise'. The account in *The Shadows of London* is at least plausible, though much of it is necessarily invented.

In October 1671, Evelyn was one of about 200 guests at Euston Hall – not quite one of the inner circle, but close enough to know what was happening. In his entry for the 9–15 October he recorded with disapproval and perhaps a hint of prurience:

It was universaly reported that the faire Lady — was bedded one of these nights, and the stocking flung, after the manner of a married Bride: I acknowledge she was for the most part in her undresse all day, and that there was fondnesse, & toying, with that young wanton; nay 'twas said, I was at the former ceremonie, but tis utterly false, I neither saw, nor heard of anything, tho I had ben in her Chamber and all over that appartment late enough; & was my selfe observing all passages with curiosity enough: however twas with confidence believed that she was first made a *Misse* as they cald those unhappy creatures, with solemnity, at this time &c . . .*

Baby Face had at last succumbed to the King's relentless advances and to the overwhelming pressure of those around her. Most commentators at the time believed that she was a grasping young woman making the most of the opportunities that fate had cast her way. Later historians have tended to follow their lead. Her subsequent career as the King's mistress gives ample evidence for this view of her.

In this novel I have tried to explore another, more nuanced possibility. At the time of her seduction, Louise de Keroualle was a defenceless young woman barely out of her teens. Her seducer was a powerful man twice her age, and his pursuit of her was not merely condoned but actively supported by some of the most influential men in Western Europe, including the King of France. Did they really allow her much of a choice?

Yes, Louise richly deserves her reputation as a self-seeking gold-digger. But that doesn't prevent her from being a victim as well.

Andrew Taylor

---

* The quotations from Evelyn's Diary are taken from the Everyman edition, edited by E.S. de Beer, selected and introduced by Roy Strong (Everyman's Library 291)

Discover how it all began . . .

**Keep reading for a sneak peek into the first book
in the Marwood and Lovett series,
*The Ashes of London***

CHAPTER ONE

THE NOISE WAS the worst. Not the crackling of the flames, not the explosions and the clatter of falling buildings, not the shouting and the endless beating of drums and the groans and cries of the crowd: it was the howling of the fire. It roared its rage. It was the voice of the Great Beast itself.

Part of the nave roof fell in. The sound stunned the crowd into a brief silence.

Otherwise I shouldn't have heard the whimpering at my elbow. It came from a boy in a ragged shirt who had just pushed his way through the mass of people. He was swaying, on the brink of collapse.

I poked his arm. 'Hey. You.'

The lad's head jerked up. His eyes were wide and unfocused. He made a movement as if to run away but we were hemmed in on every side. Half of London, from the King and the Duke of York downwards, had turned out to watch the death throes of St Paul's.

'Are you all right?'

The boy was still unsteady. I took his arm to support him.

He snatched it away. He hunched his shoulders and tried to burrow between the people in front.

'For God's sake,' I said. 'Stand back. You'll fry if you get closer.'

He wriggled to the other side of the woman next to him. The three of us were in a row, staring between the shoulders and elbows of the men in front.

The largest part of the crowd, including the royal party, was in the churchyard north-east of the cathedral. But the boy and I were in Ludgate Street, west of the portico. I was on my way to Whitehall – indeed, I should have been there an hour ago, for I had been summoned by Master Williamson, who was not a man to keep waiting.

But how could a man tear himself away from this spectacle? It was beyond imagination, beyond belief.

We were safe enough here at present, as long as we kept our distance. Some of the buildings between us and St Paul's had been demolished in the hope of making a firebreak, which gave us a view up the hill to the cathedral. But I wasn't sure how long we could stay. The heat and the smoke were already searing my lungs and making it hard to breathe.

Though the fire had now leapt the Fleet Ditch to the north and to the south, Fleet Street itself was still clear, at least for the moment, so there was no danger of it cutting off our retreat. The flames were travelling at about thirty yards an hour, much the same rate as they had since the fire started early on Sunday morning. But you could never tell. The wind might change again. Sparks might carry a hundred yards or more and find something else to act as kindling. The fire followed its own logic, not man's.

Streams of molten metal were now oozing between the

pillars of the portico and down the steps of the cathedral. It was a thick silver liquid, glinting with gold and orange and all the colours of hell: it was the overflow of the lead pouring from the burning roof to the floor of the nave.

Even the rats were running away. They streaked over the cobbles in waves of fiery fur, for some of them had already caught fire. Others were too old or too frail or too young even to flee, and they were baked alive in the heat. I watched three rats trapped in the silver rain, where they struggled and squealed and shrivelled and died.

Despite the lateness of the hour, despite the pall of smoke that blanketed the city, it was as bright as midday. By this stage – eight or nine o'clock on Tuesday evening – the cathedral glowed from within like an enormous lantern. It dominated its surroundings even in destruction.

I glanced to the left, beyond the woman beside me to the upturned face of the boy. The glare made him look less than human: it drained the life away and reduced him to a sharp but flattened representation, like a head stamped on a coin.

There was always a fascination about a fire, but this one elbowed aside all the others. I had been watching the city burn since Sunday morning. I had known London for as long as I had known anything. In a sense I was seeing my own history going up in smoke.

To my surprise, it was oddly exhilarating. Part of me was enjoying the spectacle. Another part thought: And now everything must change.

No one had really believed that the flames would reach the cathedral. St Paul's was commonly held to be impregnable. Squatting on its hill, it towered over the City and suburbs as it had for centuries. It was huge – nearly six hundred feet long. The spire had fallen in the old Queen's time, and it had never been replaced. The tower remained, however, and even the body of the church, from the new portico in the west to the pinnacled choir in the east, was more than a hundred feet above the ground. The walls were so massive that nothing could penetrate them.

Besides, everyone said that the Divine Hand was protecting St Paul's, for the fire had had ample opportunity to attack it. Its school, just to the east, had already been consumed, along with its great libraries; I had spent much of my youth there, and I did not much mourn its loss. But, until this evening, the flames had swirled around the church itself, leaving it untouched. St Paul's, they said, had always been more than a church, more than a cathedral: it stood for London itself. It was the soul of the city. It was invulnerable.

I was wearing my second-best cloak, which I had taken the precaution of soaking in the Thames before coming here. I had learned the hard way that any protection from the heat and the fumes was better than none, and a cloak could hardly make me hotter than I already was.

An almighty roar burst from within the building. A gout of fire gushed upwards above the choir. Flames spurted through the window openings. Hot air surged towards the watching people. The crowd fell back.

'Oh dear God,' the boy said in a high, agonized voice. 'The crypt's gone up.'

One of the men in front threw down his hat and stamped on it. He flung out his arms and howled. His friends tried to restrain him. It was Maycock, the printer.

It's an ill wind, I thought. At least that will please Master Williamson.

Maycock and many of his fellows had stored their more valuable books, papers and cases of type in the crypt of the cathedral, St Faith's, which served as their parish church. They had left nothing to chance: they had barred the doors with locks and bolts; they stopped up every opening that might possibly admit a spark or a draught. Even if the church tumbled about their heads, they thought, their books in St Faith's would be safe below ground for all eternity.

But they and everyone else had reckoned without the strong, capricious wind. It had set fire to goods in the church-yard. It had blown sparks from there, and from burning buildings nearby, onto the roof of the choir. The roof had been under repair for months – so exposed timbers covered places where the lead had been damaged, and these had been baked by the bone-dry summer. The sparks danced towards them, and in that hot air it was not long before the first flames appeared.

The wind fanned the flames, which ignited the network of beams supporting the roof. Seasoned oak burned almost as hot as sea coal. The heat had ruptured the vault beneath and the great stones had tumbled down into the choir and the nave. The inside of the building had been full of wooden scaffolding, which had acted as kindling. In a matter of minutes, the whole interior was alight.

Somehow the fire had reached the crypt. The rain of falling stones from the vault must have punctured the floor of the choir. The books and paper stored below in St Faith's had exploded in a gush of flame.

Already the temperature where we were standing was increasing.

The woman beside me stirred. 'Pray God no one's in there

still.' Her voice was so close to my ear that I felt her breath on my skin.

It was surely impossible to survive the heat inside the cathedral. It was bad enough out here, and it was getting worse. Anyone inside must be dead or dying, like the rats.

Maycock the printer collapsed. His friends seized his limbs and dragged him away. Their going left the boy, the woman and me in the front rank of the crowd.

'Look! Look – the roof!'

She flung out her arm and pointed. Her face glowed as if she had seen a vision of eternity. I followed the line of her finger. From where we were standing, we could see the south-west corner of the cathedral, where the little church of St Gregory nestled against the nave.

The roof fell in with a rumble that was audible above the crackle of the fire. There was a high, wordless cry.

The boy broke away from the crowd and ran towards St Paul's.

I shouted at him to stop. The fire swallowed the sound. I swore and went after him. The heat battered me. I smelled singeing hair and charred flesh. My lungs were on fire.

The boy had his arms outstretched – towards the cathedral? Towards something or someone inside?

My legs were longer than his. After twenty or thirty yards, I seized his shoulder and spun him round, knocking his hat off. I wrapped my right arm around him and dragged him backwards.

He struggled. I tightened my grip. He hacked at my shins. I cuffed him hard about the head, which quieted him for a moment.

Sparks showered over us, driven by the savage wind that

457

was driving the fire itself. Both of us were coughing. A sliver of flame danced on the front of the boy's shirt. I swatted it with my hand, but another appeared on the loose sleeve. At last he woke to the danger he was in and cried out. I tore off my cloak and wrapped his thin body in it to smother the flames.

The crowd parted as I dragged him away from the heat. I pulled him into the partial shelter of a mounting block outside a shuttered tavern on the City side of Ludgate. I slapped his face, first one cheek and then the other.

He opened his eyes. He brushed the cloak away and bared his teeth like an angry cat.

'God's blood,' I said. 'You little fool. You could have killed us both.'

The boy scrambled up and peered towards St Paul's.

'There's nothing you can do,' I said, shouting to make myself heard above the roar of the fire and the crashes from the disintegrating building. 'Nothing any of us can do.'

He fell back against the mounting block. His eyes were closed. Maybe he had fainted again. I peeled the cloak away and sat him on the step. The shirt was no longer smouldering, though the neck was ripped.

The boy was still coughing, but less violently than before. Even here, some way from the fire, it was as bright as midday, albeit the sort of flickering, orange brightness you would expect when Armageddon was raging and the end of the world was nigh.

For the first time, I saw him clearly. I saw a black smudge of soot or dirt on the thin neck. I saw the gaping shirt and the hollow below the collarbones. I saw the sheen of sweat on his chest, coloured by the fiery glow in the air.

And I saw two perfectly rounded breasts.

I blinked. St Paul's burned, the crowd jostled and the air was full of sounds of explosions, roaring flames and collapsing buildings. But in that moment all I saw was the boy.

The boy?

I pulled aside the neck of the shirt.

No, this wasn't a boy. It wasn't a girl, either. From the waist up at least, it was a young woman.

Her eyes were open and staring into mine. I let the shirt drop. She stood up. The top of her head was below my shoulder. She snatched up my cloak to protect her modesty. Despite the crowd we might have been alone, for everyone was looking towards St Paul's.

'What are you doing?' she said.

She didn't sound like a beggar or a woman of the streets. She sounded like the lady of the house addressing her maid. A lady who wasn't in a good temper, and a maid who had committed some gross error.

'What do you think?' I said. 'Saving your life.'

As if to prove my point, there was a sharp crack from the cathedral and a fragment of the portico's pediment fell with a crash that shook the ground. The blocks of stone fragmented into a cloud of rubble and dust.

'Where are you from?' I said. 'Who are you? And why are you—'

She began to move away.

'Stop – that's my cloak.'

I lunged at her hand and pulled her back. She raised my hand towards her lips. For one mad moment I thought she was about to kiss it. An expression of gratitude for saving her life.

I glimpsed the whiteness of her teeth. She bit the back of

my hand, just behind the lowest knuckle of the forefinger. The teeth dug deep and jarred against tendon and bone.

I screamed and released her.

She ran through the crowd on Ludgate Hill with my cloak floating about her shoulders. I stood there, watching her and nursing my hand. I was desperately thirsty. My head ached.

During the Fire, I saw much that seemed against custom and nature, against reason and Divine ordinance, much that seemed to foreshadow still greater disasters yet to come. *Monstra*, as the scholars called such things, meaning wonders or prodigies or evil omens. The destruction of St Paul's was one of them.

But when I fell asleep that night, I did not dream of flames and falling buildings. I dreamed of the boy–woman's face and the wide-open, unfocused eyes.

CHAPTER TWO

ASHES AND BLOOD. Night after night.
I was thinking of ashes and blood when I woke from a fitful sleep on the morning after the Fire reached St Paul's. I knew by the light that it was early, not long after dawn.

Not the hot ashes of the city last night. Not the blood from my hand, after the boy—girl had bitten me.

This blood had been dripping from a head. As for the ashes, they had been cold. A weeping man had rubbed them into his hair.

All this had given me nightmares when I was child, and for months I used to wake screaming, night after night. My mother, usually the mildest and most obedient of wives, had berated my father for allowing her son to see such things.

'Will they do it to me one day?' I had asked my mother. Night after night.

Now, on a summer morning years later, I heard a ripple of song from a blackbird. The bed creaked as my father shifted his weight.

'James?' he said in the thin, dry voice of his old age. These days he slept badly and rose early, complaining of bad dreams. 'James? Are you awake yet? Why's it so hot? Let's walk in the garden. It will be cooler there.'

Even here, on the outskirts of Chelsea, the sky was grey with ash, the rising sun reduced to a smear of orange. The air was already warm. It smelled of cinders.

After I had dressed, I removed the bandage from my left hand. The bleeding had stopped but the wound throbbed painfully. I rewrapped the bandage and helped my father down the narrow stairs, hoping we would not wake the Ralstons.

We walked in the orchard, with my father leaning on my right arm. The trees were heavy with fruit – apples, pears and plums mainly, but also damsons, walnuts and a medlar. The dew was still on the grass.

My father shuffled along. 'Why is it so black?'

'It's the Fire, sir. All the smoke.'

Frowning, he turned his face up to the sky. 'But it's snowing.'

The wind had moderated a little overnight and had shifted from the east to the south. The air was full of dark flakes, fluttering and turning like drunken dancers.

'Black snow,' he said and, though the morning was already so warm, he shivered.

'You grow fanciful, sir.'

'It's the end of the world, James. I told you it would be so. It is the wickedness of the court that has brought this upon us. It is written, and it must happen. This year is sixteen hundred and sixty-six. It is a sign.'

'Hush, Father.' I glanced over my shoulder. Even here, such

talk was dangerous as well as foolish, especially for a man like my father whose liberty hung by a thread. 'It isn't snow. It's only paper.'

'Paper? Nonsense. Paper is white. Paper doesn't fall from the air.'

'It's been burned. The stationers stored their paper and many of their books in the crypt at St Paul's. But the Fire found a way to it, and now the wind brings these fragments even here.'

'Snow,' the old man muttered. 'Black snow. It's another sign.'

'Paper, sir. Not snow.' I heard the exasperation in my voice and wished I had said nothing. I sensed rather than saw the dismay in my father's face, for signs of anger or irritation upset the old man, sometimes to the point of tears. I went on in a gentler voice, 'Let me show you.'

I stooped and picked up a fragment of charred paper, the corner of a page with a few printed words still visible on the scorched surface. I handed it to him.

'See? Paper. Not snow.'

My father took the paper and held it close to his eyes. His lips moved without sound. Even now he could read the smallest print by the dimmest rushlight.

'What did I tell you?' he said. 'The end of the world. It's another sign. Read it.'

He held out the fragment to me. The paper had come from the bottom of a page, at the right-hand corner. There were five words visible on it, taken from the ends of two lines on the page:

    ... *Time is*
    ... *it is done.*

'Well?' He stretched out his arms to the black flakes swirling in the dark sky. 'Am I not right, James? The end of the world is nigh, and Jesus will return to reign in majesty over us all. Are you prepared to face your God at His judgement seat?'

'Yes, Father,' I said.

Since May, my father and I had lodged in a cottage within the fenced enclosure of a market garden. We shared the house with the gardener, his wife and their maid. On fine days, the old man sat in the garden and shouted and waved his stick at marauding birds and small boys.

Mistress Ralston, the gardener's wife, was willing enough to take our money, and I made sure that our rent was paid on the nail. She complained about the extra work, though the maid did most of it, and she did not like having my father about the place during the day. She put up with us for the money. Of course, she said, if Master Marwood's health worsened, that might be another matter. She and Master Ralston could not be expected to nurse the sick.

I had chosen this place when my father was released on my surety, and for three reasons. The country air was healthier. The lodgings were cheap. And, most importantly, the garden was remote enough from London to reduce to insignificance the possibility that someone would recognize him; yet it was not too far for me to go daily to and from London.

My father was a marked man. When the King had been restored, six years earlier, Parliament had passed an Act of Indemnity, which pardoned all who had fought against the Crown in the late insurrection. The only people excepted from this blanket pardon were the Regicides, those who had been directly instrumental in the execution of the King's father at Whitehall.

My father was covered by the Act, for he had not been named as a Regicide. But he had thrown away the King's clemency after the Restoration, and by his own choice, and now we suffered the consequences. I loved my father, but sometimes I hated him too.

My mother had hoped I would have a different life. It was she who had cajoled my father into enrolling me at St Paul's School. She had dreamed that I might become a preacher or a lawyer, a man who worked with his mind and not his hands. But she had died a few years later. My father, whose business was declining, withdrew me from the school and bound me to him as his apprentice. Then came his last act of folly, after the Restoration, and he and I were entirely ruined.

After breakfast, I told him I must go to Whitehall.

'Ah, Whitehall,' the old man said, his face brightening. 'Where they killed the man of blood. Do you remember?'

'Hush, sir. For God's sake, hush.'

But I did not go to Whitehall. Not at first.

I had intended to walk there, but the road to Westminster, Whitehall and the City was choked with Londoners fleeing on foot and horseback, in coaches and wagons. With them they carried the elderly and sick; some of the latter showed signs of the plague, which still lingered in the town.

Others were encamped in fields and orchards along the roadside, erecting makeshift tents and shelters or merely sitting and weeping or staring vacantly towards the smoke of the Fire. Shock had made them numb.

It would take me at least an extra hour, I calculated, to

fight against the current of people and walk towards London. So I went down to the water and hailed a pair of oars to take me downriver. It was an expense I could ill afford but a necessary one.

The Fire had been good to the watermen, for everyone wanted a craft of any sort to take them and their possessions to safety. They would pay the most inflated fares without a moment's argument. Overladen craft, large and small, wallowed in the water. The Thames, even this far west, was as busy as Cheapside had been until the Fire had reached it.

But, as with the road, the traffic tended to be away from London. I haggled with the boatman, reasoning that he would prefer to have a boat with a fare in it than one that was empty when he returned to collect more refugees and their possessions.

We made good speed, with both the current and the tide on our side. The Thames was as grey as dirty pewter and littered with charred debris and discarded possessions, particularly furniture. I saw a handsome table, floating downstream, its legs in the air with a gull perched on one of them.

As we neared Whitehall Stairs, I told the waterman not to pull in but to continue downstream as far as St Paul's. I had a curiosity to see what was left of it. Part of me wondered if the boy–girl would return there, too. Something had drawn her toward the cathedral as the rats were fleeing from it, something so powerful that she had ignored the Fire.

From the river, London was a horrifying sight. Above the town hung a great pall of smoke and ash. Beneath it, the air glowed a deep and sultry red. The sun could not break through, and the city was bathed in unnatural twilight.

From Ludgate to the Tower there seemed nothing left but

smouldering devastation. The close-packed houses, built mainly of wood, had melted away, leaving only fragments of blackened stone and brickwork. Even here on the water, with a stiff breeze blowing up the Thames, we felt the heat pulsing from the ruins.

Every now and then the dull crump of an explosion boomed across the water. On the King's orders, they were blowing up buildings in the path of the flames in the hope of creating firebreaks. There was an explosion somewhere between Fleet Street and the river.

The waterman covered his ears and swore.

'We can't pull in, master,' the waterman said, coughing. 'God save us, you'll fry if you go ashore.'

A shower of cinders passed us, some clinging to my sleeve. I brushed them frantically away. 'What about downstream?'

'It's the same all the way down – and hotter than ever – they say it's the oil burning in the warehouses.'

Without waiting for my order, he pulled away from the north bank and rowed us out to midstream. I stared at St Paul's. It was still standing, but the roof had gone, and both walls and tower had a jagged, shimmering quality, like outlines seen under flowing water. Columns of smoke rose from still-burning fires within the blackened shell. It wasn't a church any more. It was more like a giant coal in an oven.

It was impossible that the boy–girl could be within twenty yards of it or more. No living creature could survive that heat.

'Whitehall,' I said.

A CITY IN FLAMES
London, 1666. As the Great Fire consumes
everything in its path, the body of a man is
found in the ruins of St Paul's Cathedral –
stabbed in the neck, thumbs tied behind his back.

A WOMAN ON THE RUN
The son of a traitor, James Marwood is forced to hunt
the killer through the city's devastated streets. There he
encounters a determined young woman, who will
stop at nothing to secure her freedom.

A KILLER SEEKING REVENGE
When a second murder victim is discovered in the
Fleet Ditch, Marwood is drawn into the political and
religious intrigue of Westminster – and across the path
of a killer with nothing to lose . . .

A time of terrible danger . . .

The Great Fire has ravaged London. Now, guided by
the Fire Court, the city is rebuilding, but times are
volatile and danger is only ever a heartbeat away.

Two mysterious deaths . . .

James Marwood, a traitor's son, is thrust into this
treacherous environment when his father discovers a
dead woman in the very place where the Fire Court
sits. The next day his father is run down. Accident?
Or another murder . . .?

A race to stop a murderer . . .

Determined to uncover the truth, Marwood turns to the
one person he can trust – Cat Lovett, the daughter of a
despised regicide. Then comes a third death. . . and
Marwood and Cat are forced to confront a vicious
killer who threatens the future of the city itself.

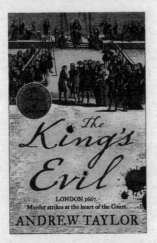

LONDON 1667.
Murder strikes at the heart of the Court.
ANDREW TAYLOR

A royal scandal . . .

In the Court of Charles II, it's a dangerous time to be alive – a wrong move may lead to disgrace, exile or death. The discovery of a body at the home of one of the highest courtiers in the land could therefore have catastrophic consequences.

A shocking murder . . .

James Marwood, a traitor's son, is ordered to cover up the killing. But the dead man is known to Marwood – as is the most likely culprit, Cat Lovett.

The stakes have never been higher. . .

Marwood is sure Cat is innocent so determines to discover the true murderer. But time is running out. If he makes a mistake, it could threaten the King himself. . .

A dangerous secret lies beneath Whitehall Palace . . .
Brother against brother. Father against son. Friends
turned into enemies. No one in England wants a return to
the bloody days of the Civil War. But Oliver Cromwell's
son, Richard, has abandoned his exile and slipped back
into England. The consequences could be catastrophic.

James Marwood, a traitor's son turned government
agent, is tasked with uncovering Cromwell's motives.
But his assignment is complicated by his friend –
the regicide's daughter, Cat Lovett – who knew the
Cromwells as a child, and who now seems to be
hiding a secret of her own about the family.

Both Marwood and Cat know they are putting
themselves in great danger. And when they find
themselves on a top secret mission in the Palace of
Whitehall, they realize they are risking their lives . . .
and could even be sent to the block for treason.

A curious death

It's winter in London, 1670. Inside a snow-patched
house two young girls plot a murder by witchcraft.
Soon afterwards, a government clerk dies painfully
in sinister circumstances.

A perilous assignment

James Marwood, a reluctant Whitehall agent, is ordered
to investigate. But the task swiftly brings unexpected
danger – both to him and those he loves the most.

A time of great treachery

Unknown to all, at the heart of this mystery
lies a royal secret so explosive that it
could not only rip apart England . . .
. . . but change the entire face of Europe.